RHYS DAVIES:
THE COLLECTED STORIES
Volume II

Rhys Davies
Collected Stories

Volume II

compiled and edited by
MEIC STEPHENS

First Publication—1996

ISBN 1 85902 485 8

Stories © The Estate of Rhys Davies

Introduction © Meic Stephens

This volume is published with the support of the Arts Council of Wales.

*Printed in Wales
at Gomer Press, Llandysul, Ceredigion*

Contents

INTRODUCTION

Rhys Davies was among the most dedicated, prolific, and accomplished of Welsh short-story writers. For more than forty years, with unswerving devotion, he practised the literary form of which he was to become a master, and on which his reputation as a prose-writer now firmly rests. He wrote twenty novels, three novellas, two books about Wales, and an autobiography, but it is for his short-stories—about a hundred in all, published in a dozen main collections—that he is remembered today.

Most of Rhys Davies's stories are set in his native Wales, whether in an unspecified but easily recognizable Rhondda, grimly proletarian, or else in fondly idealized rural parts farther west, and despite the fact that he left home for London as a very young man, it was to those landscapes that he most often returned in his imagination. Some of his later stories have characters and social milieux which are unmistakably English and middle-class, and some are set in France and Germany. Nevertheless, 'There is only one abiding classic,' he once commented, 'Wales'.

On the other hand, his long residence in England, and his refusal to be associated with any literary school or coterie, even to consider himself an 'Anglo-Welsh' writer, was to set him apart from that first generation of Welsh writers in English who came to prominence in the years between the world wars. He was, for a start, unconcerned in his writing with political or social questions, though he claimed to have had a lifelong allegiance to the Labour Party. He may have been fairly typical in his antipathy towards the narrowness of Welsh Nonconformity, and in his ambivalence towards the Welsh language, which he did not speak, but there is something wilfully wholesale about his rejection of so much that belonged to the Wales of his youth. Like Stephen Dedalus, he decided early on to fly by the nets of nationality, language, and religion. His revulsion against what he considered to be 'the tyranny of the chapels' was keenly felt and bordering on the obsessive; only Caradoc Evans was more hostile. One of the characters in his first novel, *The Withered Root* (1927), is made to say, 'You Welsh! A race of mystical poets who have gone awry . . . To me there seems to be a darkness over your land and futility in your struggles to assert your ancient nationality. Your brilliant children leave you because of the hopeless stagnation of your miserable Nonconformist towns; the religion of your chapels is a blight on the flowering souls of your young . . .' On the subject of the language he had this to say: 'To me it is a lovely tongue to be cultivated in the same way as some people cultivate orchids, or keep Persian cats: a hobby yielding much private delight and sometimes a prize at an exhibition.' Not even Caradoc Evans went as far. The price he had to pay for distancing himself by such plain speaking was that readers in Wales never really took him to their hearts: many thought he was out to caricature them for the amusement of an English audience. As a consequence, Rhys Davies's books have for long been out of print and only since his death, in 1978, has he attracted any serious critical attention in the land of his birth.

In England, too, he was always something of an outsider, a role he assiduously cultivated in defiance of all the prevailing fashions and ideologies of the day. His life, which he shared with no other person, was given up entirely to his writing. Except for a stint as a draper's assistant on first arriving in London and a few months of compulsory war-work as a civilian at the Ministry of Information, he lived for many years almost entirely by his pen, his income unsupplemented by any teaching, journalism, or broadcasting, and usually in cheap, rented accommodation. He maintained a rigorous work-schedule—eating, writing and sleeping in one small room—and seldom sought either the company or the opinion of other writers. This professional single-mindedness, which was reinforced by his equanimity, love of solitude, and modest material needs, enabled him to pursue a literary career uninterrupted by any of the emotional or domestic upheavals such as are to be found so often in his stories. The virtues he extolled were those he had learned in his youth—thrift, a horror of debt, and minding one's own business—which he also took, unusually, to be specificaly Welsh characteristics; that is why he disliked the profligate Dylan Thomas. He kept his distance, too, from London Welsh society, though was not averse to meeting other expatriate Welsh writers such as Idris Davies at Griff's Bookshop in Cecil Court. But he preferred the company of London's artistic community, taking delight in some of the more outrageous characters like the boozy Nina Hamnett, 'Queen of Bohemia', and the notorious Count Potocki, pretender to the Polish throne, who paraded through the streets of Soho in a red cloak and with his blond hair falling over his shoulders; in his entry in *Who's Who* Rhys Davies gave his recreation as 'collecting ruined characters', and it seems he had a patient way of dealing with these difficult people. Although sometimes to be seen at the Wheatsheaf, one of Fitzrovia's most famous pubs, he never took to excessive drinking and remained an urbane, mild-mannered, parsimonious man whose only extravagance was sartorial: he had a taste for fine, expensive clothes, almost to the point of dandyism. His sexual orientation was homosexual but he maintained complete discretion, never even writing about it in personal terms. It took the form of platonic friendships with younger men or else was satisfied by fleeting encounters with Guardsmen, usually strangers, about whom he is said to have had an erotic fixation. The enigmatic title of his autobiography, *Print of a Hare's Foot* (1969), is in fact a coded reference to its author's own androgynous nature. The image of the hare, a richly secretive, shape-shifting creature in folklore, was central to both his writing and his life. It also explains to some extent the detached, almost clinical way in which he observed other people and the evasiveness with which he habitually responded to enquiries about himself.

The important facts of Rhys Davies's life are few and plain, but highly relevant to his work because he often drew upon his own experiences in his writing. He was born on the 9th of November 1901 (not in 1903 as he claimed) in Blaenclydach (not Clydach Vale), a side-valley of the Rhondda, in industrial Glamorgan, which rises steeply from the town of Tonypandy. The valley was dominated by the presence of two major collieries—the Cambrian and a drift-mine, known as the Gorki, in Blaenclydach itself, quite close to the house where the author was born; both were the focus of bitter and violent industrial strife. Rees Vivian Davies, as he was christened, was the fourth child of the village grocer and his wife. His father, who voted Liberal, was the son of an illiterate Merthyr collier and his mother an uncertificated schoolteacher from Ynysybwl. On both his father's and his mother's side his people had their remote origins in north-west Carmarthenshire, always for him a lost Arcady, 'everlastingly green and sweet-smelling', despite his tenuous connection with it. The household was strongly matriarchal. Rhys Davies was to create many a female character who was as capable, shrewd, and dignified as his mother, while his men tend to be much weaker creatures, bemused, hapless victims of misfortune. The Davies's small shop, known rather grandly as Royal Stores, was at 6 Clydach Road, Blaenclydach, now a private house distinguished from others in the row only by a commemorative plaque put up by the Rhys Davies Trust in 1995; across the road stands the Central Hotel, which appears in the stories as the Jubilee. One of the Davies sons was killed in the closing weeks of the First World War; they also had three daughters and a younger son, Lewis, who is still alive. Both sides of the family were Welsh-speaking, as were Rhys Davies's parents, but they did not pass the language on to their children, and he grew up with only a few phrases at his command. As a boy he attended services at Gosen Chapel, where Welsh was in regular use, but was soon attracted to the High Anglican rite at nearby St. Thomas's Church. In later life Rhys Davies was to turn againt all forms of religious practice and declare himself an atheist. At the age of twelve he became a pupil at Porth County School, which had a reputation as the best school in the Rhondda, but he was not happy there and did not distinguish himself academically. He left two years later, much to the chagrin of his parents for whom education seemed to be the surest way of avoiding the pits, and began helping behind the counter at Royal Stores. His parents' status as shopkeepers set them apart from a community that worked in the coal-industry, to the extent that some of his attitudes in later life were distinctly petit bourgeois, but in the shop's daily routine the boy came into contact with many local people, especially women, for whom he felt a deep affection and whose gossip he relished. One of the recurring references in his prose is to 'the ledger of old accounts' in which his mother kept a record of the villagers' debts and around which more than one drama unfolds. 'I always think of this period as a burial, with myself lying somnolent in a coffin, but visually aware of the life going on around me, and content to wait until the time came for me to rise and be myself,' he told one of his earliest critics. For the next five years, having resisted parental ambition for him to work in a bank, he read avidly, mainly the French and Russian classics, and made his first adolescent attempts at writing poems and stories. A growing awareness of his own sexuality, however, eventually made life in the male-dominated society of the Rhondda unbearable and, daunted by its grime and coarseness, and by what he saw as the narrowness of its chapel-culture, he went to live for a while in Cardiff, where he found work in a corn-merchant's warehouse. He was never to live permanently in the Rhondda again, but its ethos had marked him indelibly and provided him with an inexhaustible source of material for his writing.

Soon afterwards, drawn to London, where he was determined 'to starve and suffer' for his art, he embarked on his literary career. 'I wished for no possessions and, since taking my leap over the mountains, I had learned in my initial year or two how to be alone,' he recalled in his autobiography. One wet Sunday in 1924 he sat down in his dingy lodgings in Manor Park, near Ilford, and wrote three short-stories 'as clear of fat as winter sparrows'. Set in a Welsh mining valley, these 'carnal little stories' owed more to Caradoc Evans than to Maupassant or Chekhov, except that they dealt with a brutish proletariat rather than a venal peasantry. They were first published in a small, left-wing, short-lived, avant-garde magazine, *The New Coterie*, which was distributed by Charles Lahr; a few other stories and novellas appeared in limited private-press editions which have since become collectors' items. Among other contributors to the journal were H. E. Bates, Liam O'Flaherty, and T. F. Powys. It was Lahr, a German-born bibliophile and owner of the Progressive Bookshop at 68 Red Lion Street in Holborn, who introduced Rhys Davies to the literary and artistic world of London. He also served as his amanuensis, typing the manuscript of *The Withered Root*, and publishing his first collection of short-stories, *The Song of Songs*, both of which appeared in 1927. The public response to these books was favourable: they received good reviews and the novel was published in an American edition. The author found himself taken up as an original new talent especially among those who admired the work of D. H. Lawrence, at the time a cult-figure for the young. With an advance on a second novel, Rhys Davies was able to give up the menial jobs on which he had subsisted hitherto and become a full-time writer.

The rest of his life was without great incident. During a visit to the south of France in the winter of 1928 he was invited to spend some time with D. H. Lawrence and his wife Frieda at Bandol, and the two writers, both of whom had grown up in a mining-village and whose mothers had been teachers, took to each other immediately. 'What the Celts have to learn and cherish in themselves,' Lawrence told the impressionable young Welshman, 'is that sense of mysterious magic that is born with them, the sense of mystery, the dark magic that comes with the night . . . That will shove all their chapel Nonconformity out of them.' It was Rhys Davies who smuggled a manuscript copy of Lawrence's *Pansies* into Britain and arranged for it to be published by Charles Lahr. Although his literary output throughout the 'thirties was regular and substantial—he published seven collections of short-stories, six novels (one under the pseudonym Owen Pitman), and three novellas during the decade—financial success eluded him. Unable to settle at any one address, he lived a peripatetic life until he was offered accommodation at the home of Vincent Wells, a wealthy homosexual, in the leafy village of Henley-on-Thames, an arrangement which lasted until 1945, when the house caught fire and many of the writer's papers were destroyed. Whenever his money ran out he would go home to Blaenclydach and immerse himself in his writing, turning out stories and novels with a view to selling them to magazines and publishers in London; there were, of course, no such opportunities in economically depressed Wales. The finest of his stories written at this time appeared in the collection *The Things Men Do* (1936). Much of his energy during the 'thirties, by which time the making of the young writer was virtually complete, went into the writing of a trilogy of novels chronicling life in Blaenclydach from the days of 'sylvan Rhondda', before the discovery of coal, through the years of economic boom and industrial strife—he witnessed the Tonypandy Riots of 1910—down to the onset of economic decline and widespread social deprivation after the General Strike of 1926. The best of these novels is undoubtedly *Jubilee Blues* (1938).

The outbreak of war in 1939 filled Rhys Davies with despondency, and yet the war-years—despite rationing and the blitz—were to be one of his most productive periods. Although paper was in short supply, there was great public demand for reading material, and the short-story flourished in a variety of magazines, which were exempt from rationing. Davies contributed to many of them and, with the publication of *A Finger in Every Pie* (1942), *The Trip to London* (1946), and *Boy with a Trumpet* (1949), his style as a writer of short-stories reached maturity. At about the same time he achieved his only commercial success with a novel, *The Black Venus* (1944), when it was reissued as a paperback; in the same year, however, a stage-musical adapted from his stories, *Jenny Jones*, after a short run in London's West End, turned out to be a flop. For the rest of the 'forties, and particularly after the demise of so many of the magazines where he had found a market for his stories, he concentrated on writing novels. He lived for some years with the Scottish writer Fred Urquhart in a cottage near Tring in the Chilterns, and later with other male friends in Brighton, but by 1955, the year in which his *Collected Stories* appeared, he had returned to London, where he had long felt most at home, and to his old sedentary routine. When I first met him he was living in a studio flat at 15 Russell Court in the heart of Bloomsbury, a small but compact place which he was to occupy for the rest of his life. I found him to be a friendly, courteous but reserved man, and in appearance slim, fine-boned, and with a distinctively Iberian head and complexion. He had been able to afford the flat, I remember him telling me with a wry grin, with the help of money he had inherited from his parents, who had left him a little more than their other four children because he had saved them the expense of higher education. Towards the end of the 'fifties he published a novel, *The Perishable Quality* (1957), and a collection of stories, *The Darling of her Heart* (1958), the last of his books to take the Rhondda and west Wales as their main setting. From now on he would deal with more lurid themes: incest, lesbianism, drug-addiction and murder.

The 'sixties and 'seventies were not productive years for Rhys Davies, but they were not unlucrative. Looking to America for a new market, he had several stories published in such prestigious magazines as *The New Yorker* and *The Saturday Evening Post*, including 'The Chosen One' which won the Edgar Award for Crime Fiction in 1966. Honours came his way, too. In 1968 he was admitted to the Order of the British Empire and, two years later, the Welsh Arts Council made him an award in recognition of his contribution to the literature of Wales. Two more novels appeared—*Nobody Answered the Bell* (1971) and *The Honeysuckle Girl* (1975)—but they were not particularly well received, perhaps because their subject-matter had moved beyond the taste of many of his older readers. Fortunately, he was by now no longer dependent on his books for an income, having been left two more substantial legacies. The first came from half the estate of the writer Anna Kavan, with whom he had shared a curious bond that ended only with her death in 1968. Kavan had been addicted to heroin for more than forty years and had tried several times to commit suicide. Rhys Davies had rescued her after two overdoses and arranged for her to receive medical treatment. The precise nature of the friendship between these two solitaries remains undocumented, since hardly any of their correspondence has survived. Other women had been attracted to Davies and he took pleasure in women's company, but it was perhaps only with the asexual Kavan that he was able to enjoy anything like a close relationship. Yet neither admired the work of the other and Davies turned down a suggestion from Kavan's agent that he should write a biography of her, excusing himself on the grounds that although they had seen a good deal of each other over many years, he did not know enough about her; he nevertheless carried out his duties as her literary heir and executor by editing two posthumous volumes of her work. The second legacy, of sixty thousand pounds, came a few years later from another woman-friend, Louise Taylor, an American who had been the adopted daugher and heiress of Alice B. Toklas, the companion of Gertrude Stein. She and her husband, a painter, had kept a literary and artistic salon in Chelsea, and they had been kind to Rhys Davies. He now found himself with money in the bank for the first time in his life and contemplated a trip to America to see his old friend Philip Burton, the radio producer with whom he had collaborated in the 1950s. But his deteriorating health would not allow it. A lifelong smoker and suffering from severe bronchial attacks, he was diagnosed as having lung-cancer. He died on the 21st of August 1978 at University College Hospital. After a brief secular service at Golders Green Crematorium, his ashes were scattered in the rose garden there in the presence of his brother Lewis and two or three friends, among them Keidrych Rhys.

It was the writer Glyn Jones who was among the first of Rhys Davies's compatriots to recognize his mature talent. In the inaugural issue of Keidrych Rhys's magazine *Wales*, which appeared in the summer of 1937, Glyn Jones reviewed Davies's new novel, *A Time to Laugh*. 'As Welsh writers go,' he commented, 'Rhys Davies is undoubtedly a bigshot, a good bit of a pioneer, one of the first to get the valleys across on the English in the face of indifference, prejudice and a good deal of press-engendered hostility. He has written some of the best short-stories ever published about the valleys; and his virtues, well-known by this time (fancy, salty dialogue, grotesque humour, a robust masculinity of style) are all present in this his latest novel . . . Only philosophy is missing.' He went on to regret the lack of a unifying principle, or tension, which held the characters together in an imaginative world where their co-existence might be more credible. Althought this stricture is much less true of Rhys Davies's short-stories than it is of his novels, it does contain some perceptive criticism of his work as a whole.

Rhys Davies was the first Welsh writer in modern times to live as a full-time writer in London and to exploit his Welsh background fully in his writing. He knew, too, what it was like to feel 'the ancient recoil' of English readers from Welsh life and letters. In an article in *The Literary Digest* published in 1947, one of the rare occasions on which he wrote about his craft, he revealed how conscious he was of the pitfalls lying in wait for the writer who would write about Wales in English. 'There is no decadence in Wales,' he wrote. 'Life there is lived with the bright and hard colouring, and the definite simple principles of conduct, which one sees in a child's picture-book. There are rogues and ogres, true, there is scandalous behaviour. But the Celtic simplicity and wonder lies over all.' Of his fellow-countrymen he added, 'But let a writer go beyond the border and try to shape them into English print and they begin to scowl . . . The life of this fairyland must not be told outside or to foreigners like the English. Alas, that there should be traitors like myself! But I cannot help myself—my passion for Wales, her beauty, her individuality, her quality of perpetual youth . . . must be expressed in the only way I know—words—and as truthfully as I am able.'

One of Rhys Davies's difficulties was that he had few literary models on which to base his treatment of Welsh characters and locations, and that is why so much of his dialogue and some of his plots call to mind the work of Caradoc Evans, the Welsh writer to whom he was psychologically closest. He may not have had the latter's vitriolic turn of phrase but he certainly strove for his economy of style and emulated his attempts at rendering the peculiarities of Welsh speech in English, at least in his early stories. However picturesque or outlandish the effect may have seemed to his first English readers, with its inverted syntax, literally translated idioms, singsong rhythms, and so forth, this local colour can seem dated and tedious now, especially to readers in Wales, but it should not be allowed to spoil our enjoyment of the tale. More seriously, perhaps, is that after long years of residence in England, with only occasional trips back to Wales, by the 'fifties Rhys Davies found that his memories of the Rhondda had begun to fade and date, so that Welsh readers had some difficulty in recognizing the veracity of the people and places he was endeavouring to depict. This sense of not belonging any more is most movingly treated in *The Perishable Quality* (1957), the last of his novels to have a Rhondda setting.

It may be that, in any case, a story's location for Rhys Davies was never as important as characterization and plot, for as a writer he was more interested in the play of human personality than in anything else. Only rarely does he point the moral to his tale and he never condemns his characters, not even the villains among them. He was particularly good at tracing the subtleties of the female psyche and among his most striking portraits are those women in his stories who suffer and triumph in their social and sexual relationships. His own sexual make-up may have been an advantage in this respect. Be that as it may, he is one of the few Welsh writers to have written about industrial South Wales mainly from the point of view of its womenfolk. The plots of his stories often revolve around three sisters, or a young headstrong woman, or a middle-aged spinster, or else a wife fretting against the restrictions of an unhappy marriage, who eventually rise above their circumstances and achieve a kind of liberation. Emma Bovary was ever the heroine whom Rhys Davies most admired. The women in his stories usually achieve their victories by dint of personal revolt against convention, a favourite theme of his, and by embracing the Lawrentian values inherent in a passionate response to life. This leitmotiv is linked in his work to an abhorrence of puritanism and industrialism, and to his belief that one of the specifically Welsh virtues is a joy in the natural world untrammelled by any sense of original sin. 'There is still a primitive shine on Wales,' he wrote in his travelogue *My Wales* (1937). 'One can smell the old world there still, and it is not a dead aroma.' He detected the embodiment of these virtues in the person of his great hero, the eccentric Dr William Price of Llantrisant—quack, druid, Chartist rebel, exponent of free love, nudism and moon-worship, and pioneer of cremation—whom he described as 'the seer who sought to bring back to his people the spirit of an ancient, half-forgotten poetry.' Part of this joy, for Rhys Davies, had its corollary in a fascination with death: there are more fatal accidents, bereavements, widows, murders, corpses, coffins, wreaths, legacies, funerals, cold ham, and mournful hymns in his books than in the work of any other modern Welsh writer. 'Myself, I favour a dark, funereal tale,' he wrote in the preface to his *Collected Stories* (1955), 'but not always.' Fortunately for his readers, his treatment of this theme is not at all morbid; indeed, some of the funniest scenes in his stories—he had a delicious sense of black humour—take place during the rituals of death and burial. At such moments he found his countrymen at their most primeval, their greed and hypocrisy the very stuff of satire. 'Another virtue of the short-story,' he wrote, 'is that it can be allowed to laugh.'

As for his lack of 'philosophy', Rhys Davies defended himself thus in an interview with Denys Val Baker for *John O'London's Weekly* in 1952: 'I become uneasy when a novelist begins to expound, preach or underline, state a case, even briefly, or when he douses his characters with over-personal wealth of vision. This sort of philosophising must be kept, with me, incidental.' He was against the waving of flags in public, of all kinds whatsoever, and never joined any party or group which would have required him to do so. He was, however, prepared to allow a glimpse of his political colours in private:

writing to Charles Lahr in 1929, he confided, 'Every night in my devotions I pray for a Labour Government'; and in the magazine *Wales* he once expressed support for the idea of self-government for Wales; but those are his only recorded utterances on the subject. In his stories there is hardly a hint that he had any political opinions and the reader is left to draw whatever inference is preferred. It may be that, like many other satirists, including Caradoc Evans, Rhys Davies was more conservative than his radically-minded contemporaries ever had reason to suspect. His primary aim was objectivity in the delineation of character in which there was no room for anything beyond the strictly individual, and in this he nearly always succeeded. It follows that he set his face against deliberately striving to express a specifically Welsh attitude to life and the world. 'If a writer thinks of his work along these lines,' he replied to a questionnaire from Keidrych Rhys, 'it tends to become too parochial, narrow. But if he is Welsh by birth, upbringing, and selects a Welsh background and characters for his work, an essence of Wales should be in the work, giving it a national slant or flavour.' It is an irony of Rhys Davies's career that in his determination to rebut the charge of parochialism, while at the same time giving so much of his work Welsh settings, he was sometimes considered too English in Wales and too Welsh in metropolitan England.

There is nevetheless a remarkable consistency of quality in Rhys Davies's mature work which puts him in the first rank of twentieth-century short-story writers in English. In his prodigious output he is comparable only with Liam O'Flaherty and A. E. Coppard. Whereas most writers, towards the end of a long writing career, experience a dimunition in their creative powers and tend to lapse into self-parody, often bringing out work that has long been consigned to the drawer, Rhys Davies—with the help of the legacies from Anna Kavan and Louise Taylor—was saved from the necessity of having to publish what he considered third-rate work. He continued writing during the very last years of his life, finishing another novel which was published as *Ram with Red Horns* in 1996. But there were no more short-stories. Nevertheless, he left us enough on which to base our judgement of him as a master of the form. Even in his reliance, in the early work, on melodrama and some pretty unlikely coincidences, he manages to beguile and entertain us. At his best he has an eye for significant detail, an instinct for moments of high drama, an ear for dialogue, and a delight in human nature in all its lovely and unlovely variety, which make his stories compelling reading. In practising the ancient art of the story-teller to such excellent effect Rhys Davies wrote stories that have a timeless and universal quality which will ensure their lasting appeal.

MEIC STEPHENS
Whitchurch, Cardiff   *October 1996*

THE BENEFIT CONCERT

When it was decided to give a Benefit Concert for Jenkin, so that he could buy an artificial leg, no one thought this ordinary event would lead to such strife. But then no one suspected that the loss of his proper leg—it had gone gangrenous through neglect—had turned Jenkin into a megalomaniac. The affair not only divided the valley into bitterly opposed camps but it nearly caused a strike in the colliery. Imperfect mankind is addicted to warfare and a false leg is as good a pretext for liberating smouldering passions as greed for a continent.

To begin with, the colliery where Jenkin worked was not obliged to give him compensation. He had neglected a wound received in the pit, refusing medical attention, and it was not until some weeks had passed that the leg showed signs of protest. His blood was in bad condition (as the camp later opposed to his side repeated in another sense) and the leg had always been a twitchy one. Though he could have fought his case in the courts, this wasn't done, Jenkin having a horror of courts ever since that time he was accused— unfairly, though none the less he lost his case—of buying a concertina knowing it had been stolen. Well, now he had lost his leg, too, and not a penny in the bank.

He was still convalescent in the hospital when his butties in No. 2 pit decided to give him a benefit. A committee was formed and the valley's Male Voice Choir, ever ready to open their melodious jaws, consented to give a selection from their repertoire including their famous 'Italian Salad'. This in itself would bring in sufficient money to cover the cost of a leg and the committee decided that two shillings was enough for top-price tickets. They approached the deacons of Horeb chapel for use of this big building; Jenkin, off and on, had been a member of Horeb, though he never had more than one leg—and that the twitchy one—in religion. The deacons, not liking their chapel to be taken out of their hands by a lot of more or less outsiders, said they would organise the concert themselves. The rough-and-ready committee readily agreed to this, glad to be rid of the work, and the deacons of Horeb then went into owlish conclave.

'Well, Jenkin'—one of his butties sat by the hospital bed— 'a present the boys will have ready for you after you come out. Tell that nurse by there to measure you and place the order for it at once.'

Jenkin showed one cunning eye from the bedclothes, for he liked his head covered in this draughty hospital. 'What's that, mun? Coffin is it to be, or a pair of home-made crutches?'

'Wind of it you've got already, I can see, Jenkin. Best-quality artificial leg you're going to have, the same as Samson the Fireman's got.' Samson, before wearing it, had proudly exhibited his leg for a week in his front parlour window, so that all passers-by could see the marvel with its silver joints, leather flesh, and delicate screws.

'But what I'm going to do for work I don't know,' Jenkin grunted, however. 'A 'bacco shop I'd like to open.'

'The pit's sure to give you a job on top; in the lamp-room p'raps. Don't you worry now. You get well for the concert. On the platform you'll have to sit, and if the leg comes in time it can stand on a table to show everybody.'

Jenkin got better quickly after this and was out of the hospital long before the night of the concert. The leg had been ordered, but the date of delivery was unknown. But what did become known was that the deacons of Horeb had taken full advantage of this excuse for a concert and done things on a grand scale. They had solicited the charity of four vocalists, and of these four they had persuaded—great triumph—Madame Sarah Watkins to come out of her retirement and shed her lustre, gratis, on the event.

As soon as it became known that she was to appear all tickets were sold, and as top price for these was five shillings (for the deacons were business men), a sum would be raised far beyond the leg's cost. Sarah Watkins's voice was legendary and a tale told by firesides. Still more enticing, her life had been scandalous, though of course her voice covered a multitude of sins. Wife to four men (at different times), a heavy drinker (of whisky), a constant attendant at courts (for debt), notorious for tantrums (in her heyday, that is), a wearer of flashy clothes (all belonging to the era of plush pineapples and whole cygnets on hats), she was an explosion of female vitality to be reckoned with. Though now in her retirement she lived on the coast twenty miles away, Madame Watkins was a native of the valley, where her father had been one of the pioneering miners. And she had always declared, with a heave of her bosom, that she loved dear little Twlldu. Proof of this was now evident. She hadn't sung in public for fifteen years.

'Your leg it is, mun,' people said to Jenkin. 'Your leg it is that has given her a push out again.'

What the Jenkin crowd did not know was that it was the honeyed flattery, religious blandishments, and oratorical fervour of one of the Horeb deacons that had worked a spell on Sarah; he had called on her, claiming an acquaintance with her dead father. She didn't care a rap for Jenkin's leg. But, aged now, she had begun to turn an occasional eye to the religious things of

18

her childhood; it was as well to be on the safe side. Yes, she would sing in a chapel, and not for money but for glory; and she had offered the deacon a whisky, which he at once declined.

Her name on the posters, with *London, Milan* and *Twlldu* printed under it, created a sensation. The other three soloists were of local origin, too, though of course they were not to be compared. But, what with the choir as well, a huge success was assured. The deacons of Horeb informed the hospital that the bill for Mr. Jenkin Morgan's leg was to be sent to them and same would be paid cash down. It was then that Jenkin began to wake up.

'How much the leg?' he mildly asked the hospital, going up there on crutches, and a sister who had taken a fancy to him promised to find out. 'Like to know, I do, how much money I am costing,' he explained, 'so that I can give thanks according.'

The day before the concert he called on one of the deacons in his home. 'Sit down by there,' said the deacon kindly, taking the crutches. 'Arrived has the leg in the hospital, then! Fixing it on you they'll be soon, no doubt.'

'Aye'—Jenkin blew straight, full of high stomach already because of all the talk about him— 'but what I am wanting to know, Mr. Price-Harris, is *what about the extra money?*'

'Come now,' purred Mr. Price-Harris, 'your leg you've got.'

'My benefit this concert is,' said Jenkin ominously. 'The talk is that more than a hundred pounds is left over.'

The deacon pronounced, stern at once: 'Work has been done by the deacons of Horeb, and Madame Sarah Watkins is singing out of love for the old chapel of her dead father. On the glory of Horeb the extra money will be spent. Dilapidations there are and a new coat of paint needed, and—'

Jenkin heaved himself up and took his crutches. 'Good day to you now,' he said meekly.

Half an hour before the concert's starting time the chapel was packed with women in all their beads, brooches, and furs, the men in Sunday dark and starch. A wooden platform had been erected under the pulpit; a piano, chairs, and a table stood on it. In the gallery around the pipe organ behind the pulpit the Male Voice Choir assembled in good time. But no one needed to hurry. Madame Watkins wasn't nearly ready. A turmoil was going on in the vestry behind. The diva, like an old war-horse taken out again too near the smell and roar of cannon, was behaving as in her heyday. The deacons were flustered. They couldn't be expected to know that such as Madame Watkins never got the inspiration to sing before they had torn a lion or two into pieces.

The car that had been hired to fetch her was an old decrepit one driven by the fishmonger's lout of a son. And he had taken it into his head to kill two birds on this trip by collecting a small cask of herrings from the coast; it was already beside him on the front seat when he called for Madame Watkins, who brought with her a large suitcase. Secondly, no one had remembered to welcome her arrival with flowers. Thirdly, no one had thought she would need, for changing into a concert dress, somewhere more private than a vestry filled with coming and going persons connected with tonight's affair. The other three soloists, neatly attired but of whom she had never heard, waited open-mouthed.

'Get me screens, then,' she bellowed, 'and a full-length mirror, and a dresser . . . Ach,' her body gave a great quake, 'I stink of fish . . . Violet scent too,' she screamed after people who were running out into the street in search of screens and mirrors. A deacon's wife went into the chapel to scan the tiers of people for someone known to be a dressmaker. Everything was procured in due time, though the mirror was only one taken down from someone's parlour wall. The concert began an hour late.

Yet no one would have guessed the diva's fury when at last she mounted the platform and, amid thunderous applause, gave a superb bow. She advanced like an old ruined queen majestically unaware of new fashions and systems, giving an expert kick to the billowing train of her dragon-coloured but tattered dress. At sight of her, and perhaps the train, a little hiss of awe seemed to come from the goggling women in the audience. The smile issuing from the clumps of fat, the ravines, and scarlet meadows of that face, was sweeter than Lucrezia Borgia's. An aigrette feather leaped from her auburn wig. There was a smell; a fierce perfume could be smelled even all round the gallery. It was as if Madame Wakins, a member of some mythical race, had risen through the parted earth amid the odours of flowers more gloriously ornate than were known above. The slim pianist seemed to wilt over the keys as he waited. Above, the Male Voice Choir, which had already sung an opening chorus, slunk back in abeyance.

'Fancy,' a woman upstairs reminded her companion of the diva's last appearance, 'any council summonsing her for rates!'

'Oh, there's beautiful she is!' whispered the other in an aghast voice. 'And there's glad I am I've seen her. A pity for him, but if it wasn't for Jenkin's leg—'

But the erstwhile diva was launching into something out of *Carmen*. And soon it became plain that she had already given her performance. In her voice were gaping cracks through which wheezed a ghostly wind. No matter, no matter at all! For they were cracks in a temple of glorious style. A ruined temple far away in the mists of a lonely hilltop, but grander than anything of today.

20

Everyone felt sorry for the vocalist who followed Madame Watkins; she was still of coltish age, in full possession of her voice, very popular on the radio, and spick-and-span to look at as a new button. Madame Watkins refused to give an encore, but she was down to sing 'Home, Sweet Home,' in the second half. Her exit had even more pomp than her entrance, and the applause (it was said afterwards) brought a rush of soot down the chimney of the house next door up from Horeb.

Intermission said the programme, and everyone knew what that meant. Jenkin was going to go on the platform and give tidy public thanks for his artifical leg. Ah, there he was, climbing up on his crutches and followed by a pit butty who carried the leg. Sympathetic applause greeted him. The butty stood shyly holding the limb upright on the table. Those who had missed seeing Fireman Samson's leg in his window now had their opportunity. Necks were craned and approval seemed plain in the air. It was not known then that Jenkin's crutches and his thickset butty had forced their way to the platform through a wall of hostile deacons.

'No public speaker I am,' began Jenkin in a mild kind of way, 'and not yet properly back from my serious operation under chloroform. But things must be said. The leg by there is come and very thankful I am for it—and will be more after it is fitted on and got used to my ways.' He ran a cunningly assessing eye round all the chapel and curbed the aggressive note that had crept into his voice. 'But a dispute has arose, sorry to say. For my benefit this concert was made, as my butties in No. 2 pit can prove, and over a hundred pounds is lying in the chapel safe after the leg is paid for. A little 'bacco shop I want to open, and the hundred pounds just right! But no—the respected deacons of Horeb say, "*No*." For paint and varnish on Horeb they want the money. Well, permission I am asking to say just now that it is not right!' He nodded his dead ominously and finished: 'No more now, then, thanking you one and all, and Mrs. Watkins, too, that don't know.' And nodding to the butty, who took the leg under his arm, he began to clump off the platform.

An awkward silence followed him. As far as could be judged, there were those who felt that a concert in a chapel was no place to make such a complaint. But also there were those who, ever ready to suspect ill-conduct in high places, followed Jenkin's exit with an approving eye. Then up to the platform walked dignified Mr. J. T. Llewellyn, a deacon of long and admired standing. Sternly he said in the quiet:

'Respecting the matter mentioned just now by Mr. Jenkin Morgans, the benefit that was asked by his friends of the pit is now fulfilled. A leg first-class is given to him. Success of this concert was business of Horeb's deacons and much interest in the needs of the chapel showed Madame Sarah Watkins when she remembered it was the chapel of her old father . . . Now,' he continued with an austere dismissal and looking at a copy of the programme, 'back to the concert! The choir will open again with a rendering of "Italian Salad". Ladies and gentlemen, "Italian Salad"!' And with this flourish he swept away.

While Madame Watkins in the vestry—the screens around her—was taking a secret drink of whisky out of a medicine bottle, Mr. J. T. Llewellyn thought it prudent to break into her privacy to mention the leg affair. Infuriated by (a) being caught red-handed drinking an intoxicant in a chapel vestry and (b) the deacon's tale of Jenkin's exhibition on the platform, the diva began to boil again. What, a surgical leg had been displayed on the platform a few minutes after her appearance! Her sense of style and what was fitting in a concert containing her was outraged. Amateurs, she taunted, bah! The deacon, flustered by this unaccustomed kind of high-mindedness, contined to mumble explanations uselessly. 'Interested in surgical legs I am *not*!' she stormed. 'Ring up that curtain, and let me get home.'

'No curtain there is here.' The deacon coughed. 'But a hot supper is waiting for you afer the concert, along with the other soloists.'

'What! Who are these persons?' she blew. 'Do they sell cockles and mussels in the daytime?'

And she all but ran out to sing 'Home, Sweet Home'. Yet once more the smile that greeted the loving applause was of a piercing and all-embracing sweetness which made few shiver. And the cracked voice gave an added poignancy to the old song. Not many eyes remained quite dry, for was not the celebrated Madame Watkins singing this song in her true birthplace? The concert was considered, and rightly, a red-letter one.

But the matter of Jenkin's leg did not remain there. Many of the men in No. 2 pit took umbrage at the chapel's treatment of their one-time fellow workman. These, in any case, were always critical of chapels and their power over social pleasures. Fierce arguments developed in the pits, and the ancient question of whether there is an Almighty or not was yet again raised by the opposed forces. Continued in public places on top, the dispute caused some physical combats on Saturday nights. The men's families began to take sides, too, and many were the hostilities exchanged over back-garden fences by wives pegging out washing; many were the schoolyard tumbles. After three weeks of this a meeting of miners was called in the Workmen's Hall. A strong faction of the men wanted to go on strike if Jenkin did not receive all profits from the concert.

The deacons of Horeb put on their armour. Some of them were officials in the colliery; others hoped to be. They gave emphatic 'No' to this new blackmail by men whose infamy was worsened by their being of atheistic mind. They sat tight. Out in the valley a complication was added to the affair by Jenkin's decision not to use the artificial leg till his plea had been settled. He went about the place on his pathetic crutches, thus keeping quick his supporters' sympathy.

'No,' he would say, brave, 'all right I am. But set fire to me would that leg if I put it on. Just going down to the barber's I am to read the papers.' Too poor he was to buy papers, of course.

Well, the Miners' Federation, getting wind of this unofficial strike, forbade it. Jenkin's supporters became more haughty at this. Hadn't the men of Twlldu downed tools once because an unpopular policeman was carrying on with a married woman? Wasn't this robbery of Jenkin worse? Glittering words were used at a second Workmen's Hall meeting. Finally it was decided to give the deacons another fortnight to hand over the money. There had been no sign of painters and plasteres starting work on the chapel.

'No,' said Bryn Stop Tap, an extremist, 'nor won't be. But fur coats will be seen on the deacons' wives and the ginger-beer van calling every day at their houses.'

Jenkin whimpered with devilish meekness: 'Stop the old fuss. Bad blood I am spreading.' But still he wouldn't use the leg, and his crutches and folded-up trousers were a standing reproach to everybody.

There was a nasty row in the fruit shop one Friday evening. Mrs. Evans Fruit, a suspected supporter of the deacons' side, was accused by a pro-Jenkin woman of giving her nothing but damaged apples while only healthy ones had just gone into the basket of a customer also suspected to be on the other side. The shop was full of women.

'You get out of my shop, you liar!' shouted Mrs. Evans.

Pointing at the fruiterer, another customer said two words: 'She's Horeb!'

As is known from the conduct of mobs in the French Revolution, a single accusing cry can batter down a palace and spread riot like a tornado. Soon the shop was in a very untidy state and several old insulting scandals had been referred to in the course of the row. Mrs. Evans herself collapsed on to a basket of green-gages, but by the time the policeman arrived order had been restored and everybody felt twice alive and that the world was worth living in after all. Jenkin heard, of course, of this battle on his behalf and once more called on the local reporter, trying to incite him to inform his paper. Meanwhile, he had also laboured over a long letter to Madame Sarah Watkins, soliciting her opinion. But he received no reply.

'Oh, don't you bother about me,' he whined in the Bracchi ice-cream and coffee shop a week later, as everybody offered him a seat. 'Lean on my crutches I can. Only come in to pass the time I have. If I had my little 'bacco shop, busy enough I would be.' But it was strange that no one offered him a cigarette that day, or refreshment.

A third Workmen's Hall meeting was held long after the fortnight had gone. The deacons had made no sign. But neither were the painters and ladders about Horeb. At the meeting there was a lot of high talk and everybody had a consoling word for Jenkin; the feeling was that soon as a painter's brush was put to Horeb the bomb would burst. But it was strange that the meeting got on quite soon to New Year fixtures for the Twlldu Eleven. Jenkin sat with his head on one side like a long-suffering bird.

'Waiting for the spring the deacons are,' someone told Jenkin outside the pub's closed door. 'Horeb will have a spring cleaning on your money. Better ask for a job on top of the pits, Jenkin.'

One January day Jenkin, giving vent to loud abuse, threw a crutch through a window of Horeb. But all that resulted was a summons and he had to pay the cost of the window. Feeling for and against him was revived for a day or two. Yet it was only talk and argument. Then at the end of February Mrs. Roberts the Washing's house went up in flames. A poor widow who took in washing, her cottage wasn't insured. Though she was out during the fire and didn't have to be rescued, a long sigh of sorrow for her went right through the valley. It was plain what would have to be done in her aid.

'Ask Madame Sarah Wakins to come again,' several persons said. A committee was formed.

The day after the fire Jenkin's wife took out a long cardboard box from under the bed. She was a quiet little woman who rarely put a foot into the valley's doings. But she had good eyesight and ears clear of wax. Jenkin looked at her sulkily. 'A bit tired I am,' she said, 'of idleness and sloth. Put on your leg, Jenkin, and go up to the pits to work.' On the promise of the Horeb money coming she had been lent cash by her sister. 'Come on, Jenkin,' she coaxed. And she said cleverly: 'Put not your trust in princes and the people of this earth.'

Jenkin lifted his head. A religious light shone in his eyes. 'Aye,' he said in grand contempt, 'the bull's-eye you said there! Shall a man like me be lowered because all around him are low? Help me with my leg, Maria. The hospital said like this—'

In March men placed ladders against Horeb and, carrying cans of primrose paint, they went up them unmolested. But the concert for Mrs. Roberts the Washing's benefit was not held there. And Madame Sarah Watkins did not appear for this; she wrote saying that her retirement was final unless her health

24

improved. But she was in the papers again before March was out: a firm of licensed victuallers sued her for goods delivered. She told the court that she had been too goodhearted and lately had sung everywhere for nothing, in aid of this and that charity. After the painters had done the windows of Horeb they varnished the solid pews inside.

A DANGEROUS REMEDY

I

No chance visitor to Three Saints would believe it at first. But there, alive on her three-legged stool outside her cottage door, sat Jane Puw herself, ready to tell how she was snatched out of the jaws of death by an ordinary cow. Illness can be a complicated matter of deep consultations, expensive specialists and a long rigmarole treatment. The simple remedy advocated by Dr. Vavasor Evans, who had never travelled further than Bristol, achieved a miracle the same afternoon that it was prescribed and after the doctor from the market town had given Jane Puw up as lost to this world.

Dr. Evans no longer practised. He had retired to his native village of Three Saints, half lost among big hills and where outsiders seldom penetrate, after a long life in Bristol. There, as a young man, he had known the distinguished Dr. Beddoes who first advocated a cow for the cure of certain complaints. It was true that Vavasor drank and that his housekeeper, up in the secluded house on the hillside, had often to put him to bed. But if a man can drink like a bulrush, live until he is eighty, and pull a going woman from the grave's brink, then the voice of criticism is stilled. After the cure Jane would hear no word of doubt about him; and she gave him an old cuckoo clock that he fancied instead of cash. Because of a long warfare she was carrying on with her daughter-in-law in the market town she was very pleased that he had kept her this side. She hoped to live to see the younger woman into the ground.

It was after a bout with this daughter-in-law that she had been stricken. She was already wheezing like a rusty gate, for her chest had never been strong. But she had taken her fowls and flannel to market just the same, and it was there she met her son's wife that, except to quarrel with, she had not spoken to for thirty years. They had a bout of tongues behind the flower stall, and that evening a palsy came over her. For three weeks she dwindled in loss of strength.

'Going I am,' she whimpered to her husband Watcyn in one of her clear spells. 'Under the cask in the shed my money is.'

'You want to make things up with Mali before you go?' enquired Watcyn, who hated the feud that had gone on so long.

A red began to mottle the tough old cheeks. 'That 'ooman's face you'd show in front of me while I'm lying helpless by here, Watcyn! And opening my cupboards to see if my linen is washed and prying into my pantry! For shame on you.' She began to choke in fury already.

'There now, Jane fach, there now!' soothed Watcyn, for she had been a good wife, as matters are in this world. 'No indeed, and she shan't come to your funeral either.'

But Jane began to grizzle in self-pity that she was stricken in bed, devoid of power at last, while the younger woman could have many more years of spreading calumny. She went lower that day. The market town doctor, a brisk youngster, told Watcyn that nothing could be done: It was then that Watcyn, in despair, thought of old Vavasor, come to live up there on the mountain a year ago and a man born of the district who knew the ways of its sons and daughters.

He found Vavasor with a huge bandaged foot up on a chair, one sultry eye lurking down his face lower than the other, and a mildewed tuft of hair on his speckled pate—for since coming to Wales he had ceased to wear his wig. There was a glass of whisky in his hand. 'What you want?' he shouted crossly, for he was of those physicians that are choleric of manner. 'I am retired. The whole bloody world can be on its last gammy legs for all I care. Eight hundred quid I paid for this house and the winds blow round it fit to lift it off its backside.'

But Watcyn knew that Vavasor, though odd as his unmatched eyes, had a gentle spot in his heart for the people of Three Saints. He begged him to take a peep at Jane. 'A cart I got outside to take you down,' he said. 'And plenty of straw on the bottom for your bad old foot.'

Cursing and pessimistic, Vavasor took his crutch and, wrapped in rugs and coats, descended to the village. By the time he arrived Jane was gone still lower and panted for air. She gave a little grunt when Vavasor blew into her ear but she did not open her eyes.

'Get a cow. Quick now.' Watcyn gaping and putting his hand to his ear, Vavasor shouted: 'Go on, quick. A full-sized cow in the pink, and bring her up here.'

'Upstairs?' quavered Watcyn.

'Aye. That chest of drawers got to be moved. Bring a man or two with you. Go on, I'll wait; any whisky in the house?'

Three Saints is known for its good milk, as the village across the mountain is known for its soft wool. The cows are mild and contented; the grass is moist and lush. The herd at Cefn farm ar the end of the village was first class, and as Watcyn had never had any dispute there he obtained the loan of an umber-and-white cow readily.

'More sense she's got than a lot,' Llew the farmer said, selecting her, 'and go upstairs she will easy. Just been milked she has too, so will be comfortable.' In Wales, since doctors invariably fail to cure the stricken, great belief is placed in homely remedies and odd anointments. Llew's grannie herself always said that she was over ninety because in winters she wore a sow's ear under her bodice, changing it often.

So it was that a cow, gently thwacked by a Cefn cowman, was seen to enter Watcyn's cottage door. Watcyn and a neighbour had moved all furniture out of the way. After a hesitation she mounted the short flight of stairs amiably enough and, wooed by the cowman, ambled into the low-roofed bedroom whisking her tail. Her obedient eyes were observant and curious.

Seated on a chair in a corner, his bad foot on a stool, Vavasor directed operations in that autocratic manner that had frightened the spectre from Bristol death-chambers many times in years gone by.

'Get her head over the bed, make her breathe right on the old woman's face. Get her to lick her tongue on the cheeks and mouth too . . . No, you idiot,' he shouted, brandishing his crutch angrily and his lower eye whirring in contempt, 'don't *pull* her tongue out. Don't excite the animal. There's plenty of time. Breathing first!'

Already the soft fragrant cloud of the cow's breath was filling the low room, for, when curious a cow breathes heavily and all its milky inside, composed of sweet grasses, clover and the ghosts of spring buttercups, is returned to the air, while a patina of juices stains the cool wet nose. The cow gazed in a long interested muse at Jane's face sunk in torpor on the pillow. At first it seemed she wanted to stir a horn playfully into that shut-eyed face. Lower and lower the cowman coaxed the nose. And the sweet cloud blew out of the shiny nostrils full on the twitched face.

'That's right,' croaked Vavasor. 'Now if she'll lick! Sprinkle a bit of salt on the old woman's face if she won't.' As the cow hesitated to lick, Watcyn got salt and threw it with loving but excited fingers over Jane's cheeks and lips— for sure enough there were signs already that Jane was stirring out of her uneasy coma. And the cow's long grey-and-buff tongue came out and deliciously swept over Jane's face, even over eyes and brow. The soft *clop clop* of the rub was pleased and placid.

Anyone that has felt a cow's tongue on his skin well knows that the electric touch opens up antique sensation almost lost to the human's world. Jane's lids lifted suddenly and a pair of eyes swam up from the murky fumes of death's kingdom. At first, as her eyes looked into the cow's, there was only ordinary recognition in them; the exchanged gaze was much the same as when distant relatives see each other in market. The full activity jolted into Jane's face. She snorted, she opened wide her mouth.

28

'Champion!' observed Vavasor in satisfaction, and shouted: 'Keep your mouth open far as it can, there's a good woman.'

Benign and pleased with her feed of salt the cow breathed nothing but good-will into Jane's face. And there was no doubt that the beast was a doctor whose worth was beyond crowns and kingdoms. For, as full sense grew bright blue in her eyes, Jane gave vent to a vigorous shriek that showed she was already well back in the world. It was a shriek that a woman might give if a burglar is in her house or a mouse up her skirt.

And before the month was out she was downstairs making a pie.

II

Which was all very well. But there were a few doubters in Three Saints that said it was really the shock of seeing a cow in her bedroom that had brought Jane Puw back to life. These also said that such a shock might, on the other hand, mean the final push into the abyss if someone more sensitive than Jane were subjected to this treatment. Surely it was a dangerous remedy?

Nevertheless most people declared they were ready to try Vavasor's prescription when the occasion arose. A fact cannot be dodged, and there was Jane Puw back at her handloom, going to market with her sharp eyes on Thursdays and saying she's never felt more ready to face anything. Plain there was magic healing in a cow's breath and tongue. But Three Saints is a healthy place and it was not until the next autumn that seventy-year-old Clydach Wyndham got taken to bed with a quick bronchitis.

Now, it was known that Dilys, his unmarried daughter who lived with him, was weary of the cantankerous old man. That first week of his illness she refused to have a cow brought into her little spick-and-span cottage. She had, prudently, been one of those who doubted the remedy, and also she declared now that no cow could ever get up the staircase, which was indeed very narrow. People criticised her hard, unbelieving heart and said why couldn't the old man be brought downstairs in blankets? There were mutterings against her. Finally an informer went over the mountain to tell Clydach's son who worked in a wool mill over there.

By this time Clydach was in a low state indeed. 'No use trying to put a stop to nature,' his awful daughter declared, flat. 'Gone to seed has my old datta, and time he dropped. Miserable he is to himself and me.' She was one of those women who are without the humbugs that sweeten her sex. She would inherit the cottage.

But Ellis the son came tramping over the mountain, where the first snow lay blue in the morning, and, after a look at the father, he shook his fist in Dilys's face and abused her for not calling either him or a doctor.

'Quick,' he shouted to the visitors coming in and out of the cottage—for it seemed now that Clydach wouldn't last the day, and death makes a house public— 'fetch a cow.'

'The stairs,' cried Dilys, but a bit subdued in her brother's wrath— 'very narrow they are, even for a coffin. I washed them this morning too. Some sacks I will get.' Clydach was gone too far to be moved downstairs now.

She rushed about, covering the linoleum with sacking and brown paper. Shad, a neighbour, had run for a cow. One of the Cefn farm meadows lay up the lane outside the cottage, and in it browsed fifteen cows in speculative waiting. Without asking permission or consulting the farmer, he drove the first cow through the gate and hurried her down the lane. She was a black-and-white beast of full size and her udder was full; one of Llew's best milkers. Frightened, she began to whimper and swerve. He landed her an angry thwack. She shot forward, the big udder swinging.

'Darro, Shad,' exclaimed Ellis, coming out of the cottage, 'a litter one couldn't you bring? Never mind now, no time to waste. Hee now, Shoo!' He gave the cow, hesitant outside the door, a push from the rear. Nervous, she skipped inside and at once her horn scratched the wall-paper, making Dilys screech.

Four men urged her towards the narrow stairs. 'Just take the width she will,' judged Ellis. 'Shoved past the bulge she must be; covered pretty fair her ribs are. Hee now! Shoo!' The distracted beast looked at the stairs in hostility. Thwacks descended on her rump. The men got her forelegs on the first stairs. Sweating and forgetful of the sick man upstairs, they were shouting and cursing. Joined to the uproar were the lamentations of Dilys, who foresaw disaster to her tidy and clean cottage.

'A rope!' shouted Ellis. 'Get a rope and drag the stupid old muffin up.' The cow stood on the first stairs whimpering soft moos and refusing to budge further. A rope was fetched, and the thinnest of the men climbed under the udder and up between the forelegs. The rope round the cow's neck, he stood on the landing and pulled. Behind, they thwacked and shouted. The cow heaved forward, her hoofs lifted by the men. But where the ancient wall bellied she became wedged.

It was then she lost her nerve altogether and began to bellow at the top of her voice. Her agonised exclamations shook the little cottage. In those cries were fear, protests and the anguish of her disturbed full udder. Below, the men's faces gazed up helpless, with Dilys purple in righteous anger behind them.

30

'Ah!' exclaimed Shad suddenly, 'near her milking time it is; I forgot. Nancy do milk her and sing to her.'

'Fetch Nancy, then,' shouted Ellis.

'Blow my whistle,' snapped Dilys, and fetched the second-hand policeman's whistle she had kept in the cottage since the time a tramp had broken in.

With the cow still bellowing, Shad blew the whistle on the doorstep. Several blasts he gave before, a distance away on the slope above the village, Nancy appeared on the farmhouse doorstep. He beckoned to her like a madman; she came flying down. And from the village too everybody began hurrying up to the cottage.

'A bucket!' Ellis screamed above the cow's bellows. 'A bucket get ready.'

'Serve you right,' snapped Dilys, but got a pail.

In bustled Nancy, very angry and shouting when she learned what had been done. 'No business you had to help yourself,' she shrieked. 'Curdled her you have, no doubt . . . Oh, my poor Betti, all right then; but here is your little Nancy, never mind.' Her spectacles flashing, she snatched the pail, clattered it under the udder and, kneeling on the stairs, began to milk. But there was such rage in her fingers that the weeping cow made a sudden jump. And in clumsy heaves, the pail sent flying by her hoofs, she got up the last stairs. Shouts of triumph came from the crowd below.

On the landing she stood and let out terrific bleats of renewed agony. 'Duw, duw, there's a row!' exclaimed Shad, shocked. In a temper and bawling insults at them, Nancy hurried upstairs. 'A stool!' she shouted. 'A stool bring me.' Such a state she was in, in sympathy for her loved cow, that for a while she couldn't compose herself to warble the song that best brought out the milk. Sitting on the stool, she began too high and out of tune. And still the cow noisily grieved. From the people downstairs rose a gabble of excitement.

Then someone exclaimed suddenly: 'What about old Clydach? There's upsetting it must be for him, lying there by himself!'

'Reach his room we cannot,' Dilys said, vindictive. 'Blocking my clean landing that cow is.'

But the son Ellis was squirming under the cow. He got to the front room. There he found his father gone. And it was clear that he had gone in great fear. His fingers still clutched the edge of the bedspread as if to draw it over him in terror. Out on the landing the cow's bellows began to cease.

For, her voice adjusted at last, Nancy's low, neat contralto was singing an old air of the country while some of its richest milk splashed safe into the pail.

THE LAST STRUGGLE

Grief for the newly-dead is natural in the living and thought of legacies and insurance money to be drawn from them comes second in most persons. Megan Pugh, wife of Sam Two Fingers, thought of the insurance on her husband first, that day when the pit under-manager came to her in person and sat in her kitchen telling her that all hope of rescuing Sam and the other two entombed miners had been abandoned. Megan managed to pull a face. But already her mind was wandering in speculation. A pity she would have to wear black for a time. There was a cerise dress in the window of Lewis Paris House that she madly coveted.

'The water it is,' mourned Mr. Rowlands; 'they must have been drowned.' He avoided even thinking that the three men were very likely more horribly obliterated; drowning sounded ordinary. 'Can't get at them,' he mumbled, 'for weeks, p'raps never. Blocks of stone nearly as big as a house and water running under all the time; might cause a flood of the mine if we blast the stone.' There had been a big collapse of roof four days before; four days the men had been entombed.

Fifty pounds Sam was insured for, with the Globe and Atlas people whose New Year gift calendar was on the wall; and of course there would be the compensation money from the pit too. She could go to the seaside; she could even live away from the valley at last. And why should she wear black! Black made her look sallow.

Perhaps, in a way, it was only natural that Megan should be so unnatural. Sam had always kept her short of money; you couldn't hold him off the dogs, though much of a drinker he was not and he had never hit her. He was known as Sam Two Fingers because after a previous accident in the pit one hand was left with the other fingers gone. The strange thing was those two fingers developed a peculiar iron grip.

Only a few months before she had married him—a couple of years ago it was they had hurried to the chapel—she fet it was a mistake; a false alarm the wedding had been. As a courter he had strutted cockily at her side and she took it as pleasure in being in her company. As a married man he had got bossy at once and, when she complained that he was never in the house, answered: 'You can't bring a dog race to the house, can you? Don't I sleep tidy at home every night? What more you want?'

She wanted to be taken about by him, she wanted clothes and train journeys; she did not want to become like the dumpy women of the valley, who only left their doors to go to the shops and the chapel. They had quarrelled like hell. But even in those two years she had been defeated. The valley was a man's valley, with pubs, clubs, dog tracks and football grounds for men only. Perhaps this would change if women went down to work in the pits. But not yet.

'The Company will give you compensation, I dare say,' Mr. Rowlands mumbled in embarrassment, thinking her far-away look meant shock or worry.

'How much?' she asked.

Mr. Rowlands shook his head. 'An inquest and an enquiry there'll have to be before anything is settled.' He was tired and grey from worry, but tough from long experience of these incidents. Thank goodness, though, Sam Two Fingers's wife didn't make a scene, as some wives did, especially the young ones. He heaved himself up to make the other two calls with the sad news. In their black tomb the men were lying beyond the fret of the living, sealed away for ever from the numerous details and costs of this world. Megan Pugh had sense. She did not cry out for the remains to be found and re-buried in a proper funeral.

Megan locked her front door after him. She did not want neighbours coming in to condole. There were many things to plan. She was tied in no way. Not a child to delay her. The empty days were over. Next morning she was up early and by half-past nine was sitting in a tram-car which linked the districts, colliery by colliery, of the long crab-coloured valley. The July sun shone. It would be nice by the sea if this weather kept.

At the valley's end, in a cottage overlooking the railway, she knocked at a door. It belonged to her Uncle Dai, a greaser on the railway and a private bookie. Dai was no fool with his money but could be persuaded. His wife made a cup of tea when she heard the news and, taking her cue from Megan's lack of tearful display, asked: 'What your plans now?' For Megan still had a gloss on her, knew how to wear a hat, and was a good-looker with skin and teeth still fresh as daisies.

'A little rest straight away,' Megan replied; 'a little rest by myself in Weston-super-Mare, to think things out.'

'Get married more careful next time,' Dai's wife said shrewdly.

'I've been locked up!' Megan said with violence.

'Aye, a regular old Tory your Sam was. A wife was set final for him and couldn't be broke away.'

Dai came in for his dinner at twelve. He made more money as a quiet bookie than as a greaser and did not dislike his niece. Megan produced the insurance book out of her bag and all the weekly payments for Sam were down regular.

'And there's the compensation from the pit too,' she added. 'Mrs. Bevan near me had a couple of hundred pounds when her Emlyn got killed.'

She was asking her uncle for an immediate loan of fifty pounds, since very likely, what with inquests and fusses, it would be a week or more before the insurance people paid out. For this favour she was willing to pay him two pounds interest. He could keep the insurance book for security and she would see the insurance agent and tell him that her Uncle Dai was handling her affairs. She wanted to go to Weston-super-Mare without delay; her nerves were upset from the shock.

The chance of making a couple of pounds on such a certain deal made even Dai joke: ' A fancy piece of goods in trousers you got in Weston-super-Mare, Megan? Well, well—'

So, bad though it looked, she skulked off the next day. She took train to the seaside town the other side of the Bristol Channel, did not jib at the high charge in a boarding-house, and then went at once to the drapers' shops and spent ten pounds in an hour. Her most daring purchases, owing to their colour, were a scarlet frock with handbag to match. For three days she lived in the shops and began to believe in happiness again. It was not until the Sunday that she felt appeased and, examining the beach and pier, began to wonder if she had come to the English town to look at men who did not work down under. For she would never marry another miner, coming home black and bellicose from dirty pits.

Weston-super-Mare, in the season, is bright. She sat eating striped ice-cream and one afternoon she went to Cheddar to visit the famous caves. She kept herself to herself but noticed a man looking at her instead of at the crystal grottoes and stalactites. And in the coach going back there he was sitting next to her! They got talking. He said he was from Birmingham, but he belittled the caves and said there were much finer ones in India.

A quiet-looking chap he was, chatting quite sedate. Malaria had sent him back from India. He was an electrician and had a job in a Birmingham factory now. His lean, lonely appearance was of one who wants looking after, but he ushered her out of the high plush coach with polite confidence. She accepted his invitation to take a glass of something in the lounge of a hotel on the front.

At the end of the second week she told him, grandly: 'I am a widow. Husband killed in the pits at home. But I got a bit of property. Independent.' She wished to be respected and she sounded short.

'Well,' Ted Cricks said, 'that's fine. Look here, I got to go back on Monday.

But I dare say I could do a week-end soon as you get home, if asked. Is there a pub I could stay at there?'

She got a bit flustered, thinking of the neighbouts. But, sitting on a golden beach with the sky blue and music coming from the pier, the world seemed easy. The tide was rolling in, moving with dark but careless force. She gave him her address and invited him for a week-end. He could sleep at her Uncle Dai's. He said he would wire her from Birmingham.

'Back soon, lovely weather,' was all she had said on the postcard she had sent to Uncle Dai. Forty pounds had been spent and her new suitcase was full. She stayed a few more days. After all, there was the compensation money to come, and she had a houseful of furniture, to say nothing of a promising courter from Birmingham.

On the way back she stopped in Cardiff for an hour and drank three ruby ports in farewell of the triumphant holiday. Wearing her red dress she arrived in the valley at dusk with three pounds in her handbag. But she tossed her head at the valley and admired herself for the flaunting display she was making. It was time some woman showed a respect for her own wants in this place. She did not care what the neighbours, stern guardians of the inexorable laws of the hearth, would think of the gay clothes. Sam wasn't worth mourning, the way he had treated her. She had a good mind to march into a pub there and then and scandalise those entirely male haunts.

As it happened there was no one about in her street. Preened and sunburnt, she unlocked her door. In the dusky passageway she paused just behind the door. Was that the sound of mice? Then her head hung forward and she dropped her red handbag.

The kitchen door at the end of the passage was slowly opening. A two-fingered hand came round it. She could see it distinctly in the twilight. But she could not scream. Her knees like water, she was squatting to the floor. But her face was stretched up, stiffly gazing. The door had been pushed wide open and the ghost of Sam, grey and silent, stood looking at her.

Just the same as when he sat before the fire for a while after his evening bath, before going off to the dogs, he wore trousers and sleeve-rolled shirt, a loose belt round his middle. But his cheeks were hollow and his eyes burned. It was Sam and it wasn't. And from the look of those smouldering eyes she could not move. They stood looking at each other for an age. Suddenly the ghost breathed, far away:

'You get up from there!'

'Sam . . .' she whimpered at last.

'I'll Sam you!' he panted now. 'I'll give you Weston-super-mare . . .' But she had fainted.

To her dying day Megan thought she would never forget those two fingers coming round the door. It had burned into her mind. She found herself lying on the kitchen sofa. The strange thing was that he did not attack her either with tongue or hand. He only looked at her now and again. But for her it was a dead man looking at her. He was still grey from his burial, and thinner, and in his eyes lurked the stagnant glow of one not yet fully back in the world.

'You . . .' she whispered, 'you were rescued?'

'Aye, I was rescued,' he replied, stern. 'The only one.'

For, when the cracks had sounded in the roofing, he had leapt to a manhole in the facing, a pick-axe in his hand. Two huge blocks of stone from the falling roof had sealed him in there neatly as in an upright coffin. He heard the rush of water and waited to be choked. But the water found a channel away from the manhole and it had faded to a trickling sound. And then time too had faded. The pick's wooden handle had been caught by the edge of the stone and he could not budge it in the narrow space. He had gnawed it through with his teeth, but how long this had taken he did not know, for he had slept, waking again and again to resume the gnawing. He swallowed the chewed-off wood. On the floor was a puddle of gritty water which he managed to scoop up with his hand. At last he could wrench away a stump of the handle. He had thumped with it against the stone for hours, for days, waking from sleep. The miracle had happened at last: they heard the ghostly tapping. By the time they reached him he was unconscious. But after attention he came to with a grunt. Sam Two Fingers was tough as a mule.

She did not ask for the history of his return. She only whimpered from the sofa: 'I want to go to bed.'

'Aye,' he said briefly, 'go on.'

She rose, swayed, but huddled herself to the door. He stood, looking taller in his leanness, and watched her from those resurrected eyes.

'A red dress!' was all he said. 'No mourning for me!'

He lay at her side in bed like a stranger, not moving. Even his breathing was different; soft it was, as a cat breathes. If only he would touch her she thought her fear would break; once more he would be an alive man. Yet she dreaded that he would touch her with that two-fingered hand. She forced her tongue to say: 'You are sleeping?' He did not answer but she knew he was awake. That night she went down to the last depths of the world. She slept at last and woke to find him gone from her side. And the house was empty, as a house from which a dead person has been removed.

Yet he was downstairs and she smelt something burning. She went down in her nightgown. He had kindled the kitchen fire and was burning her red dress. Under his arm was the handbag. She whispered. 'There's three pound notes in that bag.'

'Not now,' he said. 'Three pounds towards the fifty you got to save.' And he thrust the bag into the fire's core.

Her new suitcase would come up with the station lorry that morning. She went pale. Thought of the suitcase brought that Birmingham man back to her mind. What was his name? . . . Had that holiday been? She ran upstairs and threw herself on the bed in fright. She did not know his address. But perhaps he would not come, perhaps he had only been playing with her, like they did on holiday. Very likely he was married.

She crept about the house, mechanical at tasks. Sam took very little notice of her, calm in his new power. His only move from the house was to the back lane, where he gossiped with such night-shift men as were hanging about. She had to go to the shops. Women looked at her curiously but no one spoke to her; she kept her eyes down. When she arrived back he was smashing up her suitcase, a look of calm but terrible deliberation in his face.

'Well,' she panted, 'there's foolish!'

'You shut up,' he said. He glanced at her shopping basket. 'You better start saving. Fifty quid you owe your uncle.'

Three days passed just the same, Sam silent but watching her like a cat that seems not to be watching. He never touched her, day or night. Was it that, though physically he was not harmed by his entombment, the shock had unhinged his mind? From him came that new shut-in strength. He had always been bossy and a talkative strutter, but now a deeper and more tenacious power surrounded him so that she felt he was following her even when she went out alone. She wanted to run away, to plead for sanctuary at her Uncle Dai's, screaming that Sam was contemplating some awful punishment, perhaps murder. He showed no signs of returning to work and sat reading a newspaper or book for hours. If only he went to a dog race!

Several times she walked as far as the tram-car stop but always turned back. And there he was still, grey by the fireside, his thick neck bent over a newspaper. If she said something he told her to shut up. But once again he warned her to start saving; he wasn't going to have her beholden to her tyke of an uncle.

'How can I save all that?' she whimpered, but a bit rebellious too.

'Starve yourself,' he barked. 'And if you buy any clothes I'll knock you into the middle of next week.'

Bad luck follows the damned. Sam it was who, when she was out, took in the telegram and opened it. She found the slip of paper on the kitchen table— 'Arriving tomorrow afternoon. Ted.' Sam sat laboriously reading the book of Dickens lent him by a neighbour. He said nothing and she knew by his shoulders that now word could be dragged out of him. She went upstairs and lay on the bed; her stomach was plunging. But presently a new thought came to her and she sat up with a vindictive expression. Now was her chance!

Next day she dressed herself carefully, made up her face, and took several aspirins. She told Sam: 'I've got a visitor coming to tea.'

'Aye,' he said, 'I'll be here.' And turned a page of that maddening book.

'When are you going back to work?' she forced herself to ask.

'You'll know when . . . But I'm not working for you to bloody well pay your uncle fifty quid, see! You got to pay him off your own belly and back, if it takes you ten years.'

'You . . . you devil!' she breathed. But her inside was plunging again. He read on calmly.

There was only one train in the afternoon. She could have met it. But, her face set, she stayed in the house. She did not want Ted to turn back at the station. The kettle was beginning to boil on the fire when the knocker went. Sam still read, sitting in old trousers and shirt-sleeves rolled up; with him a book had to be finished once begun. Her neck throbbing, she closed the kitchen door behind her. Ted stood on the front step with an attaché-case, a new soft hat, and a raincoat neatly folded over his arm. Quite smartly dressed he was, and a man who would make such a long journey to see a holiday pick-up is clearly much attracted. Her confidence grew. 'Hello, Megan,' he said with a kind of nervous jauntiness. 'You never thought I'd come, I bet?'

She smiled gently and quiveringly, the whole appeal of an ill-used woman in it. Her eyes had both hurt and begging. And in the passage she clutched his arm, whimpered a little against his shoulder and let him smell her hair, shampooed that morning. He said, unsteadily: 'Why, what's the matter? . . . There, there now. Have you missed me?'

'Something has happened,' she whispered. 'My husband is here.'

He stiffened. 'But you told me he was dead.'

'It was a mistake. He was rescued after being buried a whole week in the pit . . . Oh, Ted, so cruel he's been to me. I've been going mad. I can't stand it any longer, no indeed I can't.' She clung to his arm.

A call made to a man's gallantry—unless he is of exceptional quality—is rarely left unanswered. Though still bewildered, Ted's face became stern. Having travelled to India he looked upon himself as a man of the world. This dour, ugly coal-mining valley with its harsh look and frowning mountains had depressed him as he walked up from the station. And here was a dainty, tragical little woman chained in it by some ruffian of a husband who was ill-treating her.

All the same, he mumbled cautiously enough: 'Well, do you want me to see him?'

'Yes,' she whispered, in a weak little voice.

'And you want to come away with me?' he asked, a trifle uneasily.

Again she laid her head in trust on his shoulder and breathed: 'Yes.'

Sam looked up from his book when they walked in. The table was laid for tea, very bright and clean, though there was not much food. Sam looked thick, squat and working-man beside Ted's slim but half-wavering height. Megan, standing with her eyes suddenly flashing, said to her husband, who had nodded briefly to the stranger: 'A friend that I met in Weston-super-Mare.'

'Your fancy man, you mean,' Sam grunted, and gave Ted another hard but not dangerous look.

'Will you sit down, Ted?' she asked in an ignoring way, and went to pour water into the teapot.

'You stop that!' barked Sam to her. 'There's no fancy man of my wife going to drink tea in my house.'

'Don't be so silly,' she said unsteadily, and went on pouring water.

He lifted his foot and neatly kicked the pot out of her hand. It smashed on the hearth. Ted involuntarily jumped up, his hat falling from his knee. Megan began whimpering; perhaps her hand was scalded. 'Here!' exclaimed Ted in a peculiar way. Sam sat back in his chair and looked at him squarely. 'What you going to do about it?' he asked, but quite polite.

'He's taking me away!' shouted Megan, enraged. Her face had become twisted and mottled, lips thin as a viper's, eyes hard and menacing. But only for a moment—for she had caught Ted's glance at her. She threw herself whimpering into the sofa, her head lolling woebegone.

Sam, quite calm, told Ted to sit down again. He then addressed the visitor exclusively and with concentration, paying no attention to Megan's sobs: 'Look, here now, Mr. What's-your-name, you listen to me . . . You're welcome to her, if you like. She's a bitch but got good points and only wants training—ever had anything to do with greyhounds?' Ted, pale at the gills, shook his head. 'Well,' Sam resumed, 'you don't know how they got to be trained, then, and what I'm meaning is that everybody's got to be trained in the same way. Everybody's got to knuckle under some way or another. I got to knuckle under to a lot of sods in the pits, and as I see it a woman's got to knuckle under to a boss of a husband . . . She,' he jerked a thumb towards Megan, 'don't want to and thinks she can break this bloody world's rules and go kicking around with no respect for anything . . . Know what she did soon as she thought I wasn't coming out of that pit alive? Raised fifty quid on my insurance and ran off to Weston-super-Mare without as much as buying a black blouse in mourning of me! That's the sort of woman she is. The old blooming place is talking about it. Why did she do it? All because I go off to the dogs when I've had a day's bellyfull of the pits and don't hang around her neck of evenings like a suckling pig.' His eyes seemed to shoot together in a righteous ferocity. 'She's one of those women that want to make a chap go wobbly at the knees before her, see? Or treat him like a concertina ready for her to play a tune on when she feels like it. She's got to be cured of it, and that's my warning to you.' He slewed a cunning little eye over the startled visitor. 'All the same, she's married to me and I'm not divorcing her, see! But if you want her, there she is and you won't be hearing from me any more.'

Ted had listened to this recital with astonishment and perhaps a bit of fear in his narrow, orderly face. He opened his mouth but closed it again. It was the decisive moment. Suddenly Megan jumped wildly off the sofa.

'You're a bully and a brute,' she flared at Sam. Her fists doubled, she heaved towards him. 'If I was a man I'd knock you down. I don't care if *he* takes me away or not. I'm going to leave you.' Glitteringly she advanced a step further towards him. He looked at her unswervingly but his eyes began to dance. 'You've never been anything else but a mean ruffian, and I hate you. I wish you were rotting now in the pit!' Their gaze was entwined like two flames. She screamed: 'I'm going, I'm going now.'

As if to ward off a blow, he lifted his hand. It was the stumpy two-fingered hand. And she stared at those fingers like someone gone daft. The shadow of a little grin seemed to lurk on his face. But all he said, coolly, was: 'Don't forget your Uncle Dai wants fifty quid off you, and if I know the tyke he'll track you down to the end of the earth for fifty bob!'

Shrinking back, she broke into sobbing and fell once more on to the sofa. 'Why wasn't you killed, why wasn't you killed!' she wept.

Sam turned to the visitor: 'Well, what you going to do? Make up your mind, man. Women don't like mild guts. If you want her, she's there.'

Ted shifted his new hat uneasily from one knee to the other. But he mumbled: 'It can't be done if you won't divorce her.'

'I see you got a respect for the wedding ring,' Sam said approvingly. He added largely: 'Seeing that you thought I was dead I'm not blaming you for chasing a skirt to where you got no business . . . Well,' he raised his voice to the still sobbing Megan, 'seems that your fancy bloke don't want you. Perhaps he thinks you'd do him in for the sake of insurance on him. So you're left on the seashore properly, eh?'

Megan wept: 'I won't be bandied about. Devils of men. I'll kill myself—' She jumped up again.

'You've brought it on your own head,' Sam barked, very severe. 'What about me, coming back after seven days in my grave and finding my wife gallivanting to the seaside on the insurance money? Expect me to sit down and eat a pork pie as if nothing had happened? By Christ, what about me! I been dead and come alive again and I find the world gone rotten because a woman haven't got even the bit of decency to pull down the blinds and sit wearing a bit of black for me.'

She gazed at him in fear. But for the first time since her return he looked more the old Sam, more alive, as if he was smashing his way through from wherever he had been, that place of stern and ghostly silence. Yet there was something new in him too, something less cocky and more mature. She shrank back from him, and at the same time her body slackened. Her face looked dwindled and older. She leaned against the dresser, hanging her head.

The visitor rose awkwardly. The room had suddenly filled with a new private tension in which he was cancelled out. He did not know what to say. Sam helped him. 'They'll give you a meal in the Tuberville Arms. Beer there is all right. So long.' Ted went out with a quick sidling movement; even his slim hips, going round the door, looked relieved.

'Done for proper, aren't you!' Sam remarked. 'Fancy man gone, fifty quid in debt, and a cruel husband back from the grave. Well, there's the door. It's a free country.'

'He wasn't ever my fancy man,' she burst out. 'Everything was respectful. We were only interested in each other . . . How was I to know they'd rescue you,' she wailed, 'after Mr. Rowlands told me there wasn't any hope!'

'You should have stayed here and gone into mourning properly,' he insisted, severe as a chapel minister. 'Coming back here dressed up in red like a Chistmas doll . . .' His voice began to boil again.

She leaned her head on the dresser shelf and wept again. Hearing him approach she lifted her head and cried out in hysteria, a long irritating howl. It was her last struggle. He gave her a crack on the jaw, not heavy but sufficient to send her against the wall, where she slumped down more in submission than because of the blow. She stopped howling. She saw him not as Sam but as some huge force not to be escaped. He picked her up. His two fingers dug into her back. His mouth caught hers like flame obliterating a piece of paper. She writhed and twisted for a few moments. But she went under, and came to life again.

PRICE OF A WEDDING RING

Big, generous and gaily dressed, Dinah Cockles was as free with herself as with the tough little sea-vermin she sold off a cart twice a week, fresh in their shells and the sharp tang of their home on them, and indeed on her. The colliers' wives would crowd round and Dinah, usually chuckling some bawdiness or other, would fill their kitchen bowls generously for a few pence, never bothering to use the pint measure. Similarly in her own life she never measured things out. It was said that in her younger days she had been a sailors' pleasure in Cardiff docks and (the romantic-minded added) had retired to the mining valleys because one particular mariner had laid waste to her over-generous heart. She looked only about forty now, as far as could be judged. But, at this time, there was something immortal about her. She had a touch of the undying pagan, flowering dingy but dauntless in an unsuitable time.

She lived in a pretty rambling old hut up by the railway near the pits, her pony stabled in a patch of vigorous garden around. In addition to the cockles she took in washing, dealt in old clothes, sold blocks of wood sawn by herself, bunches of primroses gathered in her travels, blackberries, mushrooms and other seasonal things. Her cart often was of festive aspect, like a cart in Theocritus. She rarely lacked money for drink or for the series of battered rapscallions she took under her wing. But these protégés, wandering men without roots, never stayed long with her. When wearied of them (after a few months) she chucked them out and they just disappeared without fuss. Dinah, a baleful smile on her large juicy mouth, would chuckle to the housewives: 'An old maid I am again; got any men you don't want?' Just as, blowing her toy cornet in the streets, she would shout: 'Any old waistcoats and drawers to sell?'

Despite her drunkenness, amorousness and salt tongue, she offended few. Even the chapels were silent about her, no doubt recognising—wrongly, as it happened—something irremediable in her. Her complete lack of parsimony shed a happy glow over all her doings. Even over a displeasing Saturday-night habit of hers. For this night she favoured a pub at the bottom of the steep hill. After closing-time she climbed the hill with panting but jocose insults against its steepness, and when at the summit, the rows of houses spread fan-wise beneath her, she would commit a nuisance in the middle of the road. Her loud clap of laughter seemed to crash against the mountains. People said she could he heard at this from the bottom of the hill.

On Sundays, though never an attendant at chapel, Dinah was meek as a wallflower. She never did business of any kind, wore a white apron and was highly pleased if any children—taboo though she really was—visited her for a glass of the small beer she brewed from nettles. She would call us in if we, shy and wary as swallows, skimmed about the domain of her hut in play. I enjoyed a glass of her small beer several times. The man of the moment, blear-eyed, unshaven and pondering like an owl—they always had something unlit about them—might be lolling on a kind of bed-chair stuffed gigantically with coloured old rags like some barbaric throne. I remember one of them showing me a big scar on his leg, caused, he said, in America by a Red Indian's poisoned arrow.

'Don't tell lies to children,' Dinah said indignantly. 'You never been further than Swansea all yout life.'

'I seen Niagara Falls!' the man bragged, but whiningly.

'Aye, in a penny lantern show,' she said, concise in her respect for truth.

She always showed me her two treasures—a primitive African wood-carving of a man (which she kept under the cover of a disused sewing-machine) and an albatross's egg. Dinah's eyes were dark as damsons, and in those days her voice suggested to me all kinds of purply and starry mysteries, like night. I forgot to mention that she sold herbs. Her trade was extensive and, it was whispered, peculiar. But for the drink and the men she could have been quite decently off. But she was no business woman.

Her metamorphosis into a new Dinah was achieved not by religion, illness, world economic troubles or war, but by a man. At the age of fifty or so Dinah Cockles fell with a crash into love. That is, she fell completely and wallowingly—her nature being an all-out one—under the domination of a man—*she*! There must have been something in that story of a careless sailor who, in her salad days, had rent her heart.

The new doom was an undersized little rodent of a man going by the name of Job the Grinder. He trundled a knife-sharpening machine round the streets, grinding with a glittering-eyed intensity the cutlery brought out to him, a man with the sharp-nosed exclusive concentration of a rat. With his grimy lean chops and his swift but slinking step he looked like something that dwelt in dark holes. Yet he was known to be respectable and to have a post-office savings account.

Dinah shakily informed a pub crony that the Grinder had told her he could set her up for life—meaning they could make a fortune together.

'*You* 'ont make a fortune,' the crony said, 'and that Job the Grinder's no 'andsome bit of nature for you, Dinah.'

Dinah gurgled. 'But a way he's got; I can tell. When he's looking at me it's just like a big fire warming up the old flue.'

She was overcome with respect for him when he insisted on marrying her properly, in a chapel. For a year or so they lived in the hut. But her very first week as a wife had brought an ominous change in Dinah. For the first time in her life she used the pint measure on the cockle cart, giving exact value and no more. Her manner was of one who peers over her shoulder in fright. The obliteration of her flamboyant bawdiness was more gradual, and she continued to go to the pubs for some time, for it would be a mighty catastrophe indeed that could hold such an old soaker back.

'Do that Grinder count the cockles out to you one by one?' Mrs. Evans, 36 Forest Row, complained. 'Well, Dinah, surprised at you I am. There's a paltry lot for sixpence!'

'Job,' said Dinah broodingly, 'do talk about the post-office bank in the middle of the night.'

'Good gracious,' exclaimed the customer, 'there's awful for you! Like a man swearing in chapel it must be.'

Then the prices of the herbs and the blocks of wood went up. Even worse was the apologetic hangdog manner that Dinah began to assume. Behind all her doings Job the Grinder's black shadow began to loom. Her cart ceased to be loaded with cheap bunches of flowers; Job said that the flower-trade was too unreliable, and instead he made her sell paraffin oil. Also he ordered her to hurry and not to gossip in the streets; one of his sayings was: 'A gossip is a shilling lost in profit.'

'Well, Dinah,' Mrs. Roberts, 18 Bryn Terrace, remarked, 'next time a form to fill in he'll be giving us every time we want a pint of cockles. On the Council he ought to be.'

As someone said about this new Dinah: 'It's because she's never had a husband before, only men.'

Her strange submission to the creed of profit could only be explained by a complete doting on the Grinder. But worse was to come. Not only did they move from the picturesque hut and take a slice of one of the long ugly rows of houses like everybody else, but he made her comb the tips of rubble about the colliery for sackloads of stray coal. These she would heave on her back and hawk through the back-lanes. So that she got grubby, unkempt and with a beast-of-burden look. Such is love. After moving to the house she also ceased to wear bright blouses and garish scarves. And one Sunday, in clothes of sombre hue, she walked by his side into a chapel. Yes, as a proper acceptable member. Then, last achievement of the Grinder, there was the drink, though in this she struggled against him for about three years. But there arrived a Saturday night when no pub saw her. She did not appear in the streets the whole of the following week; the Grinder said she was not well.

'One thing about it, anyhow,' someone remarked; 'the top of the hill will be dryer. An ill wind it is . . .'

It was from this time that a real and deep decline set in on Dinah Cockles. I met her once as, a bag of coal on a wall, she stood resting against it with a vaguely bewildered look. She sagged, her black cheeks were hollow, and her once-bright hair hung dank and gritty. There was no longer any sparkling dance in her damson eyes. Love still had her fast. For when Job was around her cart on cockle days she would still look at him with that submissive and shameless outpouring with which women in her state can drench men, often with refreshing effect.

She went downhill, for all the tidy lace curtains of the new house, the chapel, the teetotalism and the post-office savings. The old pagan spring in her dried up and the propriety of her tongue was like a page in the parish magazine. Her wedded life lasted five years. To the last she was apologetic when measuring the strict pint of cockles.

'How much you got in the post-office now, Dinah?' a customer grumbled.

'The Grinder do do all that,' she replied, asking forgiveness in her voice.

She died of sobriety and bronchitis one November when the wind whipped icily round the coal tips. Her coffin plate declared she was sixty. It must be said that Job the Grinder buried her tidily, taking three pounds out of the post-office for a new black suit. His lean, sharp face was quite dismal just before the funeral, and he grieved to the mourners:

'Met her too late I did. A tough little worker she was, and if I had married her twenty years earlier, from a mansion she'd be buried today.' His thin rat's whiskers sensitively quivering in the unspoken criticism around him, he added righteously: 'Gone above as a respectable member of society she has, whatever.'

But as a neighbour remarked afterwards: 'He pushed her big heart into a pint measure and it burst.' More to the point was the comment of Mrs. Jenkins, 48 Tip Terrace, who was notorious for her regular Saturday-night thrashing of her drunken husband: 'Choked she was by a wedding ring.'

THE TRIP TO LONDON

Magnificently she took her seat in the compartment, a fine sunlike woman simmering with well-being and physical vigour. The atmosphere of rich profusion she brought with her was accentuated by the shower of travel comforts she dropped to the seat—glossy magazines, sweets, cigarettes, bags of fruit. A luxurious fur bristled over her amazonian shoulders, her hands sparkled with rings, a dazzling brooch lay in her bosom. At first glance she looked like a prosperous barmaid of the traditional good-hearted type. She was about forty, though her complexion was a young girl's.

No one could remain neutral or indifferent in her presence. She was of those who are the first to break up the cautious silence of a railway carriage. 'Well,' she exclaimed, settling, 'that's over! I always enjoy a trip to London but it's nice to be going home again. A week of it is enough for me . . . And the money!' At this exclamation she bared her eyes in mock terror. They were unexpectedly black and small. And in them was a momentary whip, a flicking out of something baleful. No doubt she could be a fury when roused.

She opened her glossy handbag, took out a black cigarette case and a lighter to match. Everything looked new and shining—the handbag, the fur, her clothes, the rakish hat perched on the freshened blonde hair. 'The things I've bought! I run wild in shops, that's a fact.' Her gaze kept on darting as if expectantly towards the platform.

'You ladies,' jocularly remarked the tall man, 'go rampaging in the shops, while we men, God knows why, kill ourselves making what goes into them.'

'I never bring the wife to London if I can help,' said the stout man lugubriously. 'There's nothing you can't get at home at half the price.'

'Oh, you men!' she glowed. 'Always wanting to tie us up at home, so mean.'

And, still smoking a cigarette, she opened a packet of sweets and popped a piece of turkish delight into her mouth. Then, delving again into the crowded handbag, she extracted a lapis lazuli case and unnecessarily powdered her nose. There was something released and holiday about all her actions. She was a pleasure to watch.

A man had kept on passing the shut door. He looked into the compartment yet again, came back, and entered. He was slight, middle-aged and of respectable appearance, neatly dressed and with a narrow indecisive face. He settled himself nervously opposite the big sunlike woman. She took up one of her magazines and flicked over its pages. At the same time she was saying to the stout man, giving him a challenging dart from her eyes:

'But thank goodness *I* can't be kept at home any longer. I'm a widow and I live alone. I've got a cosy home but I won't be locked up in it any more. I go out enjoying myself in the shops, money though it costs.'

The newcomer had the disadvantage of entering a compartment where the other three occupants had already made amiable contact. But he did not look a person who wished to join in the friendliness. Except for the jumpy face he was nondescript. He seemed a man who wished to dwindle out of notice. Yet he kept on looking at the woman in a kind of half hidden anguish. She radiated such full pleasure in her secure place in the world.

'Why is it,' the tall man still jocularly mourned, 'we men sweat to make money only to let women treat it like water?'

She bustled enjoyably. 'We women want to know why too, you see!' Putting her head on one side, that black gaze darted out baleful at him. 'Perhaps it's because there's not enough in men to please us, and we've got to have something else . . . I bought a silver cake stand in Regent Street,' she went on, inconsequent, 'though I've got two already.'

'It's queer,' lamented the tall man, 'but men do get fascinated by a woman that spends his money *ad lib*—yes, fascinated, like they say a bird does by a snake.'

'Women,' she pointed out, 'got their advantages for you, haven't they? We soothe you, don't we give you home comforts, don't we put you poor cold creatures to sleep nice and comfortable?'

And her splayed fingers, with a languid ladylike gesture, took another sweet. She then vivaciously changed her magazines and pretended to peep at its pictures. Not once did she look at the slight wincing man sitting opposite her—perhaps because he rarely moved his eyes from her face.

It was true that she subsided into silence for quite a good part of the two-hour journey. But it was a silence radiating a tropical liveliness. Continually she smoked, ate, or passed rapidly from magazine to magazine. Her strong but soft-looking jaws, ceaselessly obliterating sweets, moved rhythmically as the train's wheels. Now and again she placed a hand, blind in its plump fleshiness, on her bosom and fumbled for the large brooch dripping with blue, red and lurid green clusters of imitation jewels.

The two men who had conversed with her rustled newspapers in clouds of pipe smoke. Married-looking and matured, they glanced at her now and again with a wary pleasure, delighting but also critical in her rich spread of gewgaws, eatables and frivolous women's journals. But the other man, slunk so wornly in his corner, still did not spread himself with this satisfaction.

Behind the spellbound gaze of his eyes he appeared to writhe in apprehension. He gave off an atmosphere of one who in whimpering loneliness prowls about the edges of other people's happiness. But still she did not look at him.

'I went to the Zoo,' she prattled suddenly. 'I saw the lions and tigers. They're pretty.'

'Pretty!' repeated the stout man in surprise. 'Do man-eaters look pretty?'

'I dare say,' flirted the tall man, 'you find men are more like kittens than like lions.'

'Oh, I don't know,' she smiled luxuriantly. 'I've only been married once. I lead a very quiet life. A shopping trip to London, that's all I get out of life now.'

The slight man opposite her listened to this with an awareness wistful in its intensity. Why did he not join in the conversation; was he defeated by some hungry shyness, waiting for her to look at him and to part that pink mouth in a smile for him alone? She did not do so. Instead she ate the last of her victuals—a most expensive-looking hothouse peach. She bit into its golden and rosy flesh with a relish at once greedy and delicate, dabbing at her chin and lips with a scrap of chiffon handkerchief.

It was too much for him. He closed his hypnotized eyes at last, he seemed to squirm down into himself, utterly routed.

'Well, we're drawing near,' she gurgled. 'Home! Oh, I'm looking forward to my own fireside . . . Drizzling rain as usual, Sooty too,' she said, not without pleasure. 'I must say it's nice to smell a bit of our own city soot.'

Out in the autumn dusk lay the factories, the lurking smoke, the crush of dwellings and the great black roads. There were the grunting iron-chested engines, the chimney stacks and the stern concrete yards. Out there was work and the day after day monotony . . . But she, she would shine and sparkle over these things and obliterate them. The train glided to a standstill. She arranged her fur, stepped out with quite a curt *Good evening* and refused a porter for her suitcase. And all light seemed to leave the carriage.

The slight man roused himself, jumped. Suddenly he hurtled himself out of the carriage and hurried down the platform, a chiffon handkerchief in his hand.

'You left this handkerchief behind.' There was a little nervous yelp in his voice.

She bent her glowing head down towards him; she smiled. And in her black eyes leaped out that little whiplike flame. 'Now that's kind of you! . . . You're the quiet gentlemen that sat opposite me. Did I disturb you? I'm such a chatterbox.'

48

The station's black facade towered over them like some entrance to the underworld. They stood there in its gritty maw. It was the final, the frightening and agonized last moment. He said in a vanquished yelp: 'Can we take some refreshment together?' A tram car clanked and screeched somewhere. People sped blackly through the drizzle. A faint odour of violets coming off her, she bent her head to him again. She smiled, fully and glitteringly.

It was then that he saw, in the whirring lights of cabs and buses, that she had two rows of dead-white false teeth. Somehow—perhaps it was because of their cheapness—they gave him courage. 'Please do,' he wheedled, but with decision. 'Look, we can go in there! They have a quiet lounge, very select.'

'I don't mind if I do,' she said comfortably.

They sat under an immense palm, on bony tubular chairs before a table of beetroot-coloured wicker. A melancholy old waiter brought her a port, him a whisky. Two dahlias were purply dying in a vase between them; two commercial travellers, the only other customers, held bored conference on stools at the bar. He said: 'I don't mind telling you, if you don't mind listening, that I've fallen for you.'

'Now then!' she tittered. 'That's not how a man of your sense should speak . . . But perhaps you're a bit lonely—'

'I am,' he replied, his fingers beating a tattoo on the table. And he launched at once into particulars of himself. He was an agent for manufacturing engineers and was often away from home. He was unhappy with his wife and she with him; they hadn't spoken properly for months. She didn't care a scrap what he did. There were no children. He was sick to death of his monotonous work; he had a bit of money put by. But he never mentioned his name or where he lived. The commonplace recital was jerked out anxiously but it sounded like truth.

'You want to take a holiday from your troubles,' she said kindly. 'You're not well, I can see. It just shows you that money can't buy everything.'

She seemed to bend over him in amplitude, gather him up, and at the same time obliterate him in the wealth of her bosom. For, strangely enough, his achievement in getting her to sit there with him sociably did not solidify him. He seemed to wilt, under the sprouting palm, though when ordering drinks he was lordly enough with the waiter padding about vaguely on his slouching old feet.

She met him by appointment the following evening in the city, having formally invited him to supper. But she had told him he would never find her house alone. And they must arrive after dark; the world was so full of unjust tongues. He was not allowed to take a cab even tonight. The tram car was almost full; she would not let him sit with her. The tram lines ended in a desolate half-built housing estate which seemed bitten rawly out of the land. A faint uneasy scent of the open country blew round the unlit corners.

He followed her down a new asphalt road. Unfinished houses loomed on either side. A steam roller, red light on the ground before it, stood massive; the road ended with abrupt finality. There seemed no more houses or people. She waited and, slinking and shadowy in his dark overcoat, he drew abreast with her.

'We can walk together now,' she whispered. 'We've half a mile to go yet . . . I warned you!'

'I don't mind,' he said doggedly.

'They're spoiling the country,' she prattled. 'When I was a girl I used to come out here picking blackberries . . . Still, it all makes money. I've been thinking of taking a little shop on this estate. But it needs a bit more capital than I've got.'

At the bottom of a dropping lane edged with iron railings and withering thorn bushes they came to a dim stretch of country smelling of marsh and dank vegetation. 'There's ponds here,' she said. 'Some of them are deep . . . It's not far now. My husband owned land down here; a pity it wasn't up on the estate—I would be rich now.' For the first time there was a hard rasping note in her voice.

They had passed a couple of dark, silent bungalows. The marshy odour, of reeds in rot and stagnant autumnal water, was not oppressive. In summer the place would sprout in steamy florescence and the air would be like jelly. A distance beyond the ponds a road hummed with cars and lorries; it was the arterial. 'You can get buses there,' she said. 'This lane leads out to it between the ponds.'

'The whole of England is cut up,' he yelped. 'People and noise are never far off. Roads, roads everywhere, and networks of wires above. It's a regular web.'

'There are quiet corners,' she answered, in a soothing way, 'where you can still rest peaceful . . . There's my house.'

Unlatching a gate she went with her full-rigged assurance across a garden. An earthy smell of many chrysanthemums hung in the dark. The low moaning hum of the cars had taken away the sense of lonely isolation. A dog barked. The dim house looked like a Victorian villa, brave in its aim at grandeur. There was a deep porch above a flight of steps flanked with urns.

'You'll be ready for your supper,' she said; 'I've laid it.'

She opened a dark door.

'I always say,' she smiled, 'that a trip to London does you good.'

She looked out of the cab window into the wintry afternoon street. At a traffic stop the soft yellow illumination of a jeweller's window changed her happy gaze into a childishly greedy snatching. 'Oh!' she cried, 'all that gold! . . . People are rich.'

'My trip's done *me* good, anyhow!' said the man beside her. 'When I said to myself on the ship: "I'll be in London for Christmas," I didn't think I was going to get such a present as meeting you.'

'Oh,' she expanded, 'am I a present? I began to think I was an expense to you . . . I do feel mean,' she added, in pouting self-reproach, 'but you understand, don't you, that I'm not a woman like that?'

'You're a *friend*,' he said, loyally and with simple submission. 'I'm not great shakes as a chap, I know—only an old crock from the tropics. I don't expect more than friendship, see!' His round wondering face, like an oddly matured adolescent's—for he was well into middle age—was pasty and flaccid. The tropical sun had not made him lean and wizened; it had only demolished hard bone and muscle. 'When I saw you sitting in that sedate hotel,' he went on, 'enjoying your meal, I said to myself: "That's a woman I'd like to know; there's no nonsense about her."'

'I do enjoy myself,' she admitted. Between them on the seat were a number of parcels, paper satchels and magazines. She stroked her fur coat lovingly. 'Oh, I'll have to go careful next year . . . Seventy pounds this coat cost!' she said in a hushed but gleeful way.

'Why, that's not so bad, surely?' he said with some swagger.

Her black flicking eyes peeped round at him. 'Don't you think so?'

Walking down the platform of the railway station, glistening and magnificent in her coat, she said: 'But I'm always glad to go home. I'm a woman for my own fireside. I've got a cosy little place, though I say it.'

'Home!' he sighed, trotting short and flaccid at her side like a plump schoolboy. 'I lost mine when I was seventeen. That's what made me go to the East. I haven't a single relation left now. I'm just an orphan.' A helpless little waif of humanity he seemed, trotting there by her side.

After selecting her seat and dropping the numerous parcels she came back to him on the platform. 'Never mind!' she leaned down towards him— 'You're coming to see me, aren't you! You promise? And you've got the arrangements clear?'

'Clear as daylight,' he assured with damp ardour. 'I wish I was coming now.'

'Yes, a pity it isn't convenient for me today. But, gracious, tomorrow will soon be here. I'll have a nice supper ready for you.'

Doors were slamming. The air quivered with a sense of finality, of farewells and decisive movement. Now she stood leaning out over him from the carriage window. He laid his hand yearningly over hers. She shone down on him from among an odour of carnations. But already her imminent departure was draining him of such colour and vitality as she had shed on him in the cab. He wilted in grief and mumbled: 'I shan't eat till that supper tomorrow night!'

'Till tomorrow then!' she sang from the gliding train.

There was no one of interest to her in the carriage: three women and the husband—no doubt of it—of one of them. She shut them out of her gaze relentlessly, though all were interested in the splendour of her settling to the journey, the dazzling glow of her presence, the profusion of her trinkets and parcels. Here was the good, healthy, middle-class heart of a country, well-off and assured, the daughter of a successful civilization. She was a nation in herself. Before the train was well out of the station she was eating, brought for her by a laden ship triumphantly cleaving the seas of the world, a rosy Empire apple.

Presently she took from her handbag a folded newspaper bought in the London hotel. It had been published in her native city. And she read again:

Disappearance of Local Man

Concern has been expressed at the disappearnce of Mr. James Waite of Hill Avenue, who has not been seen or heard of for two months. His wife, Mrs. Hilda Waite, fears he has lost his memory and states that her husband, a highly respected member of a City firm, suffered from a slight nervous breakdown some months ago, due to overwork. The mystery is complicated by the fact that when last heard of Mr. Waite drew from his bank two substantial sums of money within a week. The missing man is aged 47, of slight build and medium height. Anyone who may have information of him is asked to communicate with the Central Police Station.

This is the second disappearance of local business men in recent months. The case of Mr. R. Tibble, a loyal and highly esteemed member of a well known hardware house, will be recalled. Mr. Tibble has never been traced.

Suddenly it was as if a thunderous cloud passed over her face. She looked up, her black gaze thrashing across to the man sitting by his wife's side opposite her.

'This carriage is a non-smoker!' she reminded him haughtily.

'I beg your pardon,' he said and put out his cigarette.

Opening a paper satchel she selected a piece of turkish delight and passed on to other items in the newspaper. Shortly afterwards she began nipping into the many magazines strewn beside her. A blank silence, decreed by her, reigned in the compartment.

The wintry dusk was closing. Through it the train hurled its way to the industrial city whose toiling men and machines manufactured so many of the necessities of modern comfort. But she, she was taking to it warmth and seductive colours. She looked mollified now, reposed in her grandeur of flesh. She ate sweetmeats, grinding them rhythmically in her soft but powerful jaws. She shut herself in her luxurious fur coat, ignoring the other passengers again, never once offering magazine or sweet to the other women.

They, neatly turned out in unremarkable garments, eyed with distrust this dynamo in the corner. The hand of the wife stole in protection to her husband's and patted it—perhaps to soothe him after the snub he had received. For he was certainly looking uneasily roused.

GENTS ONLY

I

While he was busy burying a woman one June afternoon, Lewis the Hearse's wife left him forever, going by the 3.20 train and joining her paramour at Stickell junction, where they were seen by Matt Morgan waiting for their connection. She left a letter for her husband, a plate of tart for his tea, and that sense of awful desolation a gone person can leave in a house.

What was in that letter no one never knew, not even Lewis's sister Blodwen who—for the news was up all the hillsides of Crwtch the same evening— came flying down from her farm up where the old B.C. tomb had been found. But from that afternoon Lewis was a changed man. Not that he had been a specially bright bit of spring sunshine before, though he was quite a decent looking man in his way. His manner betokened a sombre nature which was not entirely due to his calling. Because of his reasonable prices and his craftsmanship in coffins all the people of Crwtch respected him.

'A servant you'll have to take,' Bloddie declared shrilly, and her bosom heaved like the Bay of Biscay because he wouldn't show her the letter. 'Forever running down here I can't be . . . The house she left clean, I will say.' She looked at the uneaten tart—for Lewis's wife was Crwtch's best tart maker—jealously. 'If that tart you don't want I can take it.'

Lewis lifted his brooding head at last. 'Take it!' he barked, so fierce that she jumped back. 'And your own carcass too.'

But what Crwtch never expected was the decision he came to the very next day. He tore down from outside his house the wooden tablet announcing his name and profession and in its place screwed a new one just painted in the work shed back of the house. This announced: *J. J. Lewis, Gents Undertaker.* Seeing him screw it up, Daniels Long Time, captain of the amateur Fire Brigade and so called because people said his engine was always a long time coming when needed, stopped and asked: 'What is it meaning, Lewis?'

Shaking his screwdriver, Lewis barked: 'My last woman I buried yesterday. Now on, men's funerals only.' And he went in, slamming the door.

No one could believe it. For days it was the talk at every hearth, in every shop and pub in Crwtch. Everybody waited for the next woman to go. A man died and Lewis buried him same as usual, very reasonable and the coffin up to standard. Except for this funeral Lewis had not appeared out of doors, not even to go to chapel. His sister Bloddie said he cleaned and cooked for himself, ordering things by his apprentice, Shenkin. At this funeral everybody looked at him inquisitively but could collect nothing but a bleak decision in the uprightness of his body walking behind his lovely crystal hearse.

Then Polly Red Rose went of old age. Licensee of the best pub in Crwtch (now carried on by her son), Polly was respected by both sexes and all creeds. Surely Lewis, who had often enjoyed a glass of the 'Red Rose' beer, would not say no to burying her! The son knocked at Lewis's door. But before he could take off his black bowler and step inside, Lewis said clearly, not angry, but firm as a rock:

'No use coming in. See the plate outside? Gents only, or boys, and no exceptions, sorry to say. Good day.'

Now, there was not another undertaker within fifteen miles of Crwtch, the one in Stickell, a stranger. And not only would he charge extra for travelling his contrivance thirty miles in all, but it was known that his carriages were shabby, being more used in a town the size of Stickell. Everybody knew how Lewis's coffins (to say nothing of his moderate charges) were not only good value but would surely last longer than anybody else's. And so, when the women of Crwtch began to boil against this reflection on their sex and solicited their men to do something about it, even the men more or less began to agree.

'If I was a man,' Mrs. Hopcyns the Boot declared to her husband, right in front of a woman customer buying boots, 'horsewhip him I would.'

'Sore he is,' Hopcyns the Boot said mildly. 'Give him a bit of time to get over the Mrs. leaving him like that. Come round he will in a year or two.'

'Anybody would think,' said the customer, kicking off a boot and flushed from bending, 'that men don't mind about it. Forced to bury Polly Red Rose he ought to have been.'

'How?' inquired Hopcyns. 'No law there is about it. Same as I am not bound to sell you a pair of boots!'

'Catching it is, is it!' simmered the customer. In Crwtch there was only one of all trades, except farming, so there was no competition for customers.

The first outcome of all the agitation, however, was that the Big Men of Horeb chapel went in deputation to Lewis. They wore their formal Sunday black, watch chains and umbrellas, and in array they looked impressive. Lewis received them readily enough in his parlour, where were the samples of wood, metals and glass wreaths. But he did not sit down like them, and, before they could speak, he launched like a judge having the last word:

'Lord of himself a man is. Private the soul. Between me and my destiny it is what I have decided in the matter of my funerals. But this I will say—Not only to vex the women of Crwtch is my intention; vex the women of the whole world I would. Yet small of mind that is. This is my true reason— women will see there is a man at last who will not sit down under their carryings-on and shamelessness. A good example I have begun, in a time gone loose and no respect for the vows of the marriage day. No more now. I have decided.'

The Big Men looked at each other, and it was plain there was no stout movement to contradict Lewis or attempt coaxing. At last one said, however: 'But Lewis, Lewis, come now. Surely similar all are in death, and in a hearse there are no trousers or petticoats, properly speaking. The same shroud of Heaven covers all.'

Another, who had a crinkled little old face like an old apple in the loft, added: 'Yes, persons only in the cemetery and not men and women. No carryings-on there; the only place safe from such it is. Every door marked "Private", and no back door either. Agree with you I would, Lewis, if the cemetery was a place of this and that; only right it would be for you to say no to taking women there. But surely it is not?'

'Obliged I am for the visit,' said Lewis, far away. 'Just now I am starching white collars.' Indeed, starch was whitening his fingers, and he had the air of one with many household tasks to do.

No doubt at all a door was shut fast in his soul. For him no more the peaches and the blossoms of women in the world. The Big Men filed out in the sunshine and adjourned to the vestry of Horeb to consider the manner of their report to their wives . . . But Crwtch's protest did not stop there. The following week those ten of the business men who called themselves the Chamber of Trade, meeting once a month in the 'Red Rose', sought conference with Lewis.

Though, as before, resolutely calm, Lewis made sharp interruption of their mild wheedling: 'Look now, this you must do. Put a big advertisement in the newspaper— "Chance for Undertaker in well-off small town. Present Undertaker Gents Only. Apply to Crwtch Chamber of Trade." See?'

Reproachful, one of the members protested in sorrow: 'A stranger in your business is not welcome, Lewis, and well you do know it. Surprised at you I am.' And he added significantly: 'Ointment for bruises there are always, and many in pretty boxes.'

Lewis knew what the member meant. Under the special circumstances he would not become a social outcast if he took a fancy to someone and brought her under his roof, though in Crwtch this was the most abhorrent sin of all. But he said, cynically:

'Ointments cost money, and down by half is my business. And will be forever.'

56

After the failure of the Chamber of Trade, the Society of Merched y Te itself made attempt. This society of teetotal women formed to spread the ideal of temperance was—no one knew why—of powerful influence in Crwtch and nobody willingly incurred its displeasure. The mother of one of its members having died, the daughter made great groan of the awful cost of the funeral by the undertaker at Stickell, with the coffin looking like one from a factory. The Merched, twenty strong, assembled one August afternoon and marched in procession to Lewis's house. But, appraised of their intention by his spy, Shenkin the apprentice, Lewis had not only locked and barred his door but had nailed a notice on it: '*J. J. Lewis. In Business to Men Only. No Others Admitted. By order, J. J. Lewis.*'

It is plain that women of affairs, particularly when in concourse, would not be daunted by such a notice. They knocked, they rapped and banged, called through the letterbox and rattled it with fancy umbrellas, tactless as any reforming society can be. There was no reply. Presently the noise was such—it was a hot day and tempers were rising—that a crowd of about two hundred collected, and from his cottage P. C. Evans the Spike telephoned the Sergeant in Stickell, putting on his helmet first. The Sergeant said that no man is obliged to open the door of his house to the public and that the crowd must be dispersed if it was creating a nuisance. Perspiring, Evans the Spike stepped out, went back for his baton, and then, after plunging into the crowd and inquiring the meaning of this uproar, gave the Sergeant's decision and posted himself in Lewis's doorway.

'Truth of the matter is,' called one of the Merched indignantly— 'supporting the sly old salmon the men are . . . A letter will be written!' she finished with great ominousness.

II

But it was Bloddie who moved in the affair with better craft. She became incensed that her brother persisted in deliberately throwing away good business. Some years younger than he was, she hoped to benefit one day from the tidy little fortune he could be making.

It was during a visit to her friend's farm over the hill one afternoon that she saw light—in the person of her friend's orphan niece that had just come from the mining valleys to work at the farm. About twenty, Lottie's lovely head shone fresh as a buttercup, and all her presence breathed strong of an obedient nature waiting to devote itself entire to a person. Though dainty looking she had no nerves and was strong as an axe. Better still, there was a smile behind the naughty blue of her eye, and even better still, she had deficiencies—she did not like hard work, and her lazy mind seemed vacant and only waiting for the one thing to come along and keep her comfortable.

Bloddie conferred with her old friend, who had taken Lottie to live with her because there was no one else to take her. 'Aye,' agreed the aunt at once, 'sweeten him up she could, no doubt. Welcome you are to her, Bloddie.'

'Look how he used to be,' Bloddie remembered, fired, 'as a young man! No 'ooman in Crwtch was safe from him . . . A man with extremes in his nature he is, evident,' she added, putting her finger on his character accurately.

But how to get Lottie into Lewis's notice was the problem. Bloddie lay in bed of nights brooding. She was the only woman—for a sister is not a woman—who was allowed into her brother's house, and even she was treated with short shrift though he accepted the bit of green-stuff or bacon she brought down from the farm. Then one morning she rose and said clearly to herself: 'A new shock do often kill an old one.'

Thereafter she took to calling on Lewis oftener, always with presents for his meals, and even daring to follow him into the work shed that abutted on the back lane and talking to him while he made a coffin. Subtly she got to know this and that from his short grunts. One day, splashing the varnish down on a beautifully cut coffin—for Crwtch men still remained faithful to him and his moderate charges—he growled: 'No good you keep coming here, Bloddie. Shenkin the apprentice can do my business for the house. Tomorrow, going by the first train to Stickell he is to buy wallpaper and a chicken in the market.'

'Wallpapering the parlour are you?' she said idly. 'Coffin for Josh Jones that is? There's a nice wood.'

'Going to him it is the day after tomorrow,' Lewis grunted, and drew the final brush with great delicacy along the lid.

'Would you bury *me*, Johnny?' she ventured, very sisterly.

'No,' he said.

But later he gave her a cup of tea (the first since his wife had run away, never to be heard of again), and she took it as a good omen of relenting and melting. She dared to stay until quite late that night and went out to the work shed again to fetch the bag of shopping she had left there. 'There,' she said, turning the key of the back kitchen door for him, 'all locked up and everything done for you! Surely a woman in the house is a price above rubies?' She had even washed up and polished the grate.

'You be off now,' he growled, reading a trade paper. 'Your views don't carry weight with me.'

The next morning, a mild October morning very sweet in the nose,

58

Bloddie let herself and the girl Lottie into Lewis's back-lane door as dawn was breaking. She had left the door unlocked the night before. Lottie was giggling and very ready for the prank, being bored with the lonely farm. They crept into the work shed and Bloddie lit a candle. The lid of Josh Jones's coffin lay ajar on the beautiful varnished casket resting on the trestles.

'There!' said Bloddie. 'And if you do your piece proper a man with money you might marry. Starved he is.'

She moved the lid and helped Lottie into the coffin. She arranged the bright cool yellow hair and the clean-ironed pink muslin dress that showed legs plain, and in the narrow frame the shapely girl looked like heaven come to earth. Even Bloddie herself, lifting the candle, exclaimed in wonder: 'Beautiful enough to eat you look, a wedding cake! . . . Now what are you going to say?'

Lottie, her long lashes beating her cheeks, repeated in a pleading voice: 'An orphan I am and looking for someone to take care of me. Cruel everybody has been to me. Last night I ran away from the gypsies and came in by here. Die I want to, for the world I cannot stand no more.' And she smiled a tearful and pleading smile—for the simplest girl can make a good actress when needed—and lifted her arms like swan necks. 'My father's face you got, only younger. Kiss me and let me rest by here.'

'Champion!' said Bloddie admiringly. 'Now take patience, for a long time he might be. A big piece of work you might do for Crwtch, and earn a fortune for yourself too.' She arranged the lid over the coffin as before, leaving a slit of space open, and put out the candle.

'Cosy it is,' Lottie sighed. 'There's nice the wood smells.'

But when Bloddie had gone and an hour passed without Lewis arriving, Lottie, of indolent nature and having been up early, fell fast asleep. The work shed was dark. It had only a small cobwebbed window in the shade of a tree, where a rising wind began to mutter and creak in growing noise.

III

Bloddie did not go back to the farm as she intended. She went to call on a friend in Mary Ann Street who cut dresses for her, and what with a cup of tea and one thing and another, time passed. Her friend made broth and afterwards they went to visit Mrs. Leyshon, who was confined of a son. In the afternoon Bloddie looked at a clock.

'Jawch, go I must now,' she said, suddenly feeling excited. She bought a currant loaf in the baker's and then made quick for her brother's house.

'There's pale you are looking!' her friend said in parting. 'Not well you are feeling?' But Bloddie did not know if she felt well or not.

Lewis, in his shirt sleeves, answered the door to her timid knock. He stood aside with nothing special in the grudging cast of his face.

'Well,' she said, expectant. 'Things well with you today? Down to do a bit of shopping I am.' In the living room she laid the currant loaf on the table. There was no sign of Lottie anywhere. 'A loaf of currant bread for you, Johnnie.'

There was conversation on several small matters, Lewis grunting as usual, and she tidying the hearth, her eyes restless and her ears cocked to the ceiling. 'Oh Johnnie,' she burst at last out of her dry throat, 'faint I am for a cup of tea.'

'There's the kettle,' he said, surly. 'I got work in the shed. That Shenkin haven't come back from Stickell yet.' And he went out to the back.

She drank the tea quick for strength. And her queer excitement could be held no more. She went to the back, down the slice of weedy garden, and peered into the open door of the dusky shed. A dribbling lit candle was stuck on a chest of tools, with Lewis sitting beside it polishing a brass name plate. On the trestle Josh Jones's coffin lay with the lid closed tight over it. Bloddie, stooping, twisted into the shed. Her knees were bending.

'Oh, Johnnie . . .' she began quavering, in a small going voice.

In the candlelight his shiny little eyes looked up occupied. 'What now?' he grunted, and went back to his polishing. 'You go and have your tea.'

Breathing hard, she crept across to the coffin. Her hand came out stealthily and made to lift the lid. It would not move. The six big ornamental screws were brassy in the candlelight. 'Johnnie,' she whispered, bending and feeling her head go round, 'what you screwed down the lid for?'

'Ready to go to Josh Jones tomorrow, of course. Lids don't jump about in my hearse.'

She gave the coffin a violent push. But it did not budge. Sure enough it was full as an egg. Beating the lid with her hands, she shrieked: 'Look inside you did before screwing it down? . . . Oh Johnnie!' she wailed.

'What's the matter with you, woman!' he barked. 'Look inside for what? The coffin's been screwed down since first thing this morning. You've been drinking!'

'Lottie is in there!' she screamed. 'Niece of Ceridwen.'

'I don't know any Lottie,' he shouted, irritable. 'That's enough now. I won't have you coming here in the drink.'

Babbling, and her fat little fists without real strength, she began turning the screws. He called out to her to leave his coffin alone but, still polishing the brass plate, he did not rise from his bench. Six screws she had to loosen. She flung off the lid.

The coffin was empty except for Lewis's big black ledger and many bricks. She spun round with a snarl.

'Oh, wicked old fox that you are, oh—' And this and that.

He rose tremendous, the shining plate in an arm like Moses. 'Out of my house with you, out now and till Doomsday!'

Sobbing in rage and fright, she ran up the garden, he at her heels. But she called up the criticism of hell on him, and he on her. In the living room her eye caught the currant loaf. She snatched it up and took it with her through the front door, which slammed behind her for the last time.

Up at the farm she found Lottie in bed not only with a cold but with fright. Fed and comforted, however, the girl dried her tears. 'I went to sleep,' she related, 'and I was woke up by candle grease dropping hot on my face. Red his whiskers was by the candle! I said what you said, but he shouted at me: "A good mind I got to lock you up in this coffin till I call the policeman for a burglar! You be off back to the gypsies. Supply free nights' lodging for trollops I don't." . . . And he wouldn't help me out of the coffin and wouldn't touch me at all. I lost my head and said where I was from too . . .'

Afterwards the aunt tried to console her friend. 'Let the old rascal go, Bloddie. A man he is no more. Cut off the old dolt is.'

'Pew!' breathed Bloddie, stertorous, 'but I thought poor Lottie was coffined right enough.'

'Never mind,' said Ceridwen, 'not so frivolous and empty headed it might make her.'

It was the last attempt to make Lewis Gents Only (as he came to be called) relent from his hard vow. He remained faithful to it until he retired from business and went to live in Swansea. All women continued to be buried by the Stickell undertaker, but the man who bought Lewis's business and stock in hand of course changed this. It must be said that though mention of Lewis always made Crwtch women bridle, when he left he went in dignity and with the good wishes and respect of most men. He had that upright look of a man who knows his own mind and abides by its decisions, and in his face independence mingled solemn with the natural pride of a craftsman. His history is still discussed in the parlour bar of the 'Red Rose'; and it is often the starting point of a deep debate—was he justified or not in refusing to undertake women?

THE PUBLIC-HOUSE

Opposite his home was the great public-house, a stone building edged with bright yellow bricks. The boy liked the public-house. It was clamorous with life, its interior brilliant with coloured bottles and vivid with a harsh smell; the movement of humanity in it interested him. After the staid cleanliness of his home it was satisfying to be allowed entrance, particularly in the early winter evenings, when the pink-speckled gas-lamps were lit and the floor was golden with fresh sawdust and crisp fires burned in the big grates.

He had right of entrance through friendship with the publican's sister, a gaunt spinster of forty who wore much coarse lace about her bodice, a black velvet band firmly binding a high mass of gold hair in which was a strange tint of mildew-green. Generous and lively, she spoke to him in a jokingly rancorous way as if he were grown-up, and gave him pieces of mint-toffee and often a penny. But sometimes she lifted him and stood him on the bar counter, oblivious of the men in the saloon, and, clasping his bare knees with her big moist hands, she would ask him laughingly if he loved her and would he love her always, for ever and for ever. She could make him grin, and because her manner was raucous, he was not offended or humiliated. Yet she made him feel cautious too and he experienced a vague, unformulated feeling when she gripped his knees and, lifting him down from the bar counter, her hand lingered about him. She was a strong woman.

'I don't think the boy ought to get into the habit of going into that public-house,' he heard his mother say.

'God bless my soul,' replied his father, 'he's too young to know even what they're for.'

'He'll get so used to a bar—' she went on.

'Well, perhaps he'll go into the business. There's money in pubs, Dorothy. And we'd have brandy and things cost-price, if not for nothing.'

An aloof friendship existed between the two families, though the one was chapel-going and the other, being publicans in the strict Nonconformist place, was cast out in pagan darkness. The ladies gossiped when they met on the pavement and at Christmas exchanged pieces of each other's puddings, one never failing to compliment the other on being more successful than herself. The boy's father, anxious to retain the pub's orders for decoration and painting, sometimes sat on one of its stools and slandered politicians with the publican, a bald widower who looked out on life from the grave of a ruined digestion, eating nothing but frail biscuits and watered-down soups.

'Your boy'll be a preacher,' said the publican, surveying the child, who was kneeling behind the bar rearranging some rows of brown bottles.

'He doesn't look a preacher kneeling down among those stouts,' chuckled the father. 'What makes you think so?'

'His mighty looks at us, as if he's taking us in and finding us wanting.'

Vaguely the boy heard and half understood. He got up from his knees and stared absorbingly at the warm gold of a whisky-bottle. He liked to hold the smooth, cold bottle and shake up the colour. There was the ice-like gin too, and the purple-red of the port, the tawny depths of the sherry; and strange seldom-touched bottles that were startlingly green, white like curdled milk, yellow like buttercups, a red-black like beetroot, and a whitish-gold like sunlight. He stared at them all in turn, lingering for quite two minutes over each. So absorbed was he that he did not see the publican's sister approach and stand, hands on hip, gazing at him as absorbingly.

'Well, my lord, which'll you have?'

He started, pulled from his dream, and saw her huge, gaunt nose thrust out to him, the nostrils twitching with amusement. A sudden feeling of recoil gripped him, so that he was hard and unyielding when she swept him up into her arms, exclaiming:

'One day you shall have them all. On your wedding-day. You know what that is? Ah! Your wedding-day!'

The power of her physical warmth and dominant voice encircled him. He wriggled and was subjected. She tickled his ribs and he burst into wild laughter. He slipped to the floor and kicked out his legs. When his father, rapping his empty glass on the bar counter, called out: 'Now then, whiskers, time to go home,' he jumped up with great alacrity and ran heading past the rows of stout and out into the hallway. There he joined his father, who was spitting into an enamelled pan marked *Spit Here*. Hand-in-hand they crossed the road and entered the grey evening silence of home.

He liked the public-house best on Saturday evenings. Then it was bustling and overflowing with people relaxed from the tension of the finished week and determined to enjoy themselves. It reeked of a life that seemed to sprout with raw vigour like some great healthy cabbage. The windows steamed, all the gas-lamps were ablaze, even the big unappetising 'Commercial Room' was filled with a noisy mob of swollen-faced men. He wriggled his way among a forest of thighs, now and again darting right between a pair of men's legs, accompanied perhaps on these occasions by another boy: they played hide-and-seek among the crowded bodies. The publican's sister had no time for him on Saturday evenings. But sometimes she allowed him to climb on to a chair inside the bar and peer over into that narrow dark section of the pub reserved for women. It was shut-away and secretive, that section, and always shadowy, having no lights of its own. These drinking women fascinated him; they appeared only on Saturday nights; they squatted over their glasses of black stout and talked in low, whining voices; they seemed to hide under large dark hats and they wiped their noses on the backs of their hands. There seemed something mournful about them.

Whenever there were apple-fritters Miss Sanders invited him to tea. He ate of them prodigiously, in the sitting-room behind the bar, which, to his great surprise, was like anybody else's sitting-room, containing neither rows of coloured bottles nor sawdust on the floor. Sometimes, after tea, Miss Sanders would play the piano and sing in a deep voice *Oft in the Stilly Night*. She would then turn to him and say in a bantering way that she sounded like a cockerel. Her voice was a hoarse contralto. Once, when it was time for her to go to the bar, she asked him if he would like to screw on her ear-rings for her, but he was so awkward at the job that she did not repeat the invitation. She smelled of violets and the back of her neck was brown as an autumn leaf. But, in spite of the apple-fritters, he preferred being in the public-house proper to sitting there at the back with Miss Sanders.

One afternoon he was playing on the river bank with another boy. They quarrelled, the boy gave him a push and he fell into the water. His opponent, frightened, ran off. But he had only squelched into some mud, dirtying himself up to his waist. Indignant and alarmed, he gazed in horror at his slimy legs and knickerbockers. How was he to get himself dry and clean before going home! Some particularly unpleasant punishment would be given him if he went home like this. And quickly he thought of his friend Miss Sanders, who never criticised him and would only laugh at his state.

By roundabout back-lane ways, not daring to show himself in the main street, he reached the back of the public-house, scrambled up its wall and dropped into the yard. He crept down some steps and peered into the sitting-room window. Yes, she was on the sofa reading a book. He tapped nervously at the window; in his miserable wet state he dared not go to the door. When Miss Sanders had got him inside, her mouth gaped and she screwed up her eyes with laughter.

'Can you,' he stammered, 'can you give me a pan for me to wash my knees? And then I'll stand in front of the fire and get dry.'

She stood in the middle of the room, her arms lifted, both her hands holding the high tower of her green-gold hair; she was looking at him meditatively now, having stopped laughing. 'You come with me,' she said at last. And she patted his head, took his hand and drew him upstairs. The swish of her hard shiny skirts was full of determination.

What a big bathroom they had! And it was white and splendid and not like the poked-away corner of the one in his home. Miss Sanders was turning on the taps in the enormous bath; he did not think anything; he gazed inscrutably before him. Briskly, with quick firm gestures, Miss Sanders took hold of him and whipped off his jersey.

He stood very still but once, as if trapped, he gazed round wildly at the door. Miss Sanders's well-known arms, hard and brisk with power, encircled him. They dexterously peeled off his clothes. He was clammy and shivering, and he was overcome with some strange new feeling that presently solidified into a knot of resentment in his mind. Too late! She had got him into the bath.

She rolled up her sleeves and, telling him that presently they would have some nice hot tea and pineapple together, she soaped him. There was no denying her. Busily, talking all the while with a bright, hard gallop of words, she kneaded and rubbed his flesh. The resentment swelled into anger. At home he washed himself without help now. But he could not bring his tongue to protest. She had the large, high power of the adult, and before this she had always behaved as a friend.

'There now, there now, all white and clean again! My word, look at the water! Eh, your mother would have carried on, I'm glad you came to me first . . . I'll wrap this hot towel round you and you must wear a little jacket of mine till your clothes are dry . . .' She had lifted him out and was drying him vigorously, kneeling before him now, her breast oppressively against his face.

He did not enjoy his tea, sitting in the woman's jacket. Something had changed. He kept on gazing straight into the bunch of snapdragons on the table, eating with grave austerity and refusing a second helping of pineapple. He was glad when the publican came into the room. When his clothes were dry, Miss Sanders insisted on dressing him. Once she glanced sharply into his face and said:

'You mustn't be frightened, your mother won't be angry now. We won't tell her if you like.'

And she pushed two pennies into his hand. He saw that she was in extraordinary good temper, her grey eyes, under which were mauve patches, bright-eyed as diamonds. The bar was open as he made a slow, almost funeral way through it. A resolve was at the back of his mind but did not declare itself: he made his exit with only a vaguely troubled emotion.

For he never returned to the public-house. Daily it was before him, bright and tempting and full of gaiety. He scudded past its steps, kicked a ball on its pavement, played marbles in the road before it. Garlanded with light in the evenings, the piano in the 'Commercial Room' sometimes rollicking out its strident songs, men singing, tales told in the bar, snatches of mysterious phrases over which he used to ponder interestedly—he ignored and forsook them all. He regretted the loss. The public-house had been a whole world of marvels and attractive discoveries, and he remembered that part of it with pleasure. And then something happened which made it disagreeable, which ought not to have entered into that particular world. One afternoon as he strolled along the pavement, an upstairs window opened and Miss Sanders popped out her head.

'Hello, there, hello!' she called. 'Why haven't you been to see me lately, you bad boy?'

Hesitating, he looked up but did not answer. She was smiling down at him, a smile of friendly mockery. He remembered thinking that the tower of her hair was in danger of toppling over. She was leaning out in such great eagerness, her bantering smile thrown down to him invitingly. He looked at her with curiosity but had nothing to say. Again asking for an explanation, she added:

'Well, at any rate, come in now. I want to talk to you.'

He did not move. Suddenly she dropped a coin to him. 'There's sixpence for you!' she cried, her smile breaking into a laugh. 'Now come in to see me.'

Picking up the sixpence, he began to slowly walk away, without comment, even to himself. He only remembered that for a long time he had wanted a certain penknife. Miss Sanders did not call out again, and when he reached the corner he made a sudden headlong dive out of sight.

RIVER, FLOW GENTLY

The Malt Shovel Inn was on the river's edge, with a narrow slip of lawn between. For a month or so in the summer it was moderately popular with river enthusiasts who did not mind the slack, humid air of such a low-lying place. Three miles from Honeybridge, and the lane down to the door off the beaten track, there was not much casual bar trade. If the summer was wet, even the regulars who came for a holiday were apt to cancel their rooms; there is no place more oppressive in a rainy week than a quiet river valley, with the air hanging flaccid and turning one's very bones to jelly.

Carrie Neap, after her first year in the Malt Shovel, knew that the place was a mistake. Her gentlemen had not followed her, after all; none arranged to stay or brought their fine cars down the lane. She had to admit that the Malt had no modern comforts like the Swan at Honeybridge, where she had reigned as chambermaid for many years, but nevertheless she had hoped that she would be able to make the gentlemen feel at home.

'A *home*, that's what the Malt's going to be, and no blooming list of regulations over the bed, neither . . . How's that boy of yours getting on in college, Mr. Mills?'

The regulars at the Swan were mostly comfortable, middle-aged regatta men, coming down for week-ends, and sometimes an annual week, to renew acquaintance with the river of their youth. They seldom brought wives with them, and in the evening they gathered in the lounge bar and talked of bygone boat races. Real gentlemen, and she was proud to do her best for them. One and all, they had shown interest in her great venture of getting married at last and taking an inn of her own, and nearly all made those promises.

'What, Carrie, you getting married! Lord, what's the Swan going to do! . . . There, there, never mind, we'll all be following you.' And that season they gave her extra good tips, and when they left she offered them her cheek, shedding a tear, which they nipped in their friendly way, nice and proper gentlemen that they were.

She missed them, she mourned them. There was Mr. Clarke, for instance, whose purplish-red face so worried her. Every night, after a day in his boat, he would get under the influence and rely on her not only to put him to bed but to haul him out in the morning. He would never get up unless she threw back the sheets off his curled body, give him a resounding smack, and bawl:

'Hoy! Now then, ten o'clock. Where d'you think you are? Come on, I got my work to do here.'

But God help any newcomer—the old regulars knew better—who mistook her friendliness and tried any hanky-panky with her. There was that old rip Mr. M. who one morning had made this mistake. She had given him a biff in the stomach and then soundly lectured him. Even her starched apron (she was famous for her stiff and always snowy aprons) crackled in wrath. He was in the tea trade and when she got married sent her a small chest of best Orange Tips.

Eighteen years she had been in the Swan, going as a kitchen girl in plaits and in the end all but running the whole place. She had saved money, but not enough to buy a hotel on her own. And with thirty-five not far off she had felt that if she was to do anything ambitious she'd better be hurrying. Then George Neap had turned up.

She had known him before, up on the downs where they were both reared. Since then he had been in the Navy, but had come back to his old job in his father's wheelwright shed up at Wipberry. After seeing her one Saturday night in the Swan taproom, where she had gone to help for an hour, he got courting her. He was a lean, brown-skinned man with not much to say for himself. She had seen with approval that though he could put away a tidy amount of beer—she herself rarely touched anything—he knew when to stop. There seemed a certain dogged austerity about him. Also an obstinacy in his blue thin eyes. When she had asked him what he intended doing with his life, he said concisely:

'Take a pub. The old man'll let me have some dough. Got any?'

'Close on two hundred pounds,' she said openly.

'They're skinning you in the Swan. A woman like you ought to have her own place.'

She had told him that the Malt Shovel, down the river, was on the market. He went off alone one evening and had a sniff round there. It was autumn, the air was stagnant, the willow leaves lay thick on the misty water. The report he brought back was not enthusiastic.

'Bar empty and fly dirt on everything. Smelled, as if nobody's been there for a drink for weeks. It's ramshackle.'

''Course it is,' she had said. 'Look who's got the place! A couple of drunkards. They've let it go down. That's why it's so cheap.'

He had frowned. She pointed out, with the energy which got drowsy City gentlemen out of their beds and cleaned their rooms while they were putting on a shirt, that what the Malt Shovel needed was herself. She knew it had a regular clientèle of young boarders in July and August; not much class, like the

Swan, but this she would soon change. She told George about her faithful gentlemen, whose socks she darned.

George had been obstinate for a while. She bridled, she withheld herself, she bristled. And because, in his spare, unvocal way, he was in love with her and they were not married, he had given in at last, though sulkily. His father gave him fifty pounds and lent him two hundred; they got the Malt Shovel, partly furnished and with two punts, a rowing boat and a canoe, for three hundred and fifty, and they spent another hundred in preening the place up. Carrie, ar first, had worked like a demon; George more carefully, in his silent fashion, carpentering and repairing.

But what neither had bargained for was the air of the place. A river valley is various as a woman. At Honeybridge the valley opened out, and the air, though never so vigorous as on the downs, kept on the move; on draughty days it fair waltzed round the girdle of hills. But down by the Malt Shovel it seemed never anything but stagnant. In high summer it was like living in a conservatory of tropical plants: sapping and insidious air that took the stiffening out of your spine.

'Air here,' George had remarked at first, 'got no guts in it. We're too much in the lee.' He was sweating, making a new bench in the taproom.

'Oh,' she panted—she was distempering the walls and secure in her energy then—'we'll get used to it. We're not a couple of old crocks.'

Even in winter the sheltered air was mild, and the pink roses bordering the narrow lane flowered into December. In summer all growing things flourished with lush abundance, especially willow herb, which had to be curbed every day. Nature, if allowed, seemed bent on choking the Malt Shovel with creepers, gigantic fronds and leaping bushes. And fat muscular toads jumped and big lusty spiders wove massive webs in the dank alley behind the house, under the bank's slope.

Wasps, too, found the place a companionable headquarters for a river holday; that first summer they were a cruel scourge and zoomed about the inn with a derisive energy. Their holes could not be found in the wild tangle of weeds, briars, and willows beyond George's vegetable patches. One day Carrie saw a very thick grass snake languidly pulling its length into this hot little jungle, and she uttered a rare old scream that went back to her primitive ancestors. George came out of the taproom, wiping his mouth. Still bellowing, she was plunging regardless over his young carrot bed.

'Take care of them carrots,' he bawled crossly.

'There's a big snake!' she shrieked.

'Aye,' he said briefly, 'I've seen him often.' He went back into the taproom.

There were rats too. At evening they plopped into the river from holes in the clay just above the water, visiting each other or lithely easing their bodies in the placid river. She found one on the taproom counter one early morning, sitting up on its hind legs and licking beer off its front paws. On seeing her it did not seem unduly incommoded and took its time in whisking away. George set traps, but observed in that exasperatingly indifferent way he had developed lately: 'You'll never get rid of rats in a ramshackle old place right on the river like this.'

But worse than anything was the air. On some warm days Carrie felt her blood was turned to greasy dishwater. It was an effort even to go upstairs, it was a greater effort to turn out a room with that old energy which had been her pride. She would stand gazing out of the window—she had a terror of sitting down—and the river's soft prowl seemed to bear away all her strength. And the water's soft *lap, lap* seemed to say: 'Why bother? Move slowly. There's nothing worth getting into a rage about.' A peculiar smooth tranquillity lay in the river's unhurried urge; something seductive and enticing, yet indifferent.

And the mists! The mists were worse in spring and autumn. They dampened everything and laid a thin mildew on cheese, bread, and George's boots lying under the sofa. The really bad ones hid everything outside in a world of dripping pale wool, so that it was dangerous to go out; you might step into the river. They shut off the Malt Shovel from the rest of the earth and muffled every sound. You might be hundreds of miles from other people.

One evening, when a particularly bad mist had lasted two days, imprisoning both her and George in the house, she had peered through the taproom hatch and found George mumbling to himself by the counter. She watched. He finished a pint of strong ale and went to draw himself another, spilling much of it into the zinc catch. It was plain there had been several. She pulled herself sharply out of her own torpor, went round into the bar, and said ominously:

'You putting the money for those pints into the till, are you, George Neap?'

He swivelled round in bleared astonishment. His thin eyes cocked across to her, he mumbled: 'Someone's got to drink the bally stuff. I'm playing at customers, I am.'

'Out of my bar with you, go on!' she screeched. And, panting, she began for the first time to use those classic phrases of marital rebuke common to most disputatious couples. None of her City gentlemen would have recognised the old Carrie in this termagant of swelling bosom and writhing brow. She reached home at last and, with a turn to the hangdog, George swayed out to the sitting-room and fell into a deep snooze on the soda.

Carrie dropped panting to a bench. Lord, the air was thick as jam. She was soaking. And weak as a straw. It didn't do the heart any good to work herself into a rage like that. Better take something for it.

She heard George's snores. She went behind the bar and took down the bottle of brandy. Not for the first time, on the quiet.

In September of the second year, after a poor summer, Mr. Chambers stepped off his luxurious launch, tied her up, and paid a call on his friend. He was a beaming man of prosperous port; in his smart blazer, spotless white trousers, and expensive Panama hat, this was the sort of gentleman that should have occupied the Malt Shovel lawn. Not those bits of larking chaps and giggling girls with twopennorth of manners who had cluttered up the place in August.

The river shimmering demurely behind him, Mr. Chambers entered the unswept lobby and was greeted by a swarm of flies. The sitting-room door was open on the left; he glanced inside and saw a cat with four kittens on a dirty cushion in the sagging sofa, a smudged calendar askew on the wall, a flyblown mirror over the mantelpiece, and a biscuit crushed on the dirty linoleum. There was a stagnant odour.

'Carrie!' he called in his old jovial way. 'Carrie, ooh, ooh!' Someone tramped downstairs. A woman in a soiled dress over which was a grimy unstarched apron. Her hair was slack and her face pouchy. But undoubtedly, on a second look, Carrie. Her dulled brown eyes peered at Mr. Chambers for a puzzled moment. Then she went right over to him and, with a little whimper of pleasure, held up her cheek for his nip.

'Well, Carrie, my dear, this is a treat.' And not a flicker of astonishment had he betrayed. He gallantly brushed her cheek, as of old. 'I was taking a jaunt down-river today, for a change,' he purred, 'and thought I'd look you up.' He tweaked her ear and sailed behind her into the empty bar, laying his glistening Panama on a table where unwashed beer rings entranced numerous flies.

But Carrie had become oddly shy. She stood almost furtively behind the bar, looking at him and not looking. She asked something about the Swan; she listened to his reply with a little expression of dulled eagerness.

'And now, Carrie, what are you having? . . . Ah, don't say you're still teetotal! Not with a place of your own. Look here, it won't do.' She finally agreed to take a brandy. He tilted the bottle for her, laid a pound note on the counter, and beamed: 'There, there, buy yourself a box of those chocolates you used to like. I didn't have time to get one.' His boyish eyes shone on her roguishly.

'It's been a bad season,' she said morosely. 'A tyke of a season.'

Mr. Chambers was not a man who allowed dismal thoughts around him. In his City office he continually preached the business value of cheerful countenance. So he did not realise that Carrie would have been vastly comforted if he had shed a mourning tear with her over the Malt Shovel's failure. All the comfort he offered taking out a long gold cigarette-case, was: 'Ah, the Swan is not at all the same without you, Carrie.'

She quivered. Though her brown eyes were still shy of looking at him directly, something seemed to stir in their torpid depths. She glanced round furtively at the slovenly bar; quietly she moved an unwashed tumbler out of sight. But of course she did not remind him of the gentlemen's promise to come and stay in the Malt Shovel. And not until he had gone, waving his Panama at her from the elegant launch, did she quiver into life.

She had stood on the lawn in the flaccid air out of which all vitality was wrung; she had uttered that little whimper as Mr. Chambers swayed away. Then she bounced in search of George. He was behind the boat-house, lazily planing a piece of wood. A man with a piece of wood is often completely happy and content with his world. So perhaps it was not the best moment for Carrie to announce aggressively: 'George, we've got to give up and clear out. It's no good. I've made up my mind.'

'Well, I haven't, see!' Unshaven and collarless, he went on planing the wood.

'No,' she said bitterly; 'while there's a drop of drink left in the stock you'll cling on like a leech. But,' she prophesied direly, 'it won't last, George Neap. *What about the bills?* You're going to wait till you're chucked out? . . . Bankruptcy,' she hissed. 'Summonses.'

'You wanted the place,' he said briefly. 'And now we're in, I'm staying till we've got to go—and if.' They had made a few pounds on the summer visitors.

It was a revenge for overruling his pre-marriage objections to the Malt. The air had worked in him like a slow poison, making him foolish and petty. She became very angry and assailed him with blistering words; he went on planing the wood. She threatened to leave him, and knew she'd never do that—not Carrie Neap, whose name had never been touched with scandal. But at this threat he looked up, and there was that bit of fright in his eyes. There were times even now when they cooed together in loving recognition. She noticed his fright.

'Yes, I'll leave you!' she shouted.

Maddeningly he bent again to the wood. 'Well, clear off, then,' he said shrewdly.

She flounced away, feeling defeated. She found herself behind the taproom bar, her hand lifted to the brandy bottle. She stopped herself just in time. *No, not another drop.* Instead, fuming and bridling, she scrubbed the tables, though after a few minutes she had to stop. The air made her gasp; sweat streamed down her cheeks.

During the next week or two she tried to battle against the languor of the autumn days. The air was even more enervating than usual. The river seemed dreamily without urge, only the first fallen leaves indicating it was prowling silently onwards, peaceful and enticing. She would pull herself away from contemplation of it and, working herself into a rage, attack George. He bore with her in a kind of pondering sloth. A worse effect was that he skulked oftener to the bar and, if allowed to remain there, slunk into a gross lethargy and childishly agreed to everything she said, except her wish to abandon the Malt.

One evening, when he was like that and her fury recoiled on her, she suddenly lowered her voice and whispered with awful distinctness: 'The river . . . the river . . . I'll drown myself.' She swayed in grief; she gazed out at the dusky water with its gentle flow of red and yellow leaves.

'We'll both drown ourselves, Carrie girl,' he hiccupped. Yet that fright flickered into his face again.

'There's nothing to live for,' she whimpered. Their money gone, debts, and heaven knew what the future held. Not a customer in the bar for four days. No company. The winter coming. Not even a boat passing on the river.

Then the autumn mists began. She hated these above everything; they drove her frantic. Creeping and ghostly, they thickened towards evening, and in her hysteria she swore she could hear them prowling outside, like soft-padded animals. Yet if she plunged, out there was nothing but a blind white silence, a world of dead. And the mists passed through the walls like ghosts, and after dark, as if seeking company, clotted and writhed in yellow murkiness in any lit room.

George couldn't go out to his jobs in the garden. The only outside noise she heard was the unearthly whirr and beat of the swans in flight, cleaving the mists with their great shuddering wings and swordlike necks. She thought of the black poisonous viciousness of their eyes and felt a sudden intimacy with these cold, savage creatures . . . And all day there she was imprisoned with George, watching each other—he furtively waiting an opportunity to skulk into the taproom, she neglecting her work to keep a sultry eye on him, at the same time fighting that soaking inertia in the air; and through it all feeling the soft strength of the river, oh, so softly flowing past the willow herb's withering purples, the loosetrife, the grey reeds.

One of those first autumnal mists lasted for three days. At about eight o'clock on the third night she missed George and found him in the taproom rapidly finishing a glass of whisky.

'Whisky now, is it!' she panted.

'A double.' He nodded. 'Put it down on the slate.'

She burst like a rocket. The concentrated trials of the past three days exploded in her shrieking voice, combined with all the terror of the Malt Shovel's failure. Amid extreme abuse she accused him of lacking all that which made a man a man. He was a slothful tapeworm with no right to existence.

'Here,' he stuttered, 'lay off.' But he had gone white. There seemed a madness in the air.

Her voice rose in frenzy. A hank of hair writhed down her neck, her cheekbones leaped up and down. 'I'm sick to death of you! I've had enough of it all. My life isn't worth living. I've married a dud and I've taken a dud house!' Then, with a strange and awful cry, she ran out. He heard that cry out in the mist. It rose to a wild shriek, followed by a heavy splash.

'Carrie!' he bellowed, and leaped over the counter.

It was no good; he had to give up. The mist had beaten him from the first, when he had dived in. He had heard a choked cry yards ahead down-river, but when he got there nothing was to be seen or heard. Nothing but the smooth mingling of mist and water. She could swim, but if she intended committing suicide . . . Calling, he had thrashed about under the devilish mist until he was icy cold. He couldn't find the bank—and then it was the opposite side. But from there, on the towpath, he had stumbled a mile to the lock-keeper's cottage, still calling her name.

They had given him a change of clothes and hot rum; they had telephoned the Honeybridge police station. But what was to be done? In his terror George had spilled out everything, and it was plain that poor Carrie had meant to end her life. There had been outside talk already of the disputes in the unlucky Malt Shovel.

'But if she could swim,' the lock-keeper suddenly said, 'she might be back by now . . . 'They get a change of mind sometimes, once they're in the water—'

They had decided to row back. That mile up-river was extreme agony for George. He kept calling her name through the mist. When they found the Malt Shovel bank at last, he leaped out and sped blindly into the house. He sobbed her name in the lobby; distraught, he stumbled through the rooms.

Silence. The house was dark, silent, and empty. The following hour, after the lock-keeper's departure, his thought were scarcely coherent. A policeman arrived on a bike and questioned him. Was it fancy that there was a suspicious note in his voice? George trembled anew. But nothing could be done till the mist cleared and the body was found.

Left alone to face the night, he went to the whisky. His nerve couldn't stand any more. Huddled on a bench in a corner of the taproom, he put the bottle to his mouth and drank neat. He dared not think of the dreadful morrow. The lamp shed a dim light through the mist. It had penetrated and thickened with the night, and outside the silence was like the end of the world. He peered about him. Pale shadows curled and rose from corners, wraiths of the mist. The bar was swaying. He had a fancy that the river had risen and was gently swallowing up the house.

'Ah, Carrie girl,' he whimpered, huddling farther into his corner. Swathed in mist, she stood looking at him with dreadful eyes of accusation. Was that sound the *drip, drip* of ghostly water running from her clothes? Had her soul risen already from the river bed to come and look at him in awful judgment! A spectral shawl draped the ghost in biblical fashion.

'Carrie girl,' he sobbed, 'I'll come with you. Wait for me.' To get up courage for the act, he lifted the bottle yet again.

But the wraith advanced and he stared in awful fear, the bottle poised. A white arm came out, pointing as if to eternity. 'George Neap,' a voice ordered, 'stop!'

'Carrie!' he whimpered.

'Yes, Mr. Chambers,' she said, heaving the matttress over, 'it took some doing. But I had come to the end of my patience. 'Course the water was cold, but I was out of it in a nick and hid behind the boat-house till he had gone off to the lock-keeper's. Then I ran indoors and got myself warm till he came back. I went under a bed while he ran about calling. 'Course I took a risk, but I was determined to budge him before another winter set in.'

Mr. Chambers beamed. 'Well, the Swan's a brighter place with you back, my dear . . . But some men, you know, would have got mad at your playing a trick like that; they'd have turned more obstinate.'

'Oh,' she said, shaking his pillow out of the window, 'he doesn't know it was a trick. He thought I just changed my mind when I began choking in the water. And I said I was in bed all the time, fast asleep from hot rum, when he ran about the house so demented, calling my name in the dark and mist . . . And mind,' she frowned, 'you don't tell him when he serves you in the bar. Now off with you. I've got ten rooms to do, and you can't hang about like this.'

Her tips from her regular gentlemen that week-end alone were more than a month's profit in the Malt Shovel. And down in the Swan bar George earned three pounds a week. But it wasn't so much the money. She valued the homage and tweakings of her gentlemen far more. They made her feel a woman full of use and standing, and she liked company. Nothing would ever take the starch out of her apron again.

DEATH OF A CANARY

In war-time the death of a bright yellow canary may seem a trivial occurrence. But Joey's owner, a widow evacuated from Bermondsey, took his end hard. She and Joey had survived some of the worst of the London raids and here, safe in the peace of the country and still in the prime of life, he had chosen to die on her. He was Bermondsey born and bred. She had accidentally dropped his cage to the floor the evening before his end.

Finding him dead in the morning, she rushed out of her tiny cottage—one of four sixteenth-century ex-almshouses—and wailed to us all: 'Joey's a goner! Joey's dead! Joey's passed away!'

The Russian princess—a real one—visiting at Number Two, threw back the lattice and said in her tinkling sugar-plum voice: 'How sad! Poor Joey.' She was tying up her flaxen hair in two-pennorth of rather dirty ribbon, and yawned. She had seen the Revolution with goggling childish eyes, but had escaped with her family and a few jewels.

I went with the widow to view the corpse. Joey lay on the floor of his cage in stiff yellow peace. It was his scraps of legs that looked so dead; they seemed to have retreated into his bright body, the claws bunched up.

'It must have been his heart,' the widow wailed. 'But when I dropped his cage last night he seemed all right. Oh, Joey! Was it those bombs in London,' she asked fiercely, 'that weakened your poor heart?'

'Very likely,' I said.

'But he's never been the same since I brought him here,' she rebuked herself. 'Off his seed one day, his water another. You'd think, wouldn't you, they'd like the country! Even in his cage he could see the fields and trees from the winder there. D'you think he was pining to get back to London?' she asked, and fear that I'd agree was in her voice.

'They are delicate things, I believe,' I said soothingly. 'No doubt it was his cage crashing last night that upset him.'

'Perhaps he thought it was more bombs,' she mourned. 'But he never turned a feather in London, he didn't—no, not even when the pub nearly opposite us went. He was with me in my neighbour's shelter and he just cocked his eye up and clung to his perch like a Christian and never squeaked once.'

She brewed a second pot of tea. She was of those who take their grief in hard gasps and fierce exclamations. In the kennel bedroom her bemused and trying old mother, for whose sake—and perhaps Joey's—she had at last

76

consented to be evacuated to the country, waspishly muttered in vain for attention. The princess, by now dressed and her fine family nose powdered, came in with condolences and to borrow a needle. She wore bazaar pearls, but still managed to trail a regal air, as of palaces, rubies, and plush footmen, behind her. We had been trying to persuade her to become a bus conductress, for she was looking for work. She was followed by the sole occupant of Number Four, a purple-faced old woman of eighty, who was in the habit of preparing her dinner and leaving it forgotten for days on a plate under the stove, while she suspiciously inquired of her neighbours if they had seen her dinner; she didn't really trust these Londoners.

'He *may* be dead,' she said, matter-of-factly. 'Birds can't live forever.'

The village postman, arriving then, thought Joey might have expired of the night's sharp November frost. We all drank tea. The princess told us of her parrot in Moscow which had to be left behind for the Reds. 'Probably they ate him,' she said, darning a big hole in her cotton stocking. The widow did not really like the princess, but she was too vexed to bother about her now. She kept on re-iterating—as is the way of those who are numbed in grief— that Joey must have died of a mixture of sheer country boredom and a heart which, though brave, had been weakened by London's bombs.

'I'm burying him at four o'clock this afternoon,' she suddenly announced. 'I hope everybody will come.' Before her marriage she had been a midwife; her pastry was light as a feather, and her tongue laden with tales.

At four we attended the burial. Behind Number Two the widow had a prosperous garden, oddly obedient to her Bermondsey hand—which, however, had a country ancestry. Her great bustling cabbages were lusty as the many babies she had brought into the world; her leeks, parsnips and beetroot were our envy. She could be generous with them. We attended Joey's funeral.

Outside the back door was her 'lawn,' table-cloth size. Edging it, the last bronze and white chrysanthemums were hesitating to die, her final flowers of a successful year. But last week she had tramped to town and bought four rose-bushes: red, yellow, white and pink. They were already planted. No doubt next summer her roses too would be a lesson to us all. A little hole was dug under one of these straggly bushes.

The widow came out, dry-eyed but melancholy of mien. In her hands a screw of blue tissue paper. We were allowed to take a last look inside the paper. She had wrapped Joey in cotton-wool.

We followed her to the grave. Her dog Nip, unnaturally quiet, walked soberly ahead. The princess, in a tattered white velvet jacket, was eating an apple. She was always eating, as if she would never be free of the hunger she had endured after the Revolution.

'I'm burying him under the yellow rose bush,' the widow said, gasping hard as she bent.

I admired her sense of fitness. Did she think the yellow rose would bloom more yellow with her canary under it? But covering the grave she went on: 'I thought he'd lie more happy under a rose of his own colour.' Stolid and square, she lifted herself, creaking a little. The November sun was dipping behind the well-behaved Hampshire slopes. She looked at the tawny flaring disc for a moment and murmured, trying to ease herself of the clumsy dropping of Joey's cage last night: 'Yes, he came through the London raids like a true cock bird, but the quiet of the country was too much for him. My husband bought him off a porter working in London Bridge Station and carried him home to me on an Easter Sunday. Both of 'em gone now, as well as the pub where he was bought.'

'Look at those two blue-tits in the hedge!' I pointed. Some redbreasts haunted the garden too, to say nothing of a pair of flashing jays—though these had stolen all her cherries in the summer. But her Bermondsey canary was more to her than all these.

'I've made a cake,' she said in a depressed way. 'Let's go and have a slice.' She turned to the princess. Previously she had treated this sprig of bygone imperialism with short shrift, instinctively disapproving of something that had failed. 'Well, it's not every canary has a Russian princess at its funeral, is it! Come in, my dear, and I'll tell you about some of my maternity cases.'

In isolated rural parts small events are apt to attain enormous significance. The widow remained unusually depressed for a long time; the death of her canary was to her greater than the death of kings. And that evening I watched the princess (whose aunt in Russia used to have the town's trams stopped when they disturbed her afternoon nap) elegantly peeling potatoes. She peeled them remarkably well, carefully removing all eyes. I do not know why I was impressed by this.

THE DILEMMA OF CATHERINE FUCHSIAS

Puffed up by his success as a ship-chandler in the port forty miles away, where he had gone from the village of Banog when the new town was rising to its heyday as the commercial capital of Wales, Lewis had retired to the old place heavy with gold and fat. With him was the bitter English wife he had married for her money, and he built the pink-washed villa overlooking Banog's pretty trout stream. And later he had set up a secret association with an unmarried woman of forty who was usually called Catherine Fuchsias, this affair—she received him most Sunday evenings after chapel in her outlying cottage—eluding public notice for two years. Until on one of those evenings, Lewis, who for some weeks had been complaining of a 'feeling of fullness', expired in her arms on the bed.

In every village there is a Jezebel or the makings of one, though sometimes these descend virtuous to their graves because of lack of opportunity or courage, fear of gossip or ostracism. Lewis the Chandler was Catherine Fuchsias' first real lover, so that for her to lose him like that not only dreadfully shocked her but, it will be agreed, placed her in a serious dilemma. She was not a born bad lot and, as a girl, she had been left in the lurch by a sweetheart who had gone prospecting to Australia and never fulfilled his promise to call her there. Thereafter she had kept house for her father, a farm worker, until he had followed her mother into the burial-ground surrounding Horeb chapel, which she cleaned for five shillings a week; in addition she had a job three days a week in the little wool factory a mile beyond Banog. It was in Horeb chapel during service that Lewis first studied her and admired her egg-brown face, thick haunches and air of abundant health. Her cottage stood concealed on a bushy slope outside the village, and she had a great liking for fuchsias, which grew wonderfully in the rich lap of the cottage.

When her paramour died on her bed she at first refused to believe it, so pertinacious and active was he and so unlike her idea of a man of sixty-four. Nevertheless, she ran howling downstairs. There she madly poked the fire, flung the night cloth over the canary's cage, ran into the kitchen and swilled a plate or two in a bowl, straightened a mat, and tidied her hair. In the mirror *there* was her face, Miss Catherine Bowen's face, looking no different, a solid unharmed fact with its brown speckles. The autumn dusk beginning to arrive at the window was quiet and natural as the chirp of the bird winging past the pane. For a moment she listened to the grandfather clock ticking away the silence. Then, with a bustling haste, she filled the kettle, lit the oil cooker, took an apple tart out of a zinc safe, looked at it, and put it back. She stood still again. And groaned.

She crept half-way up the stairs and called: 'Mr. Lewis . . . Mr. Lewis, here I am! Just put the kettle on. Time's going, boy. Come down straight away . . . Mr. Lewis!' She raised her voice. 'Lewis, stir yourself, boy. Come on now!' Only the clock replied. She sat on the stairs and groaned. 'Lewis,' she whimpered, 'there's a trick you are playing on me! Don't you come here again, I am offended . . . Yes, offended I am. I'll go for a walk, that's what I'll do. And don't you be here when I'm back.' She tramped noisily down the stairs, unlocked the front door, and slammed it behind her.

Bats were flying round the cottage. The sunflowers were hanging their half-asleep heads, and the old deep well among the luxuriant chrysanthemum bushes at the bottom of the garden, on which her eye rested for a dazed but speculative minute, stood in secret blue shadow. But she hurried out of the garden by the side gate where a path led into a coppice of dwarf trees and bushes. 'I'll go and pick mushrooms in Banner's fields, that's what I'll do,' she assured herself. 'Gone he'll be by the time I'm back.' But she did not descend the slope to the farm's fields. She scrambled into a ring of bushes and hid herself there on a patch of damp grass. One eye remained open in palpitating awareness, the other was half closed, as if she was in profound thought.

A bad shock can work wonders with a person's sensibility. Buried talents can be whisked up into activity, a primitive cunning reign again in its shady empire of old instincts. Or such a shock can create—women especially being given to escape into this—a fantasy of bellicose truth, a performance of the imagination that has nothing to do with hypocrisy but is the terrified soul backing away from reality. Catherine sprang up and hurried back to her whitewashed cottage. Already in the long dusky vale and the distant village a few lights shone out. She shot into the cottage and ran upstairs.

'Well, Mr. Lewis,' she exclaimed loudly, 'better you are after your rest?' She went close to the bed and peered down at the stout dusky figure lying on the patchwork quilt. 'Well now, I am not liking the look of you at all,' she addressed it, half scoldingly. 'What have you taken your jacket off for? Hot you were? Dear me, quite bad you look. Best for me to fetch your wife and the doctor. But you mustn't lie there with your coat off or a cold you will catch.' Volubly tut-tutting, she lit a candle and set about the task. Already, in the hour that had elapsed, he had begun to stiffen somewhat. She perspired and groaned, alternately blenching and going red. He was heavily cumbersome as a big sack of turnips: she was obliged to prop up his back with a small chair wedged against the bedstead. Luckily he had removed only his jacket, but (since of late he had got stouter) this, which was of chapel-black vicuña, fitted tight as the skin of a bladder of lard. Downstairs, the grandfather clock ticked loud and hurried.

Finally, buttoned up complete, he rested tidy, and she staggered back sweating. To lay out her father she had got the assistance of the blacksmith's wife.

For a minute she stood in contemplation of her work, then ran downstairs to fetch up his hat, umbrella, and hymn-book. She dropped the umbrella beside the bed, placed the hat on the bedside table, and laid the hymn-book on the quilt as though it had fallen from his hand. And all the time she uttered clamorous remarks of distress at his condition— 'Oh, Mr. Lewis, you didn't ought to have taken a walk, unwell like you are. Climbing! Lucky I saw you leaning over my gate. Dropped dead in the road you might have, and stayed there all night and got bitten by the stoats! You rest quiet now, and I won't be long.' At another thought she placed a glass of water by the bedside. Then, giving her own person a quick look-over, she put on a raincoat and a flowered hat, blew out the candle, and hastened from the cottage. It was past nine o'clock and quite dark, and she never rode her bicycle in the dark.

Half an hour later she banged at the costly oaken door of the pink villa, calling excitedly: 'Mrs. Lewis, Mrs. Lewis, come to your husband!' Milly Jones, the servant, opened the door, and Catherine violently pushed her inside. 'Where's Mrs. Lewis? Let me see her quick.' But Mrs. Lewis was already standing, stiff as a poker, in the hall.

'Catherine Fuchsias it is!' exclaimed Milly Jones, who was a native of Banog. 'Why, what's the matter with you?'

Catherine seemed to totter. 'Come to your husband, Mrs. Lewis, crying out for you he is! Oh dear,' she groaned, 'run all the way I have, fast as a hare.' She gulped, sat on a chair, and panted: 'Put your hat on quick, Mrs. Lewis, and tell Milly Jones to go to Dr. Watkins.'

Mrs. Lewis, who had the English reserve, never attended chapel, and also unlikably minded her own business, stared hard. 'My husband has met with an accident?' she asked, precise and cold.

'Wandering outside my gate I found him just now!' cried Catherine. 'Fetching water from my well I was, and saw him swaying about and staring at me white as cheese. "Oh, Mr. Lewis," I said, "what is the matter with you, ill you are? Not your way home from chapel is this!" . . . "Let me rest in your cottage for a minute," he said to me, "and give me a glass of water, my heart is jumping like a toad." . . . So I helped him in and he began to grunt awful, and I said: "Best to go and lie down on my poor father's bed, Mr. Lewis, and I will run at once and tell Mrs. Lewis to fetch Dr. Watkins." . . . Bring the doctor to him quick, Mrs. Lewis! Frightened me he has and no one to leave with him, me watering my chrysanthemums and just going to lock up for the night and seeing a man hanging sick over my gate—' She panted and dabbed her face.

Milly Jones was already holding a coat for her mistress, who frowned impatiently as Catherine went on babbling of the fright she had sustained. Never a talkative person, the Englishwoman only said, abrupt: 'Take me to your house . . . Milly, go for the doctor and tell him what you've just heard.' And she did not say very much as she stalked along beside Catherine, who still poured out a repeating wealth of words.

Arrived at the dark cottage, Catherine bawled comfortingly on the stairs: 'Come now, Mr. Lewis, here we are. Not long I've been, have I?'

'You ought to have left a light for him,' remarked Mrs. Lewis on the landing.

'What if he had tumbled and set the bed on fire!' said Catherine indignantly. In the heavily silent room she struck a match and lit the candle. 'Oh!' she shrieked.

Mrs. Lewis stood staring through her glasses. And then, in a strangely fallen voice, said: 'John! . . . John!' Catherine covered her face with her hands, crying in dramatic woe. 'Hush, *woman* . . . hush,' said Mrs. Lewis sternly.

Catherine moved her hands from her face and glared. *Woman*, indeed! In her own house! When she had been so kind! But all she said was: 'Well, Mrs. Lewis, enough it is to upset anyone with a soft heart when a stranger dies in her house . . . *Why*,' she began insidiously, 'was he wandering in the lanes all by himself in his bad state? Poor man, why is it he didn't go home after chapel? Wandering lost outside my gate like a lonely orphan child!'

Mrs. Lewis, as though she were examining someone applying for a place in her villa kitchen, gave her a long, glimmering look. 'Here is the doctor,' she said.

'Yes indeed,' Catherine exclaimed, 'and I am hoping he can take Mr. Lewis away with him in his motor.' The glance she directed at the corpse was now charged with hostility. 'He is a visitor that has taken advantage of my poor little cottage.' And was there a hint of malice in her manner as she swung her hips past Mrs. Lewis, went to the landing, and called down the stairs: 'Come up, Dr. Watkins. But behind time you are.'

Having verified the death and listened to Catherine's profuse particulars of how she had found him at the gate and strained herself helping him up the stairs, Dr. Watkins, who was of local birth and a cheerful man, said: 'Well, well, only this evening it was I saw him singing full strength in chapel, his chest out like a robin's. Pity he never would be a patient of mine. "You mind that heart of yours, John Lewis," I told him once, free of charge, "and don't you smoke, drink, or sing." Angina he had, sure as a tree got knots.'

'He liked to sing at the top of his voice,' agreed Mrs. Lewis. She took up the hymn-book from the quilt, turned quickly to Catherine, and demanded: 'Did he take this with him to bed, ill as he was?'

'No!' Catherine's voice rang. With Dr. Watkins present, the familiar local boy, she looked even more powerful. 'After I had helped him there and he laid a minute and went a better colour, I said: "Now, Mr. Lewis, you read a hymn or two while I run off; strength they will give you".'

'But you put the candle out!' pounced Mrs. Lewis. 'It must have been getting quite dark by then.'

'There,' Catherine pointed a dramatic finger, 'is the box of matches, with the glass of water I gave him.' She stood aggressive, while Dr. Watkins's ears moved. 'Candles can be lit.'

'This,' proceeded Mrs. Lewis, her eyes gazing around and resting in turn on a petticoat hanging on a peg and the women's articles on the dressing table, '*this* was your father's room?'

'Yes,' Catherine said, defiant; 'where he died and laid till they took him to Horeb. But when the warm weather comes, in here I move from the back; cooler it is and the view in summer same as on the postcards that the visitors buy, except for the old Trout Bridge . . . What are you so inquisitive about?' She began to bridle. 'Tidy it is here, and no dust. You would like to look under the bed? In the chest?'

Mrs. Lewis, cold of face, turned to the doctor. 'Could you say how long my husband has been dead?'

He made show of moving the corpse's eyelids, pinching a cheek, swinging an arm. 'A good two hours or more,' he said with downright assurance.

'Then,' said Mrs. Lewis, 'he must have been dead when he walked up those stairs! It takes only half an hour to reach my house from here.' She turned stern to Catherine: 'You said you came running to me as soon as you helped him up here to your father's room.'

'A law of the land there is!' Catherine's voice rang. 'Slander and malice is this, and jealous spite!' She took on renewed power and, like an actress towering and swelling into rage, looked twice her size. 'See,' she cried to Dr. Watkins, 'how it is that kind acts are rewarded, and nipped by a serpent is the hand of charity stretched out to lay the dying stranger on a bed! Better if I had let him fall dead outside my gate like a workhouse tramp and turned my back on him to water my Michaelmas daisies. Forty years I have lived in Banog, girl and woman, and not a stain small as a farthing on my character.' With her two hands she pushed up her inflated breasts as though they hurt her. 'Take him out of my house,' she sang in crescendo, 'my poor dead visitor that can't rise up and tell the holy truth for me. No husband, father, or brother have I to fight for my name. Take him!'

'Not possible tonight,' said Dr. Watkins, bewildered but appreciative of Catherine's tirade. 'Late and a Sunday it is, and the undertaker many miles away.'

'The lady by there,' said Catherine, pointing a quivering finger, 'can hire the farm cart of Peter the Watercress, if he can't go in your motor.'

'I,' said Mrs. Lewis, 'have no intention of allowing my husband to remain in this house tonight.' The tone in which she pronounced 'this house' demolished the abode to an evil shambles.

'Oh, oh,' wailed Catherine, beginning again, and moving to the bedside. 'John Lewis!' she called to the corpse, 'John Lewis, rise up and tell the truth! Swim back across Jordan for a short minute and make dumb the bitter tongue that you married! Miss Catherine Bowen, that took you innocent into her little clean cottage, is calling to you, and—'

Dr. Watkins, who had twice taken up his bag and laid it down again, interfered decisively at last, for he had been called out by Milly Jones just as he was sitting down to some slices of cold duck. 'Hush now,' he said to both women, a man and stern, 'hush now. Show respect for the passed away . . . A cart and horse you would like hired?' he asked Mrs. Lewis. 'I will drive you to Llewellyn's farm and ask them to oblige you.'

'And oblige me too!' Catherine had the last word, swinging her hips out of the room.

The corpse, though not much liked owing to its bragging when alive, was of local origin, and Llewellyn the Farmer agreed readily enough to disturb his stallion, light candles in the cart lanterns, and collect two village men to help carry the heavy man down Catherine Fuchsias' stairs. Already the village itself had been willingly disturbed out of its Sabbath night quiet, for Milly Jones, after calling at the doctor's, was not going to deprive her own people of the high news that rich Mr. Lewis had mysteriously been taken ill in Catherine's cottage. So when the farm cart stopped to collect the two men, news of the death was half expected. Everybody was left agog and expectant of the new week being a full one. What had Mr. Lewis been doing wandering round Catherine's cottage up there after chapel? Strange it was. Married men didn't go for walks and airings after chapel.

On Monday morning, before the dew was off her flowers, Catherine's acquaintance, Mrs. Morgans, who lived next door to the Post Office, bustled into the cottage. 'Catherine, dear,' she exclaimed, peering at her hard. 'What is this, a man dying on your bed!'

'My father's bed,' corrected Catherine. And at once her body began to swell. 'Oh, Jinny Morgans, my place in Heaven I have earned. I have strained myself,' she moaned, placing her hands round her lower middle, 'helping him up the stairs after I found him whining like an old dog outside my gate. A crick I have got in my side too. So stout he was, and crying to lay down on a bed. I thought he had eaten a toadstool for a mushroom in the dark.'

'What was he doing, walking about up here whatever?' Mrs. Morgans breathed.

'Once before I saw him going by when I was in my garden. He stopped to make compliments about my fuchsias— Oh,' she groaned, clasping her stomach, 'the strain is cutting me shocking.'

'Your fuchsias—' egged on Mrs. Morgans.

'Very big they hung this year. And he said to me, "When I was a boy I used to come round here to look for tadpoles in the ponds." Ah!' she groaned again.

'Tadpoles.' Mrs. Morgans nodded, still staring fixed and full on her friend, and sitting tense with every pore open. As is well known, women hearken to words but rely more on the secret information obtained by the sense that has no language.

Catherine, recognising that an ambassador had arrived, made a sudden dive into the middle of the matter, her hands flying away from her stomach and waving threatening. And again she went twice her size and beat her breast. 'That jealous Mrs. Lewis,' she shouted, 'came here and went smelling round the room nasty as a cat. This and that she hinted, with Dr. Watkins there for witness! A law of slander there is,' she shot a baleful glance at her visitor, 'and let one more word be said against my character and I will go off straight to Vaughan Solicitor and get a letter of warning sent.'

'Ha!' said Mrs. Morgans, suddenly relaxing her great intentness. 'Ha!' Her tone, like her nod, was obscure of meaning, and on the whole she seemed to be reserving judgment.

Indeed, what real proof was there of unhealthy proceedings having been transacted in Catherine's cottage? Mrs. Morgans went back to the village with her report and that day everybody sat on it in cautious meditation. In Catherine's advantage was the general dislike of proud Mrs. Lewis, but, on the other hand, a Jezebel, for the common good and the protection of men, must not be allowed to flourish unpunished! All day in the Post Office, in the Glyndwr Arms that evening, and in every cottage and farmhouse, the matter was observed from several loquacious angles.

On Wednesday afternoon Mr. Maldwyn Davies, B.A., the minister of Horeb, climbed to the cottage, and was received by his member and chapel cleaner with a vigorous flurry of welcome. Needlessly dusting a chair, scurrying for a cushion, shouting to the canary, that at the minister's entrance began to chirp and swing his perch madly, to be quiet, Catherine fussily settled him before running to put the kettle on. In the kitchen she remembered her condition and returned slow and clasping herself. 'Ah,' she moaned, 'my pain has come back! Suffering chronic I've been off and on, since Sunday night. So heavy was poor Mr. Lewis to take up my stairs. But what was I to be doing with a member of Horeb whining outside my gate for a bed? Shut my door on him as if he was a scamp or a member of the Church of England?'

'Strange,' said Mr. Davies, his concertina neck, that could give forth such sweet music in the pulpit, closing down into his collar, 'strange that he climbed up here so far, feeling unwell.' He stared at the canary as if the bird held the explanation.

'Delirious and lighted up he was!' she cried. 'And no wonder. Did he want to go to his cold home after the sermon and singing in chapel? No! Two times and more I have seen him wandering round here looking full up with thoughts. One time he stopped at my gate and had praises for my dahlias, for I was watering them. "Oh, Mr. Lewis," I said to him, "what are you doing walking up here?' and he said, "I am thinking over the grand sermon Mr. Davies gave us just now, and I would climb big mountains if mountains there were!" Angry with myself I am now that I didn't ask him in for a cup of tea, so lonely he was looking. "Miss Bowen," he said to me, "when I was a boy I used to come rabbiting up here".'

'Your dahlias,' remarked Mr. Davies, still meditatively gazing at the canary, 'are prize ones, and the rabbits a pest.'

'Oh,' groaned Catherine, placing her hand round her lower middle, 'grumbling I am not, but there's a payment I am having for my kindness last Sunday! . . . Hush,' she bawled threateningly to the canary, 'hush, or no more seed today.'

Mr. Davies, oddly, seemed unable to say much. Perhaps he, too, was trying to sniff the truth out of the air. But he looked serious. The reputation of two of his flock was in jeopardy, two who had been nourished by his sermons, and it was unfortunate that one of them lay beyond examination.

'Your kettle is boiling over,' he reminded her, since in her exalted state she seemed unable to hear such things.

She darted with a shriek into the kitchen, and when she came back with a loaded tray, which she had no difficulty in carrying, she asked: 'When are you burying him?'

'Thursday, two o'clock. It is a public funeral . . . You will go to it?' he asked delicately.

This time she replied, sharp and rebuking: 'What, indeed, *me*? Me that's gor to stay at home because of my strain and can only eat custards? Flat on my back in bed I ought to be this minute . . . Besides,' she said, beginning to bridle again, 'Mrs. Lewis, the *lady*, is a nasty!' She paused to take a long breath and to hand him a buttered muffin.

'Her people are not our people,' he conceded, and pursed his lips.

Fluffing herself up important, and not eating anything herself, Catherine declared: 'Soon as I am well I am off to Vaughan Solicitor, to have advice.' Black passion began to scald her voice; she pointed a trembling finger ceilingwards. 'Up there she stood in the room of my respected father, with Dr. Watkins for witness, and her own poor husband not gone cold and his eyes on us shiny as buttons, and her spiteful tongue made remarks. Hints and sarcastic! Nearly dropped dead I did myself . . . The hand stretched out in charity was bitten by a viper!' She began to swell still more. 'Forty years I have lived in Banog, clean as a whistle, and left an orphan to do battle alone. Swear I would before the King of England and all the judges of the world that Mr. John Lewis was unwell when he went on the bed up there! Swear I would that my inside was strained by his weight. A heathen gypsy would have taken him into her caravan! Comfort I gave him in his last hour. The glass of water by the bed, and a stitch in my side racing to fetch his wife, that came here stringy and black-natured as a bunch of dry old seaweed and made evil remarks for thanks . . . Oh!' she clasped her breasts as if they would explode, 'if justice there is, all the true tongues of Banog must rise against her and drive the bad-speaking stranger away from us over the old bridge. Our honest village is to be made nasty as a sty, is it? No!'

Not for nothing had she sat all these years in close attention to Mr. Davies's famous sermons, which drew persons from remote farms even in winter. And, as she rocked on her thick haunches and her voice passed from the throbbing of harps to the roll of drums, Mr. Davies sat at last in admiration, the rare admiration that one artist gives to another. She spoke with such passion that, when she stopped, her below-the-waist pains came back and, rubbing her hands on the affected parts, she moaned in anguish, rolling up her big moist eyes.

'There now,' he said, a compassionate and relenting note in his voice, 'there now, take comfort.' And as he pronounced: 'There must be no scandal in Banog!' she knew her battle was won.

'Put your hands by here,' she cried, 'and you will feel the aches and cricks jumping from my strain.'

But Mr. Davies, a fastidious look hesitating for a moment across his face, accepted her word. He took a slice of apple tart and ate it, nodding in meditation. A woman fighting to preserve the virtue of what, it is said, is the most priceless treasure of her sex is a woman to be admired and respected. Especially if she is a Banog one. And it was natural that he was unwilling to accept that two of his members could have forgotten themselves so scandalously. Nevertheless, as Catherine coiled herself down from her exalted though aching state and at last sipped a little strong tea, he coughed and remarked: 'It is said that nearly every Sunday night for two years or more Mr. Lewis never arrived home from chapel till ten o'clock, and no trace is there of his occupation in these hours. "A walk," he used to tell in his home, "a Sunday-night walk I take to think over the sermon." That is what the servant Milly Jones has told in Banog, and also that in strong doubt was Mrs. Lewis concerning those walks in winter and summer.'

'Then a policeman she ought to have set spying behind him,' said Catherine, blowing on a fresh cup of tea with wonderful assurance. 'Oh, a shame it is that the dead man can't rise up and speak. Oh, wicked it is that a dead man not buried yet is turned into a goat.' Calm now, and the more impressive for it, she added: 'Proofs they must bring out, strict proofs. Let Milly Jones go babbling more, and *two* letters from Vaughan Solicitor I will have sent.'

'Come now,' said Mr. Davies hastily, 'come now, the name of Banog must not be bandied about outside and talked of in the market. Come now, the matter must be put away. Wind blows and wind goes.' He rose, gave a kind nod to the canary, and left her.

He would speak the decisive word to silence offensive tongues. But, as a protest, she still stayed retreated in the cottage; serve them right in the village that she withheld herself from the inquisitive eyes down there. On Friday morning the milkman told her that Mr. Lewis had had a tidy-sized funeral the previous day. She was relieved to hear he was safely in the earth, which was the home of forgetfulness and which, in due course, turned even the most disagreeable things sweet. After the milkman had gone she mixed herself a cake of festival richness, and so victorious did she feel that she decided to put an end to her haughty exile on Sunday evening and go to chapel as usual; dropping yet another egg in the bowl, she saw herself arriving at the last minute and marching to her pew in the front with head held high in rescued virtue.

On Saturday morning the postman, arriving late at her out-of-the-way cottage, threw a letter inside her door. A quarter of an hour later, agitated of face, she flew from the cottage on her bicycle. The village saw her speeding through without a look from her bent-over head. She shot past the Post Office, Horeb chapel, the inn, the row of cottages where the nobodies lived, past the house of Wmffre, the triple-crowned bard whose lays of local lore deserved to be better known, past the houses of Mr. Davies, B.A., and Mrs. Williams Flannel, who had spoken on the radio about flannel-weaving, past the cottage of Evans the Harpist and Chicago Jenkins, who had been in jail in that place, and, ringing her bell furious, spun in greased haste over the cross-roads where, in easier times, they hanged men for sheep stealing. She got out on to the main road without molestation.

'Judging,' remarked Mrs. Harpist Evans in the Post Office, ' by the way her legs were going on that bike the strain in her inside has repaired quite well.'

It was nine miles to the market town where Vaughan the solicitor had his office, which on Saturday closed at midday. She stamped up the stairs, burst into an outer room, and demanded of a frightened youth that Mr. Vaughan attend to her at once. So distraught was she that the youth skedaddled behind a partition of frosted glass, came back, and took her into the privacy where Mr. Vaughan, who was thin as a wasp and had a black hat on his head, hissed: 'What are you wanting? Closing time it is.' Catherine, heaving and choking, threw down the letter on his desk and, after looking at it, he said, flat: 'Well, you can't have it yet. Not till after probate. You go back home and sit quiet for a few weeks.' Accustomed to the hysteria of legatees, and indeed of non-legatees, he turned his back on her and put a bunch of keys in his pocket.

She panted and perspired. And, pushing down her breasts, she drew out her voice, such as it was—'Oh, Mr. Vaughan,' she whimpered, 'it is not the money I want. Come I have to ask you to let this little business be shut up close as a grave.' A poor misused woman in mortal distress, she wiped sweat and tears off her healthy country-red cheeks.

'What are you meaning?' He whisked about impatient, for at twelve-five, in the bar-parlour of the Blue Boar, he always met the manager of the bank for conference over people's private business.

She hung her head ashamed-looking as she moaned: 'A little favourite of Mr. Lewis I was, me always giving him flowers and vegetables and what-not free of charge. But bad tongues there are in Banog, and they will move quick if news of this money will go about.'

'Well,' he said, flat again, 'too late you are. There is Mrs. Lewis herself knowing about your legacy since Thursday evening, and—'

Catherine burst out: 'But *she* will keep quiet for sure! She won't be wanting it talked that her husband went and left me three hundred pounds, no indeed! For *I* can say things that poor Mr. Lewis told me, such a nasty she was! It is of Horeb chapel I am worrying—for you not to tell Mr. Davies our minister or anyone else that I have been left this money.' She peeped up at him humble.

'Well,' he said, even flatter than before and, as was only proper, not sympathetic, 'too late you are again. Same time that I wrote to you I sent a letter to Mr. Davies that the chapel is left money for a new organ and Miss Catherine Bowen the cleaner left a legacy too: the letter is with him this morning. In the codicil dealing with you, Mr. Lewis said it was a legacy because your cleaning wage was so small and you a good worker.'

The excuse would have served nice but for that unlucky death on her bed. She groaned aloud. And as she collapsed on the solicitor's hard chair she cried out in anguish, entreating aid of him in this disaster. Pay him well she would if he preserved her good name, pounds and pounds.

'A miracle,' he said, 'I cannot perform.'

Truth, when it is important, is not mocked for long, even in a solicitor's office. The legatee went down the stairs with the gait of one whipped sore. She cycled back to her cottage as though using one leg, and, to avoid the village, she took a circuitous way, pushing the cycle up stony paths. At the cottage, after sitting in a trance for a while, she walked whimpering to the well among the chrysanthemums, removed the cover, and sat on the edge in further trance. An hour passed, for her thoughts hung like lead. She went into the dark night of the soul. But she couldn't bring herself to urge her body into the round black hole which pierced the earth so deep.

Then, on the horizon of the dark night, shone a ray of bright light. For the first time since the postman's arrival the solid untrimmed fact struck her that three hundred pounds of good money was hers. She could go to Aberystwyth and set up in partnership with her friend Sally Thomas who, already working there as a cook, wanted to start lodgings for the college students. The legacy, surprising because Mr. Lewis had always been prudent of pocket—and she had approved of this respect for cash, believing, with him, that the best things in life are free—the legacy would take her into a new life. She rose from the well. And in the cottage, shaking herself finally out of her black dream, she decided that Mr. Lewis had left her the money as a smack to his wife the nasty one.

No one came to see her. She did not go to chapel on the Sunday. Three days later she received a letter from Mr. Davies, B.A., inviting her to call at his house. She knew what it meant. The minister had sat with his deacons in special conclave on her matter, and he was going to tell her that she was to be cast out from membership of Horeb. She wrote declining the invitation and said she was soon to leave Banog to live at the seaside in quiet; she wrote to Sally Thomas at the same time. But she had to go down to the Post Office for stamps.

She entered the shop with, at first, the mien of an heiress. Two women members of Horeb were inside, and Lizzie Postmistress was slicing bacon. Catherine stood waiting at the Post Office counter in the corner. No one greeted her or took notice, but one of the customers slipped out and in a few minutes returned with three more women. All of them turned their backs on Catherine. They talked brisk and loud, while Catherine waited drawn up. Lizzie Postmistress sang: 'Fancy Lewis the Chandler leaving money for a new organ for Horeb!'

'The deacons,' declared the wife of Peter the Watercress, 'ought to say "No" to it.'

'Yes, indeed,' nodded the cobbler's wife; 'every time it is played members will be reminded.'

'Well,' said single Jane the Dressmaker, who had a tapemeasure round her neck, 'not the fault of the organ will that be.'

They clustered before the bacon-cutting postmistress. On a tin of biscuits, listening complacent, sat a cat. The postmistress stopped slicing, waved her long knife, and cried: 'Never would I use such an organ—no, not even with gloves on; and *I* for one won't like singing hymns to it.'

'A full members' meeting about *all* the business there ought to be! Deacons are men. Men go walking to look at dahlias and fuchsias—'

'And,' dared the cobbler's wife, 'drop dead at sight of a prize dahlia.'

Catherine rapped on the counter and shouted: 'Stamps!'

The postmistress craned her head over the others and exclaimed: 'Why now, there's Catherine Fuchsias! . . . Your inside is better from the strain?' she enquired. The others turned and stared in unison.

'Stamps!' said Catherine, who under the united scrutiny suddenly took on a meek demeanour.

'Where for?' asked the postmistress, coming over to the Post Office corner, and snatching up the two letters Catherine had laid on the counter. 'Ho, one to Mr. Davies, B.A., and one to Aberystwyth!'

'I am going to live in Aberystwyth,' said Catherine grandly.

'Retiring you are on your means?' asked Jane the Dressmaker.

'Plenty of college professors and well-offs in Aberystwyth!' commented Peter's wife.

'Well,' frowned the postmistress, as if in doubt about her right to sell stamps to such a person, 'I don't know indeed . . . What you wasting a stamp on this one for,' she rasped out, 'with Mr. Davies living just up the road? Too much money you've got?'

'Ten shillings,' complained unmarried Jane the Dressmaker, 'I get for making up a dress, working honest on it for three days or more. Never will *I* retire to Aberystwyth and sit on the front winking at the sea.'

'What you going there so quick for?' asked the cobbler's wife, her eyes travelling sharp from Catherine's face to below and resting there suspicious.

'Two stamps.' The postmistress flung them down grudgingly at last, and took up Catherine's coin as if she was picking up a rotten mouse by the tail. 'Wishing I am you'd buy your stamps somewhere else.'

Catherine, after licking and sticking them, seemed to regain strength as she walked to the door, remarking haughtily: 'There's wicked jealousy when a person is left money! Jealous you are not in my shoes, now *and* before.'

But, rightly, the postmistress had the last word: 'A cousin I have in Aberystwyth. Wife of a busy minister that is knowing everybody there. A letter *I* must write to Aberystwyth too.'

BOY WITH A TRUMPET

All he wanted was a bed, a shelf for his trumpet and permission to play it. He did not care how squalid the room, though he was so clean and shining himself; he could afford only the lowest rent. Not having any possessions except what he stood up in, the trumpet in an elegant case and a paper parcel of shirts and socks, landladies were suspicious of him. But he so gleamed with light young vigour, like a feather in the wind, that he kindled even in those wary hearts less harsh refusals.

Finally, on the outer rim of the West End, he found a bleak room for eight shillings a week in the house of a faded actress purply with drink and the dramas of a succession of lovers.

'I don't mind a trumpet,' she said, mollified by his air of a waif strayed out of a lonely vacancy. 'Are you in the orchestra, dear? No? You're not in a jazz band, are you? I can't have nightclub people in my house, coming in at all hours. No? . . . You look so young,' she said wonderingly. 'Well, there's no attendance, my charwoman is on war work; the bathroom is strictly engaged every morning from ten to half-past, and I do not allow tenants to receive visitors of the opposite sex in their rooms.' Behind the blowsiness were the remnants of one who had often played the role of a lady.

'I've just committed suicide,' he said naïvely. She saw then the bright but withdrawn fixity of his eyes, single-purposed.

'What!' she said, flurried in her kimono, and instinctively placed a stagey hand on her bosom.

'They got me back,' he said. 'I was sick. I didn't swallow enough of the stuff. Afterwards they sent me to a—well, a hospital. Then they discharged me. From the Army.'

'Oh dear!' she fussed. And, amply and yearning: 'Did your nerve go, then? . . . Haven't you any people?' There had been a suicide—a successful one—in her house before, and she had not been averse to the tragedy.

'I have God,' he said gravely. 'I was brought up in an orphanage. But I have an aunt in Chester. She and I do not love each other. I don't like violence. The telephone is ringing,' he said, with his alert but withdrawn awareness.

She scolded someone, at length and with high-toned emphasis, and returning muttering; she started to find him still under the huge frilled lampshade by the petunia divan. 'Rent is in advance,' she said mechanically. 'Number eight on the second floor.'

He went up the stairs. The webby carpet, worn by years of lodgers, smelt of old dust. A gush of water sounded above; a door slammed; a cat slept on a window-sill under sprays of dusty lacquered leaves. Later, as he was going out to the teashop, two young girls, silent and proud, sedately descended the stairs together in the dying sunshine. They, too, had that air of clear-cut absorption in themselves, unacknowledging the dangerous world. But they were together in that house of the unanchored. And he was alone, not long back from the edge of the dead land, the intersecting country where the disconnected sit with their spectral smiles.

That evening, in the tiny room, he played his trumpet. His lips, as the bandmaster of his regiment had told him, were not suitable for a trumpet; they had not the necessary full, fleshy contours, and also there were interstices in his front teeth; his face became horribly contorted in his effort to blast 'Cherry Ripe' out of the silver instrument. Nevertheless, when the benevolent spinster in the cathedral town where he had been stationed and sung Elizabethan madrigals asked what she could buy him after he had left the asylum, he said: 'A trumpet.' And, alone, he had come to the great city with his neurosis and a gleaming second-hand trumpet costing sixteen guineas. On arrival he spent half his money on four expensive poplin shirts and in the evening went to a lecture on world reform; the night he had spent in Regent's Park, his trumpet case and parcel on his lap.

The landlady rapped and came in. Violet circles were painted round her eyes and her hair was greenish. Within a wrap large, loose breasts swam untrammelled as dolphins. She looked at him with a speculative doubt.

'It's very noisy. Are you practising? There are neighbours.'

'You said I could play my trumpet,' he pointed out gravely.

She said: 'I am artistic myself, and I have had actors, writers, and musicians in my house. But there's a limit. You must have a certain hour for practice. But not in the evenings: the mornings are more suitable for a trumpet.'

'I cannot get up in the mornings,' he said. The trim, fixed decision of the young soldier stiffened his voice. 'I need a great deal of sleep.'

'Are you still ill?' She stepped forward, her ringed hands out-stretched. He sat on the bed's edge in his clean new shirt, the trumpet across his knees. From him came a desolate waif need. But his round, fresh-air face had a blank imperviousness, and down his indrawn small eyes flickered a secret repudiation. 'Are you lonely?' she went on. 'I play the piano.'

'I don't like trembling young girls,' he said. But as if to himself: 'They make me unhappy. I usually burst into crying when I'm with them. But I like babies; I want to be a father. I used to go into the married quarters in barracks and look after the babies . . . Sometimes,' he said, with his grave simplicity, 'I used to wash their napkins.'

In her slovenly fashion she was arrantly good-natured and friendly. 'Did you have a bad time in the orphanage, dear?'

'No, not *bad*. But I cannot stand the smell of carbolic soap now; it makes me want to vomit . . . I would like,' he added, 'to have known my mother. Or my father.'

'Hasn't anyone ever cared for you?' she asked, heaving.

'Yes. Both girls and men. But only for short periods.' Detached, he spoke as if he would never question the reason for this. The antiseptic austerity of his early years enclosed him like a cell of white marble; later there had been the forced, too early physical maturity of the Army, which the orphanage governor had induced him to join as a bandboy, just before the war. He had no instinctive love to give out in return for attempts of affection: it had never been born in him. 'People get tired of me,' he added, quite acceptingly.

After that, in her erratic fashion, he obsessed her. She occasionally fed him; in his room she put cushions and a large oleograph of Dante and Beatrice on a Florence bridge; she even allowed him to play the trumpet when he liked, despite complaints from the other lodgers. She badgered her lover of the moment, an irate designer of textiles, to find him a job in the studio of the huge West End store. But the boy categorically refused all jobs that required him before noon. His head like an apple on the pillow, he lay in bed all the morning sunk in profound slumber.

In the afternoons he would sit at his window drinking her tea or earnestly reading a modern treatise on religious problems. He insisted to her that a fresh upsurge of religious awareness was about to arrive in the world. He had already passed through the hands of a hearty, up-to-date Christian group, and he corresponded regularly with a canon whose sole panacea, however, was an exhortation to pray.

'But I can't pray,' he grieved to her. There was a deadlock of all his faculties.

Only when playing his trumpet he seemed a little released. Harshly and without melodic calm, he blew it over a world in chaos. For all the contortions of his round face he bloomed into a kind of satisfaction as he created a hideous pattern of noise. Cast out of the Army as totally unfit for service, it was only in these blasts of noise that he really enjoyed his liberty—the first that had ever come to him.

'Your rent is a fortnight overdue,' she reminded him, with prudent urgency. 'You really must find work, dear. Think of your future; now is your opportunity, with so many jobs about.'

'What future?' he asked curiously. 'Why do you believe so confidently in the future?'

He could always deflate her with this grave flatness. But her habit of working up emotional scenes was not easily baulked. She would call him into her sitting-room and, stroking his hand, among the billowy cushions, heave and throb about the rudeness of her lover, who was younger than herself. 'We are two waifs,' she said, while the telephone concealed under the crinoline of a doll rang yet again.

But he did not want the sultry maternalness of this faded, artificial woman; unerringly he sensed the shallow, predatory egotism of her need. Yet neither did he want to know the two beautiful and serious girls, flaxen-haired and virginal, who lived on the same floor; he always ducked his head away from them. He wanted to pick up a prostitute and spend a furtive quarter of an hour with her in the black-out. But he could not afford this. He was destitute now.

'You are horrible,' she exclaimed angrily when, in a long talk, he told her of this. 'You a boy of nineteen, wanting to go with prostitutes!'

'You see,' he insisted, 'I would feel myself master with them, and I can hate them too. But with nice, proud girls I cannot stop myself breaking down, and then I want to rush away and throw myself under a Tube train . . . And that's bad for me,' he added, with that earnest naïveté of his.

'But *is* it bad for you to break down?' she asked with some energy.

'Yes; I can't stand it.' Beyond the fixed calm of his small crystal eyes something flickered. 'When I was discharged from the Army the M.O. advised me to attend a clinic. I've been to one. It made me feel worse. I don't want to feel I'm a case.'

'The clinic,' she said sagely, 'couldn't be expected to provide you with a mother. You've got nineteen years of starvation to forget.'

She had got into the habit of giving him a glass of milk and rum at nights. Nevertheless, she had her real angers with him, for she was of tempestuous disposition. She knew that he would not—it did not occur to her that he could not—unfold to her other than in these talks. He did not weep on her waiting bosom; he did not like his bright glossy hair to be stroked. And sometimes when he played the trumpet in his room she was roused to a transport of queer, intent fury and she would prowl about the staircase in helpless rage.

He had been in the house a month when one afternoon, after he had been playing for an hour, she walked into his room. Her green hair was frizzed out, the heavily painted eyes sidled angrily, the violet lips twisted like a cord. There was something both pathetic and ridiculous in the frenzy of this worn and used woman gallantly trying to keep an air of bygone theatrical grandeur and,

96

indeed, of ladylike breeding. But she was so brittle. Carefully looking at her, he laid the trumpet on his knees.

'Why must you *keep on!*' she fumed. 'That everlasting tune, it's maddening. The neighbours will ring up the police and I shall have them calling. You are not in a slum.'

'You said I could play my trumpet!'

And still there was about him that curious and impervious tranquillity, not to be disturbed, and, to her, relentless. It drove her to a vindictive outburst, her gaze fixed in hatred on the trumpet.

'Why don't you go out and look for *work*? Your rent—you are taking advantage of my kindness; you are lazy and without principle. Aren't you ashamed to sit there doing nothing but blowing noises on that damned thing?' She heaved over him in the narrow room, a dramatic Mænad gone to copious seed and smelling of bath salts.

He got up from the bed's edge, carefully disconnected the trumpet's pieces and put them in the elegant case and his shirts and socks into a brown paper carrier. She watched him, spellbound; his crisp, deliberate decision was curbing. At the door he raised his hat politely. All recognition of her was abolished from the small, unswerving eyes.

'Good afternoon,' he said in a precise way. 'I will send you the rent when I earn some money. I am sure to find a position suited to me before long.'

He stored the trumpet in a railway station. On no account would he pawn it, though there was only a shilling or two left of the pound the canon had last sent him, together with a copy of *St. Augustine's Confessions*. He knew it was useless to look for a job even as second trumpet in the cabarets; not even his fresh, shiny, boy appearance, that would look well in a Palm Beach jacket, could help him.

That night he hung about the dark, chattering Circus, not unhappy, feeling vaguely liberated among this anonymous crowd milling about in an atmosphere of drink, flesh, and boredom. He listened carefully to the soldiers' smudged catcalls, the female retaliations, the whispers, the ironical endearments, the dismissals. But as the night wore on and the crowd thinned, his senses became sharpened, alert, and at the same time desperate. Like a young hungry wolf sniffing the edge of the dark, he howled desolately inside himself. In the black-out the perfumed women, dots of fire between their fingertips, passed and repassed, as if weaving a dance figure in some hieratic ceremony; his mind became aware of a pattern, a design, a theme in which a restated lewd note grew even more and more dominant. He wanted to play his trumpet. Startle the night with a barbaric blast.

97

He began to accost the women. He had heard that some would give shelter to the temporarily destitute, exercising a legendary comradeship of the streets. But none had use for him. After a brief assessment of his conversation they passed on rapidly. Only one was disposed to chatter. She told him he could find a job, if his discharge papers were in order, as a stagehand in a certain theatre; she gave him a name to ask for.

'Nothing doing, darling,' she replied promptly to his subsequent suggestion. 'No fresh pineapple for me to-night.'

Waiting for morning, he sat on a bench in the ghostly Square garden and returned to an earlier meditation on the nature of God. In this mental fantasy he continually saw the embryo of a tadpole which split into two entities. The force that divided the embryo was God, a tremendous deciding power that lay beyond biology. It was eternal and creative, yet could one pray to it, worship it? Would it be conscious of a worshipping acknowledgement, and if so, could it reward with peace, harmony, and contentment? He ached to submerge himself in belief and to enter into a mystic identification with a creative force; he wanted to cast himself at the knees of a gigantic parent of the universe. But on every side were frustrations, and the chaotic world, armed for destruction, was closing in on him triumphantly. Yet he knew it was that creative force that had driven him to attempt suicide as a solution and a release; he had believed that the power within him would not die but return to the central force and be discharged again. But he shivered at the memory of the hours before the act of suicide, those furtive, secret hours that had ruptured his mind. Outside himself he had never been able to kill even a spider.

'You must think of your future!' he suddenly whinnied aloud, causing a bemused sailor on an adjacent bench to lift his round cap off his face. He tried to envisage a concrete picture of that future, but saw only a ravaged place of waste with a few tufts of blackened vegetation against a burnt-out sky.

He began working among acres of painted canvases depicting idealised scenes in a world devoted to song, hilarity, and dance. Rainbow processions of girls passed in and out, pearly smiles stitched into glossy faces, the accurate legs swinging like multi-coloured sausages. Watching these friezes in tranced gravity, he sometimes missed a cue, rousing the stage manager to threats of instant dismissal, despite the labour shortage. The hard-working young girl dancers, lustrously trim and absorbed in professional perfection, took no notice of the new stagehand fascinated in attempts to adapt their integrated patterns to his consciousness. But though hypnotised by this new revelation of idealised flesh and movements, he still could not identify himself with them.

He was still cut off, he had not yet come through to acceptance that the world breathed, and that these pink and silver girls actually could be touched.

He started and listened carefully when a distinguished young man, a hero of the sky, sent a message backstage that he 'would like to collaborate' with a certain starry beauty of the chorus. 'She'll collaborate all right,' remarked another of the girls in the wings; 'I never heard it called that before.' That night he went home straight from the theatre and filled the house with the blasts of his trumpet.

He had rented a small partitioned space in the basement, its window overlooking the back garden. It contained a camp-bed and one or two bugs which he accepted as outcomes of the God-force. The street was not of good repute, but it was beyond the West End, and an amount of lace-curtained and funeral-oak respectability was maintained.

'You can blow your trumpet as much as you like,' Irish Lil said. 'Blow it in the middle of the night if you like—it might drive some of the bastards out. Can you lend me five bob till tomorrow morning?'

There had been a quarrel among the five prostitutes upstairs: four accused the fifth of bringing in clients during the daytime—they declared the house would get a bad name. They were entirely daughters of the night; in daylight there was a moon glisten on their waxen faces, their hair looked unreal, and their voices were husky fretful. They called him the Boy with a Trumpet, and he was already something of a pet among them. He shared the roomy basement with four refugees off the Continent who came and went on obscure errands and everlastingly cooked cabbage soup.

Irish Lil was the disgrace of the house. Though she always had real flowers stuck in the two milk bottles on her sideboard, she was a slut. Her slovenly make-up, her regular Q.M.S. lover in the Guards who got roaring drunk, and her inability to discriminate and to insist on pre-payment angered the four younger women. Blonde Joyce carried on a year-old vendetta with her. Over a stolen egg. Irish Lil was creeping downstairs one evening with the egg, which she had taken from Joyce's room, when a bomb fell in the Avenue. Kathleen rushed out of her room with a Free French client and found Lil struck daft on the stairs with the crushed egg dribbling through her fingers.

'Don't trust your trumpet to her,' Joyce said. 'She'll pawn it.' For, as his room had no lock, he asked where in the house he could hide his trumpet while he was at the theatre.

'She weeps,' he said gravely. 'I've heard her weeping.'

'If,' Joyce said, hard, 'she was on fire, I wouldn't pee on her to put her out.'

But they all, in their idle afternoons, liked him about their rooms. He fetched them newspapers and cigarettes; he was a nice boy and, yawning in their dressing-gowns and irremediably nocturnal, they discarded their professionalism with him. Their calm acceptance of the world as a disintegration eased him; his instinct had been right in seeking a brothel to live in.

Yet he saw the house, for all its matter-of-fact squalor, as existing in a world still spectral to him. Still he lived behind thick glass, unreleased and peering out in dumb waiting. Only his old Army nightmare was gone—the recurrent dream in which he lay sealed tight into a leaden pipe under a pavement where he could hear, ever passing and returning, the heeltaps of compassionate but unreachable women. But the tank-like underwater quiet of the observation ward in the asylum was still with him, always. And he could not break through, smash the glass. Not yet.

It was Kathleen who took quite a fancy to him. They had disconnected conversations in her room; she accepted him amicably as a virginal presence that did not want to touch her. She was plump as a rose, and a sprinkle of natural colour was still strewn over her, the youngest girl in the house. She promised to try to find him a job as trumpeter in one of the clubs; he could earn a pound a night at this if he became proficient.

'But I don't want to earn a lot of money,' he said earnestly. 'It's time we learned how to do without money. We must learn to live and create like God.'

'I've met all types of men,' she said vaguely, tucking her weary legs under her on the bed. 'And I hate them all. I tell you I've got to have six double gins before I can bring one home. That costs them a quid or two extra; I make the sods spend.'

He said dreamily: 'When I took poison I felt I was making a creative act, if it was only that I was going out to search.' He could still rest in the shade of that release; the mysteriousness of that blue underworld fume was still there, giving him a promise of fulfilment. 'I saw huge shapes . . . they were like huge flowers, dark and heavy blood-coloured flowers. They looked at me, they moved, they listened, their roots began to twine into me, I could feel them in my bowels . . . But I couldn't rise, I was lying in the mud. I couldn't breathe in the new way. I tried to struggle up . . . through. But I fell back, and everything disappeared—'

'Don't you go trying to commit suicide in this house,' she said. 'Mrs. Walton would never forgive you. That Irish tyke's doing enough to advertise us already . . . You're not queer, are you?' she asked, desultory. 'I like queer men, they don't turn me sick . . . Always at one,' she ruminated of the others.

She attracted him more than the other four, but, to content his instinct completely, he wished her more sordid, lewd, and foul-tongued, more disintegrated. The ghostly lineaments of a trembling young girl remained in her. They conversed to each other across a distance. But she was the only one

100

of the women who still appeared to observe things beyond this private world of the brothel. He sometimes tried to talk to her about God.

The taxicabs began to purr up to the front door any time after midnight. Sometimes he got out of his bed in the basement, mounted the staircase in trousers and socks, and stood poised in the dark as if waiting for a shattering revelation from behind the closed doors. There was the useless bomber pilot who broke down and shouted weepingly to Joyce that his nerve was gone—'Well,' Joyce had said in her ruthless way, 'you can stay if you like, but I'm keeping my present all the same, mind!' That pleased him, as he carefully listened; it belonged to the chaos, the burnt-out world reduced to charcoal. He laughed softly to himself. What if he blew his trumpet on this phantasmagoric staircase? Blew it over the fallen night, waken these dead, surprise them with a new anarchial fanfare?

One week when the elder tree and the peonies were in blossom in the once-cultivated back garden, Irish Lil declared she had a birthday. She opened her room on the Monday night—always an off night—to whoever wished to come in. Ranks of beer flagons stood on the sideboard, and Harry, her Guards sergeant regular, roared and strutted before them in his battle-dress like David before the Ark. Three refugees from the basement ventured in; Joyce forgot her vendetta, but refused to dress or make up; Pamela sat repairing a stocking. When he arrived from the theatre the beer was freely flowing. Irish Lil, in a magenta sateen gown, was wearing long, ornate earrings in a vain attempt to look seductive. Kathleen, on this off-night occasion, gazed at him with a kind of sisterly pensiveness.

'Heard that one about Turnham Green—?' bawled Harry, and took off his khaki blouse before telling it, owing to the heat.

He was a great tree of flesh. His roots were tenacious in the earth. The juice in his full lips was the blood of a king bull; the seeds of war flourished in the field of his muscular belly. For him a battle was a dinner, a bomb, a dog bark, a bayonet, a cat scratch, and in the palm of his great blue paw statesmen curled secure. He was the salt of the earth. The limericks flying off his lips became more obscene.

But they fell flat. The prostitutes were bored with obscenity, the refugees did not understand English humour. Joyce yarned markedly.

'Hell, what's this?' Harry panted a bit— 'The funeral of the duchess? . . . Reminds me. Heard that one about Her Grace and the fishmonger?'

'What!' shouted Harry, delighted. 'He's got a trumpet? I been in the band in my time. A kick or two from a trumpet's just what's needed.'

He snatched the beautifully shining instrument and set it to his great curled lips. The bull neck swelled, the huge face glowed red. And without mistake, unfalteringly, from harmonious lungs, he played the 'Londonderry Air'. A man blowing a trumpet successfully is a rousing spectacle. The blast is an announcement of the lifted sun. Harry stood on a mountain peak, monarch of all he surveyed.

Kathleen came in, hesitating, and sat beside him on the campbed. 'What's the matter?' she asked. He had flung away with the trumpet as soon as Harry had laid it down. He sat concentratedly polishing it with a bit of chiffon scarf she had once given him, especially the mouthpiece. 'Has he spoilt it then?' she murmured.

He did not answer. But his fingers were trembling. She said wearily: 'He's started reciting "Eskimo Nell" now.'

'I wish I could play like him,' he whispered.

'You do make an awful noise,' she said in a compassionate way. 'You haven't got the knack yet, with all your practising . . . I wonder,' she brooded after a while, 'if it's worth going down West. But they're so choosy on a Monday night.'

'Don't go.' He laid down the trumpet as if abandoning it for ever. 'Don't go.'

She seemed not to be listening, her preoccupied eyes gazing out of the window. The oblong of garden was filled with the smoky red after-fume of sunset. Their low voices drifted into silences. Two pigeons gurgled in the elder tree; a cat rubbed against the window-pane and became intent on the pigeons. Kathleen's mouth was pursed up thoughtfully. He was conscious of the secret carnation glow of her thighs. Her thick hair smelled of obliterating night.

'I won't ever play my trumpet.' His voice stumbled. 'I have no faith, no belief, and I can't accept the world . . . I can't *feel* it.'

'Christ, there's enough to feel,' she protested. 'This bloody war, and the bombs—'

'In the Army they taught us to get used to the smell of blood. It smells of hate . . . And to turn the bayonet deep in the guts . . . There were nice chaps in our battalion who had letters and parcels from home . . . from loving mothers and girls . . . and they didn't mind the blood and the bayonets; they had had their fill of love and faith, I suppose. But I was hungry all the time, I wanted to be fed, and I wanted to create, and I wanted children . . . I am incomplete,' he whispered— 'I didn't have the right to kill.'

'But you tried to kill yourself,' she pointed out, though vaguely, as if her attention was elsewhere.

'My body,' he said— 'that *they* owned.'

'Well, what can you *do*?' she asked, after another silence. 'You ought to take up some study, a boy with your brains . . . It's a shame,' she cried, with a sudden burst of the scandalised shrillness of her kind: 'the Army takes 'em, breaks 'em, and chucks 'em out when they've got no further use for 'em . . . What *can* you do?'

'There's crime,' he said.

'It don't pay,' she said at once.

'I believe,' he said, 'there'll be big waves of crime after the war. You can't have so much killing, so much teaching to destroy, and then stop it suddenly . . . The old kinds of crime, and new crimes against the holiness in the heart. There'll be fear, and shame, and guilt, guilt. People will be mad. There's no such thing as victory in war. There's only misery, chaos and suffering for everybody, and then the payment . . . There's only one victory—over the evil in the heart. And that's a rare miracle.' His voice faltered in defeat. 'I've been trying to make the attempt. But the air I breathe is full of poison.'

She let him talk, pretending to listen. Clients sometimes talked to her oddly and, if there was time, it was professional tact to allow them their airings.

'Harry, up there,' he went on dejectedly, 'carries the world on his shoulders. But he'll rob his mother and starve his wife and pick his neighbour's pocket.' He took up the trumpet off the bed, turned it over regretfully, and let it drop back. 'I can't even play my trumpet like him,' he reiterated obsessively. 'Would I make a better criminal?'

'Now, look here,' she said, her attention arrested, 'don't you go starting down *that* street! Boys like you alone in London can soon go to the bad. I've seen some of it. It won't pay, I'm telling you.'

'But crime as a protest,' he said earnestly. 'As a relief. And don't you see there's nothing but crime now, at the heart of things?'

Professionally comforting, she laid her hand on his, which began to tremble again. Yet his small crystal eyes remained impervious, with their single-purposed rigidity. She stroked his hand. 'Don't tremble, don't tremble . . . Do you ever cry?' she asked, gazing into his face in the last light.

He shook his head. 'I can't.' But something was flickering into his eyes. He had leaned towards her slowly.

'If you could,' she said, but still with a half-vague inattentiveness— 'I'm sure you ought to break down. You're too shut in on yourself.'

He breathed her odour of flesh. It seemed to him like the scent of milky flowers, living and benign, scattered in a pure air. As if it would escape him, he began to breathe it hungrily. His hands had stopped trembling. But the rigid calm of his appearance, had she noticed it in the dusky light, was more disquieting.

103

'There!' she said, still a little crouched away from him; 'you see, a little personal talk is good for you. You're too lonely, that's what it is.'

'Will you let me—'

'What?' she asked, more alert. The light was finishing; her face was dim.

'Put my mouth to your breast?'

'No,' she said at once. She shook her head. 'It wouldn't be any use, anyhow.'

But, now that the words were out, he fell on her in anguish. 'Stay with me! Don't go away. Sleep with me tonight.' He pressed his face into her, shuddering, and weeping at last. 'Stay!'

She heaved herself free, jumping off the bed with a squirm, like anger. 'Didn't I tell you that I hated men!' She raised her voice, very offended. 'I could spit on them all—and you, too, now.' She opened the door. 'But I will say this'—her voice relented a degree— 'I wouldn't sleep with you if you offered me ten pounds! I know what I am, and I don't want any of your fancy stuff.' She flounced out with scandalised decision.

He rolled over and over on the bed. Shuddering, he pressed his face into the pillow. When the paroxysm had passed he half rose and sat looking out of the window. In his movement the trumpet crashed to the floor, but he did not pick it up. He sat gazing out into the still world as if he would never penetrate it again. He saw grey dead light falling over smashed cities, over broken precipices and jagged torn chasms of the world. Acrid smoke from abandoned ruins mingled with the smell of blood. He saw himself the inhabitant of a wilderness where withered hands could lift in guidance no more. There were no more voices and all the paps of earth were dry

CANUTE

As the great Saturday drew nearer most men asked each other: 'Going up for the International?' You had the impression that the place would be denuded of its entire male population, as in some archaic tribal war. Of course a few women too intended taking advantage, for other purposes, of the cheap excursion trains, though these hardy souls were not treated seriously, but rather as intruders in an entirely masculine rite. It was to be the eternal England versus Wales battle, the object now under dispute being a stitched leather egg containing an air-inflated bladder.

The special trains began to leave round about Friday midnight, and thereafter, all through the night and until Saturday noon, these quaking, immensely long vehicles feverishly rushed back and forth between Wales and London. In black mining valleys, on rustic heights, in market towns and calm villages myriads of house doors opened during the course of the night and a man issued from an oblong of yellow light, a railway ticket replacing the old spear.

The contingent from Pleasant Row, a respectable road of houses leading up to a three-shafted coalmine, came out from their dwellings into the gas-lit winter midnight more or less simultaneously. Wives stood in worried farewells in the doorways. Their men were setting out in the dead of night to an alien land, far away from this safe valley where little Twlldu nestled about its colliery and usually minded its own business.

'Now be careful you don't lose your head, Rowland!' fretted his wife on their doorstep. 'You take things quiet and behave yourself. Remember your trouble.' The 'trouble' was a hernia, the result of Rowland rescuing his neighbour, Dicky Corner House, from a fall of roof in the pit.

Rowland, grunting a repudiation of this anxiety, scuttled after a group of men in caps. 'Jawl,' shouted one, 'is that the whistle of the 'scursion train? Come on!' Out of the corner house ran Dicky, tying a white muffler round his neck. Weighted though they all were with bottles for the long journey, they shot forward dramatically, though the train was still well up the long valley.

The night was clear and crisp. Thousands of stars briskly gazed down, sleepless as the excited eyes of the excursion hordes thronging all the valley's little stations. Stopping every few minutes, the train slid past mines deserted by their workers and rows of houses where, mostly, only women and children remained. It was already full when it stopped at Twlldu, and, before it left, the smallest men were lying in the luggage-racks and sitting on the floor, placing their bottles safe. Some notorious passengers, clubbing together, had brought crates of flagons.

Dicky Corner House, who was squat and sturdy, kept close to Rowland, offering him cigarettes, or a swig out of his bottle and a beef sandwich. Ever since Rowland had rescued him he had felt bound to him in some way, especially as Rowland, who was not a hefty chap, had that hernia as a result. But Rowland felt no particular interest in Dicky; he had only done his duty by him in the pit. 'Got my own bottle and sandwiches,' he grunted. And: 'No, I am not feeling a draught.' The train rocked and groaned through the historic night. Some parts of it howled with song; in other parts bets were laid, cards played, and tales told of former Internationals.

Somewhere, perhaps guarded by armed warriors, the sacred egg lay waiting for the morrow. In its worship these myriads had left home and loved ones to brave the dangers of a foreign city. Situated in a grimy parish of that city, and going by the name of Paddington, the railway terminus began to receive the first drafts at about 4 a.m. Their arrival was welcomed by their own shouts, whistles and cries. From one compartment next to the Pleasant Row contingent a man had to be dragged out with his legs trailing limply behind him.

'Darro,' Rowland mumbled with some severity, 'he's started early. Disgrace! Gives the 'scursionists a bad name.'

'Hi,' Dicky Corner House tried to hail a vanishing porter, 'where's the nearest public-house in London?'

'Pubs in London opened already then?' asked Shoni Matt in wonder and respect, gazing at 4.30 on the station clock.

'Don't be daft, man,' Ivor snarled, surly from lack of sleep. 'We got about seven hours to wait on our behinds.'

A pitchy black shrouded the great station. Many braved the strange dark and wandered out into it. But in warily peering groups. A watery dawn found their numbers increased in the main thoroughfares; early workers saw them reconnoitring like tribal invaders sniffing out a strange land.

'Well, well,' said Rowland at ten o'clock, following his nose up the length of Nelson's column, 'how did they get that man up there? And what for?'

'A fancy kind of chimney-stack it is,' Dicky declared. 'A big bakehouse is under us.' He asked yet another policeman—the fourth—what time the public-houses opened, but the answer was the same.

'Now Dicky,' said Rowland, in a severe canting voice like a preacher, 'you go on behaving like that and very sorry I'll be that I rescued you that time . . .

We have come here,' he added austerely, 'to see the International, not to drink. Plenty of beer in Wales.'

'I'm cold,' bleated Shoni Matt; 'I'm hungry; I'm sleepy.'

'Let's go in there!' said Gwyn Short Leg, and they all entered the National Gallery, seeing that Admission was Free.

It was the Velasquez *Venus* that arrested their full attention. 'The artist,' observed Emlyn Chrysanthemums—he was called that because he was a prize-grower of them in a home-made glasshouse— 'was clever to make her turn her back on us. A bloke that knew what was tidy.'

'Still,' said Rowland, 'he ought to have thrown a towel or something across her, just by here—'

'Looking so alive it is,' Ivor breathed in admiration, 'you could smack it, just there—'

An attendant said: 'Do not touch the paintings.'

'What's the time?' Dicky Corner House asked the attendant. 'Are the pubs open yet?'

'A disgrace he is,' said Rowland sharply as the contingent went out. 'He ought to have stayed home.'

By then the streets were still more crowded with gazing strangers. Scotland had sent tam-o'-shantered men, the North and Midlands their crowds of tall and short men in caps, bowlers, with umbrellas and striped scarves, concertinas and whistles. There were ghostly-looking men who looked as if they had just risen from hospital beds; others were unshaven and still bore the aspect of running late for the train. Many women accompanied the English contingents, for the Englishman never escapes this. By noon the invaders seemed to have taken possession of the metropolis and, scenting their powerful majority, they became noisy and obstreperous, unlike the first furtive groups which had arrived before dawn. And for a short while a million beer-taps flowed ceaselessly. But few of the visitors loitered to drink overmuch before the match. The evening was to come, when one could sit back released from the tremendous event.

At two-thirty, into a grey misty field surrounded by huge walls of buzzing insects stickily massed together, fifteen red beetles and fifteen white beetles ambled forward on springy legs. To a great cry the sacred egg appeared. A whistle blew. The beetles wove a sharp pattern of movement, pursuing the egg with swift bounds and trim dance evolutions. Sometimes they became knotted over it as though in prayer. They worshipped the egg and yet they did not want it: as if it contained the secret of happiness, they pursued it, got it, and then threw it away. The sticky imprisoning walls heaved and roared; myriads of pin-point faces passed through agonies of horror and ecstasies of bliss. And from a great quantity of these faces came frenzied cries and urgings in a strange primitive language that no doubt gave added strength to the fifteen beetles who understood that language. It was not only the thirty below the walls who fought the battle.

The big clock's pallid face, which said it was a quarter to midnight, stared over the station like an amazed moon. Directly under it was a group of women who had arranged to meet their men there for the journey back. They looked worried and frightened.

And well they might. For surely they were standing in a gigantic hospital-base adjacent to a bloody battlefield where a crushing defeat had been sustained. On the platforms casualties lay groaning or silently dazed; benches were packed with huddled men, limbs twitching, heads laid on neighbours' shoulders or clasped in hands between knees. Trolleys were heaped with what looked like the dead. Now and again an ambulance train crawled out packed to the doors. But still more men kept staggering into the station from the maw of an underground cavern and from the black foggy streets. Most of them looked exhausted, if not positively wounded, as from tremendous strife.

But not all of them. Despite groans of the incapacitated, grunting heaves of the sick, long solemn stares of the bemused helplessly waiting for some ministering angel to conduct them to a train, there was a singing. Valiant groups of men put their heads doggedly together and burst into heroic song. They belonged to a race that, whatever the cause, never ceases to sing, and those competent to judge declare this singing something to be greatly admired. Tonight, in this melancholy place at the low hour of midnight, these melodious cries made the spirit of man seem undefeated. Stricken figures on floors, benches and trolleys stirred a little, and far-gone faces flickered into momentary awareness. Others who still retained their faculties sufficiently to recognise home acquaintances shouted, embraced, hit each other, made excited turkey-cock enquiries as to the activities of the evening.

A youngish woman with parcels picked a zigzag way to under the clock and greeted another there. 'Seen my Glynne, have you?' she asked anxiously; 'I've been out to Cricklewood to visit my auntie . . . Who won the match?' she asked, glancing about her in fear.

'You can tell by the state of them, can't you!' frowned the other.

Another woman, with a heave of hostility, said: 'Though even if Wales had lost they'd drink just the same, to drown the disappointment, the old beasts . . . Look out!' The women scattered hastily from a figure who became detached from a knot of swaying men, made a blind plunge in their direction, and was sick.

'Where's the porters?' wailed one woman. 'There's no porters to be seen anywhere; they've all run home . . . Serve us right, we shouldn't have come with the men's 'scursion . . . I'm feeling ill, nowhere to sit, only men everywhere.'

Cap pushed back from his blue-marked miner's face, Matt Griffiths of Gelli bellowed a way up No. 1 platform. He was gallantly pulling a trolley heaped with bodies like immense dead cods. 'Where's the backwards 'scursion train for Gelli?' he shouted. 'Out of the way there! We got to go on the night-shift tomorrow.'

'The wonder is,' said a woman, fretful, 'that they can find their way to the station at all. But, there, they're like dogs pointing their snouts towards home.'

Two theological students, solemn-clothed as crows, passed under the clock. They were in fierce converse and gesticulated dangerously with their flappy umbrellas. Yet they seemed oblivious of the carnal scenes around them; no doubt they were occupied with some knotty Biblical matter. The huddled women looked at them with relief; here was safety. We'd better get in the same compartment as them,' one of them said to her friend, 'come on, Gwen, let's follow them. I expect they've been up for a conference or an exam.' Soon the two young preachers-to-be were being followed by quite a band of woment though they remained unconscious of this flattering retinue.

'That reverse pass of Williams!' one of the students suddenly burst out, unable to contain himself, and prancing forward in intoxicated delight. 'All the matches I've been to I've never seen anything like it! Makes you want to grab someone and dance ring-a-ring o'roses.'

Elsewhere, an entwined group of young men sang *Mochyn Du* with an orderly sweetness in striking contrast to their mien; a flavour of pure green hills and neat little farmhouses was in their song about a black pig. On adjacent platforms other groups in that victorious concourse sang *Sospan Fach* and even a hymn. As someone said, if you shut your eyes you could fancy yourself in an eisteddfod.

But in the Gentlemen's Convenience under No. 1 platform no one would have fancied this. There an unusual thing had occurred—the drains had clogged. Men kept on descending the flight of steps only to find a sheet of water flooding the floor to a depth of several inches. They had to make-do with standing on the bottom steps, behind them an impatient block of others dangerously swaying.

And this was not all. Far within the deserted convenience one man was marooned over that sheet of water. He sat on the shoe-shine throne which, resting on its dais, was raised safely—up to the present—above the water. Astonished remarks from the steps failed to reach him.

'Darro me,' exclaimed one man with a stare of respect across the waters, 'how did he get there? No sign of a boat.'

'Hoy,' another bawled over, 'what train you want to catch? You can't stay there all night.'

'Who does he think he is,' someone else exclaimed in an English voice— 'King Canute?'

The figure did not hear, though the head dreamily lolled forward an inch. Impatient men waiting on the crowded steps bawled to those in front to hurry up and make room. Soon the rumour that King Canute was sitting below passed among a lot of people on No. 1 platform. It was not long before someone—Sam Recitations it was, the Smoking Concert Elocutionist— arrived at the bottom step and recognised that the figure enthroned above the water was not King Canute at all.

'I'm hanged if it isn't Rowland from Pleasant Row!' he blew in astonishment. 'That's where he's got! . . . Rowland,' his chest rose as in a recitation, 'wake up, man, wake up! Train is due out in ten minutes. Number 2 platform . . .'

Rowland did not hear even this well-known Twlldu voice. Sam himself not in full possession of his faculties, gazed stupidly at the sheet of water. It looked deep; up to your calves. A chap would have soaking wet socks and shoes all the way back to Wales. And he was appearing at a club concert on Tuesday, reciting four ballads; couldn't afford to catch a cold. Suddenly he pushed his way through the exclaiming mob behind him, hastened recklessly through the platform mobs, reached No. 2 platform and began searching for the Pleasant Row contingent.

They were sitting against a kiosk plunged in torpid thought. Sam had to shake two or three of them. 'I've seen him!' he rolled. 'Your Rowland! He isn't lost—he's down in the men's place under Number 1, and can't budge him. People calling him King Canute—'

They had lost him round about nine o'clock in crowded Trafalgar Square. There the visiting mob had got so obstreperous that, as someone related later at a club in Twlldu, four roaring lions had been let loose and stood lashing their tails in fury against these invaders whose nation had won the match; and someone else said that for the first time in his life he had seen a policeman who wore spectacles. While singing was going on, and two or three cases of assault brewing, Rowland had vanished. From time to time the others had missed him, and Dicky Corner House asked many policemen if they had seen Rowland of Twlldu.

Sam Recitations kept on urging them now. 'King Canute?' repeated Shoni

Matt in a stupor. 'You shut up, Sam,' he added crossly: 'no time for recitations now.'

'He's down in the Gents under Number 1,' Sam howled despairingly. 'English strangers poking fun at him and water rising up! He'll be drowned same as when the Cambrian pit was flooded!' He beat his chest as if he was giving a ballad in a concert. 'Ten minutes and the train will be in! And poor Rowland sitting helpless and the water rising round him like on the sands of Dee!'

Far off a whistle blew. Someone near by was singing *Cwm Rhondda* in a bass that must have won medals in its time. They shook themselves up from the platform, staring penetratingly at Sam, who was repeating information with wild emphasis. Six of them, all from Pleasant Row. Awareness seemed to flood them simultaneously, for suddenly they all surged away.

By dint of pushing and threatening cries they got down all together to the lower steps of the Convenience. Rowland had not moved in the shoe-shine throne. Still his head lolled in slumber as if he was sitting cosy by his fireside at home after a heavy shift in the pit, while the waters lapped the dais and a yellow light beat down on the isolated figure indifferent to its danger. They stared fearfully at the sheet of water.

'Shocking it is,' said Gwyn Short Leg, scandalised. 'All the Railway Company gone home, have they, and left the place like this?'

'In London too!' criticised Ivor, gazing below him in owlish distaste.

Then in one accord they bellowed: 'Hoy, Rowland, hoy!'

He did not stir. Not an eyelid. It was then that Shoni Matt turned to Dicky Corner House and just looked at him, like a judge. His gaze asked— 'whose life had been saved by Rowland when that bit of roof had fallen in the pit?' Dicky, though he shivered, understood the long solemn look. 'Time to pay back now, Dicky,' the look added soberly.

Whimpering, Dicky tried to reach his shoe-laces, on the crowded steps. But the others urged excitedly: 'No time to take your shoes off. Hark, the train's coming in! Go on, boy. No swimming to do.'

Dicky, with a sudden dramatic cry, leapt into the water, foolishly splashing it up all round his legs. A pit-butty needed to be rescued! And with oblivious steps, encouraged by the applause of the others, he plunged across to the throne. He stepped on the dais and, being hefty, lifted Rowland across his shoulders without much bother. He staggered a bit as he stepped off the dais into the cruelly wet water.

'Careful now,' shouted Emlyn Chrysanthemums; 'don't drop him into the champagne.'

It was an heroic act that afterwards, in the club evenings, took precedence over tales of far more difficult rescues in the pits. Dicky reached the willing arms of the others without mishap. They took Rowland and bore him by his four limbs up the steps, down the platform and up the other, just as the incoming train was coming to a frightened standstill. After a battle they got into a compartment. Dicky took off his shoes, hung up his socks over the edge of the track and wiped his feet and calves in the white muffler that had crossed his throat.

'Wet feet bad for the chest,' he said fussily.

All the returning trains reached the arms of Wales safely, and she folded the passengers into her fragrant breast with a pleased sigh of 'Well done, my sons'. The victory over her ancient enemy—it was six points to four—was a matter of great Sunday celebration when the men's clubs opened in the evening, these having a seven-day licence, whereas the ordinary public-houses, owing to the need to appease old dim gods, were not allowed to open on Sundays.

The members of the Pleasant Row contingent, like most others, stayed in bed all the morning. When they got up they related to their wives and children many of the sights and marvels of London. But some weeks had passed before Rowland's wife, a tidy woman who starched her aprons and was a great chapel-goer, said to him in perplexity: 'Why is it people are calling you Rowland Canute now?'

Only that evening, Gwyn Short Leg, stumping to the door on his way to the club, had bawled innocently into the passage: 'Coming down, Rowland Canute?' Up to lately Rowland had been one of those who, because he seemed to have no peculiarity, had never earned a nickname.

'Oh,' Rowland told his wife, vaguely offhand, 'some fancy name or other it is they've begun calling me.'

'But a reason there must be for it,' she said inquisitively. 'Canute! Wasn't that some old king who sat on his throne beside the sea and dared the tide to come over him? A funny name to call you.'

'What you got in that oven for my supper?' he asked, scowling at the news in the evening paper.

She knew better than to proceed with the matter just then. But of course she did not let it rest. It was the wife of Emlyn Chrysanthemums, living three doors up, who, in the deprecating way of women versus the ways of men, told her the reason. There are nicknames which are earned respectably and naturally, and indeed such nicknames are essential to identify persons in a land where there are only twenty or so proper baptised names for everybody. But, on hearing how Rowland earned Canute, his wife pursed in her lips like a pale tulip, opening them hours later to shout as Rowland tramped in from the pit:

'Ah, *Canute* is it! . . . . Sitting there in that London place,' she screamed, 'and all those men—' She whipped about like a hailstorm. 'You think I'm going to stay in Twlldu to be called Mrs. Rowland Canute, do you? We'll have to move from here—you begin looking for work in one of the other valleys at once.'

And such a dance she led him that in a couple of months they had left Pleasant Row. Rowland got taken on at the Powell pit in the Cwm Mardy valley, several stout mountains lying between that and Twlldu.

Yet give a dog a bad name, says the proverb, and it will stick. Who could have thought that Sam Recitations, growing in fame, would visit a club in far-away Cwm Mardy to give selections from his repertoire at a Smoking Concert? And almost the first man he saw when he entered the bar-room was Rowland. 'Why now,' his voice rolled in delight, 'if it isn't Rowland Canute! Ha, ha—' And not noticing Rowland's dropped jaw of dismay, he turned and told all the clustering men what hat happened under Paddington platform that time after the famous International—just as the history of the rescue had been told in all the clubs in the valley away over the mountains.

A HUMAN CONDITION

Having done the errand at the Post Office, which he had timed with a beautiful precision that he imagined completely hoodwinked those left at home, Mr. Arnold crossed the Market Square just as the doors of the Spreadeagle inn were opened.

This morning he was in lamentable condition. He felt he would never get through the day without aid. Never, never, never. Deep inside him was a curious dead sensation of which he was frightened. It lay in the pit of his stomach like some coiled serpent fast asleep, and he was fearful that at any moment the thing would waken and writhe up in unholy destructive fury. And ultimately *he* would be destroyed. Not his critics, today collected in dark possession of his home.

He sailed into the pub with his ample, slightly rolling strut, a man of substance handsomely ripe of body and face, his attire as conservative as a psalm to godliness; no one could say Mr. Arnold neglected his person. Of the town's few pubs the Spreadeagle was his favourite haunt. It was cosily shut in on itself and dark with shadows; it had low, black-beamed ceilings, copper gleams, honest smells, and morose windows hostile to light. In the hall a torpid spaniel bitch looked at him with the heavily drooping eyes of a *passée* actress; she knew Mr. Arnold, and there was no necessity for even a languid wag of her tail. Always the first customer, he stepped into the bar parlour with his usual opening-time briskness. But Mrs. Watson, polishing glasses behind the bar, looked at him with a start. 'Well!' she seemed about to exclaim, but only pursed her lips.

'A whisky,' he said; 'a double.'

'A double?' Something was concealed in her tone.

'Yes, for God's sake.' The false briskness was suddenly deflated. 'And pour another for me while you're about it.'

'*No*, Mr. Arnold,' she said, flat; 'no. Not *two* doubles . . . It isn't right,' she bridled; 'not today. Good heavens! Don't forget you've got to be there sober at two o'clock. *No*, Mr. Arnold.'

'Hell!' he muttered. He looked over his shoulder with child-blue eyes round in fear. 'Where's Alec?' A man would understand, must surely understand, what that day really meant. Women were incalculable in the domain of the affections, could run so drastically from the extremes of loving solicitude to the bleakest savagery. 'Where's Alec?' he peered.

'Gone to London for the day,' his wife said. 'Gone to buy me a budgerigar.'
'Gone to London,' he mumbled, preoccupied.

'They can chirp ever so sweet,' she said tightly, 'and intelligent, my goodness!—my sister had one that would hop on the table when she was making cake and stone the raisins for her.'

'What?' He started from his glassy preoccupation.

'The budgerigar she had. With its beak. Intelligent, my stars! . . . I've known many a human being,' she said forbiddingly, 'that could do with their brains and feelings.'

Both the Malt Shovel and the Bleeding Horse, which were on his way home, were only beer houses. No licence for spirits. But there was plenty of time. He would climb to Cuckoo Ridge, up to the Self Defence. Its landlord, whose wife had been in an asylum for years, would understand. There was the Unicorn too, nearer, but repellent with its horrible modern cocktail bar, its café look, and its dirty waiters.

Mrs. Watson, solicited with flattery and whining, allowed him a single whisky more. She asked him what would be said in the town if she allowed him to have all he wanted on that morning of all mornings. He left the house with dignity, part of him pre-occupied with feeling offended, but the greater part obeying a huge desolate urge to complete the scarcely begun journey into that powerful state where he would feel secure, a captain of his fate, if a melancholy one. He had never been able to take to drinking at home. Besides, Susan never encouraged it. Never a bottle of whisky in the house.

In the shopping street, those people who knew Mr. Arnold—and they were many, for by now he was a local celebrity—looked at him with their cheerfulness, due to the brilliant day, wiped momentarily from their faces. But he encouraged no one to pass a few words with him; time must not be wasted. He took a side turning and began to climb among loaded apple and pear trees spread over garden walls. The whole fragrantly warm little town was fat with sunlight, fruit and flowers. Mr. Arnold began to pant and lean on his expensive malacca stick.

Above, on the bright emerald slopes with their small well-groomed fields, cows stood like shiny china ornaments. The short local train from London puffed a plume of snowy cotton-wool. It was toy countryside, and Mr. Arnold felt obliged to admire its prettiness; it had been Susan's idea to live here on his retirement from his highly successful career in the City lanes near Tower Bridge, where scores of important men knew him. He liked to feel that London was still near, he liked to see, on Sundays and Bank Holidays, clumps of pallid cockney youths and girls in cycling knickers dotting those slopes like mushrooms. The high air, clear as mineral waters, was supposed to be good

115

for one. Susan said it eased her chest, and she had become a leading voice in the Women's Institute . . . Ah, Susan, Susan! Her husband panted in sore distress, climbing.

On Cuckoo Ridge the landlord of the Self Defence greeted him, after a slight pause, courteously. But Mr. Arnold saw at once that he was in the know. Rapidly he asked for a second double. The landlord, a stout, placid man in braces, looked at him. Perhaps he saw a man in agony of spirit; he served the drink. Mr. Arnold thought he felt deep sympathy flowing from this man whose own wife had been shut away from him for several years already. He asked for a third double.

The landlord mournfully shook his head. 'Best not, Mr. Arnold.'

'One more,' panted Mr. Arnold. 'Only one. I've got a day in front of me.' In the pit of his stomach was a stirring of fear, as if the sleeping coil shuddered. 'Never be able to face it,' he whimpered.

The landlord shook his head in slow, heavy decision. 'There's the circumstances to consider,' he said.

Mr. Arnold attempted a hollow truculence. 'My money's as good as anyone's—'

'Now, sir,' said the landlord distantly, 'best be on your way.' And, solemnly: 'You've got a job to do, Mr. Arnold.'

Mr. Arnold walked out with deliberate steadiness. A clock had struck twelve-thirty. It would have to be the Unicorn, and time was pressing now. Actually he had already taken his morning allowance, but today . . . today . . . He descended from the Ridge with a careful step, crossed the watercress beds into the London road, and looked sourly at the gimcrack modern façade of the Unicorn, a rebuilt house done up for motoring whipper-snappers and their silly grinning dolls. He went in like an aggressive magistrate with power to deprive the place of its licence. But he cast himself into a bony scarlet-and-nickel chair with a groan, wiping his brow. A white presence slid up to his chair.

'Double whisky,' he said.

'Yes, Mr. Arnold,' said the waiter.

He cocked up his eye sharply. Known here too! In a blurred way, the grave young face looking down at him was familiar. Ha, it was Henry, who used to come with his father to do the garden! Quickly Mr. Arnold assumed the censorious glare of a boss of substance. 'And mind it's genuine Scotch, Henry,' he said. He did not like the boy's solicitous look as he withdrew to the blonde cinema star serving behind the jazzy zigzagged corner counter. He took out his big presentation gold watch and looked at it importantly. Was there a pausing at the bar, a whispering? Surely he, who had been a guest at Lord

116

Mayors' banquets in the Mansion House, was not going to be dictated to in a shoddy hole like this? Henry brought the double. 'Get me another, my boy,' Mr. Arnold said. Henry hesitated, but withdrew; came back— 'Sir,' he said awkwardly, 'sir, there's no more except this single. Our supplies haven't arrived; they'll be here by tonight.'

Was everybody his enemy that day? Was there a plot against him? After that long walk, to be allowed only this! Mr. Arnold pushed back his chair, made an effort to collect his forces for dire protest. But somehow—was it because of guilt or the heat?—they would not assemble. He could only gaze fixedly at Henry in silent reproach, anger, and finally, entreaty. 'Very sorry, sir,' mumbled Henry from far away. 'Can I call up the garage for a taxi, sir?'

'A taxi? Certainly not.' He swallowed the single, tipped lavishly, rose like an offended emperor, sat down, and rose again, thunderous yet dignified.

'Your stick, Mr. Arnold.' Henry handed it.

He needed it now. Outside, his eyes could focus neither on the shifting ground nor the burning pansy-coloured sky. The soft amateur hills ran into each other like blobs of water-colours imperfectly handled. But he would walk, he would walk. Anything rather than be in the house before it was quite essential. Not with *them* there . . . The town hall clock, its notes gently without chiding, struck the quarter after one. Yet those chimes were like knells bringing grief. Grief, grief. A sensation of burning grief, physical and staggering, pierced him. He sat gasping on the low roadside wall. The day was no longer brilliant, crackling with sun. The desolation of what awaited his presence swept down on him in gusts of black depression. God above, he could never face it. Not without—. He rose with remarkable celerity.

Fool, fool! Why had he forgotten the Adam and Eve? He walked rapidly, a man refreshed, stick striking the road almost evenly . . . But outside the Adam and Eve, a sixteenth-century house sagging in a dark medieval alley hidden in the town, he paused to arrange himself into the aspect of a man with a grip on himself, and he rolled into the pub with a lordly assurance.

The poky, cool bar parlour was deserted except for a cat enormously asleep on the counter. Mr. Arnold called: 'Hey! Customer here!' He banged the counter with his stick. No one appeared. Not a sound shifted into the stagnant air. He gave the cat a sharp dig with his stick; it did not stir or open an eye. He shouted, thumped the counter. A dead petal of plaster fell from the ceiling. But no one came. The silence closed impervious over his shouts of anguish. No one passed in the shadowed alley outside. His stick rang frenziedly on the counter. He had the feeling he was in a dream in which a ghostly, senseless frustration dogs one's every move. The cat slept. The hands of a dusty old clock remained neatly and for ever together at twelve o'clock.

The bottles on the shelves looked as if they were never opened. He jabbed at the cat again; it did not move out of its primeval sleep.

Mr. Arnold whimpered. He lurched over to the door in the crooked bellied-out wall and lifted the old-fashioned latch. But the door wouldn't open. Had it been locked behind him? Was he being imprisoned? 'Who's there?' he screamed, banging his stick furiously against the rickety panel. The after-silence did not budge. He tore madly at the latch. Suddenly the door flew open; it had jammed in the ancient frame. Raging, Mr. Arnold stamped down the passage, threw back another door.

A dazzle of pink interior light struck into his eyes. He stepped into a hot living-room with a huge window and an opened door leading to a garden blazing with snapdragons, roses and hollyhocks. A blue-gowned woman, immensely fat, was pegging out washing over the gush of flowers. Mr. Arnold all but sobbed with relief. 'Customer!' he yelled.

'Be there in a minute,' she called affably. 'It's a beautiful drying day.'

'Got a train to catch,' he bellowed. 'I want a double Scotch.'

'All right, all right.' Smooth and brown-faced as an egg, and with a dewlap of Turkish chins, she indolently left her basket, saying: 'No need to be crotchety. Where there's one train there's another; they've got the extra summer service now to London. I'm going up myself on Thursday; my daughter's going to be examined . . . Why, it's Mr. Arnold!' She paused, in pastoral caution. 'Are they taking her by train, then? I didn't know.' As if this settled her doubt, she hurried into the bar.

Mr. Arnold said nothing. He drank the double in two gulps and asked for another, saying quickly: 'Then I've got to hurry.' The woman talked of her daughter with soft, unstressed tact. He paused uncertainly after the second double.

'No, Mr. Arnold,' she decided for him, 'I can't give you any more.'

'Mrs. Busby,' he said grandly, grasping his stick as for a march, 'I know when to stop.'

'Gents always do.' She nodded approval. 'God bless you.'

Now he felt translated into the desired sphere, where he could survey his kingdom without lamentations. Power radiated in him. As in the old days of his office fame, he could have settled a ledger page of complicated figures in a twinkling. And that menacing dead weight in the pit of his stomach had vanished. He felt himself walking erect and proud though the luncheon-quiet town. He required no one's compassion. This heady brilliance lasted him all the way home. And he would not be late; a fixed stare at his watch testified to that. He congratulated himself on the efficient way he had handled his time. *They* would not be able to rebuke him for being late, on this day of all days.

118

Yet sight of his well-kept villa at the edge of the town struck a note in his soul like a buried knell. The garden, green-lawned and arched with trellises of roses, was trim beyond reproach—the packet he spent on it every year! And the house was cleanly white as a wedding cake. But quite suddenly now he felt that its walls and contents, its deeds and insurance policies, no longer interested or concerned him. At the gate he paused in panic. Was this, the first faint rising of the horror he thought was obliterated from his being? . . . But almost at once this fear became blurred. His stick decisively tapping the crazy paving, he rolled up under the arches of roses with an air of having unfortunate business to transact.

The white-porched door was wide open. He entered bustlingly. Out of the drawing-room came Miriam, his elder sister-in-law; the woman in charge now, and his enemy. She looked at him and shrank. 'We waited lunch as long as we could,' she said, in her hard, gritty way. Her husband hovered behind her, thick horn glasses observant. 'I wanted George to go into the town and look for you—' she said hopelessly.

'Food!' Mr. Arnold said, in high rebuke. 'You didn't expect me to eat lunch *today?*'

They all advanced out of the drawing-room into the hall, looking at him sideways. Ellen, the younger sister-in-law, and her husband, the dentist's assistant; their grown-up daughter; and Miriam's adolescent son. Alert but careful, visitors and yet that day not visitors, they were all dressed up and important, as if they were going to be photographed. Mr. Arnold stretched his hat to a peg on the stand but miscalculated its position— 'Cursed thing,' he remarked solemnly to the fallen hat. He sat heavily in the hard oak hall chair and wiped his brow. 'In good time,' he observed. 'Five minutes yet . . . What . . . what you all standing there for?' He jerked up his head despotically. He saw tears streaming down Ellen's face before she turned, and hurrying into the drawing-room, moaned: 'I shall be ashamed to go. He's ruined the day. Something must be done. Henry—' she motioned to her husband. But Miriam, stark and glaring, stood like judgment.

'They're coming,' called her son, who had gone to the open door and was keeping a watch on the lane.

'Two o'clock!' said Mr. Arnold in a solemn but strangely forlorn voice. 'Two o'clock!' Still collapsed in the chair, he groaned; his glassy eyes rolled, then stonily looked forth like tortoise eyes.

Henry and Ellen came back and whispered to Miriam's husband; they advanced briskly to Mr. Arnold. 'Look, old boy,' George attempted male understanding. 'We think you'd better not go with us. We will see to everything. Take it easy and have a rest.' Enticingly he laid his hand under Mr.

119

Arnold's armpit, while Henry gripped the other arm. 'They're here; come upstairs,' he coaxed. The two sisters watched in pale, angry withdrawal.

Mr. Arnold, shaking away the possessive hands, rose from the chair tremendously. 'What!' he panted. 'Better not go!' Masterfully he drew himself up. 'Me! *Me!*'

'*You are drunk,*' pronounced Miriam in icy rage. 'You are blind drunk. It's shameful.' Ellen wilted with a bitter sob against the wall.

Mr. Arnold's eyes bulged. Their devilish shine enveloped Miriam with a terrible contempt, restrained for many years. 'This,' said Mr. Arnold, '*this* is no time for insults. The pack of you can clear out now if you like. *I will go alone,*' he said defiantly.

'Now look here—' George began, conciliatory but aghast.

At that moment four men loomed at the open doorway. Four tall men, sleek and black-garbed, leanly efficient of aspect. With everyone in the hall black-clothed, too, the fair summer day seemed turned to shadow. The drawing-room clock struck two dainty *pings*. At the sound the four men entered, admirably prompt. There was something purifying in their sinewy impersonality. 'Upstairs,' Mr. Arnold, steady as a stout column, told them, 'in the dark room.' The black quartet filed up the staircase. Out of the kitchen came Mrs. Wills, her apron removed, and stood apart with her kind cook's fist under an eye.

'Have you decided to risk it?' Henry muttered to the women, while Mr. Arnold reached down with glacial but careful dignity for his black hat. There was whispering, a furtive watching of him.

Down the staircase came the four men with the coffin tilted on their shoulders. The severn mourners stood back. Mr. Arnold's face was stonily set again. He followed the quartet out with a stern and stiff gait. George and Henry, watchful, went close behind him. After them, in ceremonious orderliness, the others. But the two sisters, under their fashionably crisp black hats bought especially for the journey, crept forward with heads bowed very low, asking pardon of the world for this disgrace.

Mr. Arnold negotiated half the length of the crazy paving with masterful ease. Then he began to sway. A hand grasped the trellis of an arch, and a shower of pink and white petals fell on his head and shoulders; his hat dropped out of his hand. The two men took his elbows, and now he submitted to their aid. Ellen sobbed anew; and Miriam moaned: 'We can only hope people will think it's grief.' Then she hissed frantically: 'Brush those petals off him, George; he looks as if he's getting married.'

The hearse contained its burden, the three limousines behind were elegant. 'Four wreaths,' said the supported Mr. Arnold, hanging out his head like a bull. While the impersonal mutes went back to the house, the mourners disposed themselves in the cars. Though the two sisters had planned to occupy the first car with Mr. Arnold, their husbands went in with him instead. 'There, take it easy, old boy,' said George, over-friendly now. Mr. Arnold was well off and a triumphant example of industrious rectitude in the City.

'Eh? . . . eh?' said Mr. Arnold vacantly. And, sunk between the two men into luxurious cushions, he straightway went into a doze. The car began its two-mile journey with a silent, soft glide.

'We mustn't let him go right off,' Henry worried. 'Hey! Mr. Arnold, hey!'

Mr. Arnold opened his eyes ferociously. 'The best wife a man ever had,' he groaned. 'Susan, Susan !' he called wildly. The driver turned his head for a moment. 'Ha, shameful, am I! . . . That woman hasn't got the intelligence of a . . . of a . . . budgerigar! And no more Christian feeling than a trout. Who'd have thought she and Susan were sisters! . . . And that other one,' he grunted, 'what's her name . . . Ellen, always grizzling and telling Susan she was hard up and her husband kept her short—pah! . . . A depressing lot,' summed up Mr. Arnold, staring rigidly into space. Then again he called in loud anguish: 'Susan, Susan, what will I do now?'

Beads of perspiration stood on Henry's forehead. But George remained cool; despite the abuse of his wife, he even sounded affectionate—'Never mind, old chap,' he comforted the bereaved, 'it'll be over soon. But keep awake, don't let down the whole family.'

'What family?' asked Mr. Arnold. 'Got none.' And, sunk down and torpid, he seemed a secret being gathered eternally into loneliness. The two other men glanced at each other. 'Susan,' whispered Mr. Arnold, chin on chest, 'Susan . . . God above!' he wailed again, 'what will I do now?' They were going through the full shopping street; people stopped to look, with arrested eyes. 'The only one of the bunch to keep her sweetness,' muttered Mr. Arnold. 'Coming here in their showy hats!' he chuckled. 'But they couldn't make a man feel proud like Susan did. That time I took her to the Mansion House banquet—' But wild grief engulfed him anew. 'Susan, Susan,' he called, 'what'll I do now?'

'Here, pull yourself together,' Henry protested sharply at last, and, perhaps feeling Mr. Arnold had gone far enough in insults, 'We're coming to the cemetery.'

Mr. Arnold heaved into physical alertness for the ordeal. In a minute or two the car slid to a delicate standstill. Inside the cemetery gates was a group of half-a-dozen women, representatives of the institute for which Susan had organised many an event. Out of the lodge came the surpliced vicar, prayer-book in hand. Henry got out first and, red-faced, offered a hand to Mr.

121

Arnold, who ignored it and alighted without mishap. But for an awful moment the widower's legs seemed boneless. Then he drew himself up nobly, stood rock-like in ruminative strength, while the coffin was drawn out and borne ahead.

The two sisters stood in helplessness, hiding their faces, but peering like rabbits. The procession began to form. The vicar turned the pages of his book in mild abstraction. George and Henry sidled up beside Mr. Arnold. 'I'll walk alone,' hissed Mr. Arnold, and he reminded them fiercely that Miriam and Ellen were entitled to follow immediately behind him. He insisted on that being arranged. The institute women, who seemed unaware of anything unusual, took their places in the rear. The cortège moved.

The cemetery was cut out of a steepish slope, and the newly acquired section was at the top. It was quite a climb for elderly mourners; a discussion had waged in the local paper about the lack of foresight in not making a carriage road through the place. Mr. Arnold, close behind the coffin and without his well-known stick, negotiated the climb with an occasional lapsing of his knees, a straightening of his back, or a rigid turning and jerking of his head, like a man doing physical exercises. But he achieved it victoriously. Behind him Ellen wept and Mirian stared in blank fear.

It was not until all were assembled before the graveside and the service had begun that Mr. Arnold began to display signs of collapse. He vaguely swayed; his head lolled. George and Henry took a step nearer him. The abstract vicar droned unseeing; the institute women remained tactful behind the chief mourners. The attendants took up the roped coffin; it disappeared; a handful of earth was thrown in after it. Presently the vicar's voice stopped. George and Henry took Mr. Arnold's elbows to assist him for the last look.

'Leave me alone,' Mr. Arnold muttered, drawing his elbows angrily away. What had these to do with him! He advanced with renewed dignity to the brink of the grave. Looked in as if into an abyss of black tremendous loneliness. Stood there staring down in concentrated intentness, prolonged, fascinated. The vicar waited in faint surprise at the mourner's lengthy scrutiny.

George and Henry darted forward. Too late. While a single hysterical woman's cry shot up, Mr. Arnold shot down, falling clumsily, arms flapping out, his disappearing face looking briefly astonished, the mouth wide open and showing all his artificial teeth. There was a moment's hesitation of unbelieving dismay. Then the bustling began. Mr. Arnold lay down there on his stomach across the coffin. An upper denture gleamed out in the clay beside him.

'I knew it,' said Miriam, later, 'I felt it in my bones when you two allowed him to walk alone to the graveside. Thank heaven we don't live here.' They were in the villa in conference. Mr. Arnold had been taken to the county hospital with a fractured leg.

He stayed there two months. The first patient to be received out of a grave, he was the talk and pet of the hospital; as the night sister remarked: 'He must have been a devoted husband to throw himself into his wife's grave like that! I've never known a man grieve so much. How he calls out in the night for his Susan!' . . . Cantankerous at first, he became astonishingly meek. The doctor allowed him a certain amount of whisky. The night sister, perhaps because she was shortly due for retirement, secretly allowed him a little more. She took quite a fancy to him, and some months later, thinking he had detected in her a flavour of Susan's character, Mr. Arnold married her.

FEAR

As soon as the boy got into the compartment he felt there was something queer in it. The only other occupant was a slight, dusky man who sat in a corner with that air of propriety and unassertiveness which his race—he looked like an Indian—tend to display in England. There was also a faint sickly scent. For years afterwards, whenever he smelled that musk odour again, the terror of this afternoon came back to him.

He went to the other end of the compartment, sat in the opposite corner. There were no corridors in these local trains. The man looked at him and smiled friendlily. The boy returned the smile briefly, not quite knowing what he was thinking, only aware of a deep, vague unease. But it would look so silly to jump out of the compartment now. The train gave a jerk and began to move.

Then, immediately with the jerk, the man began to utter a low humming chant, slow but with a definite rhythm. His lips did not open or even move, yet the hum penetrated above the noise of the train's wheels. It was in a sort of dreamy rhythm, enticing, lonely and antique; it suggested monotonous deserts, an eternal patience, a soothing wisdom. It went on and on. It was the kind of archaic chant that brings to the mind images of slowly swaying bodies in some endless ceremony in a barbaric temple.

Startled, and very alive to this proof of there being something odd in the compartment, the boy turned from staring out of the window—already the train was deep in the country among lonely fields and dark wooded slopes— and forced himself to glance at the man.

The man was looking at him. They faced each other across the compartment's length. Something coiled up in the boy. It was as if his soul took primitive fear and crouched to hide. The man's brown lips became stretched in a mysterious smile, though that humming chant continued, worldlessly swaying out of his mouth. His eyes, dark and unfathomable, never moved from the boy. The musk scent was stronger.

Yet this was not all. The boy could not imagine what other fearful thing lurked in the compartment. But he seemed to sense a secret power of something evilly antipathetic. Did it come from the man's long pinky-brown hands, the sinewy but fleshless hands of a sun-scorched race? Long tribal hands like claws. Or only from the fact that the man was of a far country whose ways were utterly alien to ours? And he continued to smile. A faint and subtle

124

smile, while his eyes surveyed the boy as if he contemplated action. Something had flickered in and out of those shadowy eyes, like a dancing malice.

The boy sat stiffly. Somehow he could not return to his staring out of the window. But he tried not to look at the man again. The humming did not stop. And suddenly it took a higher note, like an unhurried wail, yet keeping within its strict and narrow compass. A liquid exultance wavered in and out of the wail. The noise of the train, the flying fields and woods, even the walls of the compartment, had vanished. There was only this chant, the man who was uttering it, and himself. He did not know that now he could not move his eyes from those of the man.

Abruptly the compartment was plunged into blackness. There was a shrieking rush of air. The train had entered a tunnel. With a sudden jerk the boy crouched down. He coiled into the seat's corner, shuddering, yet with every sense electrically alive now.

Then, above the roar of the air and the hurling grind of the train, that hum rose, dominantly establishing its insidious power. It called, it unhurriedly exhorted obedience, it soothed. Again it seemed to obliterate the louder, harsher noises. Spent and defeated, helplessly awaiting whatever menace lay in the darkness, the boy crouched. He knew the man's eyes were gazing towards him; he thought he saw their gleam triumphantly piercing the darkness. What was this strange presence of evil in the air, stronger now in the dark?

Suddenly crashing into the compartment, the hard blue and white daylight was like a blow. The train had gained speed in the tunnel and now hurled on through the light with the same agonising impetus, as if it would rush on for ever. Spent in the dread which had almost cancelled out his senses, the boy stared dully at the man. Still he seemed to hear the humming, though actually it had ceased. He saw the man's lips part in a full enticing smile, he saw teeth dazzlingly white between the dusky lips.

'You not like dark tunnel?' The smile continued seductively; once more the flecks of light danced wickedly in his eyes. 'Come!' He beckoned with a long wrinkled finger.

The boy did not move.

'You like pomegranates?' He rose and took from the luggage-rack a brown wicker basket. It was the kind of basket in which a large cat would be sent on a journey. 'Come!' he smiled friendlily and, as the boy still did not move, he crossed over and sat down beside him, but leaving a polite distance.

The staring boy did not flinch.

'Pomegranates from the East! English boy like, eh?' There seemed a collaboration in his intimate voice; he too was a boy going to share fruit with his friend. 'Nice pomegranates,' he smiled with good-humour. There was also something stupid in his manner, a fatuous mysteriousness.

The basket lay on his knees. He began to hum again. The boy watched, still without movement, cold and abstract in his non-apprehension of this friendliness. But he was aware of the sickly perfume beside him and, more pronounced than ever, of an insidious presence that was utterly alien. That evil power lay in his immediate vicinity. The man looked at him again and, still humming, drew a rod and lifted the basket's lid.

There was no glow of magically gleaming fruits, no yellow-and-rose-tinted rinds enclosing honeycombs of luscious seeds. But from the basket's depth rose the head of a snake. It rose slowly to the enchantment of the hum. It rose from its sleepy coil, rearing its long brownish-gold throat dreamily, the head swaying out in languor towards the man's lips. Its eyes seemed to look blindly at nothing. It was a cobra.

Something happened to the boy. An old warning of the muscles and the vulnerable flesh. He leapt and flung himself headlong across the compartment. He was not aware that he gave a sharp shriek. He curled against the opposite seat's back, his knees pressing into the cushion. But, half turning, his eyes could not tear themselves from that reared head.

And it was with other senses that he knew most deeply he had evoked rage. The cobra was writhing in disturbed anger, shooting its head in his direction. He saw wakened pin-point eyes of black malice. More fearful was the dilation of the throat, its skin swelling evilly into a hood in which shone two palpitating sparks. In some cell of his being he knew that the hood was swelling in destructive fury. He became very still.

The man did not stop humming. But now his narrowed eyes were focused in glittering concentration on the snake. And into that hum had crept a new note of tenacious decision. It was a pitting of subtle power against the snake's wishes and it was also an appeasement. A man was addressing a snake. He was offering a snake tribute and acknowledgment of its right to anger; he was honeyed and soothing. At the same time he did not relax an announcement of being master. There was courtesy towards one of the supreme powers of the animal kingdom, but also there was the ancient pride of man's supremacy.

And the snake was pacified. Its strange reared collar of skin sank bank into its neck; its head ceased to lunge towards the boy. The humming slackened into a dreamy lullaby. Narrowly intent now, the man's eyes did not move. The length of tawny body slowly sank back. Its skin had a dull glisten, the glisten of an unhealthy torpidity. Now the snake looked effete, shorn of its venomous power. The drugged head sank. Unhurriedly the man closed the basket and slipped its rod secure.

126

He turned angrily to the boy; he made a contemptuous sound, like a hiss. 'I show you cobra and you jump and shout, heh! Make him angry!' There was more rebuke than real anger in his exclamations. But also his brown face was puckered in a kind of childish stupidity; he might have been another boy of twelve. 'I give you free performance with cobra, and you jump and scream like little girl.' The indignation died out of his eyes; they became focused in a more adult perception. 'I sing to keep cobra quiet in train,' he explained. 'Cobra not like train.'

The boy had not stirred. 'You not like cobra?' the man asked in injured surprise. 'Nice snake now, no poison! But not liking you jump and shout.'

There was no reply or movement; centuries and continents lay between him and the boy's still repudiation. The man gazed at him in silence and added worriedly: 'You going to fair in Newport? You see me? Ali the Snake Charmer. You come in free and see me make cobra dance—'

But the train was drawing into the station. It was not the boy's station. He made a sudden blind leap away from the man, opened the door, saw it was not on the platform side, but jumped. There was a shout from someone. He ran up the track, he dived under some wire railings. He ran with amazingly quick short leaps up a field—like a hare that knows its life is precarious among the colossal dangers of the open world and has suddenly sensed one of them.

THE FASHION PLATE

I

'The Fashion Plate's coming—' Quickly the news would pass down the main road. Curtains twitched in front parlour windows, potted shrubs were moved or watered; some colliers' wives, hard-worked and canvas-aproned, came boldly out to the doorsteps to stare. In the dingy little shops, wedged here and there among the swart dwellings, customers craned together for the treat. Cleopatra setting out in the golden barge to meet Antony did not create more interest. There was no one else in the valley like her. Her hats! The fancy high-heeled shoes, the brilliantly elegant dresses in summer, the tweeds and the swirl of furs for the bitter days of that mountainous district! The different handbags, gay and sumptuous, the lacy gloves, the parasols and tasselled umbrellas! And how she knew how to wear these things! Graceful as a swan, clean as a flower, she dazzled the eye.

But, though a pleasure to see, she was also incongruous, there in that grim industrial retreat pushed up among the mountains, with the pits hurling out their clouds of grit, and clanking coal-wagons crossing the main road twice, and the miners coming off the shift black and primitive-looking. The women drew in their breaths as she passed. She looked as if she had never done a stroke of work in her life. Strange murmurs could be heard; she almost created a sense of fear, this vision of delicate indolence, wealth and taste assembled with exquisite tact in one person. How could she do it? Their eyes admired but their comments did not.

Yet the work-driven women of this place, that had known long strikes, bitter poverty and a terrible pit disaster, could not entirely malign Mrs. Mitchell. Something made them pause. Perhaps it was the absolute serenity of those twice-weekly afternoon walks that nothing except torrential rain or snow-bound roads could prevent. Or perhaps they saw a vicarious triumph of themselves, a dream become courageously real.

There remained the mystery of how she could afford all those fine clothes. For Mrs. Mitchell was only the wife of the man in charge of the slaughter-house. She was not the pit manager's wife (indeed, Mrs. Edwards dressed in a totally different style, her never-varied hat shaped like an Eskimo's hut). Mr. Mitchell's moderate salary was known, and in such a place no one could possess private means without it being exact knowledge. Moreover, he was no match to his wife. A rough and ready sort of man, glum and never mixing much in the life of the place, though down in the slaughter-house, which served all the butcher shops for miles, he was respected as a responsible chap whose words and deeds were to be trusted. Of words he had not many.

The women wished they could curl their tongues round something scandalous. Why was Mrs. Mitchell always having her photograph taken by Mr. Burgess in his studio down an obscure yard where he worked entirely alone? But nobody felt that suspicion of Mr. Burgess, a family man and a chapel deacon with a stark knobbly face above a high stiff collar, sat comfortably in the mind. The bit of talk about the two had started because one afternoon a mother calling at the studio to fix an appointment for her daughter's wedding party found Mrs. Mitchell reclining on a sofa under a bust of Napoleon. She was hatless and, in a clinging dress ('tight on her as a snake-skin') and her hand holding a bunch of artificial flowers, she looked like a woman undergoing the agonies of some awful confession. Mr. Burgess certainly had his head under the black drapery of his camera, so everything pointed to yet another photograph being taken. But to have one taken *lying down!* In the valley, in those days, to have a photo taken was a rare event attended by tremendous fuss. Accompanied by advising friends or relations, one stood up to the ordeal as if going before the Ultimate Judge, and one always came out on the card as if turned to stone or a pillar of salt.

The whispering began. Yet still everyone felt that the whispering was unfair to Mr. Burgess. For thirty years he had photographed wedding parties, oratorio choirs and silver cup football teams in his studio, and nothing had ever been said against his conduct.

Mrs. Mitchell, coming out of her bow-windowed little house as out of a palace, took her walks as if never a breath of scandal ever polluted her pearl ear-rings. Was she aware of the general criticism? If so, did she know that within the criticism was homage?—the homage that in bygone times would begin a dynasty of tribal queens? Was she aware of the fear too, the puritanic dread that such lavishness and extravagance could not be obtained but at some dire cost greater even than money?

I

This afternoon her excursion was no different from the hundreds of others. It was a fine autumn day. The tawny mountains glistened like the skins of lions. She wore a new fur, rich with the bluish-black tint of grapes, and flung with just the right expensive carelessness across her well-held shoulders: it would cause additional comment. With her apparently unaware look of repose she passed serenely down the long drab main road.

Down at the bottom of the valley the larger shops, offices, a music-hall and a railway station (together with Mr. Burgess's studio) clustered into the semblance of a town. She always walked as far as the railway station, situated down a hunch-backed turning, and, after appearing to be intent on its architecture for a moment, wheeled round and with a mysterious smile began the homeward journey. Often she made small domestic purchases—her clothes she obtained from the city twenty miles away—and as the ironmonger's wife once remarked: 'Only a rolling-pin she wanted, but one would think she was buying a grand piano.'

Today, outside the railway station, she happened to see her young friend Nicholas and, bending down to his ear, in her low sweet voice breathed his name. He was twelve, wore a school satchel strapped to his back, and he was absent-mindedly paused before a poster depicting Windsor Castle. He gave a violent start and dropped a purple-whorled glass marble which rolled across the pavement, sped down the gutter and slid into a drain— 'It's gone!' he cried in poignant astonishment. 'I won it dinner-time!'

'And all my fault.' Her bosom was perfumed with an evasive fragrance like closed flowers. 'Never mind, *I* have some marbles—will you come and get them this evening? You've been neglecting us lately, Nicholas.' She was neither arch nor patronising; he might have been a successful forty.

'I'll have to do my homework first,' he said with equal formality.

'Well, come in and do it with us. You shall have your own little table, and I'll be quiet as a mouse.'

They lived in the same street and though no particular friendship existed between the two households, he had been on visiting terms with the Mitchells, who were childless, for a couple of years. The change from his own noisily warring brothers-and-sisters home to the Mitchell's, where he was sole little king, nourished him. To his visits his mother took a wavering attitude of doubt, half criticism and compassion; before becoming decisive she was waiting for something concrete to happen in that house.

That evening Mrs. Mitchell had six coloured glass marbles ready for him on a small table on which also, neatly set out, were a crystal ink-well, a ruler, blotter and pencils and . . . yes! a bottle of lemonade with a tumbler. Very impressed by the bottle, which gave him a glimpse of easy luxury in a world hard with the snatching and blows of his brothers and sisters, he made little fuss of the glitteringly washed marbles, which he guessed she had bought in Watkins's shop after leaving him—and in any case they had not the value of those won from bragging opponents kneeling around a circle drawn in the earth.

'Is the chair high enough, would you like a cushion? . . . You must work hard if you want to get near the top of your class, but you must *enjoy* working . . . There! Now I'll do my sewing and not say a word.'

Hers was not big industrious sewing, complete with bee-humming machine, as at home. She sat delicately edging a tiny handkerchief with a shred of lace, and on her face was a look of minutes strained to their utmost; she had the manner of one who never glances at a clock. The house was tidy, clean, respectably comfortable. But it was shabbier than his own home. And somehow without atmosphere, as if it was left alone to look after itself and no love or hate clashed within its shiny darkly-papered walls. Occasionally this lack of something important vaguely bothered the boy. He would stand with his lip lifted, his nostrils dilated. He had never been upstairs, and he always wanted to penetrate its privacy. Was the thing he missed to be found there? Did they live up there and only come downstairs when there were visitors? Down here it was all parlour and Sunday silence, with for movement only the lonely goldfish eternally circling its bowl.

Mr. Mitchell came in before the homework was finished. 'Good evening, *sir*,' he greeted Nicholas. 'Doing my accounts for me?' He seemed to look at the boy and yet not look at him. And he was not a jocular man. He had a full, dahlia-red, rather staring face of flabby contours, sagged in on its own solitude, and the eyes did not seem to connect with the object they looked at. His face had affinities with the face of some floridly ponderous beast. He had a very thick neck. It was strange, and yet not at all strange, that his work had to do with cattle.

'Do you want a meal now,' Mrs. Mitchell asked in the heavy silence, 'or can you wait?' Her voice was crisper; she stitched in calm withdrawal; she might have been an indifferent daughter. Though bent at the table, the boy sensed the change. There was a cold air of armistice in the-room, of emptiness. Nervously he opened his bottle of lemonade. The explosion of the uncorking sounded very loud.

'I'll go upstairs,' Mr. Mitchell said. 'Yes, I'll go upstairs. Call me down.'

'You'll hear the dishes,' she said concisely. The boy turned and saw her stitching away, like a queen in a book of tales. Mr. Mitchell went out bulkily; his head lolled on the fleshy neck. It was as if he said 'Pah!' in a heavily angry way. His footsteps were ponderous on the staircase.

Had he come straight from the slaughter-house and was weary? Had he a short time ago been killing cattle? Nicholas, like all the boys of the place, was interested in the slaughter-house, a squat building with pens and sties in a field down by the river. Once he had been allowed inside by an amiable young assistant who understood his curiosity, and he saw in a white-washed room hung with ropes and pulleys a freshly dead bullock strung up in the air by its legs; it swayed a little and looked startlingly foolish. Blood spattered the guttered floor and some still dripped from the bullock's mouth like a red icicle. In a yard another young man was rinsing offal in a tub filled with green slime. 'No, we're not killing pigs today,' he replied to Nicholas's enquiry. Because of the intelligent squeals and demented hysteria of these intuitive beasts as they were chased from the sties into the house of death, pig-killing was the prized spectacle among all the boys. But few had been fortunate enough to witness it; the slaughter-men usually drove them away from the fascinating precincts. Nicholas, an unassertive boy on the whole, had never liked to take advantage of his friendship with the Mitchells and ask to be taken to the place properly, an accredited visitor on a big day. He wondered if Mrs. Mitchell went there herself sometimes. Could she get him a pig's bladder?

She did not bring in supper until he had finished the homework. 'There, haven't I been quiet?' she smiled. 'Did you work easily? I can see you're studious and like quiet. Do you like lobster too?'

'Lobster?' He looked at her vacantly.

She fetched from the kitchen an oval dish in which lay a fabulous scarlet beast. Cruel claws and quiveringly-fine feelers sprang from it. At first he thought that Mr. Mitchell must have brought it from the slaughter-house, but when his excitement abated he remembered they came from the sea. 'How did you get it?' he asked, astonished.

'I have to ask Harris's fish shop to order one especially for me. I'm the only person here that wants them.'

'Do they cost a lot?'

Over the fiery beast she looked at him conspiratorially. 'Nothing you enjoy ever costs a lot,' she smiled mysteriously.

Mr. Mitchell must have heard the dishes. But he same down looking more torpid than ever. 'Lobster again!' he said, sombrely. 'At night? There's stomachs of cast-iron in this world.'

Mrs. Mitchell looked at him frigidly. 'If you encourage nightmares they'll come,' she said.

'You're not giving it to the boy?' he said.

'Why not? You'll have a little, Nicholas?' Of course he would.

'I have dreams,' said Mr. Mitchell, his heavy dark-red face expressionless. 'Yes, *I* have dreams.'

'Do you?' Her husband might have been an acquaintance who had called at an inopportune time. 'A little salad, Nicholas? Shall I choose it for you?' In delightful performance she selected what seemed the best pieces in the bowl; with deft suggestions she showed him how to eat the lobster. He enjoyed extracting from inside a crimson scimitar shreds of rosily white meat. The evening became remarkable for him.

And it was because of it he added to the local legend of Mrs. Mitchell. When he told them at home about the lobster there was at first a silence. His mother glanced up, his brothers and sisters were impressed. He felt superior. A couple of weeks later, while he waited to be served in Watkins's shop just after Mrs. Mitchell had passed the window on her return from her walk, he heard a collier's wife say: 'Yes, and they say she has lobsters for breakfast nearly every day. No doubt her new hat she wears at breakfast too, to match them.' Despite his sense of guilt, he felt himself apart, an experienced being. No one else in the place was known to have dealings with the exotic fish.

'She'll be giving him champagne next,' he heard his father say to his mother. 'Mitchell, poor devil, will be properly in the soup some day.' And his mother said, troubled: 'Yes, I *do* wonder if Nick ought to go there—'

III

That winter Mrs. Mitchell won a £100 prize in a periodical which ran a competition every week. You had to make up a smart remark on a given phrase and send it in with a sixpenny postal order. A lot of people in the place did it; someone else had won £10, which set more members of both sexes running to the Post Office. It seemed quite in order that Mrs. Mitchell, who dressed like no one else, should win a cracker of a prize, but everybody was agog the day the news got around.

'You'll be going to see her every day now,' Nicholas's eldest brother jeered, adding offensively: 'Take your money-box with you.' And his father said to his mother, in that secret-knowledge way which roused an extra ear inside one: 'If she's got any feeling, she'll hand it to Mitchell straight away.' To this his mother said: 'Not she!'

A week later, with Christmas not far off, Mrs. Mitchell took her afternoon walk in a new fur coat. It shone with an opulent gleam as if still alive and its owner walked with the composure of one who owns three hundred and sixty-five fur coats. It was treated to a companionable new hat into which a blue quill was stabbed cockily as a declaration of independence. Her red tasselled umbrella, exquisitely rolled, went before her with a hand attached lightly as a flower. The women watchers down the long bleak road gathered and stared with something like consternation. Surely such luxury couldn't proceed for ever! The God of Prudence, who had made his character known in abundant scriptures, must surely hurl one of his thunderbolts right in her path some day.

133

That same evening Nicholas visited the Mitchells' house. And he found Mrs. Mitchell delicately shedding a few tears into a lacy wisp of the finest linen. He could not take this restrained sort of weeping seriously. Especially as she had just won a big prize. 'Have you got a headache?' he asked.

She blew her pretty nose and dried her tears. 'I'm glad you've come. It keeps Mr. Mitchell quiet.' Pointing to the ceiling, she whispered dramatically: 'He's just gone up . . . Oh dear!' she sighed.

'What is he always doing upstairs?' It did not now take him long to adjust himself to being treated as a grown-up.

'Oh, only sleeping . . . He's a man that seems to need a great deal of sleep. He says he gets bad dreams, but I believe he likes them.' She smiled at him with dainty malice. 'Do you know what he wanted? . . . My prize!' Nicholas looked thoughtful, like one privy to other knowledge. She went on: 'Week after week I worked so hard at those competitions, and he never helped me, it was all my own brains.' Her eyes shone with that refined malice. 'To tell you the truth, *he isn't clever*. Not like you and me.' She giggled. 'Oh dear, don't look so solemn, Nicholas; I've had a very trying day.'

'I have too,' he said.

'Have you, darling? Would you like a chocolate?' She jumped up and fetched a large ribboned box from the sideboard. They ate in release from the stress. But he could see her attention was on something else, and presently she resumed: 'He found out today that I spent the prize on a fur coat. Oh good gracious, such a fuss!' She rummaged for other chocolates. 'An almond one this time? Nougat? I don't like the peppermint ones, do you? We'll keep them for Mr. Mitchell . . . . Of course, people do criticise me,' she said, wrinkling her nose. 'You must not repeat what I've said, Nicholas.'

'Oh no,' he said, decided but flushing. Memory of the lobster affair still obscurely troubled him.

'Gentlemen do not,' she said. 'As you know.'

'I'm going to visit my grandmother after Christmas,' he said awkwardly.

Suddenly footsteps sounded on the stairs, descending with pronounced deliberation. And Mrs. Mitchell seemed to draw herself in, like a slow graceful snail into its shell. The door opened, and Mr. Mitchell stood there in a bowler hat and overcoat, bulky and glowering. Even his ragged moustache looked as if it was alive with helpless anger—anger that would never really shoot out or even bristle. 'Am going out,' he said, in a low defeated growl. Of Nicholas he took no notice. 'Going out,' he repeated. 'Yes.'

'You are going out,' she murmured, remote in her shell. Her eyelids were down as if against some rude spectacle.

'Yes.' Something in his heavy neck throbbed, making it thicker. Yet there was nothing threatening in his mien. His slow, ox-coloured eyes travelled from his wife's face to the large pink box of chocolates on her knees. 'I hope,' he then said, 'you'll always be able to afford 'um.'

She asked faintly: 'What time will you be back? Supper will—'

'Going to the slaughter-house,' he said sullenly. 'Got a job to do.'

'—will be ready at nine,' she said.

'Ha!' he said. He stared at her shut face. But the heavy gaze of his unlit eyes threw out no communication. The boy looked round. Feeling at a loss, he glanced uneasily at Mrs. Mitchell and saw that a peculiar, almost dirty grey, tint blotched her face. 'Ha!' repeated Mr. Mitchell. The large, sagged face hung down over his swollen neck. For a moment he looked vaguely menacing. Then he tramped into the hallway. The front door slammed.

Mrs. Mitchell opened her eyes wide at the slam. 'Oh dear!' she wailed faintly. Her eyes were different, darker, almost black. 'He never says very much,' she fluttered, 'but he stands there *looking* . . . Good gracious!' She bit a chocolate mechanically and winced in chagrin as if it held a flavour she did not like. 'It seems he's having a very busy time in the slaughter-house,' she went on erratically; 'some sheep have come in . . . Ah, well!' She jumped up again. 'You haven't seen my new photographs.'

Once again they sat over the album: she inserted a copy of the new photograph. There she was in about thirty different representations, but whether she was sad or smiling, dreamy or vivacious, aloof or inviting, it was clear that the eye of Mr. Burgess's camera found itself in concord with its elegant object. For nearly an hour she pored over the album with an exaggerated, detailed interest, demanding once more his opinion. Her voice was high, her manner hurried: 'Isn't this your favourite? Yes. It's mine too. Why do you like it so much?

He thought carefully. 'You look as though you're just going for a holiday to the seaside,' he said finally.

'It's true I was happy that day. At the time I thought we were going to move to London . . . Then Mr. Mitchell refused to take the job he was offered there.' Her voice sharpened remarkably. 'He refused . . . The fact is, he has no ambition.' Suddenly she snapped the album shut, rose with a bright restlessness. 'Will you come down to the slaughter-house with me, Nicholas?'

At last the invitation! He agreed with alacrity and thought of the envy of the other boys.

'If you are with me, Mr. Mitchell won't be so disagreeable.' She hurried upstairs, and returned in her new fur coat and the coquettish toque. 'Come, I didn't realise we had sat here so long . . . I can't have him sulking and going without his supper,' she explained.

The starlit night was cold. There were few people in the streets. The secret mountains smelled grittily of winter. Somewhere a dog barked insistent, shut out from a house. The public-house windows were clouded with yellow steam, and in a main-street house a woman pulled down a blind on a lamplit front parlour where sat Mr. Hopkins the insurance agent beside a potted fern. They crossed the main street and took a sloping road trailing away into waste land. Odorous of violets and dark fur, Mrs. Mitchell walked with a surprisingly quick glide; Nicholas was obliged to trot. They heard the icy cry of the river below, flinging itself unevenly among its stone-ragged banks. She said nothing now.

The slaughter-house stood back in its field, an angular array of black shadows; no light showed there. Mrs. Mitchell fumbled at the fence gate of the field. 'I've only been here once,' she said, 'when I brought down the telegraph saying his father had died.' She paused doubtfully. 'There's no light.' But the gate was unlocked.

'There are windows at the back,' Nicholas urged; 'there's a little office at the side.' But he himself was disappointed. It seemed unlikely that slaughtering was proceeding among those silent shadows.

They walked up the cobbled path. There was a double door leading into a stone-floored paddock; it swung loose. Inside, a huge sliding door led into the main slaughter-chamber; this did not yield to their push. Then Nicholas remembered the smaller door at the side; he turned its knob, and they walked into a whitewashed passage lit at the end by a naked blue gas-jet. 'The office is down there,' he said. He felt morose and not implicated; he remembered glancing into the office during his previous visit; it was no more than a large box with a table and chair and files and ledgers. They walked down the stone-flagged passage. She stopped. He heard her breathing.

'Go back,' she said.

Sharpened by her tone of command, he looked up at her. Her nostrils, blue in the gaslight, were quivering. He looked down quickly. From under a door a stream of dark thick liquid had crawled. It was congealing on the stone flag into the shape of a large root or a strand of seaweed. He looked at it, only distantly conscious of her further cry and her fingers pressing into his shoulders. 'Go back; go home,' she exclaimed. He did not move.

She stepped to the door as if oblivious of him. But she carefully avoided the liquid root. She turned the brass knob, slowly pushed back the door. Still the boy had not moved. He could not see inside the door. She gave a queer cry, not loud, a low hunted cry broken in her mouth. And Nicholas never forgot the gesture with which her hand went to her throat. He ran forward from the wall. At the same time his feet instinctively avoided the dark smears. 'Let me see!' he cried. But she pulled back the door. 'Let me see!' he cried. It was then he became conscious of another odour, a whiff from the closing door mingled with the perfume of fur and violets.

She violently pushed him back. 'Go home at once!' There was something like a terrible hiss in her voice. He looked up in confusion. Her face, blotched with a sickly pallor, was not the elegantly calm face he knew; the joints and muscles had loosened and were jerking convulsively. It was as if the static photograph of a pleasing face had in some nightmare way suddenly broken into ugly grimaces. For a moment he stared aghast at that face. Then he backed from her.

Her eyes seemed not to see him. 'Go!' she screamed, even more startlingly. Then he swiftly turned and ran.

IV

Three days later, carrying a large bunch of chrysanthemums from his mother, he walked down to the Mitchells' house. He went with a meek unwillingness. But not unconscious of the drama in which he was involved. All those three days the place had hummed with talk of the Mitchells'. Within living memory there had been only one local suicide before.

Already there was pre-knowledge of the bailiffs who were only waiting for the coffin to leave the house before taking possession. The dead man's affairs were in shocking condition. Besides forcing him to mortgage his house several years ago, the Fashion Plate had bullied him into going to moneylenders . . . And no, she was not a nagging woman, but she got her way by slyly making him feel inferior to her. She had done him honour by marrying him and he must pay for what was necessary to her selfish happiness.

At first Nicholas's mother had said he must not visit the house again. Then that evening—the inquest had taken place the previous day—she told him to take the flowers. His unwillingness surprised her and, oddly enough, made her more decided that he should go on this compassionate errand. He frowned at the flowers but sheltered them from the wind. He wondered if it was true that the Mitchells' house was going to be sold up, and if so could he ask for the goldfish.

When Mrs. Mitchell opened the door he looked at her with a furtive nervousness. But, except for the deep black of her shinily flowing new frock, she was no different. 'Oh, Nicholas darling!' she greeted him, with the same composed smile as before the event. And she accepted the flowers as if they were for an afternoon-tea vase. She was alone in the house. But twice there was a caller who was taken privately into the front room for a short while.

'You haven't brought your homework with you?' she asked. He was a little shocked. Upstairs lay the dead man in his coffin. She sat making calculations and notes in a little book. A heap of black-edged stationery lay on the table. The pit hooter sounded. There were silences. He looked at the goldfish eternally circling its bowl— 'What do you feed it with?' he murmured at length.

'Black gloves—' she said inattentively, 'do you think I could find a decent pair in this hole of a place!'

Out of the corner of his eye he kept on glancing at her, furtively. Once she remarked: 'You are very distant this evening, Nicholas.' Then, as his silences did not abate, she asked suddenly: 'Well, haven't you forgiven me?' He looked confused, and she added: 'For pushing you away so rudely in the slaughter-house.' The cloudy aloofness in his mind crystallised then, and he knew he indeed bore her a grudge. She had deprived him of something of high visual interest. In addition he was not yet reconciled to the revelation of how she had *looked* . . . 'Oh, it doesn't matter,' he mumbled, with hypocritical carelessness. He stared again at the goldfish. 'What do you feed the goldfish with?' he repeated.

'You must take that goldfish away with you tonight. Otherwise those dreadful men will stick a number on the bowl and get half a crown for it . . . Would you like to see Mr. Mitchell now?' As he did not reply at once but still looked owlish, she said: 'Well, come along upstairs.' He rose and followed her, in half forgiveness. 'I don't like being depressed, it doesn't suit me,' she complained; 'I feel quite old.'

Her fresh poplin skirts hissed as she climbed. 'Poor Mr. Mitchell,' she sighed, 'I do wish I could feel more sorry for him. But I'm afraid his nature made him melancholy, though I must say as a young man he wasn't so difficult . . . And he used to be quite handsome, in a footballer kind of way . . . Ah!' she said, shaking her head, 'these beefy sportsman types, they're often quite neurotic, just bundles of nerves . . . Oh, it's all been so unpleasant,' she went on, with a dainty squirm of repudiation, 'but I must own he had the decency to do it *down there.*'

Upstairs there were the same four rooms as in his own home. She took him into the end back room and turned on the light. It seemed to be the room where they had slept, there were brushes on the dressing-table and a man's jacket was still flung across a chair. On the bed lay a coffin. It sank heavily into the mattress. The lid lay against a wall. 'You won't want to be here long,' she suggested, and left him to his curiosity. He saw her go across the landing to the main front room and put on the light there. She left both doors open.

He looked into the coffin. Mr. Mitchell wore a crisp white shroud which

138

somehow robbed him of the full powerfulness of being a man. And his face, with the dark red flabbiness drained out of it, was not his. He looked as if he had been ill in bed for a long time but was now secure in a cold sort of health. Round his throat a folded white napkin was tightly swathed. This linen muffler, together with the shroud, gave him an air of being at the mercy of apparel he himself would not have chosen. Nicholas's round eyes lingered on the napkin.

He left the room feeling subdued and obedient. The cold isolation of the dead man lying helpless in that strange clothing made him feel without further curiosity; there was nothing to astonish, and nothing to startle one into fearful pleasure.

Mrs. Mitchell heard him come out and called: 'What do you think of this, Nicholas?' He went along the landing to the fully illuminated front room and saw at once it was where she slept. The room was perfumed and untidy with women's clothes strewn everywhere. Hadn't Mr. and Mrs. Mitchell used the same room, then, like other married people? He looked around with renewed inquisitiveness. A large cardboard hat-box lay open on the bed. From it Mrs. Mitchell was taking a spacious black hat on which the wings of a glossy blackbird were trimly spread in flight. Standing before the mirror she carefully put on the hat.

Even he could see it was an important hat. She turned and smiled with her old elegant brilliance. 'I'm wearing it to London as soon as Mr. Mitchell is buried. My sister is married to a publican there . . . Do you like it?' she asked in that flattering way that had always nourished him and made him feel that he was a full-size man of opinions.

A MAN IN HASTE

Even in Pardoe Street, where a swarm of the valley's rougher population lived, Sundays usually passed mildly and without public mishap. Though judged elsewhere to be neither morally nor materially a good street, its hardest critics admitted it was not entirely without virtues; two or three of its families were of chapel-going habits, and five of its men were members of a well-known Male Voice Party that, singing in strict white collars, had raised money for charities and also won several prizes at those eisteddfods which so busily foster art. It was adjacent—and therefore was sombre on another account—to the Bwlch coal-pits, with a bruised swirl of mountain rising beyond and very enticing to thunderous clouds.

But one October Sunday morning the street's atmosphere, at least to any sensitive visitor familiar with the usual placidity, undoubtedly contained an alien disturbance. Perhaps this was because men residents came out of their little dark houses much earlier than was their wont on this day of sloth and, squatting on their heels against the walls, conferred mysteriously with each other. And if the visitor had gone round to the backs he would have seen wives, grave of aspect, gossiping with neighbours at nearly every fence dividing the so-called gardens. All voices were on the whispering note. But for the fact that people were never buried on a Sunday anyone would have thought that the funeral of a beloved resident had just set out.

Voices went on bandying such information as up to the moment was available. One house at the top of the street was the subject under discussion. Or, rather, its tenants were—Bryn and Alice, married little more than two years and therefore not as yet solidly welded beyond the strength of the devil's interfering arm.

It had all begun exceptionally enough. The previous night, at about eight o'clock, Bryn had entered the Golden Harp pub at the bottom of the slope. Though at first he kept quiet, men noticed there was thunder and lightning in his face. It was a one-bar pub patronised mostly by Pardoe Street men and therefore almost a club. Bryn bought a pint without greeting anyone and stood staring fixedly at the Battle of Waterloo engraving framed over the mantelpiece. Luther Evans addressed him. 'No choir-practice tonight, Bryn?' he enquired in surprise. For Bryn was a valued tenor of the Male Voice Party, and every Saturday, from seven to nine, Pennsylvania Bowen, the conductor, who was a celebrated martinet, kept them sweating at some oratorio or the Miscellaneous Pieces of the repertoire.

Still glowering at the picture, Bryn gave no reply. His swarthy demeanour did not deter Luther, who testily repeated his question, adding: 'A tongue dipped in beer wakes up, they say.' So far there were only a dozen men in the bar.

'Pennsylvania's got 'flu,' grunted Bryn surlily. 'I went down to the Institute and found a notice to say: "No practice tonight".'

'No matter to sulk about, is it?' suggested Arthut Lewis. 'Cheer up, sing to us by here you can, instead.'

'I'll sing the hairs off your bloody heads!' suddenly snarled Bryn, creating a severe silence. He himself broke it by banging his pot on the counter and shouting to Mrs. Saunders: 'Drinks for everybody. No one else is going to spend a penny in this pub tonight.' And under everybody's startled eyes he took from the hip pocket of his grey flannel trousers a thick wad of pound notes clased with an elastic band. 'You start with a port for yourself, Mrs. Saunders; you're going to be busy.'

All that money! The customers looked dumbfounded, even shocked. But in such circumstances men do not question the source of their pleasure. Others entered the bar and were instantly received by Bryn as valued guests. Rumour, especially when on lucky errands, can travel with magical speed, and it was not long before the room was packed, nearly all being Pardoe Street tenants and all of the male sex naturally, hard workers engaged in the Bwlch pits.

True, perplexed enquiries were whispered now and again. Had Bryn got religious mania and taken out all his savings from the Post Office to give away? Had he won a Pool prize (but surely he would have announced this)? Been left money by an uncle who had owned a shop or a farm somewhere? He shouted, he sang (when the drink worked), he blustered. But not a word about the meaning of all this.

An even stranger action developed. Bryn took to handling out whole pound notes to selected individuals. 'Here, Ivor,' he said to one, 'you want to get a bit of paint on the front of your house, don't you? Heard that old ape of a skinflint won't do it for you.' He was referring to Joseph, the landlord of nearly every Pardoe Street house. Another tenant got a pound to 'repair those leaky slate tiles,' another got two towards buying a new cistern. Bryn seemed to be using the remissions of the hard landlord as tactful excuse to press a note on neighbours. The greater part of the money must have been handed out in this way, more than a score of Joseph's tenants benefiting. What with the processions of pint-pots as well, the whole wad of notes had changed hands before closing time. There must have been well over fifty pounds in that wad.

Oddly enough, there was only half-hearted competition for the pound-note gifts. No doubt this was because of something peculiar in Bryn's manner, something which couldn't be assessed. Was there a bitter ring in his tenor voice, so finely sweet in many a Handel anthem? Did the red under-glow in his dark eyes rise from drink? But though he drank a very good share, he didn't get drunk. He seemed to be upheld by a power that kept at bay the mischief of drink, which can undo a man by creating either unlovely arrogance or sore distress.

Congratulations on a champion evening were showered on him. The men's instinctive delicacy did not allow direct enquiry: not one of them knew clearly in his mind, but all felt that Bryn had been celebrating a private occasion which was not necessarily of hilarious flavour.

'Bryn, we'll give it all back to you when the Christmas clubs pay out,' someone told him, thumping his back on the road outside, which was black as the roads of hell. They all climbed the slope of Pardoe Street together. A chill air came down from the old rough-haired mountains. The others sang unfettered: Bryn was silent, and retained his carriage as he mounted the hill. Reaching Pardoe Steet, one by one they fell out and went in pleasantly to their hearths. To those wives who were without rebuke husbands related the strange occurrence in the Golden Harp; and many a pound note was honestly handed over. Doors were bolted for the night.

But residents were not settled many minutes beside their cosy fires when a clamour broke the silence of the road outside. As was usual in Pardoe Street, where Saturday night domestic disputes tended to become public, people at once came out, as if at first to examine the night's weather.

At the top of the street Bryn was turning his wife Alice, who was pretty but of frivolous disposition, out of their home. He flung her out like an old sack. With shouts of abuse. These she answered with howls which could have been of rage or despair, or both. But though people listened closely, no factual reason for the ejectment could be collected from the out-pouring. Bryn certainly called her hackneyed names to which through the ages women must have become accustomed. From other statements the listeners gathered that he was ordering her back to her mother, who lived five miles down the valley. And by that time the trams had stopped.

He slammed his door violently. She banged on it for a minute and then, while the listeners quickly withdrew into their dwellings, she hurried through the street, wailing. She had never really been accepted into the bosom of the street, though Bryn was liked well enough. After this the night closed down undisturbed.

'Perhaps,' suggested Llew Watkins, squatting outside a neighbour's house the next morning, 'Bryn will come and ask us today for those pound notes back. Perhaps in a trance he was, last night in the pub, and thought himself the King of Persia.'

Over the back fence one wife said to another: 'She washes on a Wednesday, if washing you can call it. Judging by what was hanging on her line last time, no shape there is in her ways. She dolls up her face even on a Monday, and it won't do, not for married women. Thinks of nothing but the pictures and silk stockings.'

By the time the church bell began to toll, no one was nearer the exact explanation of last night's events. Llew Watkins went off up to his hut on the mountain-side where he kept a vicious old billy-goat that had been famous in his time. Others went to their pigeon-coops or chicken-runs: two set out to exercise their whippets. The few who still gave the streets its bit of tone went to chapel. At two o'clock Mrs. Lewis, who lived next door to Bryn, knocked at his door with a plate of hot meat and vegetables carried under her apron— 'A pity for a man to go without his Sunday dinner,' she said later. Opening the door after a delay, Bryn bore every evidence of having just risen from his bed, flannel trousers hastily drawn on. She hovered about for a while, making remarks, but nothing could be gained from him, though he accepted the plate.

At about four o'clock the two or three people hanging about their doorways saw Joseph the landlord enter the street. This was unusual. He always collected all his rents on a Saturday afternoon. But no doubt someone had promised to pay today instead, and he was a tight one for his weekly money, was Joseph. Thick-skinned and full-cheeked as a football, his neckless head wobbled on top of a hefty body. People said he could be a tough customer.

But this afternoon he walked into the street on one leg, so to speak, as if the other didn't want to arrive. One eye seemed to pop here and there suspiciously, while the other remained fixed in cunning determination. He hadn't become a rich man by sitting at home twiddling his thumbs. Under his arm he carried a brown paper parcel.

When he stopped at Bryn's door the few onlookers blinked their eyes with a start. Perhaps it was by occult divination that, after Joseph's rat-tat, more inquisitive persons appeared out of their residences. And at Bryn's loud exclamation when he opened the door they drew nearer to the dramatic house.

'Ha, there you are, you—' The something or other which Bryn called his landlord was lost amid his bellow.

Still more doors opened. And Bryn, strutting on his doorstep, plunged at once into warfare. No, he'd be damned if Joseph should come into the house—for the landlord, glancing back furtively at his collecting tenants, had moved as if for admittance—no, not while he had a couple of fists ready to knock anybody into the middle of next week or over that falling-down chimney-pot opposite, that was a disgrace to the street, see!

For a moment they measured each other. Both were more or less of the same short, thick build, except that Bryn was youngly muscular while Joseph ran to fat. The landlord had seemed incommoded by his welcome. But he bucked and bridled now. 'Your missus I want to see, not you!' he shouted. 'She's been repairing my old trousers for me and lent me these instead.' He held out the parcel.

'Repairing your trousers, you bandy old scooter, you!' yelled Bryn.

An unusual scene then ensued. Stepping off his doorstep, and in full view of the street, Bryn whipped off the dark grey flannel trousers he was wearing and flung them at Joseph's feet. Then he snatched the parcel, tore it open, and pulled on the pair it contained; they also were of dark grey flannel. Buttoning up and glaring, he shouted: 'Satisfied? You've got yout trousers, haven't you, and I've got mine. Now you get off!' And he pointed aggressively down the street.

'Wait a minute!' squealed Joseph in anguish. He had felt into the hip pocket of the pair flung at him. 'Where's what was in it?'

Then suddenly it seemed as if Bryn's dancing fury left him. He looked at the landlord with a bitter jeer, a ferocious contempt. 'You want it back, do you!' he said. 'Man alive, if you was in London they'd cost you much more than that. Those countesses and janes on the pictures. Fur coats and jewels, hundreds of pounds! You get off now before I lose patience.'

It was Joseph who then showed fury. But it was empty fury, with a lot of frenzied fist-shaking and threats of police action. Bryn stood square in his doorway with his jeer of contempt. The little crowd, in that way of crowds when the raw stuff of life is displayed, had got nearer still. Of course, everybody was glad to see the hard landlord taken down a peg or two, though it was still not quite clear exactly how this had come about.

'You'll be hearing more of this!' shouted Joseph, with a last shake of his fist. Picking up the trousers, he thrust his way through the crowd with threatening mutters.

'You'll think twice about it,' bawled Bryn after him, assurance in his voice.

'What's it all about, Bryn?' asked Arthur Lewis in a soothing way. 'We was all here to see if you wanted help with the gentleman,' he added insidiously.

From his doorstep Bryn addressed them with some dignity, still standing proud in his doorway: 'A single man I am again; gone for ever *she* has . . . This is how it was. I went down to the choir-practice same as usual yesterday, but there wasn't any. So I came back home. Nearly dark it was by then. No one there was downstairs and I thought she'd gone down to the shops. I went into the back kitchen and helped myself to a bit of bread and cheese. I thought I heard someone on the stairs, but didn't take any notice. Wearing my best blue suit I was, and after combing a drip or two of water in my hair I went upstairs to our bedroom to change into these flannels that old fox brought back today, so as to go down to the pub.' The bitter note hardened his voice again. 'I see a pair of trousers hanging from the pegs behind the door, where mine always are, and puts them on. But they didn't seem to fit quite right and I began to feel round 'em . . .' His eyes became righteous. 'Blow me if I didn't find a wad of pound notes in the back pocket thick as a hymn-book.' That righteous gaze swept the closely listening crowd, most of them men who worked with him down in the pits, and he finished: 'See?'

'By damn, yes,' said Edgar Watkins, who had the quivering nose of a ferret. 'Tut, tut, the old cuckoo of a rent-collector!' he added, severely.

Yet one or two of the others, perhaps because their minds were like the driven snow, still seemed puzzled. Emlyn Jones spoke quite testily: 'Excuse me, seeing it I am not.'

Bryn then said, glassily clear: 'A man in haste, and with no candle lit, makes mistakes. That old stoat it was I heard on the stairs.'

'But where was *she*?' impatiently asked Mrs. Olwen Richards, one of the few wives in the crowd. 'Under the bed?'

'I never thought to look.' The shock of the discovery still lay black in Bryn's face. 'So upset I was. I just thought she'd crept out too till the dust settled. So I went down to the Golden Harp and blew all the money. See?'

With that he turned, went in, and slammed the door. It was clear that on the whole he still wished to be private with this episode that had altered his life. There were loud exclamations of condemnation of Joseph, of sympathy for Bryn and approval of his conduct. The women thought that Alice must have been living rent-free for some time; with wages in the pit what they were, face-cream, scents and silk-stockings could not have been obtained otherwise. The men felt justified in retaining their pound notes, to be used in much-needed house repairs. And they prayed that all this would be a reminder to Joseph that just because he was a rich man he couldn't walk into a decent street and behave like that without paying for it dearly.

TOMORROW

'Today!' smiled Miss Sadler, stopping a moment to touch the oak tree's bark, 'today!'

At her approach two jays had fled in sharp-eyed brilliance to a wild cherry tree up the glade. She looked at them in affection. This was a haunt of jays, as it was of hers, and they had known each other for long: she did not share the country people's hatred for these thieving beauties of orchard and garden, she only knew them as gay-plumaged witnesses of her daily happiness. 'Vermin,' the hard-worked landlady of the Loaded Shovel would curse them, making Miss Sadler flutter her slight, exquisitely-kept hands in deprecation.

She strode on down the wide lane, in her spick-and-span brogues and suit of fine greenish tweeds, an unnecessary walking-stick in hand. A country-living lady abounding with rhythmical health. Hatless, her vivid silver-spun mass of hair sprang clean as the sunshine; there was a steady light, fresh and optimistic, in her grey eyes—eyes that were arrestingly, piercingly clear. When she came to another oak—the one near the old inn drowsing inside its rose-red garden—she touched that too with her finger-tips. And said: 'Today!'

On the garden lawn in front of the Loaded Shovel a lean middle-aged woman was spreading a washed quilt over a chair, to catch the afternoon sun. She replied to Miss Sadler's greeting glumly; she had the manner of a woman who toils ceaselessly in her house and finds little reward. For her the 'picturesque' inn, visited only erratically by motorists and hikers, was a place of draughty chimneys, beetle-infested floors, and black-beamed low ceilings conducive to bad temper.

'And how is your mother today?' Miss Sadler sang, in such a manner that surely any physical ailment must seem bearable on such a hopeful day as this.

'Oh, just the same,' replied Mrs. Leach, still grudging.

Miss Sadler glanced at her watch. 'Would you like me to run up to see her? I've just a few minutes to spare.'

But Mrs. Leach made an excuse. Her mother was sleeping, and if she was woken she would fret for this and that, and grumble, and be restless. The daughter's voice trailed away irritably. Perhaps she was ashamed of what she had been obliged to do to her mother. For two years the old lady, aged seventy-eight, had been securely tied to her bed with ropes.

'Oh well, never mind,' said Miss Sadler. And it was as if she forced a little of the radiance out of her face. 'You mustn't take it to heart too much, Mrs.

146

Leach. Your mother has had a long and useful life, hasn't she?' Then, without pause, she said: 'I'm expecting my fiancé with the five-fifteen train today.'

'Oh yes?' said Mrs. Leach, uninterested. Her eye was on her husband, who had come out of a shed beyond the garden gate with a wire cage dangling from his hand. 'Have you caught one?' she called, a half-scolding, half-whining note in her voice now. Mr. Leach came towards them. A live rat, large but petrified, crouched in the cage. Miss Sadler gave a little cry. But Mrs. Leach began to bristle into ferocity, exclaiming as she peered: 'The devil . . . That snout! I'll give you snout.' Peculiarly and obsessively mad, she shook her fist at the terrified beast huddled in the corner of the cage, and turned to the shrinking Miss Sadler: 'I saw it with my own eyes one night, there was a full moon, I saw it walking on its hind legs out of the hen-coop holding up an egg in its front paws, for all the world like a child with a balloon!'

'Perhaps it wasn't this one,' said her husband. He was a rather disconsolate-faced man who suggested an obstinate stupidity which perhaps was due to a need for retaliation, and also an indefinable kindliness if only he was allowed to be kind. Something had gone wrong in his relationship with the world. His wife said he was bone-lazy; in her milder moments she said this was due to 'his funny glands'.

'I *recognise* the rat,' she exclaimed. 'Besides, it *looks* guilty . . . Where's Pete?' She looked round for their young dog. 'Pete, Pete!' she shouted. 'Where's he gone? Never here when he's wanted.'

'Best drown it,' said Mr. Leach uncertainly. He himself seemed to be crouching a little from his wife's wrath.

'*Drown it!* Pete must have it. He must get a taste of them.' She looked in sudden withering contempt at her husband. 'Anybody would think you'd like to make a pet of the brute. You look ashamed of yourself for catching it—'

Yet she too was at heart a kindly woman, and when there was woe in a village family she was the first to rush up with aid and sympathy. Miss Sadler drew away, unobtrusively, tactfully, and resumed her two-mile walk to the railway station, stepping out with decision, and observantly, those clear and steady eyes missing nothing. She knew every tree and bush, almost every stone, in the lane. And, once again, she stopped to touch a young oak growing beside a field gate: and, smiling, said aloud: 'Today!' The air smelt of meadow-sweet, clover and sun. In a field of wheat myriads of poppies drew a silkily taut strength out of the sun's splendour, each flower burning erect. The silver afternoon sparkled; the wheat ears stood packed with their fine-spun fruit.

There was time to call at Bill Tanner's tumbledown cottage, just off the lane. She wanted to give Mrs. Tanner a little box of glass beads for her crippled

147

young daughter. The poor child's left leg had a tubercular disease. Mrs. Tanner, a tough woman with a philosophic manner, accepted the box, as she had accepted all the other compassionate gifts, with her usual stolidity. There seemed no need at all for Miss Sadler's tender note of sympathy as she asked about Phyllis's state today.

'She's been behaving very annoyed and cross,' said Mrs. Tanner. 'Threw her crutch at her Dad after dinner.'

'Oh dear, oh dear,' Miss Sadler fluttered, 'how trying for you! . . . Never mind, my dear,' she comforted simply, woman to woman, and classless in distress. And at the cottage door she couldn't help saying, so eager was her wish to share her delight: 'My fiancé is arriving with the five-fifteen today.' Mrs. Tanner said nothing, and the visitor hastened away among the fruit trees, helplessly dazzled in her perhaps undeserved contentment.

It was as if with such calls as these she wanted to do penance for enjoying such luck. Luck of purse and heart. There were days when she would make detours to other houses stricken by some calamity or other.

Although there was plenty of time left, her pace increased as she entered the miniature town. She passed swiftly through the main street of friendly little shops, genteel cafés, smartened geranium-hung residential inn and busy garage; she nodded formally to some vague acquaintances, smiled fully at other passers-by. Among the shoppers and visitors she was outstanding with her youngly joyous face and curly silver mass of hair. Her cheerfulness was so straightforward, clear cut, and not to be hampered by doubts. But also it was controlled: it gave her a poise which did not jar on other people. Anyone could see that Miss Sadler was held in liking and respect.

The railway station, which smelt of fish and wallflowers, served several villages; three buses waited empty in the yard. She had many minutes to spare, but, with a smile at the young porter, she passed briskly on to the empty platform and sat on a bench. There, alone in the purring sunshine, she began to assume the private look of a woman who is shut into a completely tranquil dream which she savours in serene isolation. A woman with such orderly inner resources of strength that she could concentrate on a reverie for long periods without a single distracting movement.

The click of the signal roused her. The porter strolled to the platform, followed by a hot, perspiring woman wearing, remarkably, a bulky fur coat— oh, what strange things people did!—and who was tugged by an annoyed-looking dog on a lead. The porter patted the dog, and the woman exclaimed, panting but voluble: 'You wouldn't think he had a serious operation a fortnight ago, would you? . . . For gall-stones!' she cried, quite triumphatnly.

'Now he's strong as a wolf again, but I expect he thinks I'm taking him to the dog's hospital for another . . . Bruce! Bruce! Lovely! Don't be frightened . . .'

Miss Sadler too gazed triumphantly at the dog that had come successfully through such tribulation. And the dog's attention was suddenly arrested by the silver-haired woman's clear, steady gaze; perfectly still, he looked back into her eyes intently for a moment—and then gave a low, sullen growl, slackening the lead as he backed.

'Bruce, Bruce, now then!' his mistress scolded. To Miss Sadler she explained: 'He's all right, really. But he's had a serious operation, and perhaps he thinks you're the nurse at the hospital—she had hair just like yours.' The dog growled more menacingly when Miss Sadler, oblivious to him now, rose from the bench. The train was bustling round the bend.

She took up a position near the platform barrier. Doors swung back, slammed again. Oh, what a lot of people returning today! Most of them glanced at her as they passed through the gate: her own gaze skimmed over them swift as a clear-flying bird. A man greeted the fur-coated woman with a rough kiss. The porter stood collecting tickets at the barrier. The train began to glide from the emptying platform.

Away down the stone length a man carrying a portfolio, a town black hat and a neatly folded newspaper walked leisurely, almost tiredly, towards her. The last passenger. Youngish and darkly elegant, he seemed preoccupied, the decisive business-man's manner relaxed. There was even a fugitive suggestion of a sleepwalker in his unemphatic gait; the narrow face, pale and tired, seemed unaware. She took one step forward, a brief instinctive pace, those grey untroubled eyes full on him.

He passed her. His head bent slightly, the oblique glance he gave her seemed to hold a veiled sorrow. He went through the gate, passed into the shadows cast by the overhanging roof of the booking-hall, and vanished into the bright sunlight of the road beyond. She did not turn.

She stood there for some seconds. A petal of deep colour burned on either cheek. But otherwise she might have been a woman who was plunged into calmly puzzled thought, lightly frowning over a missed appointment. Then, her fingers gripping the stick sharply, she turned and walked out of the station as briskly as she had arrived. The young porter touched his cap to her.

She smiled at him with her quick, benevolent, feudal smile.

Mrs. Hathaway was always glad to see Miss Sadler, and this evening she felt in a particularly affable mood. There was something winking, even sly, in her round, hen-black eye. But her moods, like her physical condition, were incalculable. During Miss Sadler's last visit she had angrily demanded her to untie the ropes so that she could go down to the bar to 'see what was going on in the damn world.' This evening she seemed to have no objection to the four lengths fixed to her ankles and wrists and tied to the bed-posts. There was just enough latitude of rope to allow her full movement in the huge feather bed, and not an inch beyond it.

'I've brought you a bag of chocolate-creams,' Miss Sadler said.

The old lady gave an anticipatory gurgle, like a chuckle. 'Ah, my dear, you're a kind girl. I often tell Delia, if there were more lassies in the world like Miss Sadler . . . Who's the noisy bunch out on the lawn?' she demanded. 'They sound cheap. There's a girl with a laugh like a mare's.'

'They're very smartly dressed,' said Miss Sadler, putting a chocolate into the old lady's mouth, 'and they've got a lovely car. I think one of the young ladies has taken that new house above Fox's Gap.' She sat down close to the bed. With that benign quality of being a nurse to a whole race, she seemed not to mind the oppressive odour of a bed never left to air, or the rankly-hot sixteenth-century room with the lattice always resolutely closed.

'It's time there were some well-off customers,' champed Mrs. Hathaway. 'Trade's been shocking all the summer. Poor Delia, she keeps on worrying, but I say to her: "Well, what if you were tied to a bed like me?—count your blessings, drat you, even if that dried-up crow of a man you married isn't one of them".' She could be a rude, and even bawdy, old woman, and she hated her son-in-law.

'I've been to the station,' Miss Sadler said. 'I expected my fiancé with the five-fifteen, but he didn't catch it after all.'

'Ah! . . . Expect he's been kept busy in town.' Mrs. Hathaway swallowed the chocolate-cream with a gurgle. 'One of these days you *must* bring your young man to see me . . . I'll tell him,' she proclaimed, 'I'll tell him what a treasure he''s got . . . I bet,' she began to smoulder, 'he won't turn out like that lump my Delia married.' She peeped conspiratorially at the visitor. 'Proud as a turkey-cock, I'll go bail on that, *and* a sweet gentleman?' She sounded enticing, saying this, coaxing. 'Handsome enough, I'll be bound, to warm up even my old innards?'

'Anthony *is* attractive,' admitted Miss Sadler, a little deprecatingly, since in her milieu male good looks were not dwelt upon.

'Tell me, tell me,' egged the old lady. 'I like to hear of 'em still going on in the world . . . Does he kiss nice?' she dared.

Miss Sadler ignored the direct question, yet seemed very willing to proceed with the subject. Her delicately restless white hands, harmonious in their movements, made graphic gestures as she talked, the gestures of a woman imaginatively living her recital. The sapphire of her engagement ring caught the peach-red gleams of sunshine piercing the window.

'He's quite tall, and walks so nicely . . . unhurried but with a lively little spring in his step . . . But I like his voice best,' she smiled, clasping her nervous fingers, unclasping them; 'it's so low and sweet and *real*; he speaks like . . . like a young man who's at peace with himself.'

The old lady gave a full chuckle, like a duck's; her sly eye definitely winked; the fat body heaved. 'Ah, I *know*, my dear. I do like a voice that makes one itch like that! . . . At night, in the dark, whatever the rest of 'em is like, the way they say it counts more than anything—you see if it don't!'

Miss Sadler actually blushed, the pink face incongruously young under the silver but vital hair. But still she did not seem really distressed, and she resumed her own train of thought: 'And no one can carry an umbrella just like he does . . . Open or closed,' she laughed tinklingly. 'I love sharing his umbrella, I could walk for miles in the pouring rain with him.'

'You're healthy, dear,' judged the old lady, in a profound tone, 'you can take pleasure in things . . . Bah,' she began to smoulder again, '*you*'ll never turn sour: I can tell. And that's saying something.' The ankle ropes were tugged right, as if she vindictively clapped her feet together under the quilt.

'But all people change. Sometimes I wonder if in middle age Anthony won't show some sort of failing: he seems almost too perfect.' But, as if she couldn't really believe them, she smiled at her qualms.

'Don't worry about it now, my dear,' warbled Mrs. Hathaway. 'Enjoy yourself, enjoy yourself while the going's good. When I was courting I used to love it when my bloke had a belly-ache, I *loved* his belly-ache, and when he had a nasty boil on his neck.'

'Oh, I am enjoying myself tremendously. And Anthony is always so cheerful himself, such a high-spirited disposition . . . He's doing very well in his work,' she added, nodding like a woman outside the mysteries of business but confidently aware of success in it. 'He is to be junior partner soon.'

'What business is it?' asked the old lady, promptly inquisitive.

'Spices.' Miss Sadler laughed. 'He smells a little of cinnamon sometimes, it's quite delightful. And he never catches a cold—they say that working in a spices warehouse keeps one free of colds.'

Their conversation had the sound of following a familiar routine. Mrs. Hathaway's questions and remarks seemed expected, like the visitor's readiness to dwell on her lover's advantages: they were like confederates enclosed in a circle of secret understanding. The sly bed-imprisoned old lady, feeding tirelessly on the other's pouring out of her enchantment, went on asking highly personal questions to which Miss Sadler replied with a ready but decent eagerness. On the lawn below, younger and crisper voices laughed in holiday carelessness, though there was one feminine voice that was discordant as a peacock's— 'No class *there*,' Mrs. Hathaway paused to remark. 'Sounds as if she's getting tipsy.'

'Just pop another chocolate-cream in my mouth, will you dear?' This done, the old lady resumed effortlessly: 'It does me good to see a girl in love full-strength with her sweetheart. Nowadays half of them seem to begrudge a man his right to 'em . . . Not that some of the women hasn't cause,' she heaved again, tugging the ropes taut.

'Oh, why *do* so many marriages go wrong?' Miss Sadler looked blank in the mystery, as though never, never would she understand it.

'Count the pebbles on the shore,' grinned Mrs. Hathaway. But her visitor, the grandfather clock below the stairs striking seven, rose with surprising abruptness and flurry. 'Come to see me soon again. I do enjoy hearing about your young man.' She accepted the sudden haste without remark. 'You're a comfort to me,' she said, but sank oppressed into the bed as if deflated.

'I must go at once,' exclaimed Miss Sadler. 'Oh, dear!' And she stopped a moment to smile down benevolently on the corpulent old lady who had been bound so drastically to her bed for two years. Alive and strong, with her unquenched face, she patted the old lady's dropsical shoulder with something like gratitude. 'I enjoy talking about him too: thank you for listening. But I shall be locked out!' Miss Sadler laughed, running to the door.

Mrs. Leach, dressed for the evening session, and standing by the table with a bottle of gin in her hand, called out a farewell to her. Miss Sadler hurriedly waved a hand in return, passed into the lane, and strode alertly upwards.

'Who *is* that, Mrs. Leach? I've seen her before.'

The four customers, two young women and two young men, had paused to look at the woman who passed, so handsomely self-contained, across the lawn: instinctively their voices had fallen silent. In their coloured linen trousers and sports shirts, which both sexes wore, they gave a centre rainbow splash to the lawn. Though it was difficult to tell which was married to which, so hilariously gregarious were they, Mrs. Leach knew that the young lady who asked the question was Mrs. Lambert, the newcomer to the district; she had been down so often from Fox's Gap to fetch bottles of gin and rum.

'That,' said Mrs. Leach readily, 'is Miss Sadler. She's up at The Towers.'

Mrs. Lambert jerked her head aside, swinging her deep gold hair, and she stared with careful inscrutability at a rose-bush: something unacceptable to her might have been mentioned. The young woman they called Judy—she too wore a wire-thin wedding-ring—remarked: 'What wonderful hair she has.'

'They say,' said Mrs. Leach, 'it turned white in a month. When she was twenty-five. She must be about sixty now.'

'Surely not?' the plump young man idly said, snapping his fingers at Pete, who, playful after his meal of rat, was running round the lawn as if in pursuit of a dream one. 'Her face is quite young.'

Mrs. Leach, casually and entirely without compassion, said: 'She goes to the railway station every day to meet the five-fifteen train. She goes to meet the fiancé, as she calls him.'

'And he's never there?' said Judy, bright and light-lipped as a brittle pink columbine.

Mrs. Leach nodded, and went on baldly: 'She used to live over at Britwell, seven or eight miles from here. Her young man lived in that part too. He used to travel to the City every morning . . . Then one week he had to go to the North of England on business, and the day he was due back he was supposed to arrive with that five-fifteen train—' As though he wanted to cut off this bleak recital, the slight nervous young man—he looked like a bruised faun— held up his glass for another gin, and Mrs. Leach, still holding the bottle as if in prudence, poured into a brass measure. Mrs. Lambert frowned, and at last Mrs. Leach decided he was her husband.

'And the fiancé wasn't on the five-fifteen?' said Judy, in her quick, experienced voice. 'Had he jilted her, eloped with someone else? His typist?'

Mrs. Leach shook her head. 'No . . . There had been a terrible accident to the train he was travelling in from the North: a lot of people were killed. Miss Sadler waited for the next train after that five-fifteen one, and then the next two, till at last the station-master got news of the accident up North and mentioned it to her on the platform.'

Mrs. Lambert looked about her uncertainly: she seemed bored and ready to go. She shivered in her thin shirt: a little evening breeze had sprung up under the sun's last scarlet. 'Her young man was killed?' she said in a concise way, adding: 'Well, she must have been an unbalanced woman before that.'

'Or far too much in love with him?' Judy said, and looked at Mrs. Leach encouragingly.

'No doubt,' said Mrs. Leach. 'But you see, it wasn't only the shock of his being killed.' She paused again, but dramatically now, so that even Mrs. Lambert sat back. 'It was when his remains didn't turn up that she became like she is . . . There was a muddle. The coffin was supposed to arrive a few days after the accident, and by that same train, the five-fifteen: it was going to be buried the next morning in St. John's Church up there on the hill. They say Miss Sadler intended to sit up all night with the corpse, and no one could stop her going to meet the coffin on that train: she was there with a bunch of snowdrops—it was February, you see. But there was that awful muddle, and there was no coffin . . . not with that train or the next . . . not never!' At this

153

Mrs. Leach lifted her face with some pride: the story might have been her own.

'Oh . . . why?' asked the plump young man, idly scratching his suburnt arm, freckled like butcher's brawn.

'Well, you see, what they had thought was Miss Sadler's young man wasn't him—someone else had claimed the remains. Nothing arrived for Miss Sadler to weep over all night; she was left quite alone, as you might say.'

Mrs. Leach had told the tale in the Loaded Shovel several times before: she had even come to look upon Miss Sadler as a valuable possession of the district—and even, obscurely a woman to be envied . . . As she finished, Judy dropped her head with a sigh on the plump young man's shoulder, and he grinned down on her with the beautiful exhibitionary fatuity of early bliss: they looked as if they could linger for hours in the evening garden among the roses and the damson trees.

But Mrs. Lambert got up with a jerk from the table. 'She looked happy enough,' she commented. 'Come on, you two: that chicken's got to be put in the oven.' The worn faun-like young man jumped and suddenly gave vent to a shrill, sexless, bodiless laugh: it was the laugh Mrs. Hathaway had commented on upstairs. 'They're both coots,' he yelped; 'drunken crazies.' His odd skin-tight little face was squeezed up with something like fury. He fled light as a zephyr across the lawn, leapt into the car with a squirrel's jump, and sat there bolt upright peering out of his slitted eye-sockets, like an animal in a cage.

Mrs. Leach ignored the interruption. Taking a pound note from Mrs. Lambert, she said: 'Oh yes, Miss Sadler is quite happy. She's well off, they say, and after her parents died she went to live in The Towers, and they all love her there. We get the nurses in here sometimes. It's a wonderfully comfortable place from all accounts, everything modern, and the best attention for people like her.'

She did indeed seem undisturbedly content as she walked with such a quick and steady rhythm past the glade where the jays flew in sharp brilliance. In the high distance beyond the trees could be seen, ethereally palatial as a fairy-tale castle against the sunset, a close-packed Gothic pile of turrets, dark towers and spires. There were three wayside oaks in the mile to the gates, and Miss Sadler touched each one with her finger-tips, and with each touch she said: 'Tomorrow.'

THE FOOLISH ONE

I

That summer she would sit day after day at the open lattice, her eyelids blue, her mouth scarlet, her bay-copper hair dazzlingly burnished, and wait in a dreamy reverie for the dusk. The occasional drivers who noticed her always glanced twice at that face in the cottage window above the pretty garden opening unexpectedly beside this lonely road, with the beech-woods closing round again. From the road the painted face had a remote and even rather stupid look of vacancy, doll-like. It never seemed to return a glance.

Johanna often did sink into a mysterious open-eyed stupor. The sunshine was hot and perpetual that summer. For two or three hours before sitting at the window she amused herself washing in lotions, making up, arranging her beautiful hair in different styles, and admiring the handsome contours of her breasts, which, while she uttered a delighted little whinny, she would caress and pinch at the nipples. But all this used up so little of the long, silent afternoons. They never seemed to end.

Only that summer had she vaguely begun to realise that her life was becoming vexatious.

After her husband, William, left her, eighteen months ago, she had not for the first year felt inconvenienced by all the ensuing peace and silence. Not only was she soothed by the novelty of being an idle woman with a bit of means—she who had worked hard in the drapery trade since she was fifteen—but the drama of the separation nourished her for quite a while. And there were the front and back gardens to tend, there was her correspondence, and also her temporary lodger, Miss Munro, the village schoolmistress.

Marriage, she decided, had badly let her down; it was a fraud if you judged it by the standard of what went on in the head when you were a girl or what shook you when you saw someone on the pictures or read something in a book. She had always pictured men as magnificent creatures whose behaviour, both physical and spiritual, was fraught with powerful incident. But after marriage she found William what she called to Miss Munro 'independent'.

In her fireside talks with the schoolmistress, who, apart from her profession, was of emancipated character and had sown quite a lot of new ideas in her mind, Johanna said she thought herself a full-blooded woman who could enjoy life 'up to the hilt'; she could fully understand a love-murder or suicide. But William seemed not to have any blood in him at all, and she judged that

155

on the whole, men would always grieve women. Miss Munro asked her how many men she had really known, and this both cornered her and projected a sudden promising light into her confusion. But she sighed: 'William is paying my allowance on condition that I live chastely—as that lawyer put it, though I'm sure it was William's old cat of a mother made him put in that clause.'

From the first his mother had declared he was marrying beneath him, which was true if too much notice is taken of the different sets of manners and personal habits. He had picked up Johanna in a café in the country town where she served in a store and 'lived in' above the premises, her only relative being an uncle living at the other end of England. She felt very attracted to his saturnine appearance—surely beneath it dark wells of passion lay sealed?—to his big sprawling body, loose and needing to be made alert by a fervent woman's worship. A bout of male rebelliousness must have been working in him, or, as she thought afterwards, a fit of sulks against his mother; he had hustled her into marriage after only two months of what seemed to her a promising, nervous courtship. Presented to his mother a fortnight before the register-office marriage, Johanna never forgot the widow's swollen, silent face, like a red tea-cosy. William was her only child and she had always believed him to be sickly and made him sleep under an eiderdown quilt even in summer.

His mother's first hostile act had been to ask for a return of the purchase money of the car which was necessary for his work, and he had to promise the cash in instalments. Fortunately he was prospering. He was an agent for farming implements, and, wonderfully alive when he talked of machines and new mechanical inventions, his territory was being extended. In the car he and Johanna found the cottage a dozen miles from his mother's house, furnished it hastily, and moved in an hour after the cold wedding.

He hadn't been well that day, and he cancelled by telephone the room in the grand London hotel where they were to spend three honeymoon days. He complained of stomach cramp. It made him crotchety. In bed he said the cottage was damp. She nestled up to him crooning and warming his poor stricken stomach with her own abundance—they had neglected to buy both eiderdown and hot-water bottle. She had never imagined a young man could have such cold feet. Altogether he seemed to be chilly as a fish. But she, she would flood him with her warmth and regard. She had felt like a crusader.

During the following months she made industrious endeavours with antics, teasings, amorous whisperings, and crude challenges. He complained; very occasionally submitted weakly; took umbrage; and was for ever discovering some new physical distress. They began to bicker, for he, liverish or perhaps feeling guilty, accused her of neglecting the household work in favour of

156

slothful day-dreaming about matters unsuitable at a respectable domestic hearth. Healthy and ample, but feather-brained in her attitude to life, the constant reminder of the fact of her cosy vitality seemed positively to offend him.

If she had been clever, and not just a nicely silly woman, she would have got and kept him—or so Miss Munro thought—by pandering to his ailments and creating some of her own. Miss Munro said he sounded like one of those men that are passionate in gloom and only become alive at the sound of wails and in broodings on mortal decay. Perhaps he ought to have married a consumptive.

'No, it was only that mother of his,' said Johanna obstinately; 'she had wormed her way into him and he couldn't cast her out.'

Every month had become more disagreeable than the last. Constantly thwarted, she began to make fun of a sacred subject—his constipation. Though a big young man, with well-moulded if flaccid limbs, a childish whimper would come into his voice when his body failed to do its daily duty by him at a fixed time, 8.20 a.m. One morning he grizzled that his mother never missed a daily affectionate enquiry on the matter and this had somehow helped him. Johanna—and she was not given to taunts or jeers—replied tartly: 'So you're blaming it on me, are you? Well, I can't agree. It's because you don't take the natural exercise of a man.' After this coarseness he sulked for many days, even though Johanna, contrite and fundamentally nice, began to make regular morning enquiry as to his condition.

Their final quarrel was over China and India tea—he liked the first, which she found nauseous—and her flat refusal to continue to brew separate pots at breakfast; she had got up that morning feeling especially obstinate. He stamped out to the car after eating only a plate of bran, and he never came back: he had returned to his mother. Solicitors made contact with her, and he agreed finally to pay her £150 a year on condition that she lived in chastity. After spending hours in an abyss of heavy pondering she decided that the best away to repay his mother was to refuse the divorce William had at first suggested. Of course it was the mother who then retaliated with the chastity clause. William, she bitterly knew, could never have thought of it himself— such a matter just didn't exist for him, unless it was pushed aggressively under his nose.

'Considering,' said Miss Munro, 'what a passing amount of pleasure sex gives, it causes a very disproportionate amount of upsets and spite in life. I've often wondered why people make such a fuss of this subject.'

During the first year of the separation, so that the postman would call often, she wrote to numerous advertising firms for their catalogues, samples, or patterns, and she also corresponded with a 'pen friend' of the male sex that she obtained from a London 'friendship bureau'; he was an elderly cripple living in Glasgow and therefore quite safe even from her mother-in-law's spying; chastity couldn't be lost in the post. And there were the months when she lodged Miss Munro while her landlady in the village was in hospital after a serious operation. It was only after that year that the full malice of the condition of her allowance began to dawn on her.

'Women,' Miss Munro had said, 'are always victims unless they keep their wits everlastingly sharp. We need to depend more on our brains and less on our feelings.'

'I haven't got brains,' Johanna mourned. 'I'm a foolish one and all I need is a straightforward man who's lively.'

'William made you a victim,' said Miss Munro, 'and so did his mother . . . Be careful you don't get into a morbid state here. If I were you I would go back to the drapery.'

But she couldn't make that descending action to her old dead life. A dreamy inertia began to hold her. There was something to be concluded in this her present life. William had left her high and dry, had made her feel herself a failure, but she couldn't quite believe that he intended letting her remain in this unsatisfactory state of being a kept wife that he never used. Perhaps one dramatic evening he would walk in and say, with shamed face, that he had discovered his awful mistake; his mother was killing him . . . Oh, she would take him back and there would be a night of fire, her real wedding night, with William truly born at last. Miss Munro had told her how she thought it was with him, how there were men who were only half born, not released fully into the world.

Month followed month and nothing happened. After Miss Munro left, a heavy sluggishness began to oppress her. It sapped her will power. The cottage somehow imprisoned her, she had to force herself to go to the market town on the essential weekly shopping expedition. For days she did not open the letters from her Glasgow correspondent, though he had asked for her photograph and become quite endearing. She mooned about the stagnant house, stopping on occasion to realise that her loud remarks to herself or her cat bounded back on her emptily.

It was during the early summer that, after seeing a chemist's special window display in the market town, she bought a whole heap of cosmetics and began to amuse herself in altering and painting her face. Then she would recline on the sitting-room sofa and try to believe that a visitor, perhaps William himself, was on the way: it was said that if you wished hard enough, what you wanted sooner or later arrived. Soon she took to sitting at the open lattice. Why she sat there so long remained only a dim, unformulated idea in her listless mind. Certainly it was not likely that anything could happen on that dull road.

On an average not more than three vehicles—car, lorry, or motor-cycle—passed in an hour, and rarely a pedestrian. The obscure old road dawdled past the crooked-fenced garden, crawled up a hill between the woods, approached a couple of farms, erratically avoided a hamlet and a boys' reformatory home, crossed the quiet local railway and eventually, serving no very useful purpose, drifted into the bustling main road outside Apscombe, where a market was held on Wednesdays. The cottage stood a quiet half-mile from the village; there the bus from Apscombe, using a more important road, turned round again and, after seven o'clock, left the place to its severe thick-wooded evening silence.

II

On her twenty-fifth birthday she allowed herself a treat. She opened the bottle of expensive perfume the floor-walker of her department in the shop had given her for a wedding present, and that afternoon she sat at the open lattice in a swoonlike appreciation of the exotic odour rising generously from her bosom.

And that same afternoon it happened. Thinking it all over the next day she felt that it was no more than she justly deserved. She remembered Miss Munro saying something about a law of compensation always working in life. That it happened on her birthday seemed an extra gift of the gods, who were at last considering her case. Or, on the other hand, was it only the perfume?

Once before, a driver had stopped to ask her if that was the road to the boys' reformatory. Today a lorry stopped. It was a warm day, with the five-o'clock light in the opposite wood the colour of greengages. Still plunged into her scented dream, she only half heard the lorry driver's words as he leaned out of the cabin. Smiling, luxuriously remote but pleasant, she could feel the blue heavy on her eyelids, the red smoothly dried on her lips. But even then she wondered vaguely if it was the perfume that attracted him. Advertisements said these essences of sorcery worked that way.

He left the cabin and leaned on the fence of her garden. A brown-armed young man in flannels and open shirt. Did he think her hard of hearing? 'This the road to Apscombe?' He raised his voice again.

She smiled in brilliant recovery, fully woken by his leaving the cabin. 'Did you want the reformatory?'

'Do I look like it?'

'Cheeky!' She laughed. 'Apscombe? Well, this road gets there by and by, but

159

it isn't the best one. You should have turned left at the church. You new to these parts?'

'Worse luck.' He nodded. 'Taken a job in Apscombe, and I'm homesick . . . You got a garden here!' he admired. 'Reminds me of the one my dad's got, up outside Birmingham. Roses—' He was estimating her, glancing from the flowers to her face, quick-looking yet managing to convey politeness. Plus a natural physical vitality—and he was freshly attractive of face—a shrewd aliveness gleamed in his eye. Despite his job, a spick-and-span cleanliness hung about his person, and his curly hair was glossy, his cheeks tautly gleaming. He was a credit to his employer, whose lorry, a well-kept one of the van type, was inscribed *Joseph Wells & Co., Apscombe*. 'He's got arum lilies too,' he went on chatting. 'I like a bit of gardening.'

'My garden,' she sighed, 'is running to waste this summer. I've got bored with it.'

'It's a picture!' he protested, sincerely. 'Your cottage too—I'd like to bring my camera and take a snap.' His eyes challenged her to make suitable reply to this.

But, aloofly fiddling with the lattice catch and sniffing up her own perfume, she seemed to close her painted face. It was as if a flower became appraised of an unwelcome bee humming in the vicinity. She remembered she was still a married woman and, with her private means, practically a lady now. She glanced up loftily to the sky. 'So you think this fine weather is going to break?' she asked, drawing the lattice an inch or two towards her. ' My garden badly needs rain.'

'A snap of you sitting there at the window too!' he said, concentrating on his own train of thought, and gazing at her with, it seemed, objective appreciation. 'It would make a picture, it would, a prize snapshot.' And somehow in his voice was knowledge of her, instinctive knowledge of her condition, even of the fact that she was alone in the cottage, half a mile from the village, with the woods secret between them. 'Hey,' he said again, as the lattice was drawn another inch, 'I'm new to these parts. Only started with this firm a month ago. Don't know anybody. I'm lodging in Apscombe. I've got a motor-bike.'

'What make?' she asked, not knowing why.

'A Riley. Ever go to the speedway on Saturdays?' At the shake of her head, he asked: 'Come one Saturday?'

'Oh no,' she replied, starting and fluttering her eyelids.

'What I don't like,' he said in an aggrieved voice, 'about people in these parts is that they don't want to be sociable. They're cold-hearted down here in the South. I find 'em cold-hearted.'

160

'Pick yourself a rose,' she said, elegantly distant. 'From that yellow bush there.'

He leaned across the fence, plucked a rose, smelt it, and, smiling, put it behind his ear. 'Well,' he said, taking his dismissal like a man and hitching up his trousers, 'must be off now . . . Expect I'll be passing this village now and again on the bike. Like me to bring you anything from Apscombe?'

Resolutely closing the lattice, she replied: 'The evening paper.'

Afterwards she scolded herself for saying that. And she was not really surprised when just after nine o'clock she heard the distant approach of a motor-cycle. For some time its sound seemed to circle with a changing humming, as if uncertain of the way it wished to take. Once the sound completely faded out, and she plunged on the sofa again with a gasp. For, after running to make sure the door bolt was secure, she had scrambled with an alarmed whinny halfway up the stairs, returned, swiftly closed the sitting-room curtains, put out the light, switched it on again, stood aghast, and then ran to the mirror, where she made the absorbed examination of her face which the looking-glass pools in the Garden of Eden must have known.

Then, as she gasped in relief on the sofa, the cycle's distant humming began again, became more definite, began to rip the night's silence with a steady decisiveness. She leapt up, ran yet again to see that both front and back doors were securely bolted, fled here and there and, finally, upstairs. There she dabbed behind her ears several drops of the perfume. The humming thickened to a roar. She was about to plunge on the bed and bury her head in the pillows, but remembered just in time that this would play havoc with her make-up and carefully arranged hair. The roar stopped with sickening abruptness outside the cottage. She stood drawn up in the middle of the bedroom.

What a fool she'd been to leave the light on downstairs! The door knocker was carefully, even shyly, tapped. A little sound came from her throat, like the plaint of a self-pitying cat. But after the knocker was rapped twice she heard the caller begin to shuffle away. Then the thought struck her that it might not be the lorry-driver at all. Someone who had lost his way among the dark beech-woods! Or perhaps a policeman come to tell her William had crashed in his car and was calling out for her in hospital . . . The motor-bike was being revved up. She ran to the bedroom window, threw it open, and called: 'Who's there?'

'Me,' replied a meek voice. 'I brought you the evening paper. I've pushed it in the letter-box.'

There was a silent moment, into which, as a forest is contained in a seed, all her future seemed concentrated. Then, admonishing herself for being a silly

161

old-fashioned little mouse—she thought of Miss Munro's remarks on freedom—she sang out: 'Well, would you like to stay a minute and take a cup of tea for it?' Yes, he wouldn't mind a cup of tea. Happy to have found herself with a decision at last, she ran downstairs and unlocked the door.

'You mustn't leave your bike in the road,' she said, laughing. 'Will you wheel it into the garden?' By the time he stepped into the cottage she had put the kettle on and was lifting the remains of a sponge cake out of a tin. 'I hope you've had a proper supper,' she tittered, taking him into the sitting-room. 'I have mine early. In fact I was upstairs thinking of going to bye-bye.'

'Me? My landlady gives me a meat tea after I knock off at six . . . A nice night,' he said, sociably. 'Thought I'd have a run round on the old bike. Like to sit on the back and go to a pub or a roadhouse?'

'Good gracious, no . . . at this hour!' But she laughed: a loud, long laugh.

The fact of his presence filled the little room gigantically. He was without awkwardness, secure in a jaunty up-to-date acceptance of what came his way in the highways and byways of the world—she was not surprised when he told her later that he had done service as a sailor. Yet somehow he managed to preserve a deferential appearance of distance from her. He was brushed up and smartened, oil on his fair curls; his skin shone from the drive. He wore a snowily-white sweater and a check sports coat— 'It's quite close in here, mind if I sit in my sweater?' he asked. Permission given, he took off his coat and comfortably lit a cigarette.

'I must make the tea!' she shrieked, and pranced out to the kitchen.

And it was she gave the note to the ensuing atmosphere in the sitting-room. The gay run of laughter, sometimes curdled in her throat though it was, persisted; after a briefly considering watch of her he took appreciative fire. Somehow they began a consciously fictional back-chat. When he asked her name she replied, fluttering her eyelids: 'Brenda.' He said that his name was Gabriel—Gabriel Smith.

'I bet,' he darted, swallowing a lump of stale cake, 'you've got a husband tucked away on a ship somewhere; if not two.' She giggled delightedly: 'No, I'm divorced; he told me that after being in the tropics he could only fancy blacks. He's a captain.' Gabriel honked: 'No wonder my cute lorry took the wrong turning; that's a pretty dame there that makes the country worth working in.'

Enormously amused, she cried: 'Oh, you men, I've had enough of you, that's all you think about. I sit by the window because I'm bored. I play a game, gambling with myself how many squirrels will come out of the wood opposite.'

To that he jeered: 'Squirrels!'

Suddenly she became serious. Stiffening her shoulders, and putting her head on one side, she whispered: 'Oh, but I'm so bored, Gabriel!'

'Hey!' he called, bridling in his white sweater, not liking this gravity at all.

'I'm so bored,' she said, looking far away.

'You want to get out more, Brenda,' he protested.

'I'm so bored,' she said.

'—dances, the speedway, roadhouses . . . there's a dance over at Apscombe tomorrow night—'

'Bored,' she said, 'bored, bored, bored.'

'A glass or two, company or a sing-song, that's what you want, honey.'

'Life's a messy business,' she said, staring as though a funeral was passing before her eyes.

'Come out of it, Brenda!' he bawled. 'You want a man to look after you.'

She started, looked at him, and gave a great released laugh; she looked at him with liking and, plainly, trust and acceptance.

What followed a little later was natural. The note of high gaiety returned to the room; the romantic verbal sparring was resumed. She took up a Japanese fan and plied it like an opera star, she warbled out badinage equal to his. Soon, breathing her perfume, he sat beside her on the sofa. After allowing a discreet amount of fondling she jumped up with a shriek and ran out of the room into the kitchen. Dodging him round the table, she snatched up a fish-slice for weapon. Dextrously he allowed her to squirm out of his woolly arms. She ran. Looking like a confident rugger player, he leapt after her with expert lightness. Into an unused side room, stuffily dark, where she could not be seen. He crashed over a portable oil-heater, and her great abandoned whinny exploded like fireworks.

That clumsy fall seemed to make him savage. Guided by her perfume, he found her and pounded. She squeaked. He made peculiar sounds like a bark. Half carrying, half dragging her, he bore her to the staircase, and with his squat broad hands pushed her up—for still she shrieked protest. When, however, he saw her bosom, of the odour and tint of firm vanilla blancmange, he behaved with an orderly though decisive esteem. And she lay in a trance of calm surprise, her chin dropped, the heave of her breathing deeply regular. Distant, and entirely without malice, she thought of William—how, a week after their wedding, she had attempted to inspire him to the same sort of happy chasing antics downstairs, and how he had looked at her with a cold, sceptical eye.

'The headlight of my bike conked out coming here,' Gabriel said suddenly. 'Hope it'll last going back.'

'Did it dear?' she murmured. 'Get it fixed properly by next time you come.'

Downstairs she brewed more tea. In the sitting-room she took complacently to the sofa like a swan settling on water after too long an awkward treading of lumpy land. Gabriel had put on his coat and sat opposite, like a proper visitor, even to the politely neutral expression of his face; no doubt about it, working class though he was, he knew what manners were. Pouring out, she said: 'Next time I'll get something more cheerful than tea. What do you like?'

'Tea. Us lorry drivers drink tea all day. It's thirsty work.'

'When will you come?' she asked, after giving him a look of appreciation for his tact.

He thought profoundly. 'Friday,' he said finally.

'This Friday you mean?' She laughed. That day was a Wednesday.

He looked at her in surprise. 'No, next week . . . You see, Brenda, I'm going far afield with the lorry the next few days.'

'Yes, Gabriel,' she said obediently. Then, with an air of trust and honesty—all that teasing nonsense was over now and they were established in a firm and loving relationship—she said: 'There's one thing though—you must always come after dark and bring your bike inside at once . . . You see,' her voice took a parrot note, 'my husband and I are separated by mutual consent, but he pays me a hundred and fifty pounds a year on condition that I live in chastity, as they called it. Until tonight I have obeyed. I don't think *he* cares one way or another, but his spiteful mother has got her knife into me.'

He looked at her. He gave a little whistle, and exclaimed: 'You've been risking something, haven't you! A hundred and fifty—!'

She tittered, her cheeks blooming. 'I have, haven't I! Calculate it by only ten years and tonight might cost me fifteen hundred pounds. Isn't it awful!'

'Brenda, is it worth it?' he asked with great earnestness.

'Johanna's my name. What's yours?'

'What I told you . . . Look what you're risking!' he insisted, his eyes brownly round.

'Can you manage this last bit of old cake? I'll prepare a proper meal for you on Friday. Some chops . . . and I'll get a few bottles in. So don't eat much of your landlady's tea.'

'All right,' he said, getting up; 'it's your own affair, mind! As long as you don't blame *me* . . . About the same time on Friday next week, then.' He gave her an affectionate slap, kissed her on lips and ear. 'I like your scent; it smells high-class,' he said.

'It was a wedding present. I opened the bottle for the first time today . . . and it's my birthday, too, today.' She said it at last, with a celebrating smile and a delight in her eyes like a newborn happiness. She much admired his uncomplicated ways and words.

164

III

What a blessing were motor-bikes to country lovers! What an exciting music was their sound, swelling from a sweet hum to a shattering roar! She would always love motor-bikes after this. In their throats was the voice of her drama. By nine-fifteen her whole being was squeezed up into her ears.

The table, covered with a lace-edged cloth, was glitteringly ready. A bowl of asters stood in the middle. On the sideboard were a bottle each of whisky, gin and port, and on the floor beside it were four vulgar flagons of beer. She did not expect Gabriel to drink more than a fraction of these, but she wanted him to realise that she was neither a skinflint nor a prude. In the kitchen waited a couple of lovely loin chops and a highly decorative trifle. All day she had crooned over her work, polishing the cutlery and putting the finishing touches to the restaurant-looking trifle. At nine o'clock, in a crisp new voile frock and her face made up generously, she sat like a lady awaiting guests . . . Any minute now. 'About the same time,' he had said.

During the intervening days she had experienced more feelings of deliciously flinging everything to the winds. But the curious thing was that she had to make quite an effort to recall Gabriel as a concrete image of a man. He was like someone belonging to a dream, or to her open-eyed afternoon reveries at the lattice when dozens of things, ranging from Atlantic liners to lucky bangle charms, occupied her entranced mind. What remained more solid in her was a feeling of deliverance, of having been heaved up from the horrible stagnation William had cast her into. Nevertheless there were a few striking moments when memory of some of Gabriel's decisively simple actions recurred so strongly that she broke into a clap of delighted laughter. She must not let him go, no indeed, even at the cost of her allowance. He was such a gay one, a natural one. But on the whole she preferred the feeling that he belonged to her dreams—in them he was not only more handsome but more important. He was the knight with the feather in his cap who had broken into the silence of her turret.

At nine-thirty, rising frowning from the sofa, she decided the motor-bike had broken down. Often from the bus she had seen wayside drivers tinkering concentratedly at their engines. Last week his lamp had gone out. Very likely it was a cheap secondhand bike, thoroughly unreliable. Or—and for a moment she was pierced horribly yet pleasurably by this thought—he had met with an accident. Motor-bikes often had accidents. She unlocked the front door and went to the fence gate. Nothing of account to be seen or heard.

At nine forty-five she whimpered audibly in the kitchen. The dye of the cachous dotting the trifle was already smudging the wet cream. But she had barely returned to the sitting-room when the divine distant hum caressed her ears. Oh! . . . For a moment she crumpled on to the sofa, then sprang up and ran to the mirror. Had the torture ravaged her face? She felt as though she had been beaten all over with gnarled branches. The mirror comforted her. Whatever could be said against make-up, it did remain independent of the agony of the soul.

All the time the sweet humming thickened, began to buzz a louder and louder laughter, private for her ears alone. The bee was coming to his flower! Was Gabriel, as he drew inescapably nearer, himself laughing in awareness of her anxiety? Or—and more attractively—was he bad-tempered at the delay that robbed him of time with her? The humming became the authentic, the triumphant, roar. And it swept past the cottage. For an unbelieving second, before rushing out, she stood rigid. She was just in time to see a malignant red eye disappearing over the brow of the hill.

Someone visiting a farm. The humming died into the vast hollow night.

Back in the cottage she uttered a long, dry wail; it rose, circled through the stagnant air, seemed to recoil and hit her in the face, like a nasty fact flung at one. She ran about the house. In the kitchen she shot the trifle out of its bowl into the pail under the sink. The silence became like a swollen presence following her. She could not keep still: she crashed the cutlery into heaps, clattered the crockery, threw a saucepan across the kitchen, hurled an odd cup against the wall. And yet those noises of reality tore her nerves to shreds; still the interior dream bled from its wound. Then the floods of tears came and made havoc of the make-up at last. Self-pity engulfed her. Presently, stretched flat on the hearthrug, this dramatic position easing her, only an exhausted melancholy remained, strangely half-sweet. At intervals she whimpered.

How exciting he had been, what a daring one! How he had arrived magically in his lorry after she had spent all those horrid lonely afternoons dreaming at her window! No one could blame her for believing he had arrived in answer to her great yearning. The morning after his visit she had decided that she would now allow William a divorce. She had felt a wiser woman aware of what pleasure there was in the world. She had realised at last that she just did not fit into William's arms, as she snugly fitted into Gabriel's and it was cruel to make him pay for this.

When at last she rose from the hearthrug she even rebuked herself. Why was she so high-strung? A lorry driver might be seen around here at a moment's notice. He would turn up tomorrow night. 'Johanna,' she scolded herself, dropping three aspirins into water, 'you're a fool. He's had a breakdown or an accident. You know very well you're attractive and it isn't every day he meets a woman so good-hearted as you.'

IV

Four days later, unable to bear the torment any longer and by then assuring herself that Gabriel was lying heavily bandaged in a hospital, she took the afternoon bus to Apscombe, carefully dressed in her best and odorous with the high-class perfume. Yes, despite her anxiety, a sense of righteous indignation grew in her during the journey. She allowed it full entrance to her being, it seemed to give her courage; and as the bus entered the straggling town, where glossy modern shops thrust aggressively on to the ancient market place, she churned up this indignation more and more, so that her face grew red, her eyes threatening under arched-up brows.

'I asked you to put me down at the Post Office,' she snapped at the conductor.

'The stop's only a minute away,' he said, giving her a sidelong glance, his nostrils sniffing.

'Why didn't you say so at first then?' She turned to the listening passengers. 'Anybody would think the buses were run for the convenience of conductors. It's a scandal!' No one replied. But she felt better as she descended, in an aroma of fine perfume, a lady of private means giving a last baleful look at the conductor.

Borne up wonderfully by this breeze, and having made enquiry of a constable, she went at once to the warehouses of Joseph Wells & Co. They were down by the old disused canal, a sprawling collection of flour-dusted buildings and sheds. Keeping an eye open for sight of the adored lorry, she wandered about the deserted-looking place until she came to an open door with a brass plate marked *Registered Offices*. Inside, behind a partition with a little window, a young girl sat chopping off the heads and tails of sprats into a newspaper— 'Yes?' she asked.

'I would like to speak to Mr. Smith, one of your lorry drivers—Mr. Gabriel Smith. I am a relative.'

'Smith? I dunno if he's in. Expect he's out with a load. Go round to the back and you'll see a building with pulleys outside. Shout for Mr. Preen, the foreman.'

Johanna smiled at her dazzlingly. So Smith *was* his name! A promising beginning. She discovered the building and, entering it through a wide aperture with sliding doors, found herself in a huge empty space with two trapdoors above her. A ladder ran up into one of the doors. 'Mr. Preen, Mr. Preen!' she called. Footsteps tramped above, and an elderly man in a dust-coat peered down through the trap. 'There's the ladder,' he said; 'come on up. You brought the orders from Simpsons?'

Moving directly under the trapdoor she gazed up brightly. 'I want to see Mr. Smith, your lorry driver. I've come a journey. Could you tell me what time he will be in, please?'

'What,' he peered lower, more friendly, 'you're his missus? Smithy didn't tell me he was expecting you this week, I thought he said it was in a fortnight.'

Johanna stared up at him, silent for another eternal, important moment. Then, her whole being a mass of roused instinct, she said: 'Well, Mr. Preen, I've come today instead.'

'But did you know about the 'ouse? Smithy told me only yesterday that the landlord said he couldn't have it now till November. Fair upset about it he was.' At her silence he added sympathetically, while his flat face seemed to float towards her like a pancake: 'It's a devil when a man can't get his own wife with him because there's no accommodation. We all been trying to find a 'ouse or something for you and Smithy . . . You come down all the way from Birmingham today? Smith *will* have a surprise when he comes in— 'bout half-past five it will be. Pretty lonely he's been all on his own in those bad lodgings.' Very interested, he seemed now to be sniffing their perfume rising from her hot bosom.

Though her strained neck ached, she still stared up at the sympathetic foreman. 'Half-past five?' she said carefully.

'Thereabouts. Like to come up the ladder and wait here?'

She said at random: 'Oh, I'll just take a little walk . . . How is Smith getting on here?' Whether to stay or not . . . to face him . . . to denounce him to his foreman . . .

'Champion. Our best driver. Reliable and straight as a die. The boss gave him a fine reference for the 'ouse. Ah,' said the elderly Mr. Preen kindly, 'when you get that 'ouse you'll be able to settle down properly at last. You come and see my missus if you want any 'elp . . . Sure you won't come up the ladder and take a rest?'

She straightened her head. 'Thank you,' she said, 'I want to go into the town. But you'll warn him Johanna called, won't you?'

'Johanna . . . Johanna?' he said, as if puzzled.

'Yes, Johanna.' Her voice changed like a bell as she walked away. 'He will know all right, will Mr. Smith.'

Outside, her strength seemed only just enough to bear her up. Yet she walked swiftly, her burning face held down. Avoiding the direct road to the town, she took the path beside the canal, forcing herself on and on. Away from the raging temptation to stay with the foreman, to see Gabriel's face, to stand and loosen on him the anger—and the threats—the blackguard deserved. Denounce him in his place of work, make assault on the peace of

168

his marriage and the security of his job . . . But she dragged herself on, not daring to stop or look back for a second, walking towards a pink light beginning to flood the woody under-distances.

Not until she had gone about a mile did she realise that of course he could ruin her, too, spoil her good name, rob her of William's allowance. A blackguard like that would do anything in retaliation. She stopped at last, and looked. Stood looking for minutes at the sluggish water of the dead canal. But it was horrible thick brown water with a rancid smell. She swerved away, pushing herself on.

Three hours later, after climbing through a wire fence, she sat on the grass verge of the railway. Dusk was settling. An aching weariness weighted her limbs and body. In the torpor that held her mind one dull thought persisted— dread of a return to her cottage, to its silence, to a long vista of empty years there. If once she returned she would sink for ever into that silence.

During the three hours of wandering around a vaguely familiar countryside, her fury against Gabriel had exhausted itself and, in thickening inertia, she even dimly realised that he was not important and she had been right in fleeing from making an awful exhibition of herself in his place of work. The shock of discovering his baseness had cured her of *him*. What was more important was the fear that replaced the fury. Fear of the world and her helpless, silly life in it. She couldn't cope with the world and her helpless, silly life in it. She couldn't cope with the world—that was it. What had Miss Munro said?—that women, unless they had sharp wits, were always victims. William, with his mother's aid, had made her a victim. And now this other man had done it too—and in a common horrid way. A sense of uncleanliness recurred in her. She despised herself.

Sitting on the verge, she gazed fixedly at the rail track. Once she made an effort to get up, but sank bank dumpily like a drunken woman. Within the fencing behind her was a rough hedge of briars and blackberry-dotted bushes, and she had wondered if she could drag herself there and go to sleep: her eyes felt padded with swollen flesh. But she kept her gaze on the rail track. The need to punish herself remained in her like a judgment. To throw herself, she thought dimly, into some violent force and be ground down into forgetfulness; to be obliterated in a jet of scalding steam . . . At the approach of such a force she knew she would rise and go towards it with obedient steps.

A man in a peaked cap and blue cotton jacket loomed indistinctly into her gaze. She stared when he stopped and called: 'Good evening.' He carried a tin bottle under his arm. A signalman, sprightly-looking and young. 'Got many blackberries?' he asked.

Craftily she smiled back at him but said nothing. Suddenly his eyes flickered, he became alert, took half a step towards her, his nostrils sniffing the perfume still redolent about her. 'People,' he said in a teasing way, 'aren't supposed to be inside the railings. Trespassing.'

'Why?' she asked, cunning. 'What time does the next train pass?'

'Like to see 'em go by, do you? Well, there'll be no more today.'

She got up, rising with surprising swiftness, and, after giving the signalman a threatening look walked away . . . Waiting there for a train that wouldn't come! Fool, fool. Cheated again. Everything went wrong with her. She felt like hurling a stone at that grinning signalman, she wanted to shout something abusive at him. Grinning there so impudent and knowledgeable. She hated men.

It was past ten o'clock when she arrived home, having walked the six miles. After violently slamming the front door, she went at once to the sideboard. Never a drinker, it was only on special occasions she allowed herself a glass of port or sherry. Now she poured out half a tumbler of gin and drank it neat, not pausing, viciously, like a woman who wants to abase herself.

V

In the spring, after a long, bitterly cold winter, William paid her a visit. He arrived in a new and bigger car and brought, oddly, a bunch of florist's flowers. Johanna's rude reply to his diplomatic letter had not promised well, but no doubt he remembered the basic soft pliancy of the girl he had married. He was again raising the question of a divorce. His mother had not survived the winter, and a middle-aged lady of means, who in some respects resembled her, was interested in him.

Except for getting drunk, Johanna had made no preparations for his visit. When, courteously, he knocked at the door she bawled from the sitting-room: 'Walk in, can't you!—it's your own damned mansion.' He entered with a bunch of white tulips. The air of the cottage was heavy, it seemed with sloth and temper. Johanna was lying on the sofa.

'Well, William,' she greeted him, 'you look like an undertaker. Cute of you to bring those white flowers . . . 'specially,' she added, 'to one who's got to live in chastity. Sit down, dear.' Without allowing him to speak, and with a rapid change of tone, she went on: 'You staying the night, William? Or will that stop the hundred and fifty!' Easing herself with a peculiar confidence on the sofa, she rambled on: 'You're a mean old sheep with your hundred and fifty— you doing so well now; I can't dress myself properly on it, not after I've paid for my bits of comfort—a woman with the solicitor's condition on her has got to have something else, hasn't she? . . . Don't stand there staring,' she cried irritably, stretching a swarthy neck out of a limp old frock. 'Take a drink if you want one.' Under the sofa a filthy saucer stood among the scattered remnants of cat's food.

He sat down wincing. 'Now, Johanna, I'm sorry to see you so—so unwell.' He mumbled, still wanting his bearings.

'Standing there with your mouth open like a dead fish!' she said heedlessly. Then she gave him the fixed scrutiny of the intoxicated. 'You still look a gentleman at least,' she said, 'but I can't, I *can't* think what I saw in you. Still I'm a wiser woman now . . . Well, aren't you going to speak?' she demanded angrily.

'Now, look here, Johanna,' he began again, in a pleading way, 'let's talk quietly and in friendship. We've been wasting each other's life. I've brought a proposition. The time may come when you'll want to marry again—'

'What!' she exclaimed, violently roused for a moment. 'Me!' Then, with a solemn sagaciousness, she shook her head. 'I'm married to the bottle, William, as I expect even you can see. It's less troublesome than a man.'

'Well, then,' he said more briskly, and very much the businessman now. 'I'll make you an offer. Consent to a divorce and I'll increase your allowance by fifty pounds a year.'

She became still. Fifty pounds would bring a useful extra amount of forgetfulness. She looked at him. Then said sultrily: 'You're very ready with your money, William, very ready.'

'You complained I was mean with my hundred and fifty,' he pointed out, not liking her tone at all.

'Well, I don't want your extra fifty. But I tell you what, William—I'll take you back. Come back to me, William. I'll make you China tea whenever you want it; we'll be happy together as a king and queen.'

'This is not a matter for idle jokes,' he said testily, drawing in his long loose legs sharply, and a flush spreading over his forehead.

Placing an arm over the back of the sofa, she heaved herself up. She seemed to be swelling. There was something like a choking rattle in her throat. But, safely on her feet, she said quite calmly: 'That mother of yours, she's one of the women of hell now, and I hope the Old Nick's got her sizzling. The mess she made of you, William, and the spite she had for me!' Straightening herself with a jerk, she observed: 'Jokes indeed! You always were a blind fool, William—though perhaps I was as silly.' And with another change of tone she asked sociably, scratching her shoulder: 'How's your constipation now the old lady's gone?'

'Look here, Johanna—' he began, very red.

'I'm going out the back garden to pull a lettuce for my tea.' She gave a short, sharp belch— 'Excuse me, William . . . Well, good-bye—I hope you're gone by the time I'm back, dear.' Ambling across to the door while, totally at sea in this capriciousness, he stared gaping, she grieved: 'Life's awful, William. I've been so bored. But good luck to you, sweetheart.'

'Johanna, I . . . I warn you—' he stuttered, though in a small, almost wailing voice. 'I can—'

She closed the sitting-room door behind her. But he heard a shriek of laughter, and a high cry: 'I'll take you back, William; I'll make a man of you.' He got up with a threatening scowl, stood hesitating . . . The back door slammed with what seemed a fierce pronouncement of finality. Still he hesitated. Then, as though the slothful air of the cottage had become menacing, he shivered and hurried to the front door.

But as he started the car up, the sitting-room window was thrown back, and a face looked out. A blanched, indoors face, yet bold and positive. 'Good-bye, William,' its owner called. 'You'll have to live chastely yourself now, won't you? Unless you turn that woman into a trollop . . . and you're too much of a gentleman to do that.' This face of a stranger, thrust out with such truculent ribaldry at the window, while a grimy hand waved farewell, so astonished and daunted him that he could find no reply.

ALL THROUGH THE NIGHT

On this particular icy Wednesday in early January, Mrs. Bessie Evans's routine followed its normal course for a drinking evening. Rhiannon, the afternoon help from the village, safely gone, the sitting-room fire compactly built up, curtains closed against the bluely frozen night—all was set for three hours of slow pleasure. The isolation of the cottage among the cold-stiffened pines, even the ordinary fact that it was situated in a secret fold among the interior hills of Wales, seemed to give an additional relish to the coming session.

Bessie liked a hard winter: no vulgarly beaming sun nagging at one to go out and get healthy; no reproachful flowers to water in the damned garden; no malign wasps or mosquitoes; no birds yelling their little heads off at the crack of dawn. Also, a bitter frost, such as bruised the air this evening, raised (she was sure of it) a more fiery tang in her favourite beverage. She had arrived at the connoisseur's stage in such matters.

At seven o'clock, dressed in black satin, she ate boiled top-round beef with appreciation, neglecting none of the subsidiary dishes that Rhiannon—an excellent cook, ignorant village woman though she was—had prepared; there were preserved pears, a fat junket, local farm cheese and butter, home-baked bread and, finally, a slice of chocolate cake. She ate not so much out of greed as out of a realisation, based on experience, that a solid foundation of food helped to generate from whisky the special rich, luxuriant glow she desired. She would go up to bed feeling a wonderful lack of contumaciousness towards the world.

At half-past-seven, her bosom preceding her in royal solidity, she moved from the kitchen to the sitting-room, unlocked the old press of carved black oak, and drew out a glass and two bottles; one bottle was a third full, the other unopened. Her bosom, which was that of a handsomely endowed woman of forty, gave its usual preparatory heave; it suggested both a greeting and an admonishment.

Almost invariably she subjected herself to a strict practice of drinking exactly two-thirds of a bottle on alternate evenings of the week only, retiring to bed immediately after the sitting-room clock struck ten. It was a discipline from which she drew self-esteem and the deduction that she was not really going bad. On the rare occasions when she yielded to temptation and stayed up until eleven finishing a whole bottle, drastic scolding and punishment— such as doing without a meal or furiously working on the neglected garden—

173

were administered the next day. As for the whiskyless evenings, these, of course, were hard to endure; and when, still more rarely, she broke her rule completely and enjoyed two consecutive sessions of intoxication, the lapse acquired a wicked splendour that almost made her topple over into the decision to give up the tenancy of Old Well Cottage and return, contritely, to the place she had come from.

The fire burned with purplish energy. An oil lamp cast a clear glow from its pretty shade; under it, a deeply upholstered chair took Bessie's body with a companionable sigh from its springs. A lady of leisure, secure in her domain, she had no difficulty, at least on such nights as this, in enjoying vicarious ownership of the charming old cottage and its kindred furnishings. She had rented it, two years before, from a man known locally as Shadrach the Gas (he managed the gas-works in the market town), and, because of its isolation and the lack of electricity and other main services, the rent was most reasonable.

After a few preliminary sips—the whisky was never tainted with other liquids—she turned on the battery wireless. There was a programme of rollicking variety turns. She enjoyed a good dirty laugh, liked boisterous comedians with red-nosed anecdotes of undignified disasters. What she *couldn't* stand was those women who heaved their guts up in some God-awful wail about love gone wrong. One of these upset the programme tonight, and Bessie, pouring her fourth large measure by then, shouted at the wireless cabinet: 'You silly cabbage, serve you right if he let you down! We got to *fight* the devils, my gal!'

At nine-fifteen, a lecturer followed the variety turns, and she jeered good-humouredly: 'Ancient Egyptians—they were all like us, you fathead. You can't change human nature.' She shut him off, lit the single cigarette she allowed herself on whisky nights, and, as usual, sat back pondering plans.

Always, after about half a bottle had been consumed, problems acquired a roseate tinge. They would be solved with delicious ease. There was always her sister Susan, in Australia—Susan and her husband's expanding grocery business in Sydney; Susan who wanted a colleague experienced in business from the home country to help; Susan who, though she could be mean as cat's meat, valued her; Susan . . . Her drooping eyelids suddenly opened; she sat bolt upright, her eyes sidling round the room. Had a piece of coal exploded in the grate? She bent down to the low table and poured the last measured allowance from the second bottle. It was a quarter to ten.

She began to giggle. At tea-time, Rhiannon had told her more about Elfed, the widowed farmer who had been asking questions in the village about the tenant of Old Well Cottage. Why didn't she come down to the chapel on Sundays? He had seen her many times in the returning market bus, a heavily laden basket on her knees, and her face (Rhiannon herself enjoyed the inquisitive farmer's compliment) 'bright as a bunch of snapdragons.' Rhiannon thought he would soon be offering to carry that heavy basket the quarter mile from the village bus stop to the cottage above the slope of pines.

Bessie, sipping her drink and purring beautifully inside now, let out a guffaw. Those bottles in the basket! After her two years of residence, the villagers, even Rhiannon, had not found out about the whisky in the capacious wicker basket which sat, displaying a crust of groceries and fruit, on her lap in the bus after the twice-weekly visit to the market town, six miles away. But Rhiannon, her only link with the village, often hinted to her that the lone Mrs. Evans, although thought of respectfully as a dignified woman of means, still roused speculation. Why had she chosen to live among strangers in such a quiet district?

'Tell the ladies and gentlemen of Sychan,' the recluse had said, 'that I've had my day with the best man that ever lived, and I've come here to remember it undisturbed by other things.'

When she had arrived, she had told Shadrach the Gas that her late husband, William Evans, a war casualty, used to motor her on week-ends through this wonderful countryside, and that they had decided to retire hereabouts in due course. Still dressed in black, even after all that time of widowhood, she gave out the flavour of a woman who would mourn her loss forever. Yet acceptance of her became solidified when the villagers began to refer to her as Mrs. Evans Old Well, and now she could enter the bus without the babble of voices dropping. There was a very deep seventeenth-century well, still functioning, near the cottage porch. The legend was that a sinful wife, in far-off, stricter days, had been dropped down it, and her ghost was said still to haunt the garden. Shadrach the Gas pooh-poohed all that, yet after buying and furnishing the cottage he had not lived long there himself.

At five minutes to ten, she exclaimed, still giggling, 'Elfed wants to carry my basket, does he! Well, his chance *might* come—if his oats show a good profit some year!' The giggling came to an abrupt stop. Her glass was empty. She frowned.

The price of Scotch! Thirty-six shillings the bottle! Occasionally a sort of paralysis gripped her in the region of the solar plexus when she approached her bank in the market town. Otherwise, she treated her legacy of three thousand pounds—it had arrived, indeed, with a fairy-wand unexpectedness from a bachelor uncle struck down untimely and intestate—as something subject at any moment to an equally unexpected magic removal from the granite building where it lay in a deposit account yielding two and a half per cent interest. Although only a glance was required, she found it increasingly difficult to examine the state of her finances. Anyhow, she could always go back to work at the drapery. Or disappear—assuming she still had the fare—to Australia. Beautiful, beautiful Australia.

When the mantelpiece clock began striking its ten crisp pings, she sat up rigid again and, arms folded across her chest, stared thunderously at the second bottle, now a third empty. 'No, Bessie!' she cried out. 'No! You can't afford it. You've got to go to Australia. Lolling around here, you big good-for-nothing!' She thrust the cork in the bottle, gave it a bang with her fist, and heaved herself up.

Then came the satisfaction of locking up the bottles and glass in the press. Tomorrow morning, the first empty bottle would be dropped down the well. This method of disposal amused her; she liked to hear the faraway splash. Perhaps, when she was safe in Australia, Shadrach the Gas or another tenant might discover a deposit of four or five hundred bottles in that choked-up old well, which was supposed to be the residence of a ghost!

After the press key had been safely hidden from Rhiannon's prying, the usual buoyant feeling of achievement, propriety observed, and self-admiration rewarded her. Bed now! Sleep would come easily—deep, warm sleep in that lovely bed of good linen, fleecy blankets, and red eiderdown, the world obliterated. What more could a woman want? She began to sing.

She bolted the front and back doors, still humming '*Ar Hyd y Nos*'. Every downstairs window was already fastened. Not that she was a nervous woman. Besides, burglars never functioned in these tranquilly unimportant parts; neither were tramps ever seen. She took the small lamp standing on a table in the hall—a place so cold that, despite the interior whisky warmth, she shivered. As, vaguely unsteady, she mounted the crooked staircase of black oak, the lamp's flame danced within the glass funnel under the cretonne shade. On the bulgy, fortress-thick walls, shadows danced clownishly. Sleepy though she was, she still hummed the popular, dirge-like old melody.

When she opened the door of the front bedroom, her attention was caught at once by a shape in the bed. Yet she did not cry out, and the lamp did not drop from her hand. She only stared at the shape with the same thunderous intensity as that with which she had looked at the bottle downstairs when the hour struck.

The shape—clearly it was that of a man, with the head visible on the farther of the two pillows—had its back to her. The old-fashioned double bed stood against the wall, and its occupant had taken the inner position. No sound of breathing came. Bessie's eyes roved, with an effort, to garments dropped on a chair. A pair of shoes stood neatly together on a rug. Most conspicuous of all, a soft felt hat hung, rakish-looking, on the knob of one ebony bedpost.

These evidences of outrageous intrusion did not exert on her, a married woman, the effect they might have achieved with a spinster. Nevertheless, in the long moments of silence her face became drained of its opulent colour. A dim memory came to her of an old, now abandoned country custom—*caru yn y gwely*, it was called. A suitor climbed through a bedroom window—a ladder was usually left conveniently handy—and, if acceptable, was allowed to stay an hour or two, with marriage in view. It was just possible that in remote and unspoiled villages like Sychan the custom was still followed, if only in a jesting manner. Those earthy glances she got sometimes in the bus from men old enough to know better!

Fury rescued her. Her voice thick but bridling, she spoke, 'If you don't leave my house, this instant,' she declared, 'I'll call the police.' At once, she was aware of the fatuity of this—no telephone, and the nearest neighbour hopelessly beyond the range of the loudest scream.

Slowly, unalarmed, the man turned his head on the pillow. Bessie's free hand, opening and closing, clutched her satin dress. She still held the lamp; otherwise, she might have sunk to the floor. But her legs buckled somewhat. '*Will-iam,*' she stammered.

Her husband looked at her with assessing curiosity—a square-headed man with hard, unblinking eyes and a mouth that had become tightened as though from driving ruthless business transactions. 'What's that you said about the police?' he asked, still not budging from under the blankets.

'I'll—I'll call them,' she panted.

'Shouldn't think you'd want to do that.' He spoke with slow exactitude, but mildly. 'There's only one in the village, I expect, and *he* wouldn't be used to a case like this—not in these nice, respectable parts.' His steady eyes, not moving from her, shone greenish in the lamplight. 'Sit down, Bessie,' he suggested. 'Unless you're coming into bed?'

He watched her turn and, with the slow, waddling movements of a person exercising will-power after the petrification of a shock, walk to the high chest of drawers and place the lamp on it. 'What did you think was in your bed?' he asked, entirely without amusement. 'A wolf?' And suddenly, rapidly, he flung back the bedclothes and leaped out—a short, solid-fleshed man of mature cast, with strong, thick arms. He filled, with comfortable tightness, the striped shirt he had left on. Bessie shrank back a step, clutching the bodice of her dress, her eyes bared. But he did not touch her. He only locked the door, drew out the key, and leaped back into bed, thrusting the key under the farther pillow.

'Brrh! It's warmer in here,' he said. 'A pity you haven't got a stove in the room.'

She had watched with the strained inertia of someone hopelessly lost in a no man's land of mist. Then, carefully lowering herself, she sat on a hard chair placed against the wall where the chest stood. A little heat, perhaps sufficient for a doll's house, came from the lamp. The room was very cold. The sitting-room downstairs, the three hours of cosy drinking, already seemed remote. Something drastic had happened. Her mind kept on fumbling towards realisation, but so far all she felt was that a great black cloud had suddenly clamped down on the pretty cottage. She no longer looked at the man in the bed. He was saying something about having come in by the back door after keeping watch on the house for hours . . . helping himself to bread and cheese in the kitchen . . . examining the layout of the house with a torch. She made an effort to clear a way through the muddle in her mind.

'How did you find where I was living?' she whispered at last. The ordinariness of the inquiry seemed to reassure her. His presence was perfectly acceptable and, somehow, logical. But still she did not look at him—only stared in turn at the wardrobe, at the dressing-table, and, finally, up at the gently burning little lamp, as though seeing them for the first time.

'Took me a long time to track down a pal of yours,' William replied. Perhaps because of his success in this, he even sounded affable. 'She's in furs now, Monica is—a wholesale house in Cardiff. I expect you know about that. Cost me a four-quid dinner in the Angel to make her slip the bit of information—pretending she wasn't slipping it, of course.' He eased himself up, and gave the pillow a pugilist's blow. 'You shouldn't have written her asking for that twenty quid you lent her, Bessie. You must have been drunk, when you did it.'

She bridled a little. 'I don't get drunk.'

'No? Well, it was your tightness about money, then.' He chuckled, with a queer, throaty sound she had never heard from him before. He was not a man given to jokes.

'Wait till I get hold of Monica!' she said, her voice too shaky for vindictiveness.

'You won't,' William said.

She bent her head as though the strength of her neck had dwindled. There was a long silence, and when, finally, she spoke, her sluggishness suggested a lack of interest in or focus on what she was asking: 'Have you still got the restaurant?'

'No. Sold it months ago. Been on the prowl since then.' He stretched, and snuggled down like any married man in bed at home. The heavy eiderdown shone luxuriously warm. 'Got a fair price for the premises from a big firm of caterers. They said the goodwill of the business wasn't worth much—your fault, Bessie.' She said nothing, and he, calm in his deductions, although his tone seemed to imply long and bitter reveries, presently went on: 'If you'd put the money you had from your Uncle Charles—and I bet he's boiling in hell at the thought *you* got it—if you'd put it into the restaurant, we'd soon have been well off, Bess. That scheme they had to build a factory estate outside Dinas has got going—the Government is encouraging it. Dinas town is going to be a big noise in a couple of years or so.'

She drew her feet, which were getting cold, under her skirt. 'Why didn't you hold on to the premises, then?'

There was a long pause before he replied. 'I lost interest in the business. I got sour, Bessie, see? When I'd go down in the morning to let Sally and Mrs. Bevan in, and notice them looking at me sideways, wondering about my state of temper—well, I got to hate myself too. After you did a bunk from me, I took to staying at home all on my own . . . night after night.' In his voice was all the bleak solitude of the home over the restaurant, all the deserted silence of the small-town street after the shops closed.

'You used to go to meet the Chamber of Commerce men in the White Hart often enough, leaving me at home,' she reminded him.

'You drove me out, with your moods. You could have kept me at your side, loving as a silly spaniel.' Still, he sounded only mildly concerned about all that now. 'After you bunked off, leaving that note of three lines on the mantelpiece, I couldn't get myself to go to the White Hart any more, knowing how all the boys would push drinks on me and slap me on the back, cheerful as a lot of undertakers . . . But the money, Bessie, the money! If you had run off before you got the solicitor's letter about your uncle's money, it wouldn't have been quite so bad. The thought of the money stuck in my gullet. We could have used that money well, and in ten years you'd have had your jewellery and sables and ride about fat as a duchess. But, no! You wanted the legacy all to yourself. Yourself, yourself!'

She didn't like his further chuckle. Although stupor still held her body inert, her mind formulated a clear patch of opinion. Sounding detached from any wish to give offence, she began: 'I hated Dinas, and you could not have made the restaurant into anything. You're a fighter, I dare say, but you just can't think *big*. You're not the master type, William; you haven't got the employer's temperament. Those two waitresses used to laugh at you. After being in a large drapery business for fifteen years, I know what's what in business—' She stopped, dimly aware of incautiousness.

'A good woman ought to try to make a man feel larger, not smaller,' he replied to this, only a shade censorious. 'You're a mean and selfish woman, Bessie. One of the kind that only wants a man to keep her in comfort and expects it as her right—amen and no two opinions about it.'

They were approaching the old trouble, the ancient warfare, the eternal trap. For some reason, she remembered hearing, in a Welsh wireless talk on bygone courting customs, how a couple would be sewn inside a sack together by the girl's parents and left all night as a test of mutual suitability. 'I'm as God made me,' she found herself mumbling.

For the first time, his voice betrayed a dark, glowering anger. 'I wonder what we have schools and upbringing for! Did God set out purposely to make you a humbug, a liar, a greedy hypocrite, and a thief? Do you think I didn't know how you used to help yourself to money in the restaurant till and spend it in Cardiff on flighty clothes that you said you got at wholesale price? Ha! Always wanting to play the lady in Dinas, you shifty bitch!'

She did not deal with this. It seemed unimportant and normal beside the fact of his presence and the key under the pillow—unimportant, even, in comparison with the fact of her defunct feet and the moribund apathy of faculties elsewhere in her body. The room was getting colder. Or had something else—shock and fear—reduced her stamina? Whisky was fraudulent; there might be something in the belief that ale gave one more lasting warmth and energy. For a moment, she contemplated placing the lamp at her feet. But she lacked the initiative for the act; a rigid unwillingness to budge from the chair against the wall governed her. If she made a movement, would he spring? She sat with her arms folded across her chest, as if to retain the last warmth there, and still she did not look directly at him, though her eyes sidled now and again in the direction of the bed.

This silence was even longer than the others. She broke it. Again in that reminding but not conciliatory way, she said: 'I didn't run off with another man. It's what they usually get cross about.'

He replied in the reflective manner of a man who has dwelt with long deliberation on a problem or scheme but will not reveal his final decision until the time is ripe. 'It would have been better if you had run off with another chap. It was just plain, cold, murdering selfishness.'

She preferred the abusive anger. 'I can't think why you were so fond of me,' she said. 'I didn't run after you. I never thought you much of a catch.

180

You got me when I had a nasty row over pay with the firm I worked for in Cardiff—the tykes. You're no handsome oil painting, William—' Again she stopped, vaguely astonished at herself. Did she *want* him to spring?

That peculiar chuckle! He had developed into a different person, calculating, uncharacteristically voluble, chuckling to himself. Had he gone off his head? Why hadn't he called at the front door, in the normal way? The strange calculation of his trick struck her forcibly now. He had gone mad! She moved uncomfortably, and the chair creaked.

'Getting cold out there? Warm enough in here!'

'I'm all right,' she mumbled.

'That's the worst of getting yourself an outlandish cottage for a bolt hole—no heating in the bedroom when a thing like this happens. Never mind; it won't be a chill or influenza you'll be catching.'

As though rejecting what she heard, she stared more fixedly at the wall. A fancy preoccupied her that the veins of her feet had stiffened into sprays of icicles and it was impossible to walk. But her mind kept on making efforts to grapple with subjects suitable and, indeed, necessary for discussion. Anything to break those prolonged silences that were laden with something undeclared. After a while, she resumed: 'You doted on me too much, William. Your doting got on my nerves. I don't think I like men. I ought to have married a retired man who just wanted not to die alone.' A further fancy came to her that, but for the stupefying cruelty of the cold, it would be pleasant and fruitful to sit talking like this all through the night. Matters could be wound up, a personal bankruptcy declared void; pacified contestants might even make amicable farewells.

But William ignored her last observations. He asked: 'What do you do with yourself all day in this place?'

'Nothing.' She answered as if glad of his apparently social inquiry. 'At first I thought I'd stay only a few months. I wanted to think. All my life I promised myself a time to myself, with no nagging employer—or anyone else, for that matter—to answer to. I kept on trying to make up my mind to go to Susan in Australia. But somehow I couldn't make the move—'

'Ah!' he said and chuckled.

'I eat well, and take a little whisky some evenings. I keep an afternoon maid. I listen to good-class concerts and lectures on the wireless. The weeks go by . . .' The sloth of the slow, eventless days lay in her trailing-away voice.

'You mean you came here to guzzle. Australia, my Aunt Fanny! True, you've got a lot of the gypsy in you. I'm not saying that's a nasty thing; it can make a woman shine out and set a man ticking faster than usual. I bet when you'd finished guzzling your way through that legacy you'd have set about hooking some well-off fellow in these parts. You know all right there's some chaps that *like* being hooked and done down.'

'I intend going back to the drapery in Cardiff when the money is gone,' she said meekly.

'Isn't there some old buffer running after you here? I see you've got a lot of your looks left.'

At this, she turned her head and gazed at him. His eyes were fixed on her as if they had never moved away. He had placed the vacant pillow on top of his own, so that his head was propped up; he looked comfortable and warm but relentlessly wideawake, the greenish glint of his eyes clear and hard. She said: 'If you've come here thinking of a divorce, William, there isn't anyone to name. But I won't give you any trouble. I deserted you.' A glimmer of eagerness had struggled into her face.

'I don't want a divorce. No need for all that fuss and expense. Not now.'

Her mouth opened to ask the obvious question— 'Why not now?'— but she only looked at him glassily. She could hardly discern his head. Was the cold disabling her sight? Why was he there? It no longer seemed shocking that he had arrived, with such dramatic calculation, in her bed (but why, why?); she accepted the actual fact of his presence now—even, she fumblingly thought, almost welcomed it. The two dormant past years were smashed, and the thing that had fugitively haunted her had taken on, at last, concrete stature and power. She looked towards the bed as a homeless wanderer might look through a window into a firelit room.

'Come in,' he said, as if aware of her thoughts.

She did not reply but, draggingly, shook her head before turning it, with an automaton's movement, away from the hazed bed A few moments later, the lamp began to fade. 'If you give me the key,' she said, quivering out of her passivity, 'I'll fetch oil from the can in the kitchen.'

'No, Bessie.'

Her remaining vestiges of warmth and strength seemed to ebb with the sinking light. She couldn't even bring herself to get up and fetch coats and other garments from the wardrobe to wrap herself in. Neither could her mind dwell on the refusal of the key. Almost there was a sense of release, an elusive, lapping seduction, in her resolution not to move from the chair. I'll be found frozen to death in the morning, she thought. In the flickering light, the furniture began to look insubstantial, withdrawing its familiar identity; the dressing-table mirror became lifeless—an oval for ghosts to look in.

The last edge of blue on the lampwick vanished. She was surprised to find herself, suddenly conversational, saying, 'I often sit downstairs in the dark when the lamp goes out and I can't be bothered to fill it. I sit thinking. Living alone here has cured me of fright. It isn't as if you're a stranger.'

William said nothing. He was not a stranger? All people were strangers in the dark.

At the window, where the curtains were only half drawn, an anonymous night greyness seeped in, but it did not reach any object in the room. The last links with fact and reality were broken. There was not the faintest sound from the frozen world outside. All natural things were cast into the abeyance of this deepest and darkest hour. Was it midnight? What did it matter? Time mattered no more. The only thing existing—and it still remained a mystery—was the unseen element of judgement in the room; she recognised it fully now and waited for it to declare itself. It belonged to the dark.

She found herself saying, as if testing this judgement: 'You were silly to feel disgrace when I left you. A woman that runs off like that is a good riddance. Your friends at the White Hart would realise that, I expect.'

He said nothing. Had he fallen asleep? Buried his ears under the bedclothes? She could hear no breathing. Oh, if only he would hurl a heap more of abuse! Even the daft chuckle would be better than this silence. Now and again, her knees gave little convulsive jerks, as if making protest on their own account. The savage cold left her no dominon at all over her body now. Yet her mind, detached from her body, seemed to become clear of its confusion. She heard her own hesitating voice from a distance. 'William . . . If you've come wondering if I'll go back to you . . . it will need some talking . . . thinking about.' In her chest, a dead sort of pain followed the hard breathing necessary to get the words out.

Still there was no reply. Her head swerved from the direction of the hidden bed to the greyness at the window space. She thought of the bereft foothills and, beyond, the heights of the Brecknock Beacons impregnable with marble snow. All the world was pinioned in stony silence. If only she could hear the soft thud of a pine cone falling into the withered ferns of the garden! Loneliness, oblivion and freezing death were all about her. Hours must pass before a small, dim glimmer would crack the night.

When her mouth opened again, it felt grotesquely not her own. 'William . . .' Her lower jaw seemed to lock. She sat pondering.

Blue, blue . . . Why did she think of a blue, suncurled sea with foam swirling on a picnic beach? Tenby! The day trip she took to Tenby last summer . . . She saw a florist's shop filled with riotous blooms of July—

roses, sweet peas, zinnias, carnations. In a café, a sundae heaped with nuts and marshmallow cream was placed before her. A man with a sportsclub crest on his blue blazer lowered a newspaper and eyed her from a face as brown as a football. She wore a red dress and a hat she had just bought. Tenby was a good-class town. Not like rough, coal-mining Dinas, where a lady couldn't really be a lady . . . Her cheeks began twitching. Tenby vanished. Even the grey window space had gone. Her body gave a long, dislocated jerk; she was aware of it from afar.

Why was she on her feet? She did not remember getting up. Had he spoken? There was no sense of sound about her, and her eyeballs gained nothing from the dark. But she knew now where she must go. Carefully, laboriously, her feet moved. She trudged without a bending of her knees. Her body moved as towards a command, blindly without error. Her knee pressed against the bed.

'Come in,' he chuckled.

She heard the poplin swish of the thrown-back eiderdown. A faint eddy of warmth touched her face briefly. She fell into the opened bed, in all her clothes. The bedclothes closed round her. But she did not feel the warmth; the blankets seemed only to hold her immobile. When he turned and pressed the pillow over her face, she quivered only once. The long, silent apathy of the two past years contracted into a massive strength of obliteration, and acquiescent, she sank under it.

Light, a pure morning light, was seeping into her eyes. But she could not see it clearly. A pillow was on her face. Pulling it away—why was it there?—she sat up in astonishment. A shaft of sunlight came from the space between the curtains. For long moments, her mouth open like a startled child's, she remained looking down at the man beside her in the warm bed. He lay fast asleep, mouth open, too, a patina of sweat on his short, thickly rooted nose. For the first time, she recognised the nose as a pugnacious one. The wart on his chin somehow made him seem less sternly menacing.

Stealthily, keeping concentrated watch on his face, she slid a flat hand under his pillow and found the key. Then, with long pauses, she eased herself out of the bed. Her body, already wonderfully thawed, felt abounding as she stood safely on the woollen rug. She shook herself down like a dusty fowl; the black satin dress was badly creased. Her eyes did not move from William's face as she backed to the door. She unlocked and opened the door without noise, gave William a last look, and crept out.

When she returned, she carried a tray that held a teapot, two cups and a plate of biscuits. The night's residue of sloth was off her powdered face; her hair was tidied. She placed the tray on the bedside table; and stood looking at William's far-gone face again before crossing to the window. Brass rings clanged briskly as she flung back the curtains as far as they would go, releasing into the room the full, crisp morning. It was still very cold, and the light, spinning back from the dazzling frost in the garden, had the fiery bounce of diamonds. Night's claustrophobic assembly of threats had slunk away and the morning rang alive with victory.

'*William!*' At once, she reduced the hectoring shout. 'William!' There was something abridged, if not obsequious, in her gait and manner as she went to the tray and poured the tea. 'Another cold morning, William!' She did not look at him now. But she fetched a purple silk wrap from the wardrobe and, as Clytemnestra flung the net over the warrior returned from Troy, wrapped it round his shoulders. William, still a bit manacled in his heavy sleep, struggled up in the bed. Bessie found a pink woollen cardigan for herself.

As he took the cup of tea from her hand, he glanced at her from under swollen lids. He was always a thick sleeper. She shook out that other pillow, gave it a pronounced scrutiny, and placed it behind his shoulders. Bemused, he looked into the cup. 'There's nothing in it except tea,' she assured him. 'I've got no use for rat poison. When I want to get rid of you, I'll shoot you like a dog.'

She tittered as she crossed with her own cup to the chair on which such hours of agony had been endured the night before. William tasted the tea. Bessie swallowed two good mouthfuls herself, and after a silence, which seemed neutral, she asked: 'How much did you get for the restaurant from those caterers?'

'Five thousand pounds for the lease of the premises, seven hundred for the contents.' They were his first words. Had he returned to his old surly meagreness of speech?

'Why, William, that's not at all bad! Judging by the way you talked last night, anyone would think you had a grudge. You must have fought them like a man.'

He glanced at her. Something lurked in his face; it did not suggest anything to do with smiling. 'What time is it?' he asked abruptly, and looked at the soft felt hat still hanging on the ebony bedpost.

'About half-past eight. Plenty of time yet. You'll have to go by two. A woman from the village comes then. I'm supposed to be a widow.'

'I'm not going,' he said slowly.

She did not deal with this. 'I took a day trip to Tenby last summer,' she began, 'and I thought to myself, if William had adventure in him, this is a nice place to open a restaurant in. I like seaside places . . . What's the matter with you?' she suddenly challenged across the room. 'Can't you look me straight in the eye?'

He looked her straight in the eye. His thick, hard neck and square head lunged out from the purple wrap, and he growled: 'You can count yourself lucky you're sitting there drinking tea in comfort, like a bloody hypocrite sozzling after a funeral.'

A SPOT OF BOTHER

Ormond, upset by his favourite team losing the League match and, earlier in the day, a very raw shindy with his Mary Ann, so far forgot his principles as to go thoroughly astray in the city, that football Saturday. Sometimes sheepish, more often bellicose, he was a young married coal-miner endeavouring to settle down, too soon, to life. Profligacy was not his natural bent, but exceptional circumstances can achieve an exceptional breakdown of discipline, and, in addition, he was not one to halt in the thought that eccentric conduct can bring perils pertinent to it.

As dusk fell, after the disastrous match, he uncharacteristically broke away from the bunch of faithful boys who had journeyed with him from Bylau, twenty railway miles away in the swart Welsh hills, and for a time he thrust his dejected jaw through back streets whilst a drizzle wetted his well-oiled mop of curls. Then, wandering into many by-path public houses, he drank far more than was normal with him. By ten o'clock he reached the docks district, reputed place of saturnalia, and there he picked up a harlot who seemed to his (by then) illumined eyes—perhaps because of the big amber beads she wore down her front—cheerful-looking as a string of Breton onions.

He met her in a crammed pub called 'The Fireman's Larder'. After sundry conventional courtesies had been exchanged she asked him if he was married. 'I am, see!' he replied. 'To the best little Mary Ann that ever trod on a man's toe.'

'I thought so; I can always tell the married ones.'

The woman took out cosmetics and mirror from her bag and dabbed thickly at her face as though in logical comment. 'She's gone away for the week-end, I expect?'

'That's it!' Ormond said, enthusiastically recognising perception, but not mentioning that Mary Ann had torn off her thick-lensed glasses—always a bad sign—that morning and declared she was returning to her Aunt Maud's house 'for ever': she found his football excursions to the city objectionable and had not yet acclimatised herself to male isolations, though of course there were other seethings.

'She's gone by train!' he exclaimed, thumping the beer-soaked table. 'A puff-puff, see? Stops at a dozen stations before she put her lovely leg out and stares from her glasses to see who's meeting her. Short-sighted, see?'

'Sometimes they're well off, short-sighted,' the woman said, and swallowed at a gulp the single gin Ormond had bought her. He did not approve of women drinking, except a long-winded token one for sociability's sake.

She told him her name was Patricia, and in return he took out his wallet and extracted several snapshots. 'There's me!' he pointed out, unnecessarily. There, indeed, he was: uniformed in the army; bare-kneed with the Bylau Football Club; standing in a meadow among whippets and daisies; proud before a pigeon-cote in which meditated his racing birds; and one of him and Mary Ann twinly smiling a wide-open smile outside a chapel. Patricia made suitably attentive comments, and Ormond was encouraged to show, from among other documents in the wallet, the flattering character given to him by the C.O. of his regiment.

'Anyone would think,' she tittered, before excusing herself for five minutes, 'there isn't a wonky corner in you anywhere, sweetie.'

At closing time they sailed away from the wharves on a trolley-bus brilliant as a ship lit up at night. When they got off they went up to the portico steps of a tall gaunt house. Its peeling stucco was black-veined as a varicose leg. In the hallway a stately eighteenth-century staircase stretched bereft not only of people but of carpet and the wash it had long needed. A naked electric bulb, spotted with fly dirt, hung forlorn in the strange locked-up silence. To Ormond, accustomed to the poky but bustling interiors of Bylau cottages, the proportions of everything were majestic, and Patricia's flat on the second floor palatial. A begrimed plaster bust of Socrates on the mantelpiece, although an empty beer bottle stood beside it, added to the splendour. 'Who is it?' he asked, gaping. 'Your dad?'

'No, a Lord Mayor, I think.' Patricia, wheezing as she stooped, pulled off her mud-spotted shoes, which had buckles of the finest diamonds.

'Up in Bylau,' Ormond said, respectfully, eyeing the bust, 'we only have them in the cemetery, on high-class graves.' Shortly afterwards he pulled her to him by her beads. She had switched on the wireless and a dance band started to croak.

'Oh, not yet!' Patricia said.

She had small eyes lolling far down in green sockets, and he admired, in solemn illumination, all that his own bared eyes saw: it was the same

188

admiration that came from him in the cinema when actresses fabulous as mermaids waggled to and fro before their proud men. She lit a cigarette and seemed momentarily abstracted. The room was full of bulky furniture. A vast wardrobe of menacing black wood stood diagonally across a corner, near a door leading, presumably, to another room. The grand bedstead was of brass. Pink and blue articles of clothing hung over the top of a screen patched with floral wallpaper. Two windows were flimsily curtained. But the spacious room soon ceased to interest him. As is the way in drink, inquisitiveness had narrowed to a single obsessiveness. From outside came the hum of a passing trolley-bus, and this reminder of journeying pre-occupied him for only a second or two.

'Staying the whole night?' Patricia asked, suddenly eyeing him.

'If you please,' Ormond said bashfully. 'Owing to my last train being gone by now, even the one where you change at Pontypridd.'

He was undressing when a flashing explosion of light jumped through the room. 'What's that?' he called, above the wail of the dance band, trouser braces dangling in his arrested hand.

'The overhead bus wire does that sometimes,' declared Patricia. She was standing close to him. 'The flash comes through the curtains.'

'I thought it was lightning,' Ormond said, listening a moment as if for a growl of thunder.

'Perhaps it was lightning,' Patricia said indifferently. She unscrewed her pearl ear-rings, large and rosy as moons, which were almost her last coverings. ' I didn't hear a bus.' She ruffled his hair, sniffing. 'Nice hair, sweetie boy. Too much oil on it, though.'

His strong arm dotingly about her waist, he said: 'There's violets in it. Three-and-sixpence a bottle in Barney's *Cash Chemists* on the Square in Bylau.' Another flash of strange light tumbled through the room and, although engrossed in her charms, he mumbled, portentous: 'Storm brewing, right enough!' From the dance band came a jesting tune in welcome contrast to the previous wail.

'No, that one *was* a trolley-bus,' Patricia said. 'I heard it passing. The reel gets jammed on the wire. She jumped into bed quite briskly. 'Leave the light on, darling. I don't like the dark . . . No, don't turn off the wireless. I lik a bit of dance music. It goes on till midnight.'

He went into a deep cave of sleep early, lulled by the siren's croon then oozing unhurried out of Patricia's wireless.

A knock on the door can mean anything, even in Bylau, or as in those places of the still older world where men believed that a stranger at the door is sent by the ever-watchful gods. Mary Ann answered the knock, peering from her thick glasses at the tall, thin man standing, politely enough, on the beautifully whitened steps.

Following his inquiry, she bawled down the short passage to the kitchen: 'Ormond! A fellow to see you.' When Ormond appeared, shirt-sleeves rolled up, she retreated to the kitchen with a sniff. The breeze of her transit proclaimed that, in her judgement, the caller had to do with whippet racing, gambling, or other anti-home pursuits of the various male clubs in Bylau and thereabouts.

'Can I see you in private?' asked the caller. He wore a long black overcoat of flappingly thin material. His long thin nose was of startling, Caerphilly cheese whiteness, and it twitched whenever a vowel came into his words. 'Down the road, perhaps?' he invited, jerking his head towards the street of squat four-roomed dwellings, all alike and stuck together in well-kept solidity. A patch of waste ground, where children played, lay at the end.

'What for, down the road?' Ormond blew, sleepily astonished. He was not long home from the day shift, after a hot pit-head bath, and he had just eaten one of Mary Ann's meat broths, full of root vegetables, and a milky rice and egg pudding. 'I've got a house of my own. Come in . . . No,' he warned, in sudden afterthought, 'I don't want any vacuum cleaners, electric washing machines, or encyclopædias. The money in the pits won't allow them. No free samples, either.' Mary Ann closed the kichen door with a concurring slam; she too disapproved of hire-purchase goods and cheeky salesmen besieging orderly homes.

'It's a personal matter.' The caller's simple words came sliding out of the corner of his mouth. But his eyes gleamed with messages, to be revealed only in strict confidence: one moment they seemed probingly impudent, the next wooingly adulatory.

Ormond, yawning and scratching his curls, took him into the parlour. Languid tolerance lay in his flesh and muscles. Everybody had their living to earn. Perhaps this thin, black-overcoated chap wanted him to take out a life insurance on Mary Ann. Soon as a man got married, the insurance companies began to solicit him to think of burials.

The stuffy front parlour was seldom used. Its furnishings had belonged to Mary Ann's parents and included their bygone portraits in heavy golden frames. A mulberry plush cloth, thick as a carpet, covered a round table; on its centre lay a Family Bible of ornate leather and gilt clasps which had never been opened. Two china stallions of ferocious demeanour reared matched on the mantelpiece. The honeyed late afternoon light filtered in through foaming lace curtains kept clean as an angel's nightgown.

'Nor we don't want a television set,' Ormond added, absently. 'Owing to me being out a lot and Mary Ann's weak eyes.'

Standing by the round table, the caller showed sudden decision. A narrow hand of peculiarly swift pouncing whisked an envelope out of an inner pocket of the black overcoat. He drew three small limp cards from it and passed them across the table. Ormond gazed at each card in turn. Wonder slowly accumulated in his absorbed face.

'Well, well!' he remarked. He returned to the first card for further scrutiny, and said: 'Who's this? Not me, is it? Not with a pair of braces dangling from my hand!' He took the cards to the window, where the light was stronger.

The caller looked down his long white nose in deprecatory regret, though a smile of placating coyness went on and off his lips: he himself, saying: ' Excuse me,' had shut the parlour door, as if he feared draughts. 'It's you, plain enough, chum,' he now whispered. 'The one of you in bed is the best.'

It was. Ormond peered at it so concentratedly that his eyes squinted. There, solidly full-faced, was his head asleep on a white pillow, and, beside it, another head recognisable to the meanest intelligence as a woman's, complete with hair. 'Ay, it's the best,' he grunted, from down his throat. He spent quite a time in further study of the prints.

'Works of art!" the caller said, no censoriousness in his tone.

Ormond returned to the table and spread the three cards on Mary Ann's prized family plush. He pointed with a thick, strong forefinger. 'First class!' he agreed, congratulatingly. 'I'll have half a dozen of those two, postcard size . . . and an enlargement of *that* one, big enough to frame.'

The man, collecting the flaps of his long overcoat together with a wriggle of enjoyment, uttered a whinny of mirth. 'That's good, chum!' he jerked out, his manner, still man-to-man. 'Negatives only for sale, though. Worth a lot, those negatives. Sale to be completed on Saturday, if you can't manage it now.' He ended with accommodating comradeliness.

Ormond crossed to the door, opened it, and bawled into the passage: 'Mary Ann? Come here!'

She appeared with such rapidity that his call might have concealed

191

some private bird-note understood by her ears alone. 'This chap wants to sell some photos of me,' Ormond announced, giving her an unncessary push to the table. 'There they are!' The man drew his overcoat about him, blinked, but remained still.

Mary Ann, squarely short-bodied, fiery-coloured and altogether local-cast as her husband, but wearing a flowered voile frock, settled her glasses before taking up the cards for the important scrutiny due to any photographs of close relations or self. She, too, carried them to the window. Ormond followed her. 'I told him,' he said, pointing, 'six postcard-size of those two . . . and an enlargement of *that* one for framing.'

She peered at them with the suspicious intentness of the near-sighted, silent for long, long moments. Ormond stood waiting, hands on hips like an athlete poised for direction or assessing a distance. The caller had stepped back a yard from the table, towards the door: he had replaced the envelope in his pocket. But, upper lip lifted, he too waited.

'No,' Mary Ann decided at last, with mistress-of-the-home finality, 'not an enlargement of that one. It wouldn't frame well . . . not for the parlour or anywhere else, Ormond, dear.'

Ormond sprang. But the man, agilely black as an eel, was out, slithering down the passage before Ormond's raised foot could find relief. 'Ormond!' Mary Ann shouted, sprang too, and grabbed her husband by the waistband of his trousers seat. 'Think of the neighbours!' she hissed. The man escaped.

'Fetch my coat!' Ormond's snort was that of a boiling full-back cheated of the ball by a fouling opponent. Mary Ann, babbling, held on to her husband. He butted her backwards, so that she fell against the oak umbrella stand. Not more than a few seconds elapsed before he had put on his hairy Harris tweed jacket of myrtle green and, oblivious to Mary Ann's winded exhortations, streaked out of the house. The man was just disappearing round the corner at the end of the street.

Bylau is not of important dimensions; in fact, it is seldom spotted on maps. Under beetling hills rich with coal, it lies in uncaring sloth towards modern developments, though its little railway station functions, and buses ply in and out of it in haphazard easy-going. The natives know its every cranny, the various treads of its half-dozen police, and exactly what to do in time of trouble. Within three minutes Ormond had collected the following men: Goronwy Jones (from off the steps of the Miners' Institute), Wyn Davies (snatched out of the

White Hart bar), Pennar Bevan (coming out of a convenience), and Aneirin Evans (standing in reverie before a Labour Party poster). All were miners and members of the Bylau Football Club.

Information was conveyed mostly by gesticulations, Ormond's only vocal explanation being: 'That bloke in the black overcoat has stolen something from me; it's in his pocket.' (For theft, of course, it was; dastardly theft of his good name and odour in Bylau.) The stranger, sliding round corners, jerking his head back, clutching his flapping overcoat about him, was kept securely in view all the time.

They headed him out of the shopping Square and away from the railway station, dribbled him through law-abiding Coronation Street and intersecting Pleasant Terrace. Neither pursuers nor pursued hurried now. Outside the colliery manager's villa, the group was joined by Reverend Meurig Morris, a useful inside-right in his day and still a stand-by for an occasional match. 'I've got to go to Miss Lloyd-Trealaw's house,' the Rev. declared. 'I can only give you ten minutes.' With his starched dog-collar and round clerical hat he lent the affair a suitable pomp.

Their non-committal progress became that of men enjoying a promenade among well-beloved nooks and haunts too familiar for discussion: silence hung about their prowl. The stranger, kept twenty yards ahead, seemed for a while to pretend that he too was lightly engrossed in a walk among quiet back streets which, however, did not lead him back into the Square with its traffic, plashing fountain, and dutiful policeman standing impartial. Soon three of the group sauntered up a steep street while the other three cut through an alley. Thus they manoeuvred the culprit into a shady cul-de-sac under the disused colliery coke-ovens.

He cowered, spittle on his lips, against the padlocked door of a shed. But the half-hour of plodding pursuit was his sole punishment, and in any case the Rev. would not have countenanced physical blows. Whilst the others stood in a semi-circle of thick-set criticism, Ormond inserted his hand into the overcoat pocket, drew the envelope out, carefully looked in it, and stepped back with a mien of completion. 'Let him go, now,' he said graciously. Only the Rev., naturally a dab at recognising evil, had a word to say to the man.

'Better mend your ways, whatever you've done,' he pronounced; 'otherwise perdition will be your lot.' But the man's eyes had become unseeing slits refusing knowledge of anything.

They left him crouched into his overcoat like a bat closed on itself under a barn eave. 'Pickpocket!' Ormond mumbled to his friends, as they emerged from the cul-de-sac. 'Robbed me last Saturday when I was down in Cardiff for the match. No value in the envelope, except what's sentimental to me.' Tactful grunts came from the others, and they parted in the Square for their various evening pleasures. The noses of the cronies had sensed outrage against a son of clean Bylau, and it was enough.

His exalted shout, as he strutted down the passage, proclaimed that all was well. 'Mary Ann!' he bellowed, 'where are you? Let's go to the pictures. Best seats tonight!'

The kitchen door stood half open, and as he pranced round it something which seemed tremendous smacked him on the crown of his head. He staggered, stood still in shock, and another blow thumped on the same place; it was followed immediately by a shower of hard-dried haricot beans. He gazed in stupor at the pallid stuff gushing around his feet. Above him, standing on a chair behind the door, stood a young Queen Boadicea upraised in powerful moral wrath. She had half-filled an artificial silk stocking with the beans and twisted the top, but this cudgel had split with the second blow.

Staring up at her, he experienced the impact of a stranger exploding into vengeful revelation, a secret enemy erupting into bitter truth. Mary Ann's glasses shone from a domain of dragons.

'What's the matter?' he growled, taking offence up to a point. They had fought innumerable verbal contests, but she had never assaulted him before. 'Beans!' he grunted, and stared down again at the floor, perhaps furtively. 'Try a bottle next time,' he said, attempting bravado. But as he stepped to the fireplace rug, crunching the beans, the strut was out of his gait.

Mary Ann did not dismount from the chair, though she gave the door a push, so that it slammed and left them enclosed from any neighbour rash enough to pop in just then. And from that dais she launched a tirade. Anciently hackneyed of theme, it sprang out in rhythmic congress with the heavings of her bosom. It placed his sex low in the structure of the universe. Nameless beasts crawling out of primeval slime, baboons of later date but scarcely more attractive, speaking but no-forehead creatures ambling out of dank caves with clubs in their hirsute hands—these, and marginal embroideries such as serpents, hog-pigs, toads and billy-goats, haunted her abuse. Yet she did not snatch off her glasses with that ominous gesture her husband

194

had learned to dread. The broken stocking waved from her hand as if she had enchanted it into a whip.

'A woman,' she shouted, apparently reaching crescendo, 'marries a man with two legs and finds he's got four like the dogs of the street!'

Ormond, twenty-five next birthday, stood on the rug with arms folded and eyelids stretched back as far as they'd go. Instinct informed him that it is always best, in such circumstances, to remain silent (but silent with an engrossed attention and not an insulting indifference). He continued to stare at her whilst she fulfilled herself in speech. When she stopped, he only remarked: 'You said last Saturday you were leaving me for your Anutie Maud's for ever. How was I to know you'd come bouncing back so quick the next day? I'm not God Almighty. I'm only a man.'

Still up on the chair, but looking as though she needed a glass of water, Mary Ann panted: 'Excuses! Being a man excuses everything?'

'That's how they are,' he said, even sombrely. He wanted to light a cigarette but somehow could not, as one can't in a solemn court of law. 'How would you like to be married to that crocodile in the black overcoat?' he inquired. 'Count your blessings, Mary Ann.'

She jumped down from the chair, went to the table, and banged a pot or two about. Although the onslaughting fury had sunk, still she disclosed an identity new to him. 'There's a bit of that villain in every man,' she said rhetorically.

Ormond bridled. 'Here, that's a nasty insult!' In stern rebuke, he added: 'Not so insulting, though, as a married woman running away from her husband to her silly auntie's. A woman that won a scholarship in school, too . . . *and* top prize for good general conduct!' A certificate of these merits hung framed in the parlour: Mary Ann had a passion for framing everything framable.

'Ha!' She banged the lid on the casserole dish. 'A pity they don't give us girls lessons about men; we all leave school as big dunces about *them*.'

'Boys don't have lessons about women,' Ormond said, and, looking surprised himself at his ruminations, proceeded: 'That's proper enough; otherwise, we wouldn't have a champion time making big mistakes before settling down.'

She jabbed at the wilting dahlias in a pottery vase they had bought during a seaside holiday that summer. 'A pretty champion mistake *you* made last Saturday!' she exclaimed.

'And have dealt with it today in a champion way,' he retaliated, not without pride.

The dew was finally off the garden. They recognised it. Ormond crossed to her, took her shoulders, turned her round from the table. She had to be re-discovered. He gave her a shake. A bean fell out of his tight-knit curls and dropped into her bodice of flowered voile. Two pairs of tears also fell from behind her glasses.

'Let me find my bean,' he begged.

Later, tidily with hand-brush and pan, he swept up all the beans from the floor. This was exceptional. In Bylau men are not much addicted to domestic jobs, and Ormond in particular, always out with the boys, was not partial to them. There was a vague aspect of compliant reformation about his figure as he stooped to the task.

AFTERNOON OF A FAUN

No one took any notice of the ordinary, strong-legged mountain boy as he stood, in truant-looking calculation, on a street corner one golden October afternoon. The day-shift miners were clattering their way home; a few women scuttled, concentratedly as crabs, in and out of the shops; in the gothic-arched porch of Lloyds Bank the minister of the prosperous Baptist chapel stood brandishing an unnecessary umbrella in debate under the long, doubtful nose of the Congregational minister, whose sermons were much bleaker than his rival's. Even the constable stepping out from the police station, which had eight cells for violent men, did not rest his pink-lidded eyes on the meditating boy. The afternoon remained entirely the property of grown-ups.

A few minutes earlier, Mr. Vaughan, the head-master, had walked into his classroom in the grey school up behind the main street. After beckoning to the boy from behind the big globe atlas, which had just been wheeled in for a geography lesson, Mr. Vaughan had whispered: 'You have to go home at once, Aled; your mother has sent for you . . .' The old duffer, in that unreliable way of his, had smiled, hesitated, attempted to pat the pupil's ducking-away head; then, giving the globe —skittishly it seemed—a spin in its sickle, he had stalked off to his own quarters.

Had he come with good news which, in his punishing way, he decided finally to withhold? A back-row boy had made a whinnying neigh, and Aled's own departure was accompanied by a chorused groan from the others of Class IV: they thought he was summoned out for the usual. In those days, corporal punishment was rife in the schools, and Mr. Vaughan's only authority lay in a resined willow cane, though his incessant use of this had about as much real body as a garrulous woman's tongue. All the boys of Class IV despised him, unerringly divining his lack of true moral stature, unforgiving him for not being masterful as a bloody oath.

Humming like a bee with a ripe peach in its vicinity, Aled had swooped down the hill from the stone jail and come to a bouncing halt in the main street. It was a full hour before the school would close for the day, and the liberation made time prodigal. A yellow sun wallowed high above the mountains.

He half guessed why he had been called from school. His father, who lately had become more bad-tempered, was due to go to Plas Mawr, the hospital and rest-home for sick miners, away in another valley, and the horse-drawn ambulance van must have arrived that afternoon; no doubt his mother had gone in it too, to see his father installed. He was only needed to look after the house until she returned by train. It wasn't necessary, he decided, to hurry home just for that. Willie Dowlais's mother, who lived next door, would be keeping an eye on the house meanwhile.

But what was there to do? He gazed dreamily at the Baptist preacher. Then, in the style of a pigeon-fronted old gentleman of well-behaved disposition, he took an imitative strut down the main street, hands clasped behind him, a leisurely eye cocking into shop windows. Suddenly he halted again. Neck out, he advanced closer to a window of Morgan's General Emporium, stared into it intently, and loped a rapid step backwards. The afternoon lost all its festival tints.

Morgan's hotch-potch window display included a bulky perambulator, and in it sat, among silken cushions, a most successful-looking wax baby. Cosy as a cauliflower among leaves, its face bulged out from a price-ticketed bonnet of green ribbons, and a snowy napkin, also priced, dangled from a triumphantly lifted hand. Other articles relevant to worship of this enthroned pest were scattered below its carriage— garish toys, shoes of knitted blue wool, a little pot painted with garlands of roses, and embroidered bibs to catch dribbles from that smirking and overfed mouth.

Nose puckered, he continued to stare at the omen in mesmerised suspicion. *That* was why Mr. Vaughan had twitched into a smile and attempted to pat his head! About a month ago, while she was ladling baked custard on his plate, his mother had confided in him that he might expect either a sister or a brother soon. Although withholding comment at the time, he had not been favourable at all. The sovereignty of his reign, now in its eleventh year, had never been disputed before.

'I'm sure it's a sister you'd prefer,' his mother had added, in that deciding-for-you manner of grown-ups, and looking at him as if it was only for his comfort that this act was being done. 'She'll be company for you . . . But, of course, they *might* send you a brother instead. They handle so many that often they get careless and stupid.'

'They', 'they'—who were these mysterious, two-faced 'theys'? He didn't believe in them, they were invented by cowardly and treacherous

198

grown-ups who wanted to hide their own mistakes. He had stared angrily at the photo of his grandfather, which hung above the chiffonnier, and muttered: 'Why don't *they* go on strike for shorter hours or more money, like the miners do?' It was his sole pronouncement at the time.

'That's enough, Aled!' his mother had said, escaping into another of the despotisms of grown-ups. 'You're a spoilt boy. Eat your custard.'

Since then, the news had been too outlandish to preoccupy him. He turned from the grinning wax horror at last, hesitated, and stood frowning on the gutter kerb. Further brooding weighed him down. The thought of Ossie Ellis had arrived logically, and, also logically, his stomach sank lower.

Ossie, often seen obediently pushing a battered old pram—usually it contained two babies—through the streets, was the derision of his fellow-pupils of Class IV. He was seldom in the position to enjoy a cowboy Saturday in the mountains because he was obliged to stay at home to look after his brothers and sisters, all unjustly younger than himself. One Saturday, when called for at his home to go on a pre-arranged spree, he had put his head round the door and said, depressingly: 'Can't come, Aled. I'm the old nanny-goat again today; four to mind and feed, and one of them's got measles, I think.' His shirt-sleeves were rolled up, he wore a girl's stained pinafore, and a smelly noise came out of the ramshackle house. His mother was a befeathered tartar, his father a drunkard, but Ossie, always solemn behind steel-rimmed spectacles, never took umbrage when taunted by Class IV with its terrible kow-towing to domestic tyranny.

'Do a bunk from home some day,' Aled advised, on another thwarted occasion. 'Run away and get lost all night—that will teach them.'

Ossie had blinked owlishly, and said: 'No, it won't. But I'll never get married, Al.'

'Nor me,' Aled said, without just cause then.

He looked up. The pink-lidded eyes of the policeman, who was patrolling the main street in the usual suspicious manner of his kind, rested assessingly on him now. Without futher delay, Aled turned on his heel, walked with laborious meekness up the street, and vanished into a quiet turning. He even hurried down the rough-stoned, deserted alleyway: it lay in a homewards direction, and it approached the bridge which he crossed twice a day, to and from school.

He looked back over his shoulder furtively. It was as though the golden day had darkened into night and avenging footsteps plodded behind him—the inescapable feet of pursuit in a nasty dream.

Forebodings of drastically curtailed pleasures, and of assaults to dignity, bereft his sandalled hooves of their usual nimble leap as he climbed the gritty steps which led to the old iron footbridge. On the top step he paused to gaze up at the bluish green mountains encircling the valley. It was a look of farewell. He was a great lover, even in winter, of the coarse high-ways and by-ways in the mountains, and he knew their secrecies as shrewdly as the rams and ewes inhabiting those antique places. A baby's perambulator could never reach them.

Ahead, on the shivering middle span of the old bridge, tramped a last day-shift miner. The rickety Victorian structure linked, with three long, nervously zigzagged spans, the valley's two hillside communities. It was a short cut for pedestrians, and it crossed the big, sprawling colliery yard. In winter storms uneasy people avoided it. Two pit shafts, aerial wheels whirling, towered a quarter-mile up the narrowing valley. Downwards lay a long view of swirls of mountain flank retreating from the valley in flowing waves ungrimed as a sea.

He began to increase his step after a last backwards glance. The miner ahead had stopped to peer over the bridge railing—the colliery yard ended just there with a steep 'tip', down which rubble, slag and useless coal dust was thrown every day—and Aled, when he reached him, stopped to peer down too, looking through an opening in the trellised ironwork.

What he saw below made him grip the railings. The afternoon flowered.

'His back got broken,' the old miner said, casually noticing the boy standing beside him. 'There's been a fall of roof down in Number Two pit today. They had to stun him to put him out of his misery.' His voice was casual too, and his hands hung from the dirtily ragged sleeves of his pit jacket like crumpled shapes of old black paper. For a miner he looked frail and ghostly.

Aled drew away for a moment and, astounded, asked: 'They are going to throw him on the tip?'

'No. The wagon will be shunted back after they've emptied the stuff from the others. He was called Victor in Number Two.' The miner, his face anonymous in its mask of negroid dust (there were no pit-head baths in those days), looked at the boy again. The whites of his eyes shone glossy as candle-wax. 'Dan Owen's boy, aren't you?' he asked. 'How's your dad getting on?'

'He's going to Plas Mawr,' Aled replied, inattentive, a foot jerking in excited impatience. Why didn't the man go?

200

'Oh, aye. A good place for them.' The miner tramped off, unconcerned. The middle span quaked under his studded boots.

Expert as a squirrel, Aled scrambled up the railing and sat on the shaky ledge. Now he could view unimpeded the train of four small-size wagons below. It had run on a narrow-gauge track from the pit shafts and stood drawn up to the tip's edge. But no labourer was in attendance. A horse lay in the end wagon. The boy sat rigid. All the wealth of the Indies might have been below in the monotonous yard.

If only because of its size, a collapsed horse is an arresting spectacle, and this one—he was of the cob breed suited to the pits—had been dumped into a wagon much too mean for his awkward proportions. From the chained body a foreleg was thrust up stiffly into the air. The long neck, a sorrel gush under the dishevelled, grit-dulled mane, hung inert over the wagon's end. But the staid profile of the head could be seen, its eye open in a dull, purposeless fixity. Gaunt teeth showed yellow under lips drawn back as if in a snarl, and from the mouth dripped—yes!—an icicle of purplish fluid. Victor looked an old horse. Had he been stunned on that bone inset so strongly down the long, desolate face?

No one crossed the bridge now, no one was visible in the whole yard. All the smashed horse was his. He stared down calculatingly, wanting to retain the exclusiveness of this treat, jealously to store this gala exhibit. An item from an elementary school lesson of the past returned to him: *The horse is a quadruped, a beast of burden, and a friend to man*, and he felt a brief compassion. Everybody spoke well of horses. He remembered seeing a couple of young ones trotting in fastidious energy, tossing their bright manes, as they were led up the valley for their life down in the pits. Horses dragged the small wagons of coal from the facings to the bottom of the pit shafts, and he had heard that when they were brought up for retirement, or to be sent to the knackers, they could no longer see clearly in daylight: they would stand bewildered at the pit-head, neighing in chagrin, lost from their warm dim-lit stables deep under the earth . . .

He jerked up his head, glanced swiftly at the sky, swivelled round the ledge, made a clean jump, and galloped over the bridge. Willie Dowlais's camera! The light would be good for a long time yet, but the horse might be removed at any moment. With snap-shots of this treasure in his possession he would be a prince among the other boys.

Anxiety began as he leapt the far steps and it occurred to him that Mrs. Dowlais the Parrot might not be at home or, alternatively, would be unwilling to lend Willie's camera.

Springing up the path on the slope, above which the piled streets and terraces began, he heard Angharad Watkins singing as she pegged washing on a rope in the tilted, flower-cushioned garden of her old cottage, which stood isolated on the slope. She called to him when he stampeded past her gate, but he only waved an impatient hand; they were old friends and he owed money in her amateur shop. Above, the length of Noddfa Terrace was abolished in a flash.

On the corner of Salem Street, swarthy old Barney Window Panes shouted his customary: 'Hey, boy, know anyone with a broken window?' Barney was also called The Wandering Jew, because, with a load of glass pieces strapped to his bowed, homeless-looking back, he tramped over the mountains, never using trains even after sunset, and no one knew where he lived. He gave pennies to boys for information of people's broken windows. Although Aled knew of a couple, he dashed past heedlessly, rounding the corner into the empty roadway of Salem Street in champion style.

His shouted name brought him to an abrupt halt. The call home! He had forgotten about it. He stood poised in the road, glaring sideways towards the open door of his home, a leg still lifted. 'There you are at last!' Aunt Sarah's voice cried, further. 'Come here, Aled. You've taken a long time.'

Why was *she* there? She stood just inside the door-way with Willie Dowlais's mother. He lowered his leg and cautiously approached them. 'What do you want?' he demanded, his voice rising to a shout—'I've got to go back to school . . . For the geography!'

Mrs. Dowlais the Parrot—as, usually, she was called—gave Aunt Sarah a bunch of chrysanthemums which grew in her back garden and waddled past him silently to her own door: he watched her go in despair. Aunt Sarah never failed in reducing him to a surly feeling of guilt. She lived across the bridge, in the fashionable part, and always looked as though she had been awarded medals all her life. The owner of five terrace houses, and an influential member of the Baptist chapel, she sang solo in the chapel's famous annual performance of Handel's *Messiah*, heaving herself out of her seat on the specially erected platform when her items came, and growing twice her size as she gave vent. Even now, statuesque, she stood as if expecting applause that she was there.

His kingdom came toppling down. He had forgotten about her, too, and anguish became more acute as he realised she would have been called across the valley for such a ceremonious event as the arrival of a baby. The usurper *had* arrived!

'Come in, Aled,' Aunt Sarah said, her voice different. He edged a step or two inside the doorway, avoiding her hand, and throwing a glance of extreme anxiety in the tip's direction. 'Your father asked for you,' she said. 'He has left us.'

'Gone to Plas Mawr?' He still breathed heavily—half in relief now. But he did not proceed farther into the house. A peculiar silence, such as comes after an important departure of a person, lurked about the interior.

'No.' Aunt Sarah's pince-nez glimmered down on him. 'He died this afternoon, Aled.' She added, in comforting afterthought: 'You wouldn't have arrived here in time, in any case.'

'Died?' The word dropped down his throat like a swallowed sweet. He stared at her. 'Why?'

'Why?' The familiar, other tone returned. 'He had a relapse . . . hæmorrhage.' She used the word importantly and, noticing his uncomprehending stare, added: 'His lungs, my boy. The silicosis.'

Silicosis. It was a word he knew well. The blight word of the valley. Some men of the pits stayed at home with the disease for years, living on the compensation money paid by the colliery owners; others went to Plas Mawr for cure or not. Men got it from breathing the gritty dust of the pits. Now and again, in streets or shops, he had heard gossiping women relate: 'The test says he's got it hundred per cent.' Or it would be the gamble of eighty per cent; or a more cheerful fifty. Even men who were cured never went down the pits again, and always there were others, younger, coming up the valley to take their places.

'Your mother is upstairs with him,' Aunt Sarah said, returning to her grown-up oblivion. She bunched the neighbour's chrysanthemums and began to mount the staircase. Her voluminous grey skirt swished majestically.

'Shall I come up?' he mumbled, stretching his neck as he advanced. He wanted a cup of water.

'No; wait,' she replied, not turning. 'I'll call you when we're ready.'

He stood baulked before the staircase, gazing up. The sense of frustration became more desperate. That unfamiliar silence came down the stairs like an exhalation; it made his scalp contract. Yet he could hear the gentle press of feet shifting across the floor above. Then he heard his mother's voice—it sounded both swollen and hollow—saying: 'Give me the sponge, Sarah.' He made a headlong plunge to the open front door.

A new agony, as he banged on the neighbour's door, was the sudden thought that there would be no reel of negatives in the camera, though he knew Willie had bought one on Saturday . . . Mrs. Dowlais the Parrot was ages in answering the bang. 'Yes, Aled?' she said, bending a puce ear closer, as if she hadn't heard his immediate babbling request. 'Your mother wants something?'

'Willie's camera—' he panted.

'Willie's camera!' Her eyes widened in astonishment. Within the house, her aged parrot gave a squawk that sounded mocking.

His feet strutted on the doorstep like a dancer's. But he sensed that she was willing to grant any request because of what had happened next door. 'I've got to take photos of a horse on the tip, before it's taken away!' he shouted. 'For school. We're having lessons about horses. Willie said I could borrow his camera . . . The *camera!*'

His crescendo yell did not upset her. A comfortable woman, very esteemed in the valley, she waddled and sighed her way into her sympathetically darkened house, its blinds down. She rummaged there for an unbearably long time. A whine came from him when he snatched the camera from her hand. Running, he examined the reel indicator of the black, ten-shilling box, saw that only three negatives had been used, and streaked round Salem Street corner. The Wandering Jew was still there, sunk in reverie, waiting for informing boys to come from school. In the sky the mountain-blue of early October had darkened a shade.

He had scrambled down to the yard by a workmen's path on the slope and, chest bursting in foreboding of this last frustration, arrived at the exact place below the bridge. But the horse was gone. The three wagons of waste stuff remained. But, again, no labourer was visible. He could have gone in pursuit of the shunted wagon; the man in charge would have understood this special flouting of the *Trespassers will be Prosecuted* notices posted at the yard's main entrances. But he did not move. All desire to photograph the horse left him.

A fanfare of approaching yells made him start into attention, and, immediately, he dashed to the shadows under the bridge. The boys were out of school. They stampeded over the spans in whooping droves. Leaning against a trembling stanchion, he listened to their cries as though hearing them for the first time: he had no wish for their confederacy now. The last feet pattered away into the distance. Still, passive and exhausted, he lingered in the hiding-place, gazing at a heap of mildew-green tree trunks maturing for use down in the pits.

He knew, now, that he would never brag to the boys about the horse, never mention it. He could hear them—'Hark at Al! . . . You saw a dead horse, eh? Shoved into a little wagon on top of the tip! Purple stuff dropping from its mouth, eh? Sure he didn't have billiard balls for teeth, too?'

The yard stretched unfamiliarly silent and deserted. Had he really seen a horse? Had a man with an unknown, dustily black face spoken to him on the bridge, and asked a question about his father? It seemed a long time ago, though yellow sunlight still splashed on the tenacious clumps of seeded thistles and thorn bushes growing from this grit-thick waste ground. He looked about him vaguely. It no longer seemed unusual that he had not seen a labourer. This closed territory, where he trespassed, was not the same yard which he viewed daily from the footbridge. It was his first visit below.

When he came from the hiding-place he stood irresolutely on the tip's crest. The sun, veering towards a mountain, had become a deeper gold; a seagull visitant winged through a shaft of thickening light, returning down the quiet valley to its coastal haunts. People were gathering into their houses. He took a few slow steps homewards, stopped, and moodily kicked a piece of slag down the tip.

Forgetful of prosecution, he stood looking everywhere but in the direction of his home. A rope of lazily flapping coloured garments caught his eye—Angharad's washing, hung above a spread of dahlias, chrysanthemums and Michaelmas daisies. He hesitated, remembering his debt, then crossed the yard and scrambled up a slope to the path beside which her old, silverstone cottage stood alone, the only one remaining from the valley's remote rural days.

Angharad's grandmother had left the house as a legacy to her, together with its litter of pigs and a cow. After the funeral, about a year ago, she instantly got rid of the pigs and cow and almost as instantly married Emlyn Watkins, a sailor conveniently home on leave from the Royal Navy. But Aled could never think of her as a woman shut-up properly by a wedding: she didn't have that style.

A chewing woman customer, chronically married-looking and with a ponderous goitre, came out of the cottage. To companion herself during Emlyn's long absences—she had no children to bother her, so far—Angharad had opened a shop in her front parlour, the stock consisting mainly of confectionery, cheap remedies for sickness, household oddments, and cigarettes for workmen dashing in off the colliery yard. Credit was allowed some children, who were selected emotionally and not according to social prestige. He owed her for three lots of stopjaw toffee, a bag of marbles, and two cartons of chalk crayons.

A dramatic soprano shriek greeted him as he walked into the odorous parlour. 'Aled!' Angharad cried, 'I've only just heard about it from Mrs. Price the Goitre!' And full-based, down she collapsed to a chair behind the big table, which was heaped with open boxes of sweets, satchels and bottles of stuff for toothache, bellyache and headache, culinary herbs, pencils and cotton-reels, cards of hairpins, illustrated packets of flower seeds, and the kitchen scales of burnished brass on which she usually gave very good measure to favoured children. 'Another good man gone!' she wailed. 'It's wicked.' She might have been bewailing the loss at sea of her own husband.

A chair, for gossiping, stood on the customer's side of her well-spread table. Aled sat on its edge, eyeing a newly-opened box of Turkish Delight. The rose and yellow chunks, elegantly perfumed and pearl-dusted, were always beyond his means. He felt he was there under false pretences. Why had he come?

'They're upstairs with him,' he mumbled, waiting for her outburst to subside, but also relieved by it.

'I'd close all the damned pits!' she went on, shrilly. 'Or make people dig for their own dirty coal!' Momentarily the origin of all sorrow, she yet managed to remain lavish as a lot of lambs gambolling on a hillock. A tight heliotrope frock, stamped with a design of pineapples and pale shells, held her body in precarious bondage.

He dreaded that she would ask him what she wanted—the room, after all, was a shop. Simmering down in her abuse of the pits, she peeped at him out of the corner of her blue eyes. At random, he said: 'My mother made a lemon jelly this morning—she said it would set in time for his tea. Dad liked lemon jelly . . .' He lapsed into pondering. Because of all that was going on upstairs, he thought, no one would prepare a meal now, and the jelly would remain forgotten in a cool place under the kitchen sink.

Angharad's woe entirely ceased. She dabbed at her fresh-coloured face with a man's large handkerchief, and invited: 'Take a piece of

206

Turkish Delight.' When, slowly, he shook his head, she urged: 'Aled, I'll let you off your account. You don't owe me anything!' She jabbed a tiny gilt fork into a yellow chunk and, smiling, held it out.

'My Aunt Sarah is there,' he said, taking the honey-soft chunk. He heard the hiss of the goose-grey bombazine skirt going upstairs.

'*She's* got a good voice in the *Messiah.*' Angharad wagged her head. 'Too loud and showy for my taste, though.' She pushed a piece of Turkish Delight in her own mouth, which, shaped like a clover-leaf, was surprisingly small.

He sat back. The scented luxuriance melted in his mouth. 'She's always criticising me,' he remarked.

'A rose one this time?' Angharad held out another chunk, dismissing Aunt Sarah. A drop of juice, like a golden ooze from fruit, came from the corner of her mouth, and for a moment, staring, he remembered the horse. 'It's what they eat in harems in the East,' she said, and she, too, eating a rose piece, seemed to purr in understanding of women reclining lazy in satin bloomers on a marble floor. 'But these are made in Bristol,' she said.

'Have you been in a harem?' he asked, exact.

'No, certainly not! And neither has Emlyn, though his ship's been to the East.' Angharad remained amiably regal as her ancient name.

No one came in to buy; everybody, by that time, was gathered about the routine teapot and a plate of bread and butter. Angharad, after giving him another peeping glance, placed the lace-frilled box of Turkish Delight in a position convenient to both of them and took a letter from a fat cookery book, lying on the table. 'From Emlyn!' she whispered, confidentially. 'I'll read it to you . . . Help yourself,' she said, pointing.

It was a long letter, and she read it in leisurely gratification, a hand reaching occasionally for Turkish Delight. Emlyn seemed to be exceedingly fond of her and interrupted anecdotes of life in ship and port to reiterate, like the last line in a ballad's verse: 'Angharad, girl—roll on, Christmas leave! You'll have to shut shop then!' Once or twice, she paused to omit something, shaking her head and peeping at her guest.

Interest in Emlyn's ramblings dwindled from him. He watched her hand playing with beads distributed about her freckled throat, where it went into her sleepy-looking chest. Vaguely he thought of something tucked-in and warm, and, for some reason, he remembered the speckled thrush's egg which he and Willie Dowlais had taken from a nest last spring: the startling private warmth of the nest, as he put his hand in it, returned to him.

She folded the letter at last and gave a heave, murmuring: 'Home by Christmas! My big Santa Claus . . .' She stared, looking at Aled guiltily, craned her neck, and squealed: 'My God, we've eaten the whole boxful! Seven shillings' worth, at cost price! No wonder Emlyn always asks me what I've done with my profits.'

Aled said rapidly: 'I've got a loan of this camera. I thought I'd take photos of you, to . . . to send to Emlyn.' He glanced at the window. 'We'll have to be quick.'

She jumped up with alacrity, crying: 'Oh yes, yes! But let me get my new hat and fur.'

Willie Dowlais would need appeasing for this unsanctioned use—far less understandable than for the eccentric treasure of a dead horse—of his negatives. They hurried into the garden. He took nine shots of her, among the explosive dahlias, lolling chrysanthemums and dried washing; for some, the expert in charge, he commanded her to remove the cygnet-winged hat of Edwardian dimensions which was balanced on a head which always he had trusted. She posed with proud docility. The cherry-red sun leaned on a mountain top. He guessed the prints would be dim.

'Sailor though he is, Emlyn will break down and cry, when he sees me among my dahlias and washing.' Angharad, after stretching a hand to feel if a pale blue nightdress had thoroughly dried, began to pluck the freshest dahlias and chrysanthemums. 'But serve him right for joining the Navy!' She turned, quickly. 'All the same, Aled, don't go down the pits when you grow up! Join the Navy. It's healthier.'

He wound the completed reel, and said: 'There was a dead horse on the tip this afternoon. I was going to take photos of it. But it had disappeared . . .' His voice loitered and his eyes wandered in the tip's direction.

Angharad paused, turned to look at him again, then only remarked: 'Well, better a live woman inside that box than a dead horse, don't you think?'

Her face was serious, but, within the clear eyes, smiled. She began to walk towards him, flowers—milky purple, golden, sorrel-red, russet, deep claret—in the crook of her arm. As, vaguely, he stood watching her approach, the apparition came again. But, now, the defeated neck, the dead eye, the snarling yellow teeth, the mouth from which thick liquid dropped, were like glimpses recalled from a long-age dream . . .

Angharad had come close to him; he did not look up to her face. Her right hand pressed his head into her, under the breast. He seemed to smell a mingle of earthily prosperous flowers, sweets and herbs, and warm flesh. She had to pull his head away by the hair.

'Aled,' she said, 'I've kept you too long. You must go home now. You'll be needed.'

'Yes,' he agreed, waking.

'Take these flowers with you?' she suggested.

He shook his head, definitely. 'No; I can't carry flowers through the streets.'

'What!' But she smiled at once, and, walking down the garden with him, only said: 'Men!'

'Bring them up to the house tonight?' he invited, adding, without dubiousness: 'My mother is going to have a baby.'

'Aren't you lucky!' Angharad said, unsurprised. 'When my time comes, you'll be able to advise me how to bring them up.' At the garden gate, she promised: 'I'll come up tonight with the flowers.'

'You can have the prints on Saturday,' he shouted from the slope, waving the camera.

The sun was slipping out of sight. Greyish fumes already smudged the valley's far reaches. Soon the air would stir under the crescent moon's rise, with the evening star sparkling in clear attendance. He hurried, without anxiety.

THE DARLING OF HER HEART

The key of the cottage lay hidden in its customary place under the lavender clump beside the front porch. She unlocked the door and found everything as usual in the dusky living-room, its odour of Saturday morning wax-polishing still mingled with the scent of bunched herbs maturing under the pitted ceiling beams. The burnished brass candlesticks and the cherished pieces of old china on dresser and in cabinet were undisturbed; not a petal had fallen from the bowl of damask roses on the tawnily gleaming table. Nevertheless, all the house was desecrated.

As if following the intuition of her roused nose, its bird's curve quiveringly alert, Siân Prosser darted up the staircase of ancient oak rising direct from the living-room. She went into one of the two spick-and-span front rooms. A taut, small-assembled woman of sixty, in whose autumnal brown face the eyes had become blazingly renewed, she stood by the single-size bed for two or three minutes, while the sunset light thickened to a violet hue at the window. She stood as though gone into a trance in which unimpeachable knowledge was being given her.

Suddenly, and with furious speed, she stripped the bed, taking the two blankets, the sheets, the pillow and bolster out to the landing and hurling them down the stairs. Next she dragged the mattress down the stairs and into the back garden. Getting the mattress through the gate into the rough, lumpy field behind the cottage was quite a task. After placing it over a molehill, so that air could circulate beneath it, she sped to fetch the pillow, bolster, sheets and blankets. Made locally, the blankets were of excellent Welsh flannel, which lasts for generations. She piled all on the humped mattress. Finally, she ran for a can of paraffin oil from the kitchen, liberally sprayed the big heap, and struck a match.

Flames spread over the heap with a soft, eating pleasure. Siân did not wait; the evening dew on the grass would prevent the flames spreading over the field. Back in the cottage, she peered up at the clock. Over an hour remained before the Rising Sun would close its doors. Everybody's social—and indeed private—habits are known in small country villages. Catrin Lloyd would be alone in her cottage until about half-past-ten. Siân hastened out, replacing the key under the lavender bush.

Hatless, walking with the trot of a vigorously small woman out on an important errand, she climbed a road bordered with fields in which, here and there, a farm cottage nestled. The Rising Sun, which she passed, lay cosily sunk in a fruiting apple orchard. Her own husband and the husband of the woman she was about to visit were inside it drinking together with the other village men in Saturday night freedom from woes. Not once had her husband picked a quarrel with Catrin's husband. But men were weak in such matters.

Arrived on the hill's crown, where, had she not been so heated, dowdy St. Teilo's church might have reminded her of Christian forbearance, Siân paused a moment. She looked back and, like Lot's wife, saw a glowing red confusion in the field behind her cottage. She resumed her trot with a pinched smile. A few lights began to gleam in windows of the cottages scattered spaciously in the well-ordered domain down the other side of the hill. Nobody else trod the road. At the bottom of the hill she turned off into a lane smelling of meadowsweet and clover, and at last came to a thatched, bulgy-walled old cottage.

Above its front flower garden, the twilit cottage stood pretty as a calendar picture, though in daylight it showed decayed and tumbledown, the thatch unkempt as the hair of the slut dwelling within. As her feet skipped up the garden path Siân could see, beyond an uncurtained window, an oil lamp burning inside. The window-sill was crowded with sickly potted plants, and, for some reason, Siân gave a grimace at sight of these: she had already peered contemptuously at the waif-like plants and bushes in the garden.

She gave the door a peremptory blow with her first, lifted the latch without delay, and entered. It was her first visit to this cottage of Catrin's married life, and, intent on her errand though she was, her glance swept disdainfully over the gimcrack contents of the living-room. The front door opened into it immediately.

'Catrin Morgan,' commanded the visitor, using the maiden surname with a grimly pointed return to the past, 'get your feet out of that water and stand up.'

Catrin, who was giving her feet their Saturday soaking in a bowl on the hearth-rug, astonishingly obeyed this hectoring order. At sight of Siân, the jaw of her big, round, nefarious face had dropped. Her milky eyes sidled as she dried her feet in a ragged towel and reached, bulkily, for her slippers. During this, a stream of calmly enunciated opinion came from Siân. She compared her erstwhile friend, not to the beasts

211

of the fields, which country people respect, but to villainesses of Biblical and local fame, and she used adjectives applicable to evil human failings.

Catrin seemed unaffected by these preliminaries. 'Marching in!' she mumbled. An imposing but pulpy woman standing five or six inches taller than her opponent, she rose, and added: 'What do you want, Siân *Williams?*' Her own retaliatory use of Siân's maiden surname blew away not only forty years of married life, but a silence of the same period.

'You know why I've come.'

A large oval table stood between them. On it rested the oil lamp, its glass funnel unwashed for many a week. Catrin, her pale eyes absorbing without expression the menace shooting from those of the structurally-inferior woman opposite her, groped for her dentures on the mantelpiece and slipped them in. Possession of them seemed to give her a little more confidence, for she protested, with a certain amount of indignation: 'There's a knocker on my door. Marching in!' Perhaps it was shock that curtailed her and made her seem halted in stupor.

Siân, taking a short step round the table, came to the matter in hand. 'You set her on him! A stoat on a young rabbit! Your red-haired daughter on *my* son!' She gave a quick yelp, such as a terrier might release. 'Plotting it all in revenge on me! No doubt you're hoping he gets her into trouble, so that he's got to marry her. *My* Oliver! *Your* Muriel! Ha!'

She took another step, and another, round the table, while Catrin, in obedient rhythm, backed round it. During Siân's next pronouncements they moved thus, in the manner of some solemn folk-dance figure, twice round the table.

'You plotted with your Muriel to do her business even in my house! To spite me! . . . I saw them coming out when I came back early from my married daughter—*you* know I go to see her every Saturday evening, while my husband is in the Rising Sun and Oliver supposed to be gone on his bike to the cinema in Morpeth, the house locked up and the key under the lavender bush—*you* knew it all, and set your red-haired daughter to Delilah tricks with my son. *You* know he's my favourite, the darling of my heart—'

There was no hauteur, insult or mockery in her manner, only a bristling condemnation born of long breeding and decent taste. But still Catrin's faculties seemed to be entirely occupied in obediently, if warily, backing a step in unison with Siân's approach round the table,

212

and still no word of denial or retaliation had come from her. All she said, repetitiously, was: 'Marching in!'

'For a month I've been smelling that something like this was going on. So I came back early tonight from my married daughter's house, an hour before my usual time. I saw them coming out when I was up on the main road. They went down into Bruchan Lane. Courting, are they?' Siân's beak darted towards the culprit she stalked, a degree faster, round the table. 'A red hair on the pillow! . . . I burned the bed in the field—' she allowed herself a menacing hiss as her hand moved towards the lamp—'as I'll burn down this sty of a house, with you in it punched to Jerico, if that daughter of yours gives another look at my boy! See?'

Without further ado, she made a leap, head down, towards the momentarily paused woman. Accurate as a goat, she butted her head under Catrin's chin. There was a clicking sound of dentures sharply meeting. Otherwise, a choked gasp was all that Catrin manifested. But she backed a foolish step, thus allowing Siân space to take another leap and repeat the butt. Grunting and backing, Catrin flung out her arms. The main features of her face, blurred in fat, expressed an alarmed demise of the shifty elements governing her character. The physical pain of assault is trivial compared with the revelatory power of its criticism, and blows (the only method, unfortunately, in some cases) are also a short cut to clarification of a disputatious matter. Catrin's girlhood friend had gone into action once more, and she knew what she was about.

'Now you can put your feet back in that water,' she pronounced, still amazingly brisk of wind.

Catrin, an expiring heap of plump mounds and flabbergasted limbs, collapsed into the fireside armchair. It was guilt again. Also, after forty years of silence, the incident was a tremendous recognition of undying bondage. Siân trotted to the door, looked back over her shoulder with a single threatening glance, and whisked out like a fox with dismissing celerity in its tail.

In the garden she heard a bellow. It came from delayed shock: all of Catrin's faculties moved cumbersomely. In the lane, additional bellows could be heard, swelling and lowing. Yet they were not truly agonised. Did they contain, besides hints of recovery, an undercurrent of satisfaction?

She got home with time to spare. A quarter of an hour later, Oliver walked in. His father would be there in a few minutes. It was their customary Saturday night arrival, in circumstances and time, for supper and bed.

Siân gave her son a fair preliminary hint. 'You didn't go to the cinema in Morpeth?' she said absently, without blunt questioning. 'When I came back from Barbara's I saw your bike in the shed.'

He sat down and took off his shoes, which had been beautifully polished by her and were now dust-spattered. 'I went for a walk with Ivor to the farm,' he said, 'to see his new sheepdog.'

Glad of the lie, which showed a proper sense of uneasiness, she said nothing and went on preparing the supper table. Oliver pulled on the soft calfskin slippers which had been a present from his mother on his nineteenth birthday a month ago. None of her other children had obtained such tributes as he enjoyed. She eyed him once or twice as she laid down crockery. He lit a cigarette without looking at her, but he went so far as to mention the price of the new sheepdog. She only said, 'Ah!' As she passed him, a frail breeze of opposition must have reached him. 'Ivor asked me to help in the trials,' he mumbled, still on the dog. She smiled at the back of his auburn head.

He was her best and different one, the last flower of her season. Particularly she delighted in his pale, well-bred little ears; her four other children, now out in the world, owned big purplish ones like their father. Oliver, by her determined efforts, had been put out to superior employment as a clerk in the Morpeth Rural Council offices; barring setbacks, he would never follow the agricultural pursuits of his family. But did his melancholy fine-cut nostrils still quiver at the aroma of ploughed soil? That he had responded to the wiles of Catrin's daughter, whose rufus hair was of a kind common in several unredeemed families of the district, deepened her suspicion that his physical delicacy was only a brittle shell.

When Prosser stumbled in, pompously holding his ham-shaped head erect, as always in liquor, she fetched the minced-liver faggots from the kitchen oven. At the same time she reiterated the scolding of hundreds of Saturday nights. He accepted it as his due, only interjecting a doomed 'Aye' and 'True, true!' and 'Correct as a tombstone, Siân,' his florid face smokily matured. His son sat waiting, slim legs stretched out, contrastingly not yet crystallised in his being.

'Well, come to the table, both of you,' Siân said.

She sat there in the quiet yellow lamplight. Her well-kept dishes shone, the hearth was shinily black as an empress housewife could make it; the herbs festooned on the beams sent down a pleasing odour

214

to the delicious faggots which contained, together with apple and onion, a sprinkling of them. Even the clock, under its porcelain garland of cherub-borne flowers, seemed to tick in clear approval of its habitation.

At the table, Prosser's insecure attention became focussed. At the side of his plate, instead of the usual everyday cup and saucer, stood a painted china mug. It had been taken from the glass cabinet of never-used domestic treasures. He gazed at the ceremonious piece in thunderstruck silence while Siân, talking of her routine visit to their daughter, dished out the Saturday night faggots. Did she, at the end of the meal, intend pouring tea into that old mug painted with medallions of a crowned king and queen? At the side of her own and Oliver's plates rested an ordinary cup and saucer.

Presently she scooped an extra faggot on to her son's rapidly emptied plate. 'Oliver,' she prattled absently, 'walked with Ivor to the farm to see the new sheepdog. A long walk!'

Prosser, in his stupor betraying the son whom he too admired, said with surprise: 'Ivor was in the Rising Sun with the sheepdog all the evening.'

Oliver bent over his faggot to hide his flush. Siân gave a squeezed-in laugh that made both father and son wince. 'I expect Oliver has started courting then,' she said. 'They often tell lies at first, as if they're doing something wrong.'

'I did go walking,' Oliver muttered, head still over his plate.

Prosser, more himself after food, began to spread himself. 'Is it Gwyneth Vaughan?' he boomed up to the beams. Going sententious, perhaps because he was a churchwarden of St. Teilo's and it was Sunday tomorrow, he rambled on: 'We all got to come to it. Man that is born of woman hath but a short time to live. He cometh up, and is cut down, like a—'

'Be quiet, Joseph Prosser!' his wife put a stop to this. 'Mixing up the funeral service with the marriage one!"

'I will keep my mouth as it were with a bridle,' he quoted further, however.

She rose and fetched the teapot from the hearth. Holding the pot high, but with a hand so accurately steady that the pouring seemed baleful, she filled the mug. The jet of dark tea descended to the mug long and thin as a whip. Prosser watched it go into the receptacle. Siân then walked round the table to her son. But he refused tea. He sat looking remote now, if not offended, and also not fully adjusted to

215

whatever rankled within him. He got up. A waxen pallor had replaced the flush in his face. His mother did not question the unusual refusal of tea.

'I'm going to bed,' he mumbled.

He went to the dresser cupboard for his candlestick, lit it, and tramped up the stairs without another word, taking his mystery with him. Prosser sat with eyelids down, palms crossed over his stomach like a meditating monk, not touching the mug of tea. He waited until his son was safely in his room before saying, 'You've got to face it, Siân, my girl. You can't keep him to yourself for ever. I wonder is it Gwyneth Vaughan? She's always hanging round him in St. Teilo's.' It would be a desirable match. Gwyneth was sole offspring of a reasonably well-off family.

Siân assembled the table dishes. 'Gwyneth is a nice girl,' she said, in full approval. 'Aren't you going to drink your tea?'

'Don't hurry me, Siân,' he said, not looking at the mug.

She had taken two journeys with dishes to the kitchen before Oliver, candlestick still in hand, began to descend the stairs. His mother crossed to the table as though unnoticing. He put his feet down with slow care, stopped on the bottom stair, and asked: 'Where's my bed?'

'I burnt it,' his mother said, sugar basin in hand.

The only sound came from Prosser's scratching of his walnut-shell cheek. He stared fixedly at the mug again. Then the extraordinariness of the two events seemed to penetrate him with considerable force. 'Why have you burnt Oliver's bed?' he demanded, even aggressively. Oliver, sensing mysterious support, stood behind his candle, looking glassy as a young saint in a church window.

'Yes,' he said, though there was an under-squeak of dread in his voice, 'and where am I to sleep?'

Siân laid the sugar basin on the table, and spun round fast as a weathercock in a sudden blast of wind. She faced both the men in turn. 'That bed is burnt in the field!' she rapped out. 'And I've been to Catrin Morris's house tonight and knocked the wickedness out of *that* plotting old witch! See?' To her husband she exploded: 'Like mother, like daughter! And like father, like son! That daughter of Catrin's was in this house tonight! With *him*! But never again while I've got an ounce of strength to pull the trigger of your gun, Joseph Prosser . . . And you, Oliver,' she rasped to her overcome son, totally unlike the woman who purred in ministration to his every wish and need, 'no more from *you*! Get up to bed in the back room—and,' she added, 'don't forget to fall down on your knees by it and ask forgiveness . . . before you set foot in St. Teilo's tomorrow!' In a white surplice, perfectly starched and ironed by her, he sang a pure tenor in the choir.

The candle unsteady before him, Oliver returned up the stairs at once. A silence, bleak but seemly, followed Siân's outburst. Prosser moved from the table and the accusing mug. He unlaced his size eleven boots, bending from the arm-chair at his solidly-established hearth. Siân held out the painted mug to him.

'You haven't drunk your tea,' she said, with her pinched smile. 'You'll be thirsty in bed, after all those salty faggots.' She went off to the kitchen to wash up.

He drank the cooled tea with pondering slowness. The clock, flouting its heirloom age, ticked with a speedy clarity which always seemed to him mysteriously united with Siân's unwearied energy. Women, he ruminated, could seldom forget mischief done to them, however petty; and they had to be humoured; unlike men, they were unable to accept certain worldly matters with calm. Yet, as he remembered the gala Coronation Day of 1911, part of him seemed to become Siân. He experienced an approximation to her scorching fury on that day. That was what long marriage did to one, he thought: a bit of one became like a woman.

Burning a good bed! But he experienced the drastic fury of that act too. He also heard a connecting explosion of fireworks. He remembered the laden tables in the meadow behind St. Teilo's, the gay marquee, the barrels of strong ale, the games and competitions, the commemorative mugs, painted with the crowned heads, King George and Queen Mary, which were presented to every villager by Sir Llewellyn's wife on that 1911 afternoon. He remembered how, after dark had fallen, Catrin Morris had wheedled him—yes, wheedled him—into the copse below the meadow, when everybody's attention was on the opening of the fireworks display. He had been drunk by then, and it seemed only a minute before Siân had leapt in on them, snatched up Catrin's coronation mug from the grass, and smashed it to pieces on her red head. From where he lay, pushed over disregarded on the ground, he saw a soaring rocket burst into blue stars and fiery rain. He and Siân weren't married then, of course; only courting.

She came in from the kitchen, too briskly, and asked: 'Finished your tea?'

'Men,' he said, still pondering, 'they don't mean to do harm. They only get helpless in their nature. A man goes weak in the joints sometimes, and his mind goes dark . . . yes,' he brooded, 'dark'. He handed her the drained mug.

Her nose quivering over these obscurities, she observed: 'It's a good thing a woman stands watching from the other pan of the scales, then.'

Prosser continued to stare up at the pitted ceiling beams as he went on: 'Something there is that tells a man to take advantage of what's going.' He added, 'It's nothing serious, Siân.'

'What!' she exclaimed, thunderstruck.

'Not in young men, Siân,' he said in some haste. 'Their heads are in the clouds and they can't see plainly what's going on below.'

'You mean,' she clarified for him, not displeased by this paternal concern, 'Oliver hasn't been wicked on purpose, bringing that fire-haired demon into the house. Well, I didn't say *he* was wicked. But *someone* had to fetch his head out of the clouds.'

'Well, you've put the fear of God into all concerned now, Siân.' He suppressed a belch, but managed to add, with some assertion of justice: 'She isn't a bad little whelp, on the whole, that girl isn't. But not suitable for Oliver, of course, of course.'

'Oh, go up to bed,' she said, only impatient, sure of her power in her own important territory.

A MAN UP A TREE

When the corpse of her husband, whom she had not seen for seventeen years, was delivered to Mari Lloyd's farmhouse it caused her a most disagreeable upset.

Not only was the farm busy in the last days of harvest, with all her daughters out in the fields and her alone in the house, but a most disordering sense of guilt sprang up in her from its hiding-place, quick after the first shock of this peremptory delivery of the body. She had not been informed that her husband was on his way to her, alive or dead. 'Wife of John Lloyd you are?' was all one of the two green-uniformed men said when she opened the door to their knock. An unvarnished coffin, made of cheap box-wood, lay on a sort of stretcher behind them. The engine of their motor-van in the lane had not been shut off.

'Not one word to warn me!' she stormed at the men as they carried the coffin—it even looked dirty—into the house. 'No feelings they've got in that place?' The guilt made her the more vehement. Crimson of cheek, and still under fifty, she looked a ripely handsome widow despite her wrath. 'Bringing him back like this! In *that!*'

'We've got a letter from the Superintendent's office,' said one of the asylum men, unconcerned. They laid the paltry coffin across two chairs in the best parlour where she had led them, and, unaware that he was adding fuel to the burning guilt, the other man explained: 'The office had to phone the policeman in your village to find if your husband's next of kin was still living here. The policeman said you and your daughters were here just the same, so we brought the deceased, along with the letter that would have been posted to you yesterday, otherwise. He went sudden, I think.'

As the widow gazed in horror at the box, he laid the letter on a table and, apologetic now, added: 'Our Superintendent is away on holiday this month, and his office is very busy just now. Mention there'll be in the letter about the coffin; our usual one it is.' Underlings not responsible for this official disregard of human emotions, they edged towards the door, and were gone.

Did she deserve this? For another minute, but backing away, she stared at the coffin. Then she snatched up the horn of an old-style gramophone standing on the chiffonnier and ran out to the yard behind the house. Setting the horn in turn towards east, north, and west, she trumpeted the names, in order of their birth, of her daughters: Cadi, Marged, Gwynneth, Ceinwen, Efa.

At the noise, rooks took black flight from a cluster of elms fringing a nearby meadow, in which three dozen Welsh-faced sheep looked up, censorious of the disturbance. A despot since her husband's breakdown —and even before that event—she looked like a roused Queen Boadicea calling her clan of warriors to battle.

From the fields of ripened wheat where they laboured like men paid full union rates, her down-trodden daughters came hurrying to this unusual summons. Only Efa, lackadaisical as her namesake of Eden, dawdled as though the world and all its time were before her: she was nineteen and seemed to be admiring the landscape while her mother, horn still in hand, waited in the cobbled yard. It was a lonely and beautiful landscape, uninhabited hills soaring to the moist blue in the far distance; but a glimpse of Miskin village, where men lived, could be seen below, looking deceptively near and peaceful.

'I thought the house was on fire,' Cadi panted, arriving first. Her mother, motionless now, stood staring bemused at the group of elms.

Marged, the only daughter who wore trousers, demanded crossly: 'What's the matter? Not another war?' The horn hadn't been used like that since the last war was declared, an insurance collector having brought the news to the isolated farm. Mari never would spend money on a radio set, which in any case might unsettle her daughters' minds with its frivolous programmes. She believed that the business of working a farm and of rearing, without aid of husband, five daughters cannot be done by living soft and easy.

Efa entered the gate at last, and Mari, still without a word, led the five into the house and down the sunset-reddened passage to the parlour. 'A visitor has come?' asked Ceinwen, pushing forward for the first glimpse of such a phenomenon.

'A widow I am!' Mari groaned, pointing dramatically. 'Your poor dead father has been brought back to you in *that*.'

The bereaved daughters did not show the high concern of the widow. So long had their father been 'put away' that almost he had ceased to exist for them, except as a dark, and more or less unspoken, reminder that they had an ominous blight in the family. The first four children could remember, in a vague way, his demeanour and flavour, but he had disappeared for ever before affection could be induced in any measure; Efa had no awareness of him at all.

What interested them now was the behaviour of their mother. They had never seen her undone like this, never heard her whimpering and moaning like an ordinary human being at the mercy of a cruel world.

Gwynneth stood gaping, sniffing the new atmosphere; and Marged, hard and curt of disposition, suddenly ordered her to fetch a screwdriver. Cadi, tall and sorrel-tinted like her mother, observed judiciously: 'Well, perhaps better off he is now.' Plump and soft-looking Ceinwen, always thirsty in the fields, waddled away to the kitchen to brew a pot of tea. Only easy-going Efa, pretty and curly-headed as a tawny chrysanthemum, sat down and took off her field boots; she assumed, mistakenly, that her mother would command a cessation of the day's toil now, harvest though it was and the weather holding good.

Marged, screwdriver in hand, said: 'Let us have a look at him.'

When she began to unscrew the thin lid, her mother burst into further cries, plainly of fear. What was the matter with her? Exchanging glances, the daughters watched her but offered no comfort. She had removed herself too long into supreme and bossy authority, and such Caesars rarely obtain human comfort when they have received sore blows.

Lifting off the lid, Marged challenged her mother: 'There he is. Come on, take your look.' But her mother did not advance.

'Shrunk he has,' Cadi said, taking a bold look, 'and all his hair gone. So thin and stern! He's like a man not belonging to anyone.'

'They must have starved him in that place,' pursued Marged, relentless. 'What can you expect of a free-of-charge asylum that's always crowded like a Michaelmas fair?'

Gwynneth and Efa, catching the subtle note of triumph of their older sisters, took their looks into the coffin and unitedly expressed their 'Oh's' of dismay. None of them could believe that their mother's remorse and terror went very deep. Ceinwen, bringing in the tea and a round of fruit cake, took her brief glance at her father and said to the widow in ironical scepticism too: 'Come on, a cup of tea will give you strength.' Even Efa's pet magpie, flying into the parlour, alighted on the edge of the coffin and cocked an eye inside.

'What did he die of, I wonder?' pursued Marged, in whose swearing, masculine-cast mind her mother's bossiness had always rankled most. 'Loneliness, was it?'

221

Justice often is tardy in arrival, but it comes. Crouching away, collapsing into a chair, refusing the tea, Mari cried: 'Oh, I ought to have gone to see him every week! Always saying: "Next week I will take him fresh eggs and a cold chicken." But never finding the time to go.'

'I never heard you saying it,' observed Marged, driving the magpie away and replacing the lid.

'To myself I used to say it,' wept Mari, oddly unable to retaliate in her old autocratic style. Catching sight of the letter on the table, she asked her first-born to read it. She could not read herself and was able to write only her signature—though, an expert mistress of crops and cattle since an early age, she had treasure in the bank, and also a pig's bladder full of old gold sovereigns tied to a hidden rafter of the house.

Cadi, sipping tea while she read the letter said: 'It only says that John Lloyd died suddenly of coronary thrombosis—what is that, I wonder? And there's a piece about the coffin.' She read out: '*A charge of five guineas will be made if the coffin is retained for burial, but if not required the Asylum must be informed and the coffin will be collected in due course by our van.* It's signed by Owen Williams, Clerk to the Superintendent.'

Mari, briefly reviving, took great umbrage. 'Who wants their second-hand coffin? Used many times before, no doubt. Oh, a lot of heartless ruffians they are in that asylum!'

'Hearts are out of place in an asylum,' hummed Ceinwen.

Efa's magpie—which she had captured and tamed that summer, lacking anything else on which to vent her loving disposition—had perched on her shoulder. Caressing it and feeding it with fruit cake, she said: 'We will have to have a funeral.'

Her sisters lowered their cups of tea. Even her mother's woe was arrested a little. Fed, the magpie flew off, jumped on the coffin lid and excitedly squawked there, its feet dancing; very intelligent, it always caught the prevailing mood of the house and when dispute was rife it would always shriek, raucous as any of the sisters or their ruler.

'Black clothes and hats,' Gwynneth nodded. 'Shoes and stockings.'

Their mother gazed at the coffin with an extraordinarily humble submission. At last she crossed to it and spread her fingers tremblingly on the lid, so that the magpie, still squawking as if its throat would burst with something important to say, scampered away to the edge.

'*Gold*,' the widow whimpered, 'pure gold is inside this box! He shall have a funeral. A coffin they call this? The box of a tramp! A funeral he shall have that will be the talk of Miskin and the farms for years to come. Yes, full mourning for us all.' Then she ordered her first-born to fetch the precious heirloom lace tablecloth from the press and cover this unseemly coffin with it.

'Time it is,' observed Marged tartly, 'that we showed everyone that we are a well-off family.'

Efa said: 'Fresh clothes we all need, certain enough. Black handbags can we buy, too?'

None of them had ever possessed handbags or the other knick-knacks of their sex, and they rarely experienced entertainment. Mari had for ever kept her purse-strings tight. By dint of the punishment-stick of childhood, belittling their aspects and characters, and keeping them protected from the dangerous world on her tucked-away acres, she had subdued them early. Even now, on market-day trips to the town, they were shooed home as soon as farm business was done. Never a cinema, a café meal, or an evening trot through the streets where the young farmers let their importuning eyes roam in search of likely sweethearts. Kept in leash like this, what opportunities had they to find husbands?

Efa had raised this point oftener than her sisters. Her mother would say, with some truth, that young men were not likely to cast a favourable eye on a family that had such a skeleton in the cupboard. Her own blighted marriage, though it had yielded five daughters in quick succession, seemed to have created a mania to keep them close to her on the lonely farm, where also they were so productive of profit, money being the only real safety on earth. But, of course, now that they were full-size they smouldered penniless in the thought of revolution, waiting for signs of decay in her. Had the first sign come?

Taking no notice of the request for handbags, but very raised up now, as often as the parsimonious are when at last they decide to loosen themselves for an occasion, she resumed: 'A tombstone memorial fit for a king he shall have. Tomorrow I will buy a patch of land in the cemetery big enough to hold us all.'

'A will was he allowed to make, perhaps?' murmured his pretty last daughter. It was shortly after her birth that he had gone totally into his strange vexation and was found up one of the elm trees near the house, where he had remained hidden for a day and night, the village policeman having been informed of his disappearance.

'Only this farm, he owned,' Mari declared, 'and I am full and legal owner of it now. Back to the fields!' There would be enough light for two hours' work yet.

'Watered black poplin I shall choose,' Ceinwen bleated, going. 'It rustles well-off as one walks.'

Cadi, draping the lace tablecloth over the closed box, remarked cryptically: 'It ought to be stood up open to keep us reminded.'

They dreaded that the shock would wear off and Mari would change her mind about the mourning clothes and the other displays of remorse for her conjugal neglect. But she kept her word, and, during the five days between receipt and burial of her husband's body, subdued her remorse in the most extravagant acts of expiation.

A spacious car was hired to take her excited daughters to Swansea, where they spent the length of daylight in a store and returned laden like a caravan of the East. All the accoutrements of loving mourning were ordered at their costliest.

'Surely,' Efa said to her sisters, trying on her hat, 'an egg or two we're laying for hatching? Men will arrive out of all this?'

Announcement of the funeral was sent to all the local farms and houses of consequence. The widow cooked two whole hams. Cadi made fancy cakes; Marged baked several loaves; Gwynneth concocted rich trifles; Ceinwen, an expert poacher, snatched trout from the forbidden Miskin river and glazed them; and Efa went off on the bicycle to order whisky, sherry and port at the Red Lion pub in Miskin.

A fine oak coffin arrived on the day before the funeral, and the undertaker's men shut themselves into the parlour for the task of removing the body from the five-guinea box to the thirty-guinea casket.

When these men had gone, Mari, who had been strange and bemused all that day, commanded: 'Take that asylum box to the sties. A trough for the pigs' feed it will make.'

Cadi, sounding oddly like her mother, exclaimed in protest: 'The letter said the cost of it is five guineas.'

'To the sties with it!' She continued to breadcrumb the hams, and further commanded her daughters to put the lid in the barn, where it could be used for patching a draughty hole in the wall.

No man or woman of Miskin district had ever been buried with such pomp. The widow of John Lloyd not only made amends for his ill-starred life but struck down at one blow her reputation for being close-fisted and closeting her daughters from showing their advantages to the world.

At noon on the funeral day neighbouring farmers, in oval black hats and vicuna odorous of moth-balls, had turned up in force. Mari Lloyd, the she-farmer who had profitably turned all her daughters into

224

labourers that, being daughters, need not be paid union rates of pay—
Mari Lloyd, a tartar at driving a bargain in market, was respected by
these farmers, though they gazed in shocked amazement at the six
gigantic wreaths of shop flowers.

And all along the miles to the cemetery, passing through three villages,
everyone came out to view the procession of eight black cars, packed
with worthwhile people of the district, and the decked hearse followed
by a limousine containing the fashionably dressed family mourners.

It was Mari, magnificently statuesque as a queen able to endure great
tribulation, who seemed to get all the attention. Back in the house
after the burial, even optimistic Efa grumbled: 'All these men married or
elderly! I couldn't see one warm little bachelor weeping for us, not one.'

'Bachelors or not,' Ceinwen lamented, 'men's thoughts are not for
such matters in a funeral.'

'They were around *her* like bees,' Marged grunted. 'She's got the
money.'

In the house was that flat aftermath air of such events. There was not
even the reading of a will to distract them, for, being out of his senses,
their father had no legal right to make a will. Their day of splendour
was over. By five o'clock, the ham, trout, sweetmeats and drink
consumed, all the sympathisers had departed.

The last to go was Shinkin Parry, owner of many local acres. With
him Mari had remained in close parlour confabulation. She looked
into the livingroom, where her daughters still sat about in their finery,
and commanded them to change into their working clothes; the pigs
and poultry needed feed and, at the field gate, the three unmilked cows
were complaining.

Already changed herself into an old black blouse and skirt rummaged
from the past, she announced: 'A talk I had with Shinkin Parry. I am
hiring from him the Melan fields for ploughing. Barley we'll sow in
them.'

They cried out. The Melan fields! Soil requiring the labour of giants
to free it of stones and briars. Was there not sweating toil enough for
them already? She was back to her old tricks after all. Guilt and
remorse had not really undone her.

She said: 'A big hole has been made in our money today. Will
husbands ever come to keep you? *Your* futures I am thinking of—do I
spend money on myself? Your poor father's monument is to cost a
hundred pounds. A column of marble I've ordered, and a size proper
for a grave that is to hold us all. We must work.'

'Men go on strike!' Marged scowled. She ventured an oath, and muttered: 'Greedy old hog.'

'Certain it is,' fumed Gwynneth, 'that the Melan fields will send us to that grave quite early. Let the mason make haste with the column.'

'Bury me in my black poplin,' spat Ceinwen, rustling about the room in it, 'and put on my horny hands my black gloves. I want to look a lady in my coffin.'

Mari took no notice. It was always her policy to allow them, by tongue, free and even insulting expression of their views, women being appeased by this. She would have her way. Her act of expiation was done, and ordinary life must be resumed.

During the next few days they muttered and smouldered among themselves. But the old childhood pattern of obedience held them. They would never achieve the drastic mutiny of leaving home to hire themselves out as common farm workers elsewhere. In their own home they were heiresses and ladies. And Mari must die some day. Then the farm, together with the money in the bank and the bladder of sovereigns, would be theirs.

Unless, of course, she married again. As Efa mocked incitingly to her sisters in the fields: 'Never one to waste time! Another husband she'll get yet. Fresh roses in her cheeks and the owner of a farm with five meek-and-mild labourers!'

'It's that monument mason she goes to see,' Cadi decided. 'He's a widower, and if she gets round him she'll have the column cost-price.'

It seemed feasible that Mari was going out courting. Wearing her expensive black, she had already made three mysterious trips from the farm, arriving back from the last looking pleased with herself, and mentioning that the mason had begun work on the memorial stone.

'Six little white marble doves I've chosen,' she had said. 'They will stand on the steps under the column. Two guineas a dove the mason wanted to charge, but I bargained and got the six for ten pounds.'

'Serpents,' Marged had growled, 'they ought to be.'

On a Monday afternoon exactly one week after the funeral, a small car drove up to the farm gate. Out of it jumped a young man. Mari was at home but all her daughters were out in the fields, ploughing for next season's sowing. She opened the door to the young man's knock and, to his affable inquiry, acknowledged that she was Mrs. Mari Lloyd.

'I am from Plas Carmarthen Asylum,' he announced, rubbing his hands like an optimistic debt-collector certain of his prey.

She lifted an arm and pointed a finger. 'Your coffin is over there in the sties. Lid is in the barn.' Not out of this swelling woman would five guineas be got.

He put his hand against the door she was about to shut. 'Never mind about the coffin!' he assured. 'Ask me in, please; I am here on important business with you and family.'

Her eye shone alert. Had John been allowed to make a will, after all? She admitted the respectably dressed young man. His nervous legs whisking in, he complimented: 'A fine spick-and-span farm you've got here, and a beauty of an old house!' In the living-room, as she stood suspiciously forbidding, his flattering manner increased. He praised the sixteenth-century room, thick-walled as a castle, the old china on the dresser. His popping eyes roved about, insecure and shifty as his smile.

'Your business?' she demanded.

'Take off your black clothes!' he said, preliminary as a doctor, but smiling at her so wide that his dry-looking tongue could be seen.

A man from the asylum! Backing away, she said, half soothing, half threatening: 'I will call my daughters. *Cadi!*' she shouted, uselessly, since they were all too far afield to hear. '*Marged—*'

Dazzling with the happy tidings he bore, he clapped his hands. '*Stop!* You must be the first to hear the good news. Your husband John Lloyd, aged fifty-three, is alive! There now!'

She turned from the door. 'Buried he was a week ago—' she began to mumble.

'No, no! Not *your* John Lloyd. Another John Lloyd was sent to this farm. A little mistake. *Two* John Lloyds we had on our register, see?' As no word came from her open mouth, he said, suddenly going severe and blustering: 'Why is it you didn't send the corpse back to us? Along with our coffin? Didn't you take a last look at what was supposed to be your own husband, same as all wives do? You buried a man you had no right to. Why?'

Still no word came from her, and, blinking his eyes, he added: 'Lucky it is that the dead John Lloyd's got no relations to make a fuss about it.'

'Ha!' she panted. 'Ha!'

And, before he could say more, she ran to fetch the gramophone horn, sped out to the yard, and called her brood. When, with wet brow but unable to wait for the five to assemble, she crept back to the living-room, the young man had become even more jumpy. 'What is it you are telling me?' she mumbled, in a weak little voice.

Watching her out of the corner of his eye, he babbled: 'Not very often can I bring good news like this! The car out there came to you fast as I could make it go. All the way from Plas Carmarthen for me to tell you in person. "No," I said to Dr. Llewellyn, our Superintendent, "*no*, not a letter; I will go to Mrs. Lloyd in person." ' He coughed behind his jerking Adam's apple. 'Mistakes are made everywhere, and Dr. Llewellyn was on holiday, and very busy we've been, only a spare-time deputy superintendent coming in while Dr. Llewellyn was on holiday—'

'*You* it was that sent the body?' she panted.

'A mistake!' he pleaded. 'Not the first one that's been made in this world. Like this it was, you see: only this morning the Superintendent returned from holiday, and after he looked at the register and saw the deaths and discharges and admittances he went on his rounds of the wards as usual, knowing all the old patients by name and history.' He swallowed, but plucked up voice again. 'And there, in the Hafod ward, he saw your husband John Lloyd. "Why," he said, "dead you are!" ' . . . Then out came the little mistake, see? It was John Lloyd in the Tenby ward, a new patient who had been sent from the workhouse in Swansea, that had gone from thrombosis; but your one it was that I ticked off in the register when the nurse came to tell me in the office. So busy we are and short-staffed, and behind with everything—' His smile came out entreating once more. 'But happy news for you! Your husband is quite well, but not ready to be discharged yet. The pleasure you will give me of driving you to the asylum to see him? There and back.'

She whispered: 'Over three hundred pounds spent and gone!' She sat down, got up; she went pale, grew red. Sounds like groans came from her. But when her daughters, even Efa prompt for once, arrived, she drew a little strength and cried out: 'One of you go to the mason. At once! On the bicycle. Stop the work on the monument!'

'My car—' began the young man. At the entrance of the five daughters he had begun to retreat towards a corner. His gaze roamed feverishly over the swarm, and, in the way natural to man, skimmed longest over unruined Efa, who always smiled a polite welcome at sight of any young man.

In a few words from down her chest, Mari informed her daughters of the awful event. Only Efa, brushing aside her magpie that had flown in too, left the room during the ensuing clamour and, very quick for her, reappeared dressed in her smart black. 'I will go to the mason,' she tried to make herself heard above the noise. 'Your car?' she hinted to the young man.

His false jerk of energy was vanishing before this covey of daughters arrived strong and healthy from the fields, and already he was too far gone to notice that, under their exclamations, no real wrath was directed at him. It was towards their mother that their eyes darted, interested. Shrunk and reduced, Mari had collapsed finally into a chair.

Efa waited, listening near the door. Still the young man made weak attempts to protect himself, whining of shortage of staff and holidays and asylum muddle for which he was not responsible. He was appealing to their mercy, And the truth came out: the monthly meeting of the Asylum Board was due in a fortnight, and if this affair was not settled and hushed-up before then, he would be sacked.

Marged, rapid in trying to snatch the authority dwindling out of her mother, turned on him then. 'And you deserve the sack. A fool like you in charge of the register! A patient you used to be in that asylum?'

Cadi, first-born, gave Marged a demolishing glance and said: 'Him getting the sack won't pay for the funeral.'

'The shop,' said Gwynneth with satisfaction, 'won't take our clothes back.'

'Over three hundred pounds spent and gone!' their mother whispered. 'A long funeral with six heavy wreaths. A big grave. The asylum will pay me back?'

The young man, pale around his nostrils, made an effort to protest. 'A man can be buried comfortable for forty pounds. It isn't the fault of the asylum if you've got five daughters and buried a man as if he was a Lord Mayor.'

Cadi, sounding more than ever like her mother, said: 'A strange man is in our grave. He must be got out. More expense!'

'Let him stay there,' barked Marged to the first-born. 'The only sweetheart he is that you will ever lay by.'

'Thirty guineas for the coffin alone!' Ceinwen gave the young man a smile of plump malice.

From the door, Efa got in at last: 'Perhaps the mason is working on the monument this very minute?'

Her mother looked up and moaned. 'What, you haven't gone yet? Go on the bike at once!'

'The gentleman,' Efa said, 'can take me in his car: it will be faster.'

'Yes, go,' jeered Ceinwen, her eyes not missing anything, 'and we will sit and judge what is to be done with your gentleman.' As the young man hurried over to her beckoning sister, she went to brew a pot of tea.

The front door slammed. Mari lifted her black apron, covered her face with it, and howled in woe: 'Oh, what is it I have done to deserve this?' But the old power was quite gone from the howl. When a despot falls the collapse is total. She, Mari Lloyd of the high farming and business reputation, had been guilty of the greatest of sins: witless and unwary, she had been cheated of money. Only a year ago, Luc Watkins, farmer over at Ystrad, had declined into a mortal illness because, in his cups, he had been sold a defective cow at market, and by an Englishman, too. 'What is it I have done?' she groaned. 'A good-living woman I've been, and a hard worker.'

Cadi fluffed up her bosom. 'But a widow you are not, after all,' she said.

'You must start a law case,' shouted Marged. 'All of us will sit in public court with you. Go tomorrow to consult Vaughan the Lawyer.'

Mari lowered her apron. In Wales mention of lawyers brings shivers to money-owners, for so often their shifty work is a fearsome gamble. Could she fight the huge asylum, kept by wily and important men of the county? 'Lawyers?' she whimpered. 'Six shilling and eightpence every time they open their mouths!'

'No doubt,' Cadi said, giving Marged another demolishing glance, 'the asylum lawyer would ask in court why you didn't look into the coffin to make sure the corpse was your husband.'

Weak and wailing, Mari tried to justify her old guilt. 'As he used to be I wanted to remember him always; a man sound and fresh, and still my loving John.' She even tried to accuse her daughters: 'You looked into the coffin, all of you!'

Her first-born declared: 'So young I was when he hid himself from us up the elm tree that I couldn't remember him properly. But I mentioned he had shrunk and gone bald.' She raised her voice threateningly: 'Blaming *us*, are you?'

'People will say,' Gwynneth hummed, 'that a wife with no feelings you were, refusing to take a last look at him. Or a coward.'

'It would come out in court,' Cadi added, 'that you never went to see him in seventeen years. The case printed in the papers! . . . No,' she swept Marged aside, 'no taking it to court.'

'If,' blew Ceinwen, bringing in the teapot, 'that young man isn't married or courting, Efa is itending to take advantage of him. Quick enough when she wants to be.'

'Judging by the hole in the heel of his sock,' Gwynneth said, 'married he is not.'

'We must take into account,' decided Cadi, just and fair, 'that if it weren't for his mistake no new clothes we'd have got to show ourselves off to the world.'

'Yes,' Gwynneth agreed, 'and now some day we can have the funeral of our proper father all over again.'

'Perhaps Efa was right,' admitted Ceinwen, pouring tea, 'when she said the funeral will hatch good things. Young men in Miskin will know that we will bury them loving. So let us not worry over the expense.'

Mari, ignored now, sank further into a stupor, though when Cadi handed her a cup of tea, she whimpered: 'A curse is on me for neglecting him.'

'In the old days,' her first daughter said, 'people would say a witch was behind this black behaviour.'

'A good witch,' purred Gwynneth.

Yet, as is the way with women roused in excitement, nothing solid came out of their conference. The tea drunk, only Marged raised the point of what was to be done with the duffer from the asylum, but to this Ceinwen said: 'Efa will have decided.'

She was gone a long time. They had lit the oil lamp before she returned, the asylum young man, pale but looking a little more hopeful, behind her. From the top of the dresser her magpie flew to her shoulder as she sat the young man considerately in a chair.

'The monument?' whispered Mari, dwindled in the shawl she had asked for in her cold distress.

'The name of John Lloyd,' Efa announced, 'was cut on the column yesterday. The mason said: "Business is business, a monument is ordered, and deposit paid." ' Mari uttered a groan of final defeat, and her youngest daughter proceeded: 'But there's a difference a man makes! Owen here, had quite a to-do with the stubborn old mason, and a half-way bargain is struck. The centrepiece to be kept till required, but no marble steps, surround or doves as ordered, and no more money to be paid. Thanks to Owen being so fierce with him.'

Owen, looking down his nose, muttered something no one could hear; plainly he was still in dread of the assembly.

Ceinwen, pursing her lips, said: 'A long time you've been settling a bit of business like that! Over five hours!'

'We went into the Red Lion for refreshment,' Efa stated.

Marged said harshly: 'The business of all the other expense is still to settle. Savings this asylum fellow has got?'

231

'Even if it is only the price of a thirty-guinea coffin?' blew Ceinwen, fixing him with her fat brown eye.

Efa, stroking her magpie, which was pecking at her ear-lobe in jealous esteem, said: 'Owen is willing to come and work on the farm for nothing on his day off every week; and for his holiday of a fortnight, starting next month. Helping us to stone the Melan fields, perhaps?'

'Ay,' Owen spoke at last, and braced his bowed office clerk's shoulders, 'ay.'

'Free to work here for ever he'll be,' jeered Ceinwen, half excited, half vexed by the suspicion that matrimony had been set going in this family at last, 'if he gets the sack from the asylum.'

'The sack Owen must not get,' Efa said, complacent. 'Soon as he marries, a little cottage he can take close to the asylum, and then every day I will be able to see our poor father, that has been neglected for seventeen years, though he has a wife and five daughters fit to travel and show love . . . Perhaps,' she said, as her mother raised slow and vanquishd eyes, 'I can make him well again, so that he can come back to you, safe and up on his two feet.'

A VISIT TO
EGGESWICK CASTLE

As was their custom when they moved for the summer months to their country house, eighty miles from London, Mr. and Mrs. Chalmers made the cook and the housemaid travel first-class on the train, while they themselves in obedience to their protesting principles (and perhaps as a hair-shirt for their well-off condition), went in the crowded third.

Dorinda Chalmers would say, to such friends as were surprised by this eccentricity: 'Bertie and I are active in our socialism, not mere theorists. Besides, the domestics have the physical work to do when they arrive at Sallows, after a restful journey.' Experienced in social work since her remote girlhood, she yet never paused to wonder if the domestics might feel ill at ease in their first-class splendour.

Cook, in particular, always thought worriedly of the elderly master and mistress getting crushed, hot, and grubby down the train among the riff-raff; faithful to the Chalmerses for a dozen years now, she still hadn't accustomed herself to this topsy-turvy example of their democratic views, although, a meat eater herself, she had rapidly adapted her talents to their strict vegetarianism.

And this year, again, there was a new housemaid—how they came and went!—and, as usual, she had to placate the girl about the summer move. 'Socialists they might be, Marjorie,' she whispered as they settled in the train, 'but in my opinion it's carrying things too far to make us travel first-class. Never mind, I do promise you that Sallows is a lovely house and the countryside the sweetest in England.'

There was only one other passenger in their compartment, an ignoring old gentleman buried under *The Times*, but after sitting *sotto voce* on the edge of the plump upholstery for the first mile or two, they kept entirely without a twitter for the rest of the journey.

Marjorie, indeed, brooded with an unwonted intensity of silence. Cook, knowing from bitter experience how London-born housemaids tended to be incommoded by isolated country parts, did not like her aspect at all. Herself of the old régime and always loyal to the family she chose to serve, she had felt uncertain of Marjorie since the girl arrived out of the foggy unknown during the winter in London.

The democratic mistress, saying she relied on her eye for character, never asked for references. But, of course, Marjorie belonged to the new, flighty brigade—girls who rankled against sleeping in at their jobs, whose corners were not good, who, off-hand with milkmen and window-cleaners, flopped down on sofas with film magazines. From the first, too, Cook had been suspicious of a sultry 'something' lurking in Marjorie's ox-blood eye, and also of her obscure allusions to a Mr. Grigson, to whom she was denying wedlock because he drank.

'I *don't* like first-class,' the girl observed pettishly when they emerged from the ordeal at Aldridge station. 'Not a soul to talk to! Often one can pick up a lively acquaintance in the thirds.'

Cook, peering down the platform for the mistress's famous cream cloak, made the best of the unwelcome luxury: 'A woman can depend on respect in the firsts.'

Her cloak—Mrs. Chalmers possessed three, of identical cut and shade —flowing from a glittering silver chain at her throat, the mistress swept up to them, while Mr. Chalmers, tall, pale green, and as distinguished-looking as a saint, supervised the luggage with the welcoming station-master (to whom he had long ago predicted the nationalisation of the railways) and two obsequious porters. It was like royalty arriving. The mistress presented Cook with a key.

'You and Marjorie can go on before us. Take either of the two cars waiting outside . . . We had such an absorbing conversation in our compartment with an Urban Council rodent operator,' she said. 'In the old days, he would have been called a rat-catcher. He told us a great deal about his work and views. Were you comfortable?'

'Yes, ma'am,' Cook said, and added, a little censoriously: 'Marjorie complained of the lack of company.'

'Oh, but both of you are rested? . . . Marjorie'—the mistress turned to the morose, shoe-gazing girl—'some day this ridiculous class distinction on the railway will be abolished and we shall all travel together happily. We are already a good step towards it with the nationalisation of the lines, and if the Labour Government returns to power next election—' There on the platform she gave quite an oration, until her husband himself released them. He reminded her that before proceeding to Sallows they were paying a call on their bank manager in Aldridge.

'You'd think,' Marjorie grumbled, in the sumptuous hired limousine, 'they'd have a car of their own, with a house in the country.' She had surveyed without enthusiasm the picturesque Aldridge street the car glided through.

'They believe in not having too much that's different from what we have,' Cook said, sounding woolly in this herself.

Now they were out in the lanes among the uninhabited fields, Marjorie began to look alarmed, and even hunted. It was fourteen miles to Sallows, and as the landscape took on a more and more lonely appearance, with the road going through deserted beech-woods ('Forests!' she muttered) of budding green, she let out a little whimper. Suddenly, when the car took a sharp turn, she sat back in a dumpy, gasping heap. 'Ah!' she panted.

Cook said warily: 'Don't you like the countryside? It's pretty. You've gone quite pale!'

Marjorie, as suddenly, sat bolt upright, her protuberant eyes fixed on the glass partition separating them from the driver. 'Have I?' she said. 'I dare say I *have* gone pale!' she added, in a smart, back-answering manner. 'So would you. You see, I'm expecting a little one at the end of September.'

'My God!' Cook, despite her previous forebodings herself went pale. 'And we're in the country! Till the middle of October!' It was late May.

'I don't care where I am,' Marjorie asserted, still bolt upright and breathing hard. 'It's Mr. Grigson.'

'*Now*,' Cook declared, quickly recovering, 'you'll have to marry him, drink or not.'

'He's married. I never seen him touch a drop of drink. I lied to you.'

Cook momentarily edged away from it all; she couldn't abide a liar. 'Well, it's a whole bottle of pickles for you to be in, isn't it!' she said, in due course and with beady satire. Then: 'Who's to tell the mistress?'

'I give her satisfaction, don't I?' Marjorie demanded, more herself now the revelation was completed. She always had difficulty in making a direct answer to any question.

No one had ever said that Bessie Allen had a hard heart, and as they drew up to the rose-brick old house, in its charming flower gardens, she announced: 'Well, I'll tell the mistress, and do the best I can for you.'

'No, I'll tell her.' Marjorie spoke with truculence. 'When we're settled in.'

'Best let me do it,' Cook fought.

'Mrs. Allen,' Marjorie said proudly, 'it's *my* affair. See?'

That day, and on many other days, they had quite a battle over the necessity of informing Mrs. Chalmers. But Marjorie refused to be overcome, and Cook saw that she was of those who always postpone unpleasantness until tomorrow. Nor would she discuss her paramour with any realism, and Mr. Grigson remained veiled in thick married-man mists. She even giggled a little hysterically when Cook tried to pin her down to some definite action against the culprit. To offset all this, however, she uncomplainingly accepted the loneliness of the countryside, and, as if her bout of wickedness had improved her character, she worked remarkably well in the house, which wasn't too large.

'I never knew the country could be so good for the nerves,' she declared, always ready to leap when Mrs. Chalmers rang the bell.

It wasn't rung often. Master was writing his book out in the garden study, with Mistress helping him. Visitors came to stay most weekends, but they were talking ones, of serious and tidy disposition, all of them elderly and socialistically considerate of domestic legs.

Then, one morning in the fourth week at Sallows, Cook remarked: 'It's beginning to speak for itself. Even the mistress will notice soon, though the master never will.'

'The mistress can see I'm a good maid,' Marjorie, aware that Cook had something else waiting under her tongue, reiterated.

Cook shook out the contents of a Nut Health Food package into a mixing bowl and said: 'Their daughter is coming down next weekend. She's going to have a baby, too. The mistress told me this morning. Of course, *she* is entitled to one.'

Marjorie, as if abruptly deflated of all power, sat down. 'Ah!' she breathed. 'Ah!'

'The daughter's having hers round about your time, too, I think. So you'll have a rival.'

'I'm an orphan,' Marjorie panted. 'I'll tell Mistress today.'

'Get ready what you're going to say about Mr. Grigson,' Cook advised, relenting. 'If you want any help from them, you must blame *him*.'

'Tell them, you mean, I didn't know he was married till too late?'

'Say what you like,' Cook replied, pursily withdrawing. 'Sometimes I believe you've got a mind besides your other things.'

Mrs. Chalmers, as her housemaid stood before her with dropped head and made confession, was delighted; she had expected to be given notice when Marjorie requested a private interview. 'Remarkable!' she

236

said. 'This is the second time I have been told such happy news today. I am to be a grandmother early in October, Marjorie.'

'Soon after my time,' Marjorie whimpered, head drooping lower, the unfortunate one in contrast with the other.

Dorinda Chalmers had not been a public-speaking woman and a Fabian for nearly half a century without learning, she thought, the art of being firmly authoritative while retaining her warm human interior. Confronted with disaster in the lower classes (she had worked for years, early in the century, at one of the idealists' settlements in the East End of London), she always wanted to comfort first, before dwelling on a concrete remedy. 'Now, my dear girl,' she said, 'don't cry. Has the father any plans about it?'

'He broke my heart,' Marjorie sobbed. 'Mr. Grigson by name. I found out that he's married.'

At this, Mrs. Chalmers bridled up into full alertness. One of her earliest campaigns had been of the feminist persuasion; it was rather old hat now, but a whiff of it was still not offensive to her. An uneducated young woman had been downtrodden in the way that still gave meaning to the ancient crusade. 'Has this man left you entirely to your own resources?' she asked.

Marjorie uttered a sound that seemed an affirmative neigh. 'I'm an orphan,' she added further.

'You poor girl. No doubt that is why you felt the urge to motherhood at all costs. But you are still enamoured of this man?'

The victim managed a straight reply. 'I won't ever see him again.'

'Then we must see what we can do for you,' declared Mrs. Chalmers, always an admirer of decisiveness. 'You are fortunate,' she went on, the public-speaking clatter beginning to mount into her voice, 'that we are now living in what is termed—imprecisely as yet, I admit—the Welfare State. This includes a sensible attitude towards unmarried mothers. There is every provision for your category. I can remember, Marjorie, when it was very different! Nowadays you will not want for advice, the finest treatment, and even money.' Always at her best in opportunities for her organising ability, she was in full and pleasurable flow. 'The State apart, the master and I will not let you down, Marjorie. I would like to arrange your lying-in and convalescence. Meanwhile, of course, you will remain in our employment.' As Marjorie, the emotional crisis of confession over, lifted her head at last, the mistress proceeded: 'But surely you wish to sue the father? If so, we will take legal advice for you.'

'I couldn't face a court, madam,' whimpered Marjorie, becoming agitated again. ' I couldn't, I couldn't.'

'Is this Mr. Grigson a scoundrel?'

'I don't want to break up his home.'

'Pride is often a mistake, Marjorie. Don't you think this man should be taught a lesson? Demands on their pocket is the thing that teaches them! Probably you could obtain cash by merely *threatening* proceedings.'

'Mr. Grigson is a respectable man,' the girl wept.

Mrs. Chalmers, controlling her indignation under these tears, resumed: 'Come, we don't want to make a tragedy of it. With the State so helpful, the moral stigma of your condition is entirely a personal affair nowadays; certainly the retributive element has been abolished and—' Her attention arrested by the apathy settling in the housemaid's face, she pulled herself up. 'Cook knows about this? She is not upset with you?' It was the working class that displayed the most drastic feelings in such a matter.

'Cook has been a married woman,' Marjorie replied obscurely.

'And she has lived in my household a good many years!' the mistress clarified Cook's apparently sensible attitude. 'Now, my dear girl, go and lie down. You are overwrought.'

She stepped briskly into the garden, to tell Bertie without delay. In the country, so little happened. And to ensure that Marjorie obtained all those benefits for which pioneers such as she and Bertie had preached and fought, she could go into action again. Although such old fellow-campaigners as remained were ready enough to visit comfortable Sallows, and the flow of talk never lapsed, she faced the fact that they all were stagnant back-numbers now. The fate of pioneers! And she and Bertie were pioneers who had never achieved fame or notoriety. Vigour unimpaired, she felt not a day over fifty.

On Saturday afternoon, she pecked at her daughter's cheek in the porch, demanding: 'Why didn't you tell us before this week?' Grace, looking in her usual state of decorative torpor, murmured something non-committal, and her mother bustled on: 'There is a pleasing coincidence. Marjorie told me on the day you telephoned that she is expecting a child, too—and more or less at your time.'

'Marjorie?' Grace said, typically blank.

'The housemaid. You visit us so very infrequently that you haven't noticed her. An illegitimate case.' By the time they had crossed the rose garden to Bertie's study, Dorinda had given an account of her plan to avail Marjorie of all State succour.

Bertie craned his long neck at his daughter, greeting her with the arch breeziness that with him took the place of parental pride. 'You bring great news,' he chuckled. 'Sly little puss, keeping it all to yourself till now!'

'David thought his family name ought to be preserved.' Grace sank into the softest chair. 'So I hope it's a boy.'

'Ah, these glamorous titles!' Bertie, shaking his greenishly leonine head, made a rhetorical platform gesture with his hands.

'They'll be totally obsolete in due course,' his wife pronounced. 'Besides, in this case, is there any money to support the glamour?' Sir Leonard, Grace's father-in-law, had nothing but a mouldy manor-house, its acres let out to the local agricultural authority at a nominal rent; the house itself would be the next to go, and probably would become a school or hostel.

'Where *is* your husband, Grace?' she continued, putting her feet up on a stool of blue velvet. It was always 'your husband'.

Vaguely stroking her cascade of fox-coloured hair, which she wore in an uninhibited style testifying to her studio *milieu*, Grace looked somewhat vanquished already. 'David? Painting in Greece.'

'How long has he been there?' The wasp hum was more definite in Dorinda's voice now.

'Three weeks. I told him to get out of the way until I was normal shape again.'

Was she a trifle furtive? That Bohemian world of revolutionary sex freedom that she inhabited! Already, at thirty, she had had two husbands, the divorce from the first decided upon as lightly as an order to the grocer. Her mother, at moments willing to be just, sometimes asked herself if this freedom was a logical development of the feminist rebellion of an earlier era. Was this wayward daughter, despite her inertia, truly the offspring of the fighting energy that was Dorinda Chalmers?

'Well,' she said, looking somewhat halted, 'I suppose he'll be back for the accouchement?'

'I don't see what use he can be with that.' Grace's strange lapis-lazuli eyes fixed themselves speculatively on her mother. 'A painter needs freedom to move about, and you know—don't you—I have the objection of a cow to travelling.'

'Ha, ha!' chuckled her father.

Dorinda, unamused, often suspected that Grace, always sitting about in sluggish reveries that had no hint of planning, secretly laughed at her long-viewing mother. Even as a child, her attitude at home had been one of orientally passive resistance. 'It's most odd that she's always so lazy!' Mrs. Chalmers frequently remarked of this disappointing daughter, born as late as possible, for which surprising event her mother had been compelled to forgo attendance at a Fabian summer school frequented by the Webbs.

'Why doesn't the Arts Council do something for your husband?' She spoke in a brisk forestalling manner, suspecting, and rightly, that Grace had made the journey to Sallows in the hope of borrowing money yet again. 'It is State-financed. But there! If he can afford to travel about Greece—'

'But without me, Mother.' Grace, looking a degree more vanquished, added: 'Perhaps his next exhibition will earn enough to buy a few diapers.'

Dorina, dismissing this frivolty, resumed the inquiry. 'Are you living alone in that Chelsea flat?'

'I go to the cinema a lot.' Unexpectedly, the examinee began to laugh, with running gurgles and queer convulsive movements of her indolent flesh, so that even her limbs seemed to exude mirth. 'To the comics, mostly. I even journey out to the suburbs . . .Oh, I saw such a funny one yesterday.' Her laughter reached boisterous force, as she attempted to engage their attention in a description of some farce.

The hysteria was, of course, a symptom of her condition. After allowing it to subside, Dorinda went on: 'Did your husband get the commission for the theatrical designs?' Grace had 'borrowed' a hundred pounds on this probability.

'No.' A giving-up-the ghost tone succeeded her mirth. 'The people thought his sketches too fantastic.'

'I'm not surprised.' His mother-in-law had been to one exhibition of his work and considered the afternoon thoroughly misspent. The catalogue introduction had suggested that this revolutionary work represented the chaos and destruction of life today . . . Chaos and destruction ! When one of the greatest experiments of modern times, the Socialist State, was in creation before the eyes of these artists and their preposterous women, whose faces, judging by her glimpses of them at David's 'private view', were depraved from inferior intoxicants and, worse, loose living. 'Revolutionary', indeed! These people contaminated the word.

She reverted dutifully to the chief matter in hand. 'Where will you have the child?'

'Oh . . . In the flat, I suppose.'

'Since we are organising Marjorie's accouchement, your father and I thought you should take advantage of it. Perhaps you could go into the same maternity home—you might have a companion in Marjorie, should your times coincide. You've kept up the National Insurance stamps, of course?'

Her daughter might have been as remote from National Insurance as a woman on the moon. 'I believe we have the card for them,' she murmured glassily.

'Well, as your husband sees fit to remain wandering about Greece at such a time, we had certainly better organise this affair for you. You would go into the same maternity home as Marjorie?'

Grace seemed roused at last. Her Modigliani-type neck, which was not so long as her father's, flexed slightly. 'Oh, there's plenty of time, Mother!' she protested. 'Why fuss?'

'Grace can look after herself,' her father crowed, belatedly interfering. 'Ha, these modern young women, they know everything, Dorrie.'

'Very well.' Dorinda spoke as if it were her last word, dismissing the matter from her aid. 'You may as well take advantage of State benefits in these things,' she added, however. 'People pay for them with the stamps, and I am informed the service is of the best, from the cradle to the grave.'

'Their funerals are not like those that used to be known as paupers' funerals?' Grace asked.

'In the Welfare State'—her mother took a firm stand, lifting the house telephone to ring for tea— 'there is no such person as a pauper.'

Grace, waiting for tea, relapsed into the silence usual with her in these rare home visits. Odour of countless roses came through the open lattices. The room seemed the tranquil haven of a well-used life; it was bright with Morris chintz, hand-thrown pottery, folk-weave rugs, crowded with books, busts, and browned old photographs autographed by Fabian celebrities, including the Webbs, Shaw and Henry Salt, and Labour Party politicians of fiery early vintage.

When Marjorie came in, Grace took a trance-like glance at her, which was returned with a behaved primness.

'I'm not sure if Marjorie ought to carry a heavy tea-tray across the garden,' Dorinda said after her protégée had retired.

241

'She looked as strong as a horse to me,' Grace made an effort into consciousness. 'How are the "Memoirs" getting on, Father?'

'I have to jog his memory so much,' Dorinda replied for him. 'It's really half my book.'

Ownership of Sallows was hers, too, in addition to the other securities. Bertie's inherited money, imprudently invested, had become negligible since the First World War. But otherwise they were socialistically united, and had never seriously crossed swords since they first met, in an East End Settlement, shortly after Bertie came down from Oxford in a Ruskin blaze of idealism.

'I want him to bring this Marjorie business into the last chapter of the "Memoirs",' Dorinda resumed, eating a buttered muffin. 'The things that will be done for her will show that the Socialist State is not founded on humbug.'

'The question arises'—Bertie attempted to start a debate—'do State benefits help the *emotional* condition of this poor girl ill-treated by a married man? What do you think, Grace?'

But Grace, cast again into reverie, only shook her head. She had given up hope of a loan; a weekend had to be got through; her parents were evangelistic teetotallers, and there was never even a bottle of brandy for possible, though unlikely, collapses of the retired old warriors who frequented the house. Her mother's heart had become an institute, and she had done nothing to earn admittance there.

Settling to supper in the kitchen that evening, Marjorie said to Cook, with satisfaction: 'That daughter has been a wild one. I can tell! But she's got caught now, and she don't welcome it. I tell you what, Mrs. Allen—it's because she's the child of vegetarians. Man and his woman was meant to eat meat, like you and me do; that's how we get the strength to take things as they come. Mark my words, she'll get a difficult time, and it's not her fault, poor thing, daughter of a woman that only eats monkey food.'

Bessie Allen was just old enough to realise the value of the hard fights the mistress and her like had waged for both the poor and her sex. 'If you are referring to the mistress,' she said majestically, 'you have cause to be thankful for what monkey food, as you call it, has done.'

Marjorie frowned at the scolding. 'I don't dispute the mistress is kind.'

'Many a one,' continued Cook, who was finding Marjorie's new, conceited manner very trying, 'would have sent you packing out of the house. Then you would be obliged to find your Mr. Grigson, since you've got no savings.'

'Wrong,' Marjorie retaliated. 'The mistress told me the Government supports and encourages a woman in my position, to keep the birth-rate up.' And to show that she was offended she refused a second helping of Cook's delicious steak pie. Mrs. Chalmers was forced to allow meat in the kitchen.

As the summer proceeded, Marjorie got more and more above herself. The mistress asked Cook not to overburden the jilted girl. Free National Health bottles of orange juice and vitamin capsules arrived regularly from a clinic in the county town to which Mrs. Chalmers had taken Marjorie in a car for an interview. There had been, too, a visit to a lady in the town's Moral Welfare Centre, where both practical and psychological advice were given to the unfortunate girl, though Marjorie still refused, in the most adamantine fashion, to allow any stalking down of Mr. Grigson. In addition, Mrs. Chalmers obtained information about a wonderful rest home for after the event.

'I hope to get you into it, Marjorie,' she said. 'It's run for such cases as yours and is a Labour Government experiment. The idea is that you can adjust yourself there to the psychological damage you may have sustained in your misfortune—if you may call it that. I don't think you are a neurotic type, but why shouldn't you take advantage of a rest in Eggeswick Castle? The National Insurance covers everything; there won't be a penny to pay.'

Returned from the drawing-room after being told of this likely treat, Marjorie announced importantly: 'I'll be going to Eggeswick Castle for three weeks' rest. Damage has been done to me.'

Cook only pursed her lips. But her choler, much as she tried to control it, was growing. She considered the mistress's zeal misplaced. Marjorie was giving herself, more and more, the most irritating duchess airs—perhaps not surprisingly, since she had not to lift a hand in self-labour over her plight, except to swallow fruit juice and capsules.

The weather, too, became torrid, and one August afternoon, when Marjorie refused to clean the cutlery, saying the heat 'daunted' her, a kitchen fracas developed. In its crescendo, Cook, at last, crystallised her dissatisfaction. She brought out, with rising colour: 'And it's my belief that there's no Mr. Grigson. Married *or* single!'

Marjorie gave her a long look of devilish subtlety before replying: 'And there you're right, for once.'

'Then who is he?' Cook demanded.

Marjorie thrust out her head. 'Go on!' she taunted. 'Go on, run to the mistress and tell her I don't know who he is! It won't make any difference.' She showed signs, nevertheless, of a reduction in her belligerent supremacy. 'I took the name out of a newspaper—Mr. Grigson, of Berkeley Square. The paper had his photo, and I liked the size and look of him.' She added defiantly: 'So there *is* a Mr. Grigson.'

Verified in her suspicion though she was, Cook collapsed in horror. The drama was of that unkempt order about which nothing can be done, except, in this case, an ultimatum that either she or the house-maid must terminate service to the household. If Marjorie hadn't herself collapsed into violent tears, prior to obediently laying out the cutlery, this drastic solution would have ensued. Cook had to admit to herself that the mistress's high code would still not have allowed her to cast Marjorie away, and it seemed she had the nation behind her.

'I'll keep my mouth shut,' she pronounced, in a tone of washing her hands of it all. 'I dare say the Government has got lovely mansions where evil liars, and worse, can go to have breakfast in bed under eiderdowns.'

'The mistress,' Marjorie said, perking up a little, 'said that the Government feels shame because of the nasty way unmarried mothers were treated in the old days. She's an education, the mistress is.'

Mrs. Chalmers, indeed, went further in kindness. So that Marjorie could obtain final metropolitan advantages, she closed Sallows a fortnight earlier than was her custom. The two domestics travelled to London first-class, as usual, while their employers went third. And from the house in Hampstead the mistress went into action the day after arrival, accompanying Marjorie to a clinic.

On other days she inspected, in her cream cloak and with her sharp eye of a regally experienced hen, three maternity homes, greatly impressing the staffs and, of course, obtaining priority of attention. In the one she chose, tea was given her up in the Matron's parlour while Marjorie remained below on an examination table.

An important point remained undecided. The mistress took it up. 'Now, Marjorie, we must decide what is to become of the child.'

Marjorie, immediately hanging her head, whimpered: 'I won't tell Mr. Grigson. I'd rather die.'

244

'The State will be a better father than that man!' Mrs. Chalmers said, with asperity. 'I have inquired most thoroughly about the Homes for these children, and during your lying-in I intend to inspect one or two that are near London.'

'Foundling places!' grieved Marjorie, who had confided to horrified Cook her hope that the Chalmerses would adopt the child. 'Orphanages!'

'Oh, nonsense. It's old-fashioned to associate these Homes with delinquency.' Mrs. Chalmers took up a document from her desk and, scanning it, continued: 'There is no need to be depressed. You are by no means a lonely pariah. I have some facts here. One in ten of the births in Great Britain in 1945 was illegitimate; there were sixty-five thousand in all. The numbers in subsequent years are somewhat lower, but not all disheartening for you. Your child won't feel out of place in our little country.'

Marjorie pleaded: 'If it is a girl, can I name her after you, and after the master if it is a boy?'

Mrs. Chalmers, remarkably, looked at a loss, but struck a lame mean in her indecision. 'There is no copyright in names. It would be delightful.'

At dinner, when she told Bertie of this compliment, he said: 'To tell you the truth, Dorrie, I will be relieved when we're rid of this problem child and it's safely shut up in a Home far from London.'

'There speaks a man! You sit upstairs in comfort while I run charitably all over London.'

'Did you succeed in getting Grace on the telephone today?' he asked, a trifle pointedly.

'Yes,' Dorinda blew. 'At last! Why is she never at home in that Chelsea flat, and why doesn't she come to see us? She said her husband is still in Greece. I couldn't get anything sensible from her about her arrangements. She thinks she has three or four weeks to go yet—imagine it, *thinks*! So typical.'

Marjorie, her time announced by a series of breakfast grunts, went off to the maternity home with such lack of dismay that Cook wondered if it was the first occasion. In conclave with the matron, Mrs. Chalmers had bespoken for her protégée the services of the best gynæcologist on the visiting National Health Service staff. So it was not surprising that a fine, sturdy girl was born in entire safety later in the day. Matron herself telephoned the news to Mrs. Chalmers, who broke into her husband's sanctum upstairs.

'Yes, yes, Dorrie,' he said, somewhat testy at the interruption. 'This birth was expected, wasn't it?'

'The sex wasn't.' Mrs. Chalmers descended to the kitchen, where Cook controlledly expressed the appropriate remarks of gratification. 'She'll settle down now,' the mistress averred. 'You and I know too well, Mrs. Allen, how difficult it is to find housemaids that will sleep in and go to Sallows.'

'We must *hope* she'll settle, ma'am,' Cook took leave to amend. 'Her nature is on the turn, and it might be to sweet or sour.'

'It could easily have been to sour in the old days, Mrs. Allen. But now she has seen what is being done for her by the Welfare State . . . And there are her three weeks at Eggeswick Castle to come, too. She'll be a welcome guest in a historic residence where ten years ago she might well have been a kitchenmaid. One could call this a National baby.'

Cook said: 'Well, we have National teeth, spectacles, wigs and whatnot—and few of us know where they really come from, do we?'

A little flurried by the rage she sensed in Cook, usually so discreet, Mrs. Chalmers pursued: 'I think I deserve an outing to Eggeswick next week, don't you? Perhaps the following week you'd like a trip there yourself?'

It was three hours by slow train from London, and then a hired car from Eggeswick station, but the castle was well worth the journey. The first glimpse of the harmonious pile, stone-blue in the mild early October sunshine, soothed the heart with a sense of unruffled eternalness. But a more personal and up-to-date pleasure was to come.

Once the fortress of thieving medieval barons, and for subsequent centuries the jewel-box home of a Tory-fisted aristocratic line, now under the portcullis of the entrance tower a new, beautifully streamlined ambulance car preceded Mrs. Chalmers's old country taxi, and in a window of one of the fairy-tale turrets above the russet bailey she caught sight of a snowy-capped nurse looking at a thermometer. Later, during her tour of the entire castle, she panted up to the battlements, where, catching the high, sweet breeze, long ropes of State diapers dried quickly above the rusty cannon balls still left there for antiquarian display.

Erring girls might well find a repairing peace here. They could be seen scattered about the greenswards of the outer domain in ruminating couples and trios. After a long, surprisingly inefficient delay in the reception hall, Mrs. Chalmers, hothouse peaches and grapes under her cream cloak, found her own protégée in converse with two other patients in a small flower garden.

'Oh, madam!' Marjorie began to rise rather languidly from the bright cushions and rugs of her chaise-longue, placed on the edge of a sunken lily-leafed pond. Her companions, pretty though sharp-faced, sat on other cushions. The trio made a delightful picture. Foolish nymphs learning wisdom, they were feeding the goldfish.

'No, no, don't get up, Marjorie. What a superb view you have from here!' Mrs. Chalmers waved the satchel of fruit at the tranquil landscape. 'A perfect retreat for convalescents. It moves me to think that ten years ago you—no, don't go, dear girls.' The visitor, never losing an opportunity to address the proletariat, detained the other two.

'Dorrie,' Marjorie broke into the oration when a chance offered, making her mistress start at this use of her name, 'is in the nursery, madam. I'll take you up.' Her companions had begun to fidget.

She led the way into the castle like a tactful chatelaine, and preceded the visitor up the great stone staircase, which was odorous of disinfectant. A giggling girl chased another down a dark corridor. The former armoury contained some three dozen occupied cribs, each with a tied-on label. Tiny Dorinda was fast asleep. Mrs. Chalmers cooed dutifully at the anonymous little face, but was much more kindled by the majestic dimensions of this spick-and-span nursery.

'Marjorie,' she declared, 'I think we can congratulate ourselves. I must drop a note to the Minister of Health.'

'We have hobbies and lectures,' Marjorie said primly. She lowered her voice out of the nurse's hearing. 'But to tell you the truth, madam, some of the girls here are too far gone for lectures. Jail is what *I* would give them. They must *enjoy* nastiness. One of them has stolen my gold locket—what I had Mr. Grigson's head in, cut out of a photo, and was keeping for Dorrie as all she'd have of her father.' Ox-blood eyes wide with anxious appeal, she added: 'But don't tell Matron, if you see her. The other girls would make mincemeat of me for carrying tales.'

Mrs. Chalmers smiled confederately. 'I won't tell. We must take the rough with the smooth, dear girl. Never mind about the locket. After all, you could have Mr. Grigson's head in reality, if you chose.'

'I'd rather die,' Marjorie said. 'Besides, I've heard he's emigrated to New Zealand.'

247

Taking full advantage of the trip, Mrs. Chalmers interviewed the Matron and was conducted by her over the castle—even to the dungeons, of evil despot's repute but now the properly ventilated larders of State-provided victuals. Matron refused to be drawn on the political and social inferences of the work under her jurisdiction but admitted that patients often were rehabilitated in the castle. Mrs. Chalmers became severe when this lady let slip the word 'delinquents'. 'Surely,' she protested, 'the patients are *victims*, and it is the *causers* of their neurotic condition that are the delinquents?'

For some reason, as happened sometimes in her public life, she did not hit it off with this official. But, leaving the castle, she signed the visitor's book with the remark 'Admirable! I am deeply moved by the Eggeswick experiment and congratulate everybody concerned, including myself.'

She arrived back in London just before midnight. Because of hunger —a vegetarian could seldom get proper food in the carnivorous by-paths of the country—she felt dispirited. As she let herself into the house at Hampstead, her thoughts on a cheese-and-mushroom soufflé, Cook came bustling up from the kitchen in a state of dire excitement.

'Oh, ma'am!' she gasped. 'The master has gone off to St. Stephen's Hospital in the East End. Your daughter is there—had her baby suddenly.' She heaved in the distress of having more to tell.

'St. Stephen's!' It was a well-known hospital deep in the docks district. 'She's not in danger?'

'Oh dear, no. I haven't got the rights of it properly, but the news on the phone was that she had her baby in some cinema in those parts, and an ambulance took her to St. Stephen's. A boy it is, I think Master said, when he hurried off.'

Revived to a bounce, Mrs. Chalmers got to the telephone. The night superintendent of St. Stephen's, who seemed not at all surprised by the extraordinary venue of the birth, verified that the mother had been sitting in a cinema. But the actual birth had taken place in the manager's office while an ambulance was being called. Luckily, a local doctor had been in the audience. The mother was quite comfortable, the baby doing well, and Mr. Chalmers had left for home a few minutes ago.

When Dorinda heard the taxi drive up, she bore down on her husband in the hall, crying out: 'Bertie! What has that madcap been up to?'

248

He hung up his umbrella with a sigh. 'The newspaper reporters have got hold of it, Dorrie. But Grace doesn't seem to mind. She said it would be good publicity for her husband's work.'

'Whatever was she doing in the East End at such a time?' Dorinda bridled impatiently.

'It seems,' he began, 'Grace has a mania for some film comedians called the Marx Brothers and goes after them wherever their pictures are shown. She took a bus to the East End and admits that she felt she ought not to go.' He coughed deprecatingly. 'The film, apparently, was particularly hilarious. She had made no plans at all for the accouchement,' he added, 'and hadn't been to any clinic or registered with a doctor under the National Health Service.'

Dorinda sat down heavily. 'A daughter of ours, Bertie! What will Sir Leonard say? In an East End cinema!'

'Grace doesn't seem at all put out,' he repeated. 'She said something about having a child in the old-fashioned way, without fuss and a lot of State interference and licking of stamps.'

'The old-fashioned way!' Mrs. Chalmers could not subdue a snort. 'Without fuss! In a cinema!'

And the next morning, prominent in one of their two newspapers, was an item: '*Heir to baronetage born in East End Cinema*'. It stated, with biographical details, that the wife of the well-known young painter had been watching a revival of *Animal Crackers*. A stevedore's wife had given birth three months before in this cinema, situated in a teeming district, and Mrs. Slocombe, the manager, hoped for the honour of becoming godfather to this second child, too. The Chalmers' other paper, the less radical-toned *Times*, ignored the outlandish event, fortunately.

Flinging her cream cloak on after breakfast, Dorinda pronounced: 'There's only one word for her— 'decadent'. If she were of a lower class, she'd be called "delinquent".'

'Oh, come, come,' Bertie protested. He added delicately: 'Grace told me last night that it was quite human in St. Stephen's, but I felt she needed money. I noticed she was wearing a very coarse-looking nightgown. It had an institute cut.'

'Nothing but *sluttishness*, all her life.' Dorinda, rummaging in her desk for her cheque-book, added: 'She deserves to go to Eggeswick. The matron there would soon know how to deal with her.'

THE CHOSEN ONE

A letter, inscribed *By Hand*, lay inside the door when he arrived home just before seven o'clock. The thick, expensive-looking envelope was black-edged and smelled of stale face powder. Hoarding old-fashioned mourning envelopes would be typical of Mrs. Vines, and the premonition of disaster Rufus felt now had nothing to do with death. But he stared for some moments at the penny-sized blob of purple wax sealing the flap. Other communications he had received from Mrs. Vines over the last two years had not been sent in such a ceremonious envelope. The sheet of ruled paper inside, torn from a pad of the cheapest kind, was more familiar. He read it with strained concentration, his brows drawn into a pucker. The finely traced handwriting in green ink, gave him no special difficulty, and his pausings over words such as 'oral', 'category' and 'sentimental', while his full-fleshed lips shaped the syllables, came from uncertainty of their meaning.

Sir,

In reply to your oral request to me yesterday, concerning the property, Brychan Cottage, I have decided not to grant you a renewal of the lease, due to expire on June 30th next. This is final.

The cottage is unfit for human habitation, whether you consider yourself as coming under that category or not. It is an eyesore to me, and I intend razing it to the ground later this year. That you wish to get married and continue to live in the cottage with some factory hussy from the town is no affair of mine, and that my father, for sentimental reasons, granted your grandfather a seventy-five-year lease for the paltry sum of a hundred pounds is no affair of mine either. Your wretched family has always been a nuisance to me on my estate and I will not tolerate one of them to infest it any longer than is legal, or any screeching, jazz-dancing slut in trousers and bare feet to trespass and contaminate my land. Although you got rid of the pestiferous poultry after your mother died, the noise of the motor cycle you then bought has annoyed me even more than the cockerel crowing. Get out.

Yours truly,
Audrey P. Vines.

He saw her brown-speckled, jewel-ringed hand moving from word to word with a certainty of expression beyond any means of retaliation from him. The abuse in the letter did not enrage him immediately; it belonged too familiarly to Mrs. Vines's character and reputation, though when he was a boy he had known different behaviour from her. But awareness that she had this devilish right to throw him, neck and crop, from the home he had inherited began to register somewhere in his mind at last. He had never believed she would do it.

Shock temporarily suspended full realization of the catastrophe. He went into the kitchen to brew the tea he always made as soon as he arrived home on his motor bike from his factory job in the county town. While he waited for the kettle to boil on the oil stove, his eye kept straying warily on to the table. That a black-edged envelope lay on it was like something in a warning dream. He stared vaguely at the familiar object around him. A peculiar silence seemed to have come to this kitchen that he had known all his life. There was a feeling of withdrawal from him in the room, as though already he were an intruder in it.

He winced when he picked up the letter and put it in a pocket of his leather jacket. Then, as was his habit on fine evenings, he took a mug of tea out to a seat under a pear tree shading the ill-fitting front door of the cottage, a sixteenth-century building in which he had been born. Golden light of May flooded the well-stocked garden. He began to re-read the letter, stopped to fetch a tattered little dictionary from the living room, and sat consulting one or two words which still perplexed him. Then, his thick jaw thrust out in his effort at sustained concentration, he read the letter through again.

The sentence: 'This is final' pounded in his head. Three words had smashed his plans for the future. In his bewilderment, it did not occur to him that his inbred procrastination was of importance. Until the day before, he had kept postponing going to see the evil-tempered mistress of Plas Idwal about the lease business, though his mother, who couldn't bear the sight of her, had reminded him of it several times in her last illness. He had just refused to believe that Mrs. Vines would turn him out when a date in a yellowed document came round. His mother's forebears had occupied Brychan Cottage for hundreds of years, long before Mrs. Vines's family bought Plas Idwal.

Slowly turning his head, as though in compulsion, he gazed to the left of where he sat. He could see, beyond the garden and the alders fringing a ditch, an extensive slope of rough turf on which, centrally

251

in his vision, a great cypress spread branches to the ground. Higher, crowning the slope, a rectangular mansion of russet stone caught the full light of the sunset. At this hour, he had sometimes seen Mrs. Vines walking down the slope with her bulldog. She always carried a bag, throwing bread from it to birds and to wild duck on the river below. The tapestry bag had been familiar to him since he was a boy, but it was not until last Sunday that he learned she kept binoculars in it.

She could not be seen anywhere this evening. He sat thinking of last Sunday's events, unable to understand that such a small mistake as his girl had made could have caused the nastiness in the letter. Gloria had only trespassed a few yards on Plas Idwal land. And what was wrong with a girl wearing trousers or walking bare-foot on clean grass? What harm was there if a girl he was courting screeched when he chased her on to the river bank and if they tumbled to the ground? Nobody's clothes had come off.

He had thought Sunday was the champion day of his life. He had fetched Gloria from the town on his motor bike in the afternoon. It was her first visit to the cottage that he had boasted about so often in the factory, especially to her. Brought up in a poky terrace house without a garden, she had been pleased and excited with his pretty home on the Plas Idwal estate, and in half an hour, while they sat under this pear tree, he had asked her to marry him, and she said she would. She had laughed and squealed a lot in the garden and by the river, kicking her shoes off, dancing on the grassy river bank; she was only eighteen. Then, when he went indoors to put the kettle on for tea, she had jumped the narrow dividing ditch on to Mrs. Vines's land —and soon after came dashing into the cottage. Shaking with fright, she said that a terrible woman in a torn fur coat had come shouting from under a big tree on the slope, binoculars in her hand and threatening her with a bulldog. It took quite a while to calm Gloria down. He told her of Mrs. Vines's funny ways and the tales he had heard from his mother. But neither on Sunday nor since did he mention anything about the lease of Brychan Cottage, though remembrance of it had crossed his mind when Gloria said she'd marry him.

On Sunday, too, he had kept telling himself that he ought to ride up to the mansion to explain about the stranger who ignorantly crossed the ditch. But three days went by before he made the visit. He had bought a high-priced suède windcheater in the town, and got his hair

252

trimmed during his dinner hour. He had even picked a bunch of polyanthus for Mrs. Vines when he arrived home from the factory— and then, bothered by wanting to postpone the visit still longer, forgot them when he forced himself at last to jump on the bike. It was her tongue he was frightened of, he had told himself. He could never cope with women's trantrums.

But she had not seemed to be in one of her famous tempers when he appeared at the kitchen door of Plas Idwal, just after seven. 'Well, young man, what do you require?' she asked, pointing to a carpenter's bench alongside the dresser, on which he had often sat as a boy. First, he had tried to tell her that the girl who strayed on her land was going to marry him. But Mrs. Vines talked to the five cats that, one after the other, bounded into the kitchen from upstairs a minute after he arrived. She said to them, 'We won't have these loud-voiced factory girls trespassing on any part of my property, will we, my darlings?' Taking her time, she fed the cats with liver she lifted with her fingers from a pan on one of her three small oil stoves. Presently he forced himself to say, 'I've come about the lease of Brychan Cottage. My mother told me about it. I've got a paper with a date on it.' But Mrs. Vines said to one of the cats, 'Queenie, you'll have to swallow a pill tomorrow!' After another wait, he tried again, saying, 'My young lady is liking Brychan Cottage very much.' Mrs. Vines had stared at him, not saying a word for about a minute, then said, 'You can go now. I will write you tomorrow about the lease.'

He had left the kitchen feeling a tightness beginning to throttle him, and he knew then that it had never been fear he felt towards her. But, as he tore at full speed down the drive, the thought came that it might have been a bad mistake to have stopped going to Plas Idwal to ask if he could collect whinberries for her up on the slopes of Mynydd Baer, or find mushrooms in the Caer Tegid fields, as he used to do before he took a job in a factory in the town. Was that why, soon after his mother died, she had sent him a rude letter about the smell of poultry and the rooster crowing? He had found that letter comic and shown it to chaps in the factory. But something had told him to get rid of the poultry.

He got up from the seat under the pear tree. The strange quiet he had noticed in the kitchen was in the garden too. Not a leaf or bird stirred. He could hear his heart thumping. He began to walk up and down the paths. He knew now the full meaning of her remark to those cats that no trespassers would be allowed on 'my property'. In about six weeks he himself would be a trespasser. He stopped to tear a branch of pear blossom from the tree and looked at it abstractedly. The pear tree was *his*! His mother had told him it was planted on the day he was born. Some summers it used to fruit so well that they had sold the whole load to Harries in the town, and the money was always for him.

Pacing, he slapped the branch against his leg, scattering the blossom. The tumult in his heart did not diminish. Like the kitchen, the garden seemed already to be withdrawn from his keeping. *She* had walked there that day, tainting it. He hurled the branch in the direction of the Plas Idwal slope. He did not want to go indoors. He went through a thicket of willows and lay on the river bank, staring into the clear, placidly flowing water. Her face flickered in the greenish depths. He flung a stone at it. Stress coiled tighter in him. He lay flat on his back, sweating, a hand clenched over his genitals.

The arc of serene evening sky and the whisper of gently lapping water calmed him for a while. A shred of common sense told him that the loss of Brychan Cottage was not a matter of life and death. But he could not forget Mrs. Vines. He tried to think how he could appease her with some act or service. He remembered that until he was about seventeen she would ask him to do odd jobs for her, such as clearing fallen branches, setting fire to wasp holes, and—she made him wear a bonnet and veil for this—collecting the combs from her beehives. But what could he do now? She had shut herself away from everybody for years.

He could not shake off thought of her. Half-forgotten memories of the past came back. When he was about twelve, how surprised his mother had been when he told her that he had been taken upstairs in Plas Idwal and shown six kittens born that day! Soon after that, Mrs. Vines had come down to this bank, where he had sat fishing, and said she wanted him to drown three of the kittens. She had a tub of water ready outside her kitchen door, and she stood watching while he held a wriggling canvas sack under the water with a broom. The three were males, she said. He had to dig a hole close to the greenhouses for the sack.

She never gave him money for any job, only presents from the house —an old magic lantern, coloured slides, dominoes, a box of crayons, even a doll's house. Her big brown eyes would look at him without any sign of temper at all. Once, when she asked him, 'Are you a dunce in school?' and he said, 'Yes, bottom of the class,' he heard her laugh aloud for the first time, and she looked very pleased with him. All that, he remembered, was when visitors had stopped going to Plas Idwal, and there was not a servant left; his mother said they wouldn't put up with Mrs. Vines's bad ways any more. But people in the town who had worked for her said she was a very clever woman, with letters after her name, and it was likely she would always come out on top in disputes concerning her estate.

Other scraps of her history returned to his memory—things heard from old people who had known her before she shut herself away. Evan Matthews, who used to be her estate keeper and had been a friend of his father's, said that for a time she had lived among African savages, studying their ways with her first husband. Nobody knew how she got rid of that husband, or the whole truth about her second one. She used to disappear from Plas Idwal for months, but when her father died she never went away from her old home again. But it was when her second husband was no longer seen in Plas Idwal that she shut herself up there, except that once a month she hired a Daimler from the county town and went to buy, so it was said, cases of wine at Drapple's, and stuff for her face at the chemist's. Then even those trips had stopped, and everything was delivered to Plas Idwal by tradesmen's vans or post.

No clue came of a way to appease her. He rose from the river bank. The sunset light was beginning to fade, but he could still see clearly the mansion façade, its twelve bare windows, and the crumbling entrance portico, which was never used now. In sudden compulsion, he strode down to the narrow, weed-filled ditch marking the boundary of Brychan Cottage land. But he drew up at its edge. If he went to see her, he thought, he must prepare what he had to say with a cooler head than he had now. Besides, to approach the mansion that way was forbidden. She might be watching him through binoculars from one of the windows.

An ambling sound roused him from this torment of indecision. Fifty yards beyond the river's opposite bank, the 7:40 slow train to the county town was approaching. Its passage over the rough stretches of meadowland brought back a reminder of his mother's bitter grudge against the family at Plas Idwal. The trickery that had been done before the railroad was laid had never meant much to him, though he had heard about it often enough from his mother. Late in the eighteenth century, her father, who couldn't read or write, had been persuaded by Mrs. Vines's father to sell to him, at a low price, not only decaying Brychan Cottage but, across the river, a great many acres of useless meadowland included in the cottage demesne. As a bait, a seventy-five-year retaining lease of the cottage and a piece of land to the river bank were granted for a hundred pounds. So there had been some money to stave off further dilapidation of the cottage and to put by for hard times. But in less than two years after the transaction, a railroad loop to a developing port in the west had been laid over that long stretch of useless land across the river. Mrs. Vines's father had known of the project and, according to the never-forgotten grudge, cleared a big profit from rail rights. His explanation (alleged by Rufus's mother to be humbug) was that he had wanted to preserve the view from possible ruination by buildings such as gasworks; a few trains every day, including important expresses and freight traffic, did not matter.

Watching, with a belligerent scowl, the 7:40 vanishing into the sunset fume, Rufus remembered that his father used to say that it wasn't Mrs. Vines herself who had done the dirty trick. But was the daughter proving herself to be of the same robbing nature now? He could not believe that she intended razing Brychan Cottage to the ground. Did she want to trim it up and sell or rent at a price she knew he could never afford? But she had plenty of money already— everybody knew that. Was it only that she wanted him out of sight, the last member of his family, and the last man on the estate?

He strode back to the cottage with the quick step of a man reaching a decision. Yet when he entered the dusky, low-ceilinged living room the paralysis of will threatened him again. He stood gazing round at the age-darkened furniture, the steel and copper accoutrements of the cavernous fireplace, the ornaments, the dim engravings of mountains, castles, and waterfalls as though he viewed them for the firt time. He could not light the oil lamp, could not prepare a meal, begin his evening routine. A superstitious dread assailed him. Another presence was in possession here.

He shook the spell off. In the crimson glow remaining at the deep window, he read the letter once more, searching for some hint of a loophole. There seemed none. But awareness of a challenge penetrated his mind. For the first time since the death of his parents an important event was his to deal with alone. He lit the lamp, found a seldom-used stationery compendium, and sat down. He did not get beyond, 'Dear Madam, Surprised to receive your letter . . .' Instinct told him he must

256

wheedle Mrs. Vines. But in what way? After half an hour of defeat, he dashed upstairs, ran down naked to the kitchen to wash at the sink, and returned upstairs to rub scented oil into his tough black hair and dress in the new cotton trousers and elegant windcheater of green suède that had cost him more than a week's wages.

Audrey Vines put her binoculars into her tapestry bag when Rufus entered Brychan Cottage and, her uninterested old bulldog at her heels, stepped out to the slope from between a brace of low-sweeping cypress branches. After concealing herself under the massive tree minutes before the noise of Rufus's motor cycle had come, as usual, a few minutes before seven, she had studied his face and followed his prowlings about the garden and river bank for nearly an hour. The clear views of him this evening had been particularly satisfactory. She knew it was a dictionary he had consulted under the pear tree, where he often sat drinking from a large Victorian mug. The furious hurling of a branch in the direction of the cypress had pleased her; his stress when he paced the garden had been as rewarding as his stupefied reading of the deliberately perplexing phraseology of her letter.

'Come along, Mia. *Good* little darling! We are going in now.'

Paused on the slope in musing, the corpulent bitch grunted, blinked, and followed with a faint trace of former briskness in her bandily aged waddle. Audrey Vines climbed without any breathlessness herself, her pertinacious gaze examining the distances to right and left. She came out every evening not only to feed birds but to scrutinize her estate before settling down for the night. There was also the passage of the 7:40 train to see; since her two watches and every clock in the house needed repairs, it gave verification of the exact time, though this, like the bird feeding, was not really of account to her.

It was her glimpse of Rufus that provided her long day with most interest. For some years she had regularly watched him through the powerful Zeiss binoculars from various concealed spots. He renewed an interest in studies begun during long-ago travels in countries far from Wales, and she often jotted her findings into a household-accounts book kept locked in an old portable escritoire. To her eye, the prognathous jaw, broad nose, and gypsy-black hair of this heavy-bodied but personable young man bore distinct atavistic elements. He possessed, too, a primitive bloom, which often lingered for years beyond adolescence with persons of tardy mental development. But this throwback descendant of an ancient race was also, up to a point, a

257

triumph over decadence. Arriving miraculously late in his mother's life, after three others born much earlier to the illiterate woman had died in infancy, this last-moment child had flourished physically, if not in other respects.

Except for the occasions when, as a boy and youth, he used to come to Plas Idwal to do odd jobs and run errands, her deductions had been formed entirely through the limited and intensifying medium of the binoculars. She had come to know all his outdoor habits and activities around the cottage. These were rewarding only occasionally. The days when she failed to see him seemed bleakly deficient of incident. While daylight lasted, he never bathed in the river without her knowledge, though sometimes, among the willows and reeds, he was as elusive as an otter. And winter, of course, kept him indoors a great deal.

'Come, darling. There'll be a visitor for us tonight.'

Mia, her little question-mark tail unexpectedly quivering, glanced up with the vaguely deprecating look of her breed. Audrey Vines had reached the balustraded front terrace. She paused by a broken sundial for a final look round at the spread of tranquil uplands and dim woods afar, the silent river and deserted meadows below, and, lingeringly, at the ancient trees shading her estate. Mild and windless though the evening was, she wore a long, draggled coat of brown-dyed ermine and, pinned securely on skeins of vigorous hair unskilfully home-dyed to auburn tints, a winged hat of tobacco-gold velvet. These, with her thick bistre face powder and assertive eye pencilling, gave her the look of an uncompromisingly womanly woman in an old-style sepia photograph, a woman halted for ever in the dead past. But there was no evidence of waning powers in either her demeanour or step as she continued to the side terrace. A woman of leisure ignoring time's urgencies, she only suggested an unruffled unity with the day's slow descent into twilight.

The outward calm was deceptive. A watchful gleam in her eyes was always there, and the binoculars were carried for a reason additional to her study of Rufus. She was ever on the lookout for trespassers and poachers or tramps on the estate, rare though such were. When, perhaps three or four times a year, she discovered a stray culprit, the mature repose would disappear in a flash, her step accelerate, her throaty voice lash out. Tradesmen arriving legitimately at her kitchen door avoided looking her straight in the eye, and C. W. Powell, her solicitor, knew exactly how far he could go in sociabilities during his quarterly conferences with her in the kitchen of Plas Idwal. Deep within those dissociated eyes lay an adamantine refusal to acknowledge the existence of any friendly approach. Only her animals could soften that repudiation.

'Poor Mia! We won't stay out so long tomorrow, I promise! Come along.' They had reached the unbalustraded side terrace. 'A flower for us tonight, sweetheart, then we'll go in,' she murmured.

She crossed the cobbled yard behind the mansion. Close to disused greenhouses, inside which overturned flower-pots and abandoned garden tools lay under tangles of grossly overgrown plants sprouting to the broken roofing, there was a single border of wallflowers, primulas, and several well-pruned rosebushes in generous bud. It was the only evidence in all the Plas Idwal domain of her almost defunct passion for flower cultivation. One pure white rose, an early herald of summer plenty, had begun to unfold that mild day; she had noticed it when she came out. Raindrops from a morning shower sprinkled on to her wrist as she plucked this sprightly first bloom, and she smiled as she inhaled the secret odour within. Holding the flower aloft like a trophy, she proceeded to the kitchen entrance with the same composed gait. There was all the time in the world.

Dusk had come into the spacious kitchen. But there was sufficient light for her activities from the curtainless bay window overlooking the yard and the flower border in which, long ago, Mia's much loved predecessor had been buried. Candles were not lit until it was strictly necessary. She fumbled among a jumble of oddments in one of the two gloomy little pantries lying off the kitchen, and came out with a cone-shaped silver vase.

Light pattering sounds came from beyond an open inner door, where an uncarpeted back staircase lay, and five cats came bounding down from the first-floor drawing room. Each a ginger tabby of almost identical aspect, they whisked, mewing, around their mistress, tails up.

'Yes, yes, my darlings,' she said. 'Your saucers in a moment.' She crossed to a sink of blackened stone, humming to herself.

A monster Edwardian cooking range stood derelict in a chimneyed alcove, with three portable oil stoves before it holding a covered frying pan, an iron stewpan, and a tin kettle. Stately dinner crockery and a variety of canisters and tinned foodstuff packed the shelves of a huge dresser built into the back wall. A long table stretching down the centre of the kitchen was even more crowded. It held half a dozen bulging paper satchels, biscuit tins, piles of unwashed plates and saucers, two stacks of *The Geographical Magazine*, the skull of a sheep, heaped vegetable peelings, an old wooden coffee grinder, a leatherette hatbox, a Tunisian birdcage used for storing meat, several rib-boned chocolate boxes crammed with letters, and a traveller's escritoire of rosewood. On the end near the oil stoves, under a three-branched candelabra of heavy Sheffield plate encrusted with carved vine leaves and grapes, a reasonably fresh cloth of fine lace was laid with silver cutlery, a condiment set of polished silver, a crystal wine goblet, and a neatly folded linen napkin. A boudoir chair of gilded wood stood before this end of the table.

When the cold-water tap was turned on at the sink, a rattle sounded afar in the house and ended in a groaning cough—a companionable sound, which Mrs. Vines much liked. She continued to hum as she placed the rose in the vase, set it below the handsome candelabra, and stepped back to admire the effect. Pulling out a pair of long, jet-headed pins, she took off her opulent velvet hat.

'He's a stupid lout, isn't he, Queenie?' The eldest cat, her favourite, had leaped on the table. 'Thinking he was going to bed that chit down here and breed like rabbits!'

She gave the cats their separate saucers of liver, chopped from cold slices taken from the frying pan. Queenie was served first. The bulldog waited for her dish of beef chunks from the stewpan, and, given them, stood morosely for a minute, as if counting the pieces. Finally, Audrey Vines took for herself a remaining portion of liver and a slice of bread from a loaf on the dresser, and fetched a half bottle of champagne from a capacious oak chest placed between the two pantries. She removed her fur coat before she settled on the frail boudoir chair and shook out her napkin.

Several of these meagre snacks were taken every day, the last just after the 11:15 night express rocked away to the port in the west. Now, her excellent teeth masticating with barely perceptible movements, she ate with fastidious care. The bluish light filtering through the grimy bay window soon thickened, but still she did not light the three candles. Her snack finished, and the last drop of champagne taken with a sweet biscuit, she continued to sit at the table, her oil-stained tea gown of beige chiffon ethereal in the dimness.

She became an unmoving shadow. A disciplined meditation or a religious exercise might have been engaging her. Mia, also an immobile smudge, lay fast asleep on a strip of coconut matting beside the gilt chair. The five cats, tails down, had returned upstairs immediately after their meal, going one after the other as though in strict etiquette, or like a file of replete orphans. Each had a mahogany cradle in the drawing room, constructed to their mistress's specifications by an aged craftsman who had once been employed at Plas Idwal.

She stirred for a minute from the reverie, but her murmuring scarcely disturbed the silence. Turning her head in mechanical habit to where Mia lay, she asked, 'Was it last January the river froze for a fortnight? . . . No, not last winter. But there were gales, weren't there? Floods of rain . . . Which winter did I burn the chairs to keep us warm? That idiotic oilman didn't come. Then the candles and matches gave out, and I used the electricity. One of Queenie's daughters died that winter. It was the year he went to work in a factory.'

Time had long ago ceased to have calendar meaning in her life; a dozen years were as one. But lately she had begun to be obsessed by dread of another severe winter. Winters seemed to have become colder and longer. She dreaded the deeper hibernation they enforced. Springs were intolerably long in coming, postponing the time when her child of nature became constantly visible again, busy under his flowering trees and splashing in the river. His reliable appearances brought back flickers of interest in the world; in comparison, intruders on the estate, the arrival of tradesmen, or the visits of her solicitor were becoming of little consequence.

She lapsed back into silence. The kitchen was almost invisible when, swiftly alert, she turned her head towards the indigo blue of the bay window. A throbbing sound had come from far away. It mounted to a series of kicking spurts, roared, and became a loudly tearing rhythm. She rose from her chair and fumbled for a box of matches on the table. But the rhythmic sound began to dwindle, and her hand remained over the box. The sound floated away.

She sank back on the chair. 'Not now, darling!' she told the drowsily shifting dog. 'Later, later.'

The headlamp beam flashed past the high entrance gates to Plas Idwal, but Rufus did not even glance at them. They were wide open, and, he knew, would remain open all night. He had long ceased to wonder about this. Some people said Mrs. Vines wanted to trap strangers inside, so that she could enjoy frightening them when they were nabbed, but other townsfolk thought that the gates had been kept open for years because she was always expecting her second husband to come back.

At top speed, his bike could reach the town in less than ten minutes. The fir-darkened road was deserted. No cottage or house bordered it for five miles. A roadside farmstead had become derelict, but in a long vale quietly ascending towards the mountain range some families still continued with reduced sheep farming. Rufus knew them all. His father had worked at one of the farms before the decline in agricultural prosperity set in. From the outskirts of the hilly town he could see an illuminated clock in the Assembly Hall tower. It was half-past nine. He did not slow down. Avoiding the town centre, he tore past the pens of a disused cattle market, a recently built confectionery factory, a nineteenth-century Nonconformist chapel, which had become a furniture depository, then past a row of cottages remaining from days when the town profited from rich milk and tough flannel woven at river-side mills. Farther round the town's lower folds, he turned into an area of diminutive back-to-back dwellings, their fronts ranging direct along narrow pavements.

Nobody was visible in these gaslit streets. He stopped at one of the terraces, walked to a door, and, without knocking, turned its brass knob. The door opened into a living room, though a sort of entrance lobby was formed by a chenille curtain and an upturned painted drainpipe used for umbrellas. Voices came from beyond the curtain. But only Gloria's twelve-year-old brother sat in the darkened room, watching television from a plump easy chair. His spectacles flashed up at the interrupting visitor.

'Gone to the pictures with Mum.' The boy's attention returned impatiently to the dramatic serial. 'Won't be back long till after ten.'

Rufus sat down behind the boy and gazed unseeingly at the screen. A feeling of relief came to him. He knew now that he didn't want to show the letter to Gloria tonight, or tell her anything about the lease of Brychan Cottage. Besides, she mustn't read those nasty insults about her in the letter. He asked himself why he had come there, so hastily. Why hadn't he gone to Plas Idwal? Mrs. Vines might give way. Then he needn't mention anything at all to Gloria. If he told her about the letter tonight, it would make him look a shifty cheat. She would ask why he hadn't told her about the lease before.

He began to sweat. The close-packed little room was warm and airless. Gloria's two married sisters lived in poky terrace houses just like this one, and he became certain that it was the sight of Brychan Cottage and its garden last Sunday that convinced her to marry him. Before

Sunday, she had always been a bit offhand, pouting if he said too much about the future. Although she could giggle and squeal a lot, she could wrinkle up her nose, too, and flounce away if any chap tried any fancy stuff on her in the factory recreation room. He saw her little feet skipping and running fast as a deer's.

The torment was coming back. This room, instead of bringing Gloria closer to him, made her seem farther off. He kept seeing her on the run. She was screeching as she ran. That loud screech of hers! He had never really liked it. It made his blood go cold, though a chap in the factory said that screeches like that were only a sign that a girl was a virgin and that they disappeared afterwards. Why was he hearing them now? Then he remembered that one of Mrs. Vines's insults was about the screeching.

His fingers trembled when he lit a cigarette. He sat a little while longer telling himself he ought to have gone begging to Plas Idwal and promised to do anything if he could keep the cottage. He would work on the estate evenings and weekends for no money; a lot of jobs needed doing there. He'd offer to pay a good rent for the cottage, too. But what he ought to get before going there, he thought further, was advice from someone who had known Mrs. Vines well. He peered at his watch and got up.

'Tell Gloria I thought she'd like to go for a ride on the bike. I won't come back tonight.'

'You'll be seeing her in the factory tomorrow,' the boy pointed out.

It was only a minute up to the town centre. After parking the bike behind the Assembly Hall, Rufus crossed the quiet market square to a timbered old inn at the corner of Einion's Dip. He had remembered that Evan Matthews often went in there on his way to his night job at the reservoir. Sometimes they'd had a quick drink together.

Thursdays were quiet nights in pubs; so far, there were only five customers in the cosily rambling main bar. Instead of his usual beer, he ordered a double whisky, and asked Gwyneth, the elderly barmaid, if Evan Matthews had been in. She said that if he came in at all it would be about that time. Rufus took his glass over to a table beside the fireless inglenook. He didn't know the two fellows playing darts. An English-looking commercial traveller in a bowler sat at a table scribbling in a notebook. Councillor Llew Pryce stood talking in Welsh to Gwyneth at the counter, and, sitting at a table across the bar from himself, the woman called Joanie was reading the local newspaper.

263

Staring at his unwatered whisky, he tried to decide whether to go to Evan's home in Mostyn Street. No, he'd wait a while here. He wanted more time to think. How could Evan help, after all? A couple of drinks—that's what he needed now. Empty glass in hand, he looked up. Joanie was laying her newspaper down. A blue flower decorated her white felt hat, and there was a bright cherry in her small wineglass.

He watched, in a fascination like relief, as she bit the cherry from its stick, and chewed with easy enjoyment. She'd be about thirty-five, he judged. She was a Saturday-night regular, but he had seen her in the Drovers on other nights, and she didn't lack company as a rule. He knew of her only from tales and jokes by chaps in the factory. Someone had said she'd come from Bristol, with a man supposed to be her husband, who had disappeared when they'd both worked in the slab-cake factory for a few months.

Joanie looked at him, and picked up her paper. He wondered if she was waiting for someone. If Evan didn't come in, could he talk to her about his trouble, ask her the best way to handle a bad-tempered old money-bags? She looked experienced and good-hearted, a woman with no lumps in her nature. He could show her the letter; being a newcomer to the town, she wouldn't know who Mrs. Vines was.

He rose to get another double whisky but couldn't make up his mind to stop at Joanie's table or venture a passing nod. He stayed at the counter finishing his second double, and he was still there when Evan came in. He bought Evan a pint of bitter, a single whisky for himself, and, Joanie forgotten, led Evan to the inglenook table.

'Had a knockout when I got home this evening.' He took the black-edged envelope from a pocket of his wind-cheater.

Evan Matthews read the letter. A sinewy and well-preserved man, he looked about fifty and was approaching sixty; when Mrs. Vines had hired him as an estate keeper and herdsman, he had been under forty. He grinned as he handed the letter back, saying, 'She's got you properly skewered, boyo! I warned your dad she'd do it when the lease was up.'

'What's the reason for it? Brychan Cottage isn't unfit for living in, like she says—there's only a bit of dry rot in the floor boards. I've never done her any harm.'

'No harm, except that you're a man now.'

Uncomprehending, Rufus scowled: 'She used to like me. Gave me presents. Is it more money she's after?'

264

'She isn't after money. Audrey P. Vines was open-fisted with cash—
I'll say that for her. No, she just hates the lot of us.'

'Men, you mean?'

'The whole bunch of us get her dander up.' Recollection lit Evan's
eyes. 'She gave me cracks across the head with a riding crop that she
always carried in those days. I'd been working hard at Plas Idwal for
five years when I got my lot from her.'

'Cracks across the head?' Rufus said, sidetracked.

'She drew blood. I told your dad about it. He said I ought to
prosecute her for assault. But when she did it I felt sorry for her, and
she knew it. It made her boil the more.'

'What you'd done?'

'We were in the cowshed. She used to keep a fine herd of Jerseys,
and she blamed the death of a calving one on me—began raging that I
was clumsy pulling the calf out, which I'd been obliged to do.' Evan
shook his head. 'It wasn't *that* got her flaring. But she took advantage
of it and gave me three or four lashes with the crop. I just stood
looking at her. I could see she wanted me to hit back and have a
proper set-to. Of course, I was much younger then, and so was she!
But I only said, "You and I must part, Mrs. Vines.' She lifted that top
lid of hers, like a vixen done out of a fowl—I can see her now—and
went from the shed without a word. I packed up that day. Same as her
second husband had walked out on her a couple of years before—the
one that played a violin.'

'You mean . . .' Rufus blurted, after a pause of astonishment. 'You
mean, you'd *been* with her?'

Evan chuckled. 'Now, I didn't say that!'

'What's the *matter* with the woman?' Rufus exclaimed. The mystery
of Mrs. Vines's attack on himself was no clearer.

'There's women that turn themselves into royalty,' Evan said. 'They
get it into their heads they rule the world. People who knew little
Audrey's father used to say he spoiled her up to the hilt because her
mother died young. He only had one child. They travelled a lot
together when she was a girl, going into savage parts, and afterwards
she always had a taste for places where there's no baptized Christians. I
heard that her first husband committed suicide in Nigeria, but nobody
knows for certain what happened.' He took up Rufus's empty whisky
glass, and pushed back his chair. 'If he did something without her
permission, he'd be for the crocodiles.'

'I've had two doubles and a single and I haven't had supper yet,'

265

Rufus protested. But Evan fetched him a single whisky. When it was placed before him, Rufus stubbornly asked, 'What's the best thing for me to do?'

'Go and see her.' Evan's face had the tenderly amused relish of one who knows that the young male must get a portion of trouble at the hands of women. 'That's what she wants. I know our Audrey.' He glanced again at this slow-thinking son of an old friend. 'Go tonight,' he urged.

'It's late to go tonight,' Rufus mumbled. Sunk in rumination, he added, 'She stays up late. I've seen a light in her kitchen window when I drive back over the rise after I've been out with Gloria.' He swallowed the whisky at a gulp.

'If you want to keep Brychan Cottage, boyo, *act*. Night's better than daytime for seeing her. She'll have had a glass or two. Bottles still go there regularly from Jack Drapple's.'

'You mean, soft-soap her?' Rufus asked with a grimace.

'No, not soft-soap. But give her what she wants.' Evan thought for a moment, and added, a little more clearly, 'When she starts laying into you—and she will, judging by that letter—you have a go at *her*. I wouldn't be surprised she'll respect you for it. Her and me in the cowshed was a different matter—I wasn't after anything from her. Get some clouts in on her, if you can.'

Rufus shook his head slowly. 'She said in the letter it was final,' he said.

'Nothing is final with women, boyo. Especially what they put down in writing. They send letters like that to get a man springing up off his tail. They can't bear us to sit down quietly for long.' Evan finished his beer. It was time to leave for his watchman's job at the new reservoir up at Mynydd Baer, the towering mountain from which showers thrashed down.

'Brychan Cottage belongs to me! Not to that damned old witch!' Rufus had banged the table with his fist. The dart players turned to look. Joanie lowered her paper; the commercial traveller glanced up from his notebook, took off his bowler, and laid it on the table. Gwyneth coughed and thumped a large Toby jug down warningly on the bar counter.

Evan said, 'Try shouting at *her* like that—she won't mind language—but pipe down here. And don't take any more whisky.'

'I'll tell her I won't budge from Brychan Cottage!' Rufus announced. 'Her father cheated my grandfather over the railway—made a lot of money. She won't try to force me out. She'd be disgraced in the town.'

'Audrey Vines won't care a farthing about disgrace or gossip.' Evan buttoned up his black mackintosh. 'I heard she used to give her second husband shocking dressings-down in front of servants and the visitors that used to go to Plas Idwal in those days. Mr. Oswald, he was called. A touch of African tarbrush in him, and had tried playing the violin for a living.' A tone of sly pleasure was in his voice. 'Younger than Audrey Vines. One afternoon in Plas Idwal, she caught him with a skivvy in the girl's bedroom top of the house, and she locked them in there for twenty-four hours. She turned the electricity off at the main, and there the two stayed without food or water all that time.' Evan took from his pocket a tasselled monkey cap of white wool, kept for his journey by motor bike into the mountains. 'If you go to see her tonight, give her my love. Come to Mostyn Street tomorrow to tell me how you got on.'

'What happened when the two were let out of the bedroom?'

'The skivvy was sent flying at once, of course. Mari, the housekeeper, told me that in a day or two Mrs. Vines was playing her piano to Mr. Oswald's fiddle as usual. Long duets they used to play most evenings, and visitors had to sit and listen. But it wasn't many weeks before Mr. Oswald bunked off, in the dead of night. The tale some tell that he is still shut away somewhere in Plas Idwal is bull.' He winked at Rufus.

'I've heard she keeps the gates open all the time to welcome him back,' Rufus persisted, delaying Evan still longer. It was as though he dreaded to be left alone.

'After all these years? Some people like to believe women get love on the brain. But it's true they can go sour when a man they're set on does a skedaddle from them. And when they get like that, they can go round the bend without much pushing.' He rose from the table. 'But I'll say this for our Audrey. After Mr. Oswald skedaddled, she shut herself up in Plas Idwal and wasn't too much of a nuisance to people outside. Far as I know, I was the only man who had his claret tapped with that riding crop!' He drained a last swallow from his glass. 'Mind, I wouldn't deny she'd like Mr. Oswald to come back, even after all these years! She'd have ways and means of finishing him off.' He patted Rufus's shoulder. 'In the long run it might be best if you lost Brychan Cottage.'

Rufus's jaw set in sudden obstinate sullenness. 'I've told Gloria we're going to live there for ever. I'm going to Plas Idwal tonight.'

When he got up, a minute after Evan had left, it was with a clumsy spring; the table and glasses lurched. But his progress to the bar counter was undeviating. He drank another single whisky, bought a half bottle, which he put inside his elastic-waisted windcheater, and strode from the bar with a newly found hauteur.

She came out of her bedroom above the kitchen rather later than her usual time for going down to prepare her last meal of the day. Carrying a candleholder of Venetian glass shaped like a water lily, she did not descend by the adjacent back staircase tonight but went along a corridor and turned into another, off which lay the front drawing room. Each of the doors she passed, like every other inside the house, was wide open; a bronze statuette of a mounted hussar kept her bedroom door secure against slamming on windy nights.

She had dressed and renewed her make-up by the light of the candle, which was now a dripping stub concealed in the pretty holder. Her wide-skirted evening gown of mauve taffeta had not entirely lost a crip rustle, and on the mottled flesh of her bosom a ruby pendant shone vivaciously. Rouge, lip salve, and mascara had been applied with a prodigal hand, like the expensive scent that left whiffs in her wake. She arrayed herself in this way now and again—sometimes if she planned to sit far into the night composing letters and always for her solicitor's arrival on the evening of quarter day, when she would give him soup and tinned crab in the kitchen.

She never failed to look into the first-floor drawing-room at about eleven o'clock, to bid a good night to the cats. The bulldog, aware of the custom, had preceded her mistress on this occasion and stood looking in turn at the occupants of five short-legged cradles ranged in a half circle before a gaunt and empty fireplace of grey stone. Pampered Queenie lay fast asleep on her eiderdown cushion; the other tabbies had heard their mistress approaching and sat up, stretching and giving themselves a contented lick. Blue starlight came from four tall windows, whose satin curtains were drawn back tightly into dirt-stiff folds, rigid as marble. In that quiet illumination of candle and starlight, the richly dressed woman moving from cradle to cradle, stroking and cooing a word or two, had a look of feudally assured serenity. Mia watched in pedigreed detachment; even her squashed face achieved a debonair comeliness.

'Queenie, Queenie, won't you say good night to me? Bowen's are sending fish tomorrow! Friday fish! Soles, darling! *Fish fish!*'

Queenie refused to stir from her fat sleep. Presently, her ceremony performed, Audrey Vines descended by the front staircase, candle in hand, Mia stepping with equal care behind her. At the rear of the panelled hall, she passed through an archway, above which hung a Bantu initiatory mask, its orange and purple stripes dimmed under grime. A baize door in the passage beyond was kept open with an earthenware jar full of potatoes and onions. In the kitchen, she lit the three-branched candelabra from her pink-and-white holder, and blew out the stub.

This was always the hour she liked best. The last snack would be prepared with even more leisure than the earlier four or five. Tonight, she opened a tin of sardines, sliced a tomato and a hard-boiled egg, and brought from one of the dank little pantries a jar of olives, a bottle of mayonnaise, and a foil-wrapped triangle of processed cheese. While she buttered slices of bread, the distant rocking of the last train could be heard, its fading rhythm leaving behind all the unruffled calm of a windless night. She arranged half a dozen sponge fingers clockwise on a Chelsea plate, then took a half bottle of champagne from the chest, hesitated, and exchanged it for a full-sized one.

Mia had occupied herself with a prolonged examination and sniffing and scratching of her varicoloured strip of matting; she might have been viewing it for the first time. Noticing that her mistress was seated, she reclined her obdurate bulk on the strip. Presently, she would be given her usual two sponge fingers dipped in champagne. She took no notice when a throbbing sound came from outside, or when it grew louder.

'Our visitor, sweetheart. I told you he'd come.'

Audrey Vines, postponing the treat of her favourite brand of sardines until later, dabbed mayonnaise on a slice of egg, ate, and wiped her lips. 'Don't bark!' she commanded. 'There's noise enough as it is.' Becoming languidly alert to the accumulating roar, Mia had got onto her bandy legs. A light flashed across the bay window. The roar ceased abruptly. Audrey Vines took a slice of bread as footsteps approached outside, and Mia, her shred of a tail faintly active, trundled to the door. A bell hanging inside had tinkled.

'Open, open!' Mrs. Vines's shout from the table was throaty, and even. 'Open and come in!'

Rufus paused stiffly on the threshold, his face in profile, his eyes glancing obliquely at the candlelit woman, sitting at the table's far end. 'I saw your lighted window,' he said. The dog returned to the matting after a sniff of his shoes and a brief upward look of approval.

'Thank God I shall not be hearing the noise of that cursed motor cycle on my land much longer. Shut the door, young man, and sit over there.'

He shut the door and crossed to the seat Mrs. Vines had indicated, the same rough bench placed against a wall between the dresser and the inner door on which he used to sit during happier visits long ago. He sat down and forced himself to gaze slowly down the big kitchen, his eyes ranging over the long, crowded table to the woman in her evening gown, to the single, red jewel on her bare chest, and, at last, to her painted face.

Audrey Vines went on with her meal. The silence continued. A visitor might not have been present. Rufus watched her leisurely selection of a slice of tomato and an olive, the careful unwrapping of foil from cheese. Her two diamond rings sparkled in the candlelight. He had never seen her eating, and this evidence of a normal habit both mesmerized and eased him.

'I've come about the letter.'

The words out, he sat up, taut in justification of complaint. But Mrs. Vines seemed not to have heard. She sprinkled pepper and salt on the cheese, cut it into small pieces, and looked consideringly at the untouched sardines in their tin, while the disregarded visitor relapsed into silent watching. Three or four minutes passed before she spoke.

'Are you aware that I could institute a police charge against you for bathing completely naked in the river on my estate?'

It stirred him anew to a bolt-upright posture. 'There's nobody to see.'

She turned a speculative, heavy-lidded eye in his direction. 'Then how do I know about it? Do you consider me nobody?' Yet there was no trace of malevolence as she continued. 'You are almost as hairy as an ape. Perhaps you consider that is sufficient covering?' Sedate as a judge in court, she added, 'But your organs are exceptionally pronounced.'

'Other people don't go about with spying glasses.' Anger gave his words a stinging ring.

Turning to the dog, she remarked, 'An impudent defence from the hairy bather!' Mia, waiting patiently for the sponge fingers, blinked, and Audrey Vines, reaching for the tin of sardines, said, 'People in the trains can see.'

'I know the times of the trains.'

'You have bathed like that all the summer. You walk to the river from Brychan Cottage unclothed. You did not do this when your parents were alive.'

270

'You never sent me a letter about it.'

'I delivered a letter at Brychan Cottage today. *That* covers everything.'

There was another silence. Needing time to reassemble his thoughts, he watched as she carefully manipulated a sardine out of the tin with her pointed fingernails. The fish did not break. She held it aloft by its tail end to let oil drip into the tin, and regally tilted her head back and slowly lowered it whole into her mouth. The coral-red lips softly clamped about the disappearing body, drawing it in with appreciation. She chewed with fastidiously dawdling movements. Lifting another fish, she repeated the performance, her face wholly absorbed in her pleasure.

She was selecting a third sardine before Rufus spoke. 'I want to go on living in Brychan Cottage,' he said, slurring the words. The sardine had disappeared when he continued. 'My family always lived in Brychan Cottage. It belonged to us hundred of years before your family came to Plas Idwal.'

'You've been drinking,' Audrey Vines said, looking ruminatively over the half-empty plates before her. She did not sound disapproving, but almost amiable. Rufus made no reply. After she had eaten a whole slice of bread, ridding her mouth of sardine taste, she reached for the bottle of champagne. A long time was spent untwisting wire from the cork. Her manipulating hands were gentle in the soft yellow candle-light, and in the quiet of deep country night filling the room she seemed just then an ordinary woman sitting in peace over an ordinary meal, a flower from her garden on the table, a faithful dog lying near her chair.

Making a further effort, he repeated, 'My family always lived in Brychan Cottage.'

'Your disagreeable mother,' Audrey Vines responded, 'allowed a man to take a photograph of Brychan Cottage. I had sent the creature packing when he called here. The photograph appeared in a ridiculous guidebook. Your mother knew I would *not* approve of attracting such flashy attention to my estate. My solicitor showed me the book.'

Unable to deal with this accusation, he fell into headlong pleading. 'I've taken care of the cottage. It's not dirty. I could put new floor boards in downstairs and change the front door. I can cook and do cleaning. The garden is tidy. I'm planning to border the paths with more fruit trees, and—'

'Why did your parents name you Rufus?' she interrupted. 'You are dark as night, though your complexion is pale . . . and pitted like the

271

moon's surface.' The wire was off the cork. 'I wonder were you born hairy-bodied?'

He subsided, baffled. As she eased the cork out, there was the same disregard of him. He jerked when the cork shot in his direction. She seemed to smile as the foam spurted, and settled delicately in her crystal glass. She took a sip, and another, and spoke to the saliva-dropping dog.

'Your bikkies in a second. Aren't you a nice quiet little Mia! A pity *he* isn't as quiet, darling.'

'Got a bottle of whisky with me. Can I take a swig?' The request came in a sudden desperate burst.

'You may.'

She watched in turn while he brought the flat, half-sized bottle from inside his windcheater, unscrewed its stopper, and tilted the neck into his mouth. She took further sips of her wine. Absorbed in his own need, Rufus paused for only a moment before returning the neck to his mouth. About half the whisky had been taken when, holding the bottle at the ready between his knees, his eyes met hers across the room's length. She looked away, her lids stiffening. But confidence increased in Rufus.

He repeated, 'I want to live in Brychan Cottage all my life.'

'You wish to live in Brychan Cottage. I wish to raze it to the ground.' A second glass of wine was poured. 'So there we are, young man!' She wetted a sponge finger in her wine and handed it to Mia.

'My mother said the cottage and land belonged to us for ever at one time. Your father cheated us out of . . .' He stopped, realizing his foolishness, and scowled.

'Mia, darling, how you love your drop of champagne!' She dipped another sponge finger; in her obliviousness, she might have been courteously overlooking his slip. 'Not good for your rheumatism, though! Oh, you dribbler!'

He took another swig of whisky—a smaller one. He was sitting in Plas Idwal and must not forget himself so far as to get drunk. Settling back against the wall, he stared in wonder at objects on the long table and ventured to ask, 'What . . . what have you got that skull for? It's a sheep's, isn't it?'

'That? I keep it because it shows pure breeding in its lines and therefore is beautiful. Such sheep are not degenerate, as are so many of their so-called masters. No compulsory education, state welfare services, and social coddling for a sheep!' Rufus's face displayed the blank respect of a modest person hearing academic information beyond his comprehension, and she appended, 'The ewe that lived inside that skull was eaten alive by blowfly maggots. I found her under a hedge below Mynydd Baer.' She finished her second glass, and poured a third.

As though in sociable alliance, he allowed himself another mouthful of whisky. Awareness of his gaffe about her cheating father kept him from returning to the subject of the cottage at once. He was prepared to remain on the bench for hours; she seemed not to mind his visit. His eyes did not stray from her any more; every trivial move she made held his attention now. She reached for a fancy biscuit tin and closely studied the white roses painted on its shiny blue side. He waited. The silence became acceptable. It belonged to the late hour and this house and the mystery of Mrs. Vines's ways.

Audrey Vines laid the biscuit tin down unopened, and slowly rang a finger along the lace tablecloth, like a woman preoccupied with arriving at a resolve. 'If you are dissatisfied with the leasehold deeds of Brychan Cotage,' she began, 'I advise you to consult a solicitor. Daniel Lewis welcomes such small business, I believe. You will find his office behind the Assembly Hall. You have been remarkably lackadaisical in this matter . . . No, *not* remarkably, since he is as he is! He should live in a tree.' She had turned to Mia.

'I don't want to go to a solicitor.' After a pause, he mumbled, half sulkily, 'Can't . . . can't we settle it between us?'

She looked up. Their eyes met again. The bright ruby on her chest flashed as she purposely moved a dish on the table. But the roused expectancy in Rufus's glistening eyes did not fade. After a moment, he tilted the bottle high into his mouth, and withdrew it with a look of extreme surprise. It was empty.

Audrey Vines drank more wine. Then rapping the words out, she demanded, 'How much rent are you prepared to pay me for the cottage?'

Rufus gaped in wonder. Had Evan Matthews been right, then, in saying that nothing was final with women? He put the whisky bottle down on the bench and offered the first sum in his mind. 'A pound a week?'

Audrey Vines laughed. It was a hoarse sound, cramped and discordant in her throat. She straightened a leaning candle and spoke with the incisiveness of a nimble businesswoman addressing a foolish client. 'Evidently you know nothing of property values, young man. My estate is one of the most attractive in this part of Wales. A Londoner needing weekend seclusion would pay ten pounds a week for my cottage, with fishing rights.'

It had become 'my cottage'. Rufus pushed a hand into his sweat-damped black hair, and mumbled, 'Best to have a man you know near by you on the estate.'

'For a pound! I fail to see the advantage I reap.'

'Thirty shillings, then? I'm only drawing a clear nine pounds a week in Nelson's factory.' Without guile, he sped on, 'Haven't got enough training yet to be put on the machines, you see! They've kept me in the packing room with the learners.'

'That I can well believe. Nevertheless, you can afford to buy a motor cycle and flasks of whisky.' She clattered a plate onto another. 'My cottage would be rent-free to the right man. Would you like a couple of sardines with your whisky?'

The abrupt invitation quenched him once more. He lowered his head, scowling, his thighs wide apart. His hands gripped his knees. There was a silence. When he looked up, she was straining her pencilled eyes towards him, as though their sight had become blurred. But now he could not look at her in return. His gaze focussed on the three candle flames to the left of her head.

'Well, sardines or not?'

'No,' he answered, almost inaudibly.

'Grind me some coffee, then,' she rapped, pointing to the handle-topped wooden box on the table. 'There are beans in it. Put a little water in the kettle on one of those oil stoves. Matches are here. Coffeepot on the dresser.' She dabbed her lips with her napkin, looked at the stain they left, and refilled her glass.

He could no longer respond in any way to these changes of mood. He neither moved nor spoke. Reality had faded, the kitchen itself became less factual, objects on the table insubstantially remote. Only the woman's face drew and held his eyes. But Audrey Vines seemed not to notice this semi-paralysis; she was allowing a slow-thinking man time to obey her command. She spoke a few words to Mia. She leaned forward to reach for a lacquered box, and took from it a pink cigarette. As she rose to light the gold-tipped cigarette at a candle, he said. 'Brychan Cottage always belonged to my family.'

'He keeps saying that!' she said to Mia, sighing and sitting back. Reflective while she smoked, she had an air of waiting for coffee to be served, a woman retreated into the securities of the distant past, when everybody ran to her bidding.

'What to you want, then?' His voice came from deep in his chest, the words flat and earnest in his need to know.

The mistress of Plas Idwal did not reply for a minute. Her gaze was fixed on the closely woven flower in its silver vase. And a strange transformation came to her lulled face. The lineaments of a girl eased its contours, bringing a smooth texture to the skin, clothing the stark bones with a pastel-like delicacy of fine young flesh. An apparition, perhaps an inhabitant of her reverie, was fugitively in possession.

'I want peace and quiet,' she whispered.

His head had come forward. He saw the extraordinary transformation. Like the dissolving reality of the room, it had the nature of an hallucination. His brows puckering in his effort to concentrate, to find exactness, he slowly sat back, and asked, 'You want me to stay single? Then I can keep Brychan Cottage?'

In a sudden, total extinction of control, her face became contorted into an angry shape of wrinkled flesh. Her eyes blazed almost sightlessly. She threw the cigarette on the floor and screamed, 'Did you think I was going to allow that slut to live there? Braying and squealing on my estate like a prostitute!' Her loud breathing was that of someone about to vomit.

With the same flat simplicity, he said, 'Gloria is not a prostitute.'

'Gloria! Good God, *Gloria*! How far in idiocy can they go? Why not Cleopatra? I don't care a hair of your stupid head what happens to you and that wretched creature. You are *not* going to get the cottage. I'll burn it to the ground rather than have you and that born prostitute in it!' Her hands began to grasp at plates and cutlery on the table, in a blind semblance of the act of clearing them. 'Stupid lout, coming here! By the autumn there won't be a stone of that cottage left. Not a stone, you hear!'

Her demented goading held such pure hatred that it seemed devoid of connection with him. She had arrived at the fringe of sane consciousness; her gaze fixed on nothing, she was aware only of a dim figure hovering down the room, beyond the throw of candlelight. 'The thirtieth of June, you hear? Or the police will be called to turn you out!'

He had paused for a second at the far end of the table, near the door. His head was averted. Four or five paces away from him lay release into the night. But he proceeded in her direction, advancing as though in deferential shyness, his head still half turned away, a hand sliding along the table. He paused again, took up the coffee grinder, looked at it vaguely, and lowered it to the table. It crashed on the stone floor.

She became aware of the accosting figure. The screaming did not diminish. 'Pick that thing up! You've broken it, clumsy fool. Pick it up!'

He looked round uncertainly, not at her but at the uncurtained bay window giving onto the spaces of night. He did not stoop for the grinder.

'*Pick it up!*' The mounting howl swept away the last hesitation in him. He went towards her unwaveringly.

She sat without a movement until he was close to her. He stopped, and looked down at her. Something like a compelled obedience was in the crouch of his shoulders. Her right hand moved, grasping the tablecloth fringe into a tight fistful. She made no attempt to speak, but an articulation came into the exposed face that was lifted to him. From the glaze of her eyes, from deep in unfathomable misery, came entreaty. He was the chosen one. He alone held the power of deliverance. He saw it, and in that instant of mutual recognition his hand grasped the heavy candelabra and lifted it high. Its three flames blew out in the swiftness of the plunge. There was a din of objects crashing to the floor from the tugged tablecloth. When he rose from beside the fallen chair and put the candelabra down, the whimpering dog followed him in the darkness to the door, as though pleading with this welcome visitor not to go.

He left the motor bike outside the back garden gate of Brychan Cottage, walked along a wicker fence, and, near the river, jumped across the ditch on to Plas Idwal land. Presently, he reached a spot where, long before he was born, the river had been widened and deepened to form an ornamental pool. A rotting summer house, impenetrable under wild creeper, overlooked it, and a pair of stone urns marked a short flight of weed-hidden steps. The soft water, which in daytime was as blue as the distant mountain range where lay its source, flowed through in lingering eddies. He had sometimes bathed in this prohibited pool late at night; below Brychan Cottage the river was much less comfortable for swimming.

He undressed without haste, and jumped into the pool with a quick and acrobatically high leap. He swam underwater, rose, and went under again, in complete ablution. When he stood up beside the opposite bank, where the glimmering water reached to his chest, he relaxed his arms along the grassy verge and remained for moments looking at the enormous expanse of starry sky, away from the mansion dimly outlined above the pool.

He was part of the anonymous liberty of the night. This bathe was the completion of an act of mastery. The river was his; returning to its depths, he was assimilated into it. He flowed downstream a little way and, where the water became shallow, sat up. His left hand spread on pebbles below, he leaned negligently there, like a deity of pools and streams risen in search of possibilities in the night. He sat unmoving for several minutes. The supple water running over his loins began to feel much colder. It seemed to clear his mind of tumult. Slowly, he turned his head towards the mansion.

He saw her face in the last flare of the candles, and now he knew why she had tormented him. She had been waiting long for his arrival. The knowledge lodged, certain and tenacious, in his mind. Beyond his wonder at her choice, it brought, too, some easing of the terror threatening him. Further his mind would not go; he retreated from thinking of the woman lying alone in the darkness of that mansion up there. He knew she was dead. Suddenly, he rose, waded to the bank, and strode to where his clothes lay.

His movements took on the neatness and dispatch of a man acting entirely on a residue of memory. He went into Brychan Cottage only to dry and dress himself in the kitchen. When he got to the town, all lamps had been extinguished in the deserted streets. The bike tore into the private hush of an ancient orderliness. He did not turn into the route he had taken earlier that night but drove at top speed through the market place. Behind the medieval Assembly Hall, down a street of municipal offices and timbered old houses in which legal business was done, a blue lamp shone alight. It jutted clearly from the porch of a stone building, and the solid door below yielded to his push.

Inside, a bald-headed officer sitting at a desk glanced up in mild surprise at this visitor out of the peaceful night, and, since the young man kept silent, asked, 'Well, what can we do for you?'

I WILL KEEP HER COMPANY

When he achieved the feat of getting down the stairs to the icy living room, it was the peculiar silence there that impressed him. It had not been so noticeable upstairs, where all night he had had company, of a kind. Down in this room, the familiar morning sounds he had known for sixty years—all the crockery, pots and pans, and fire-grate noises of married life at break of day, his wife's brisk soprano not least among them—were abolished as though they had never existed.

It was the snow had brought this silence, of course. How many days had it been falling—four or five? He couldn't remember. Still dazed and stiff from his long vigil in a chair upstairs, he hobbled slowly to the window. Sight of the magnificent white spread brought, as always, astonishment. Who would have thought such a vast quantity waited above? Almighty in its power to obliterate the known works of man, especially his carefully mapped highways and byways, the weight of odourless substance was like a reminder that he was of no more account than an ant. But only a few last flakes were falling now, the small aster shapes drifting with dry languor on the hefty waves covering the long front garden.

'They'll be here today,' he said aloud, wakened a little more by the dazzle. The sound of his voice was strange to him, like an echo of it coming back from a chasm. His head turning automatically towards the open door leading to the hallway, he broke the silence again, unwilling to let it settle. 'Been snowing again all night, Maria. But it's stopping now. They'll come today. The roads have been blocked. Hasn't been a fall like it for years.'

His frosting breath plumed the air. He turned back to the window and continued to peer out for a while. A drift swelled to above the sill, and there was no imprint of the robins and tits that regularly landed before the window in the morning, for breakfast crumbs. Neither was there a sign of the garden gate into the lane, nor a glimpse of the village, two miles distant down the valley, which could be seen from this height on green days. But the mountains, ramparts against howling Atlantic gales, were visible in glitteringly bleached outline against a pale-blue sky. Savage guardians of interior Wales, even their lowering black clouds and whipping rains were vanquished today. They looked innocent in their unbroken white.

278

His mind woke still more. The manacled landscape gave him, for the moment, a feeling of security. This snow was a protection, not a catastrophe. He did not want the overdue visitors to arrive, did not want to exercise himself again in resistance to their arguments for his future welfare. Not yet. He thought of his six damson trees, which he had introduced into the orchard a few years before and reared with such care. Last summer, there had been a nice little profit from the baskets of downy fruit. Was he to be forced away from his grown-up darlings now? Just one more season of gathering, and, afterwards, he would be ready to decide about the future . . .

Then, remembering something else, he lamented, 'They'll come, they'll come!' They had such a special reason for making the journey. And this marooning snow would give even more urgency to their arguments regarding himself. He strained his keen old countryman's eyes down the anonymous white distances. Could they come? Could anyone break a way through those miles of deep snow, where nothing shuffled, crawled, or even flew? The whole world had halted. They would not come today. There would be one more day of peace.

Mesmerized at the window, he recalled another supreme time of snow, long ago, before he was married. He and two other farm workers had gone in search of Ambrose Owen's sheep. An old ram was found in a drift, stiff and upright on his legs, glassy eyes staring at nothing, curls of wool turned to a cockleshell hardness that could be chipped from the fleece. Farther away in the drift, nine wise ewes lay huddled against each other, and these were carried upside down by the legs to the farmhouse kitchen, where they thawed into life. But Ambrose, like that man in the Bible with a prodigal son, had broken down and shed tears over his lost ram that had foolishly wandered from the herd. The elderly farmer was in a low condition himself at the time, refusing to be taken to hospital, wanting to kick the bucket not only in his own home but downstairs in his fireside chair. Quite right too.

He returned from the window at last, drew a crimson flannel shawl from his sparsely-haired head, and re-arranged it carefully over his narrow shoulders. He wore two cardigans and trousers of thick home-spun, but the cold penetrated to his bones. Still unwilling to begin the day's ritual of living down in this room, he stood gazing vaguely from the cinder-strewn fireplace to the furniture, his eyes lingering on the beautifully polished rosewood table at which, with seldom a cross word exchanged (so it seemed now), he had shared good breakfasts for a lifetime. Was it because of the unnatural silence, with not the whirr of a single bird outside, that all the familiar contents of the room seemed withdrawn from ownership? They looked stranded.

Remembrance came to him of the room having this same hush of unbelonging when he and Maria had first walked into it, with the idea of buying the place, a freehold stone cottage and its four acres, for ninety-five sovereigns, cash down. They were courting at the time, and the property was cheap because of its isolation; no one had lived there for years. The orchard, still well-stocked, had decided him, and Maria, who could depend on herself and a husband for all the talking she needed, agreed because of the tremendous views of mountain range and sky from this closed end of the valley. What a walker she had been! Never wanted even a bike, did not want to keep livestock, and was content with the one child that came very soon after the rushed purchase of the cottage. But, disregarding gossip, she had liked to go down to church in the village, where she sang psalms louder than any other woman there.

He had huddled closer into the shawl. Since he would not be staying long down here, was it worthwhile lighting a fire? Then he realized that if the visitors found means of coming, it would be prudent to let them see he could cope with the household jobs. First, the grate to be raked, and a fire laid; wood and coal to be fetched from outside. But he couldn't hurry. His scalp was beginning to prickle and contract, and he drew the shawl over his head again. Feeling was already gone from his feet when he reached the shadowy kitchen lying off the living room, fumblingly pulled the back door open, and faced a wall of pure white.

The entire door space was blocked, sealing access to the shed in which, besides wood and coal, oil for the cooking stove was stored. He had forgotten that the wall had been there the day before. Snow had drifted down the mountain slope and piled as far as the back window upstairs even then; it came back to him that he had drawn the kitchen window curtains to hide that weight of tombstone white against the panes. 'Marble,' he said now, curiously running a finger over the crisply hardened surface. He shut the door, relieved that one item in the morning jobs was settled; it would be impossible to reach the shed from the front of the cottage.

Pondering in the dowdy light of the kitchen, he looked at the empty glass oil-feeder of the cooking stove, at the empty kettle, at an earthenware pitcher, which he knew was empty, too. He remembered that the water butt against the outside front wall had been frozen solid for days before the snow began. And even if he had the strength to dig a path to the well in the orchard, very likely that would be frozen. Would snow melt inside the house? But a little water remained in an ewer upstairs. And wasn't there still some of the milk that the district nurse had brought? He found the jug in the slate-shelved larder, and tilted it; the inch-deep, semi-congealed liquid moved. He replaced the jug with a wrinkling nose, and peered at three tins of soup that also had been brought by Nurse Baldock.

Sight of the tins gave him a feeling of nausea. The last time the nurse had come—*which* day was it?—a smell like ammonia had hung about her. And her pink rubber gloves, her apron with its row of safety pins and a tape measure dangling over it, had badly depressed him. A kind woman, though, except for her deciding what was the best way for a man to live. The sort that treated all men as little boys. She had a voice that wouldn't let go of a person, but being a woman, a soft wheedling could come into it when she chose. Thank God the snow had bogged her down.

He reached for a flat box, opened it, and saw a few biscuits. Maria always liked the lid picture of Caernarfon Castle, which they'd visited one summer day; he looked at it now with a reminiscent chuckle. His movements became automatically exact, yet vague and random. He found a tin tray inscribed 'Ringer's Tobacco' and placed on it the box, a plate and, forgetting there was no milk left upstairs, a clean cup and saucer. This done, he suddenly sat down on a hard chair and closed his eyes.

He did not know how long he remained there. Tapping sounds roused him; he jerked from the chair with galvanized strength. Agitation gave his shouts an unreasonable cantankerousness as he reached the living room. 'They've come! Open the door, can't you? It's not locked.'

He opened the front door. There was nobody. The snow reached up to his waist, and the stretch of it down the garden slope bore not a mark. Only an elephant could come to this door. Had he dreamed the arrival? Or had a starving bird tapped its beak on the window? The dread eased. He shut the door with both his shaking hands, and stood listening in the small hallway. 'They haven't come!' he shouted up the stairs, wanting to hear his voice smashing the silence. 'But they will, they will! They are bringing my pension money from the post office. Dr. Howells took my book with him.' Self-reminder of this ordinary matter helped to banish the dread, and the pain in his chest dwindled.

281

Pausing in the living room, he remembered that it was actually Nurse Baldock who had taken his book and put it in that important black bag of hers. She had arrived that day with Dr. Howells in his car, instead of on her bike. The snow had begun to fall, but she said it wouldn't be much—only a sprinkling. And Dr. Howells had told him not to worry and that everything would be put in hand. But even the doctor, who should have had a man's understanding, had argued about the future, and coaxed like Nurse Baldock. Then she had said she'd bring Vicar Pryce on her next visit. People fussing! But he couldn't lock the door against them yet. It was necessary for them to come just once again. He would pretend to listen to them, especially the vicar, and when they had gone he would lock the door, light a fire, and sit down to think of the future in his own way.

His eyes strayed about the room again. He looked at the table with its green-shaded oil lamp, at the dresser with its display of brilliant plates and lustre jugs, at the comfortable low chairs, the bright rugs, the scroll-backed sofa from which Maria had directed his activities for the week before she was obliged to take to her bed at last. After the shock of the fancied arrival, the objects in the room no longer seemed withdrawn from ownership. They would yield him security and ease, for a long while yet. And the cooking stove in the kitchen, the pans, brooms, and brushes—they had belonged solely to Maria's energetic hands, but after a lifetime with her he knew exactly how she dealt with them. Any man with three penn'orth of sense could live here independently as a lord. Resolve lay tucked away in his mind. Today, with this cold stunning his senses, not much could be done. He must wait. His eyes reached the mantelpiece clock; lifting the shawl from his ears, he stared closer at the age-yellowed face. *That* was why the silence had been so strange! Was even a clock affected by the cold? Surely he had wound it last night, as usual; surely he had come downstairs? The old-fashioned clopping sound, steady as horse hoofs ambling on a quiet country road, had never stopped before. The defection bothering him more than the lack of means for a fire and oil for the stove, he reached for the mahogany-framed clock, his numb fingers moving over it to take a firm grip. It fell into the stoneflagged hearth. There was a tinkle of broken glass.

'Ah,' he shouted guiltily, 'the clock's broken, Maria! Slipped out of my hand!'

He gazed at it in a stupor. But the accident finally decided him. Down in this room the last bits of feeling were ebbing from him.

There was warmth and company upstairs. He stumbled into the kitchen, lifted the tin tray in both hands without feeling its substance, and reached the hallway. Negotiation of the stairs took even more time than his descent had. As in the kitchen, it was the propulsion of old habit that got him up the flight he had climbed thousands of times. The tray fell out of his hands when he reached a squeaking stair just below the landing. This did not matter; he even liked the lively explosion of noise. 'It's only that advertisement tray the shop gave you one Christmas!' he called out, not mentioning the crocks and biscuit box which had crashed to the bottom. He did not attempt to retrieve anything. All he wanted was warmth.

In the clear white light of a front room he stood for some moments looking intently at the weather-browned face of the small woman lying on a four-poster bed. Her eyes were compactly shut. Yet her face bore an expression of prim vigour; still she looked alert in her withdrawal. No harsh glitter of light from the window reached her, but he drew a stiff fold of the gay-patterend linen bed curtains that, as if in readiness for this immurement, had been washed, starched, and ironed by her three weeks before. Then he set about his own task. The crimson shawl still bonneted his head.

His hands plucked at the flannel blankets and larger shawls lying scattered on the floor around a wheelbacked armchair close to the bed. Forcing grip into his fingers, he draped these coverings methodically over the sides and back of the chair, sat down, and swathed his legs and body in the overlapping folds. It all took a long time, and for a while it brought back the pain in his chest, compelling him to stop. Finally, he succeeded in drawing portions of two other shawls over his head and shoulders, so that he was completely encased in draperies. There had been good warmth in this cocoon last night. The everlasting flannel was woven in a mill down the valley, from the prized wool of local mountain sheep. Properly washed in rain water, it yielded warmth for a hundred years or more. There were old valley people who had been born and had gone in the same pair of handed-down family blankets.

Secure in the shelter, he waited patiently for warmth to come. When it began to arrive, and the pain went, his mind flickered into activity again. It was of the prancing mountain ponies he thought first, the wild auburn ponies that were so resentful of capture. He had always admired them. But what did their lucky freedom mean now? *They* had no roof over their head, and where could they find victuals?

Had they lost their bearings up in their fastnesses? Were they charging in demented panic through the endless snow, plunging into crevices, starvation robbing them of instinct and sense? Then there were the foxes. He remembered hearing that during that drastic time of snow when he rescued Ambrose Owen's sheep, a maddened fox had dashed into the vicarage kitchen when a servant opened the back door. It snatched in its teeth a valuable Abyssinian cat lying fast asleep on the hearth rug, and streaked out before the petrified woman could scream.

A little more warmth came. He crouched into it with a sigh. Soon it brought a sense of summer pleasures. A long meadow dotted with buttercups and daisies shimmered before him, and a golden-haired boy ran excitedly over the bright grass to a young white goat tied to an iron stake. Part of the meadow was filled with booths of striped canvas, and a roundabout of painted horses galloped to barrel-organ music. It was that Whitsuntide fête when he had won the raffled goat on a sixpenny ticket—the only time he had won anything all his life. Maria had no feeling for goats, especially rams, but she had let their boy lead the snowy-haired beast home. Richard had looked after it all its sturdy years and, at its hiring, got for himself the fees of its natural purpose in life—five shillings a time, in those far-off days.

The father chuckled. He relaxed further in the dark chair. His hands resting lightly on his knees, he prepared for sleep. It was slow in taking him, and when, drowsily, he heard a whirring sound he gave it no particular attention. But he stirred slightly and opened his eyes. The noise approached closer. It began to circle, now faint, then loud, now dwindling. He did not recognize it. It made him think of a swarm of chirping grasshoppers, then of the harsh clonking of roused geese. Neutral towards all disturbance from outside, he nestled deeper into the warmth bred of the last thin heat of his blood, and when a louder noise shattered the peace of his cocoon he still did not move, though his eyes jerked wide open once more.

The helicopter circled twice above the half-buried cottage. Its clacking sounded more urgent as it descended and began to pass as low as the upstairs windows at the front and back. The noise became a rasp of impatience, as if the machine were annoyed that no reply came to this equivalent of a knocking on the door, that no attention was paid to the victory of this arrival. A face peered down from a curved grey pane; the head of another figure dodged behind, moving to both the side panels.

Indecision seemed to govern this hovering above the massed billows of snow. After the cottage had been circled three times, the machine edged nearer the front wall, and a square box wrapped in orange-coloured oilskin tumbled out, fell accurately before the door, and lay visible in a hole of snow. The machine rose; its rotor blades whirled for seconds above the cottage before it mounted higher. It diminished into the pale afternoon light, flying down the valley towards immaculate mountains that had never known a visit from such a strange bird.

Evening brought an unearthly blue to the sculptured distances. Night scarcely thickened the darkness; the whiteness could be seen for miles. Only the flashing of clear-cut stars broke the long stillness of the valley. No more snow fell. But the cold hardened during the low hours, and at dawn, though a red glow lay in the sun's disc on Moelwyn's crest, light came with grudging slowness, and there was no promise of thaw all morning. But, soon after the sun had passed the zenith, another noise smashed into the keep of silence at the valley's closed end.

Grinding and snorting, a vehicle slowly burrowed into the snow. It left in its wake, like a gigantic horned snail, a silvery track, on which crawled a plain grey motor van. Ahead, the climbing plough was not once defeated by its pioneering work, thrusting past shrouded hedges on either side of it, its grunting front mechanism churning up the snow and shooting it out of a curved-over horn on to bushes at the left. The attendant grey van stopped now and then, allowing a measure of distance to accumulate on the smooth track.

The van had three occupants. Two of them, sitting on the driver's cushioned bench, were philosophically patient of this laborious journeying. The third, who was Nurse Baldock, squatted on the floor inside the small van, her legs stretched towards the driver's seat and her shoulders against the back door. She was a substantial woman, and the ungainly fur coat she wore gave her the dimensions of a mature bear. She tried not to be restless. But as the instigator of this rescuing operation, she kept looking at her watch, and she failed to curb herself all the time. The two men in front had not been disposed for talk.

'I hope that thing up there won't break down,' she said presently. 'It's a Canadian snowplough—so I was told on the phone. The Council bought it only last year.'

'It took them a deuce of a time to get one after we had that nasty snowfall in 1947,' remarked the driver, a middle-aged man in a sombre

285

vicuna overcoat and a bowler hat. 'A chap and his young lady were found buried in their car halfway up Moelwyn when we had *that* lot—been there a week, if you remember, Vicar. Thank God these bad falls don't come often.'

'Councils seldom look far outside their town hall chamber after election,' mumbled Vicar Pryce, who had been picked up in Ogwen village twenty minutes earlier. Under his round black hat only his eyes and bleak nose were visible from wrappings of scarves. It was very cold in the utilitarian van, lent for this emergency expedition by a tradesman of the market town at the valley's mouth; the road from there to Ogwen had been cleared the day before.

'Well, our Council has got hold of a helicopter this time, too,' Nurse Baldock reminded them, not approving of criticism of her employers from anyone. 'Soon as I heard they had hired one to drop bundles of hay to stranded cattle and mountain ponies, I said to myself, "Man first, then the beasts," and flew to my phone. I'm fond of old John Evans, though he's so wilful. I arranged to have tins of food, fruit juice, milk, a small bottle of brandy, fresh pork sausages, and bread put in the box, besides a plastic container of cooker oil and a message from me.'

'Couldn't you have gone in the helicopter?' the driver asked, rather inattentively.

'What, and got dropped out into the snow with the box?' The nurse's bulk wobbled with impatience. 'If the machine couldn't land anywhere on those deep slopes of snow, how could I get down, I ask you?'

'I thought they could drop a person on a rope.' The driver sounded propitiatory now. For him, as for most people, the district nurse was less a woman than a portent of inescapable forces lying in wait for everybody.

'Delivery of necessities was the point,' she said dismissingly, and, really for Vicar Pryce's wrapped ears, continued, 'After getting the helicopter man's report yesterday, I was on the phone to the Town Hall for half an hour. I insisted that they let me have the snowplough today—I *fought* for it. It was booked for this and that, they said, but I had my way in the end.'

'Last night was bitter,' Vicar Pryce said, following a silence, ' I got up at 3 a.m. and piled a sheepskin floor rug on my bed.'

'Bitter it *was*,' agreed Nurse Baldock. 'We single people feel it the more.' Neither of the men offered a comment, and, with another look

286

at her watch, she pursued, 'Of course, the helicopter man's report needn't mean a lot. Who could blame Evans if he stayed snuggled in bed all day? And at his age, he could sleep through any noise.'

'One would think a helicopter's clatter would bring him out of any sleep, Nurse,' the Vicar remarked.

'I think he's a bit deaf,' she replied, rejecting the doubt. 'In any case, I don't suppose he'd know what the noise meant.' The van stopped, and she decided, 'We'll have our coffee now.'

She managed to spread quite a picnic snack on the flat top of a long, calico-covered object lying beside her, on which she wouldn't sit. There were cheese and egg sandwiches, pieces of sultana cake, plates, mugs, sugar and a large Thermos flask. A heavy can of paraffin propped her back, and, in addition to the satchel of picnic stuff, she had brought her official leather bag, well known in the valley. Nurse Baldock's thoroughness was as dreaded by many as was sight of her black bag. After determined efforts over several years, she had recently been awarded a social science diploma, and now, at forty-five, she hoped for a more important position than that of a bicycle-borne district nurse. This rescuing mission today would help prove her mettle, and Vicar Pryce, to whom she had insisted on yielding the seat in front, would be a valuable witness of her zeal.

'I'll keep enough for the young man in the snowplough,' she said, pouring coffee. 'He ought not to stop now. The quicker we get there the better.'

'Makes one think of places in the moon,' the driver remarked, gazing out at the waxen countryside.

Sipping coffee, she resumed, 'I have eight patients in Ogwen just now, and I really ought not to be spending all this time on a man who's got nothing the matter with him except old age and obstinacy. Two confinements due any day now.' The men drank and ate, and she added, 'What a time for births! There's Mavis Thomas, for instance— she's not exactly entitled to one, is she, Vicar? But at least that man she lives with keeps her house on Sheep's Gap warm, and her water hasn't frozen.'

'Nobody except a choirboy turned up for matins last Sunday,' the meditative vicar said. 'So I cancelled all services that day.'

Nurse Baldock finished a piece of cake. 'I heard yesterday that a married woman living up on Sheep's Gap was chased by two starving ponies that found a way down from the mountains. You know how they won't go near human beings as a rule, but when this woman

287

came out of her farmhouse in her gumboots they stampeded from behind a barn; with their teeth grinding and eyes flaring. She ran back screaming into the house just in time.'

'Perhaps she was carrying a bucket of pig feed and they smelt it,' the driver suggested, handing back his mug.

Undeterred, Nurse Baldock gave a feminine shiver. 'I keep an eye open for them on my rounds. We might be back in the days of wolves.' The van resumed its amble on the pearly track as she proceeded. 'But these are modern times. Old Evans would never dream he would get a helicopter for his benefit, to say nothing of that great ugly thing in front, *and* us. There's real Christianity for you! This affair will cost the Council quite a sum. It will go on the rates, of course.'

'John and Maria Evans,' Vicar Pryce said, rewrapping his ears in the scarves, 'were always faithful parishioners of mine when they were able to get down to the village. I remember their son Richard, too. A good tenor in the choir. Emigrated to New Zealand and has children of his own there, I understand.'

'Well, Vicar,' Nurse Baldock said, packing the crocks into the satchel between her knees, 'I hope you'll do your very best to persuade Evans to leave with us today and go to Pistyll Mawr Home. Heaven knows, I did all I could to coax him when I was at the cottage with Dr. Howells the other day.'

'It will be a business,' he mumbled.

She pursed her lips. 'He told me it was healthy up there in his cottage, and that he and his wife had always liked the views. "Views!" I said, "Views won't feed and nurse you if you fall ill. Come now, facts must be faced." Then he said something about his damson trees. I told him Pistyll Mawr had fruit trees in plenty.'

The driver, who lived in the market town, spoke. 'Don't the new cases take offence at being forced to have a bath as soon as they enter the doors of Pistyll Mawr.'

'So you've heard that one, have you? Why, what's wrong with a bath? Is it a crime?' Nurse Baldock had bridled. 'I am able to tell you there's a woman in Pistyll Mawr who *brags* about her baths there—says that for the first time in her life she feels like a well-off lady, with a maid to sponge her back and hand her a towel. You're out of date, sir, with your "take offence".'

'Aren't there separate quarters for men and women, even if they're married?' he persisted.

' As if very elderly people are bothered by what you mean! Besides,

288

they can flirt in the garden if they want. But old people have too much dignity for such nonsense.'

'I dare say there are one or two exceptions.'

'Ah, I agree there.' Nurse Baldock pulled gauntlet gloves over her mittens. 'The aged! They're our biggest problem. The things that come my way from some of them! One has to have nerves of iron, and it doesn't do to let one's eyes fill. Why must people trouble themselves so much about the young? My blood boils when I see all the rubbishy fuss made about the youngsters by newspapers and busybodies of the lay public. Sight of the word "teenagers" makes me want to throw up. Leave the young alone, I say! They've got all the treasures of the world on their backs, and once they're out of school they don't put much expense on the rates.'

After this tirade no one spoke for a time. As the van crawled nearer the valley's majestic closure, Nurse Baldock herself seemed to become oppressed by the solemn desolation outside. Not a boulder or streak of path showed on Moelwyn's swollen heights. Yet, close at hand, there were charming snow effects. The van rounded a turn of the lane, and breaks in the hedges on either side revealed birch glades, their spectral depths glittering as though from the light of ceremonial chandeliers. All the crystal-line birches were struck into eternal stillness—fragile, rime-heavy boughs sweeping downward, white hairs of mourning. Not a bird, rabbit, or beetle could stir in those frozen grottoes, and the blue harebell or the pink convolvulus never ring out in them again.

'Up here doesn't seem to belong to us,' Vicar Pryce said, when the van halted again. 'It's the white. If only we could see just one little robin hopping about the branches! The last time I came this way, I saw pheasants crossing the road, and then they rose. Such colour! It was soon after Easter, and the windflowers and primroses were out.'

'We might be travelling in a wheelbarrow,' sighed Nurse Baldock, as the van moved. She looked at her watch, then into her official bag, and said, 'I've got Evans's old-age pension money. Because of his wife's taking to her bed, he worried about not being able to leave the cottage. I told him, "You're lucky you've got someone like me to look after you, but it's not my bounden task to collect your pension money, Council-employed though I am. Things can't go on like this, my dear sir, come now".'

'You've been kind to him,' the Vicar acknowledged at last.

'It's the State that is kind,' she said stoutly. 'We can say there's no such thing as neglect or old-fashioned poverty for the elderly now. But in my opinion the lay public has begun to take our welfare schemes too much for granted. The other day, I was able to get a wig free of charge for a certain madam living not a hundred miles from this spot, and when I turned up with it on my bike she complained it wasn't the right brown shade and she couldn't wear it—a woman who is not able to step outside her door and is seventy-eight!'

'The aged tend to cling to their little cussednesses,' Vicar Pryce mumbled, in a lacklustre way.

'Yes, indeed.' They were nearing their destination now, and Nurse Baldock, tenacity unabated, seized her last opportunity. 'But do press the real advantages of Pistyll Mawr Home to Evans, Vicar. We are grateful when the Church does its share in these cases. After all, my concern is with the body.' This earned no reply, and she said, 'Germs! It's too icy for them to be active just now, but with the thaw there'll be a fine crop of bronchials and influenzas, mark my words! And I don't relish coming all this way to attend to Evans if he's struck down, probably through not taking proper nourishment.' There was a further silence, and she added, 'On the other hand, these outlying cases ought to convince the Health Department that I must be given a car—don't you agree, Vicar?'

'I wonder you have not had one already. Dr. Howells should—'

A few yards ahead, the plough had stopped. Its driver leaned out of his cabin and yelled, 'Can't see a gate!'

'I'll find it,' Nurse Baldock declared.

The vicar and van driver helped to ease her out of the back doors. She shook her glut of warm skirts down, and clumped forward in her gumboots. A snow-caked roof and chimney could be seen above a billowing white slope. Scanning the contours of a buried hedge, the nurse pointed. 'The gate is there. I used to lean my bike against that tree.' It was another lamenting birch, the crystal-entwined branches drooped to the snow.

The plough driver, an amiable-looking young man in an elegant alpine sweater, brought out three shovels. Nurse Baldock scolded him for not having four. Valiantly, when he stopped for coffee and sandwiches, she did a stint, and also used the Vicar's shovel while he rested. They had shouted towards the cottage. There was no response, and, gradually, they ceased to talk. It took them half an hour to clear a way up the garden. They saw the oil-skin wrapped box as they neared the door. The nurse, her square face professionally rid of comment now, had already fetched her bag.

It was even colder in the stone house than outside. Nurse Baldock, the first to enter, returned from a swift trot into the living room and kitchen to the men clustered in the little hallway. She stepped to the staircase. All-seeing as an investigating policewoman, she was nevertheless respecting the social decencies. Also, despite the sight of broken crockery, a biscuit box, and a tray scattered below the stairs, she was refusing to face defeat yet. 'John Ormond Evans,' she called up, 'are you there?' Her voice had the challenging ring sometimes used for encouraging the declining back to the world of health, and after a moment of silence, she added, with an unexpected note of entreaty, 'The vicar is here!' The three men, like awkward intruders in a private place, stood listening. Nurse Baldock braced herself. 'Come up with me,' she whispered.

Even the plough driver followed her. But when the flannel wrappings were stripped away, John Ormond Evans sat gazing out at them from his chair as though in mild surprise at this intrusion into his comfortable retreat. His deep-sunk blue eyes were frostily clear under arched white brows. He looked like one awakened from restorative slumber, an expression of judicious independence fixed on his spare face. His hands rested on his knees, like a Pharoah's.

Nurse Baldock caught in her breath with a hissing sound. The two older men, who had remained hatted and gloved in the icy room, stood dumbly arrested. It was the ruddy-cheeked young man who suddenly put out a bare, instinctive hand and, with a movement of extraordinary delicacy, tried to close the blue eyes. He failed.

'I closed my father's eyes,' he stammered, drawing away in bashful apology for his strange temerity.

'Frozen,' pronounced Vicar Pryce, removing his round black hat. He seemed about to offer a few valedictory words.

Nurse Baldock pulled herself together. She swallowed, and said, 'Lack of nourishment, too!' She took off a gauntlet glove, thrust fingers round one of the thin wrists for a token feel, and then stepped back. 'Well, here's a problem! Are we to take him back with us?'

Vicar Pryce turned to look at the woman lying on the curtain-hung bed. Perhaps because his senses were blurred by the cold, he murmured, 'She's very small—smaller than I remember her. Couldn't he go in the coffin with her for the journey back?'

'No,' said Nurse Baldock promptly. 'He couldn't be straightened here.'

291

The van driver, an auxiliary assistant in busy times to Messrs Eccles, the market-town undertakers, confirmed, 'Set, set.'

'As he was in his ways!' burst from Nurse Baldock in her chagrin. 'This needn't have happened if he had come with me, as I wanted six days ago! Did he sit there all night deliberately?'

It was decided to take him. The coffin, three days late in delivery, was fetched from the van by the driver and the young man. Maria Evans, aged eighty-three, and prepared for this journey by the nurse six days before, by no means filled its depth and length. Gone naturally, of old age, and kept fresh by the cold, she looked ready to rise punctiliously to meet the face of the Almighty with the same hale energy as she had met each washing day on earth. Her shawl-draped husband, almost equally small, was borne out after her in his sitting posture. Nurse Baldock, with the Vicar for witness, locked up the house. Already it had an air of not belonging to anyone. 'We must tell the police we found the clock lying broken in the hearth,' she said. 'There'll be an inquest, of course.'

John Evans, head resting against the van's side, travelled sitting on his wife's coffin; Vicar Pryce considered it unseemly for him to be laid on the floor. The helicopter box of necessities and the heavy can of oil, placed on either side of him, held him secure. Nurse Baldock chose to travel with the young man in the draughty cabin of his plough. Huddled in her fur coat, and looking badly in need of her own hearth, she remained sunk in morose silence now.

The plough, no longer spouting snow, trundled in the van's rear. 'Pretty in there!' the driver ventured to say, in due course. They were passing the spectral birch glades. A bluish shade had come to the depths.

Nurse Baldock stirred. Peering out, she all but spat. 'Damned, damned snow! All my work wasted! Arguments on the phone, a helicopter, and this plough! The cost! I shall have to appear before the Health Committee.'

'I expect they'll give you credit for all you've done for the old fellow,' said the driver, also a Council employee.

She was beyond comforting just then. 'Old people won't *listen*! When I said to him six days ago, "Come with me, there's nothing you can do for her now," he answered, "Not yet. I will keep her company." I could have taken him at once to Pistyll Mawr Home. It was plain he couldn't look after himself. One of those unwise men who let themselves be spoilt by their wives.'

'Well, they're not parted now,' the young man said.

'The point is, if he had come with me he would be enjoying a round of buttered toast in Pistyll Mawr at this very moment. I blame myself for not trying hard enough. But how was I to know all this damn snow was coming?'

'A lot of old people don't like going into Pistyll Mawr Home, do they?'

'What's wrong with Pistyll Mawr? Hetty Jarvis, the matron, has a heart of gold. What's more, now I've got my social science diploma, I'm applying for her position when she retires next year.'

'Good luck to you.' The driver blew on his hands. Already, the speedier van had disappeared into the whiteness.

'The lay public,' Nurse Baldock sighed, looking mollified, '*will* cling to its prejudices.' And half to herself, she went on, 'Hetty Jarvis complained to me that she hasn't got anything like enough inmates to keep her staff occupied. "Baldock," she said to me, "I'm depending on you," and I phoned her only this week to say I had found someone for her, a sober and clean man I would gamble had many years before him if he was properly cared for.'

'Ah,' murmured the driver. He lit a cigarette, at which his preoccupied passenger—after all, they were in a kind of funeral—frowned.

'People should see the beeswaxed parquet floors in Pistyll Mawr,' she pursued. 'When the hydrangeas are in bloom along the drive, our Queen herself couldn't wish for a better approach to her home. The Bishop called it a noble sanctuary in his opening-day speech. And so it is!'

'I've heard the Kingdom of Heaven is like that,' the young man remarked idly. 'People have got to be pushed in.'

Nurse Baldock turned to look at his round face, to which had come, perhaps because of the day's rigours, the faint purple hue of a ripening fig. 'You might think differently later on, my boy,' she commented in a measured way. 'I can tell you there comes a time when few of us are able to stand alone. You saw today what resulted for one who made the wrong choice.'

'Oh, I don't know. I expect he knew what he was doing, down inside him.'

She sighed again, apparently patient of ignorance and youthful lack of feeling. 'I was fond of old Evans,' she said.

'Anyone can see it,' he allowed.

She remained silent for a long while. The costly defeat continued to weigh on her until the plough had lumbered on to the flat of the valley's bed. There, she looked at her watch and began to bustle up from melancholy. 'Five hours on this one case!' she fidgeted. 'I ought to have gone back in the van. I'm due at a case up on Sheep's Gap.'

'Another old one?'

'No, thank God. An illegitimate maternity. Not the first one for her either! And I've got another in the row of cottages down by the little waterfall—a legitimate.' The satisfaction of a life-giving smack on the bottom seemed to resound in her perked-up voice. 'We need them more than ever in nasty times like these, don't we? Providing a house is warm and well stocked for the welcome. Can't you make this thing go faster?'

'I'm at top speed. It's not built for maternities of any kind.'

Nurse Baldock sniffed. She sat more benevolently, however, and offered from the official black bag a packet of barley-sugar sweets. The village lay less than a mile distant. But it was some time before there was a sign of natural life out in the white purity. The smudged outline of a church tower and clustering houses had come into view when the delighted young man exclaimed, 'Look!' Arriving from nowhere, a hare had jumped on to the smooth track. His jump lacked a hare's usual celerity. He seemed bewildered, and sat up for an instant, ears tensed to the noise breaking the silence of these chaotic acres, a palpitating eye cast back in assessment of the oncoming plough. Then his forepaws gave a quick play of movement, like shadowboxing, and he sprang forward on the track with renewed vitality. Twice he stopped to look, as though in need of affiliation with the plough's motion. But, beyond a bridge over the frozen river, he took a flying leap and, paws barely touching the hardened snow and scut whisking, escaped out of sight.

THE OLD ADAM

Scandals never disturb the placidity of Clawdd, and everybody was put about when Jane Morgan, unwittingly or not, began one by taking a simple bathe on a beautiful summer afternoon. The distressing business was the more out of key because Clawdd, which lies in one of the most secluded valleys of Wales, is noted for its small but old-established theological college. Otherwise, the place has little to recommend it, except the several pure waterfalls and a breed of sheep which, nurtured on moistly succulent pastures, become the tenderest mutton in the land.

Jane, uncumbered by a bathing suit, took the bathe in a pool formed by the river in a glade just below her home, outside the village. Fishing rights in the stretch of river tumbling thereabouts belonged to her pugnacious mother, who rented them by the season to rich anglers coming from elsewhere. But was it true (as one critic suggested that evening in the Hawk Inn) that she had been sent bathing in the pool by her mother as a trap? There was dissent to this. Why shouldn't she enjoy lolling about in out-of-doors water? The criticism was based on the fact that the Morgans couldn't always lay their hand on ready money to pay their bills.

Jane was twenty, and although in her school days, and later, she had been ferocious at all energetic sports, indolence had begun to undo her that summer. After climbing out of the pool she took a long time over drying herself, standing on the daisy-sprinkled bank. Heavy-jowled for her age, and with small grey eyes lapsed too far in, nevertheless she owned a well-off body such as is seen, as a rule, only on a plinth in a museum or, alive in a slip, being chosen for first prize at a seaside fête while the brass band waits to strike up.

Presently she lay down, forgetting that her mother had asked her to pluck a capon killed the day before—a college professor was coming to a meal on Sunday. Her amiable spaniel, a bird or two, and a few droning bees seemed to be her sole companions in enjoyment of the purring sunshine. She was on her mother's enclosed land, and no anglers had arrived that afternoon.

She was not lying there for the sake of health or beauty, either, for in ancient Clawdd, which possesses two valiantly thriving Nonconformist chapels, as well as the esteemed theological college (situated quite near the Morgans' land), the up-to-date manias for sun-therapy and tinting the flesh are not thought about. Innocent of those fads as a nymph of the old dispensation, she dozed off among the daisies.

The spaniel's sudden bark wakened her. She scrambled up and, for a moment, stood posed with wonderfully graceful alertness. The dog, wagging its tail, was ambling to the trunk of a venerable oak which cast shade twelve yards distant up the glade. Jane let out the hallooing cry foxhunters give; then, swift as a released arrow, she charged towards the tree. She did not stop to snatch up her towel. Sun and sleep (so she told Police Sergeant Pryse later) had addled her senses.

A young man fled—foolishly but perhaps naturally—from behind the tree. Jane's cries increased. They were heard by her mother in the old red brick house above. She told Sergeant Pryse that she had been in the kitchen making blackberry tart and was unaware of her daughter's habit of bathing in the pool. But for some weeks she and Jane had suspected that an intruder haunted their land, especially at night, and the sergeant had been informed of this already. One morning, indeed, Jane had found a spray of wild cherry blossom—it was too heavy for any bird to have carried—on the window ledge of her bedroom.

Shrieks from an unclothed woman in pursuit are more unnerving than from the clothed. The young man completely lost his head. Or was it that he *wished* to be captured? Instead of fleeing downwards to the left, where the public road to the college lay, he dashed upwards. The delighted spaniel barked, chased and whisked about as if in a game with its own kindred. Jane, a fine sprinter, got the intruder in a couple of minutes. He had bounded away from a barbed-wire fence enclosing staring sheep in a field rented to a farmer and, just as Mrs. Morgan rounded the house, Jane and the spaniel—not that the dog intended seizing him—cornered him where a barn joined the low wall of a disused paddock. Athletic of physique, Jane not only cornered him but leapt and brought him down under her. His head bumped against the stone cobbles.

She scrambled up. 'I know him!' she shouted to her mother, whose own jaw was clamping soundlessly as she drew up. 'He was skulking behind a tree.' A bubble broke at the corner of her mouth. 'I've seen him in chapel!' She looked down at him with the victorious gaze a hunter gives to netted prey. 'His name is Tudor . . . Tudor . . .?'

'Edwards,' supplied the supine young man, in a mumble. He seemed to be in a condition for total submission, perhaps because of the bumping. But his eyes watched her in dark tumult.

Mrs. Morgan, understandably, untied her kitchen apron to give her daughter before she found speech. 'If there was a whip—' she panted, looking round at the horseless paddock, long fallen to rack and ruin because of the sloths, dissipations and debts of her recently deceased husband. She turned to the villain, her tone grim as her eye: 'You'll be hearing more about this!'

He lay still on the cobbles, as if shocked to the core. Jane should have run off, the apron not being enough, but she had remained looking down intently at her captive. Her mother gave her a push, and, accompanied by the slavering dog, they left Tudor Edwards where he lay. He was a native of Clawdd. But he and Jane had never spoken to each other, and in this unseemly way his wooing burst into flower.

Of course, the disagreeable event became common property by that evening, though muddling gossip spread a story, at first, that the culprit was a resident student—some of them came from England—in the college. No one wanted to believe that a son of Clawdd could forget himself so far.

'There's bound to be a goat even in a little college like ours,' remarked Emlyn Prichard, in the saloon bar of The Hawk. The college was not so important as the one in Cardiganshire, but it was more exclusive.

'Students are not proper until they've passed their examinations,' said Blodwen Lewis, who, as barmaid, was the only woman allowed to tread the saloon.

'Perhaps the student just wanted to do a bit of poaching,' Llewellyn Morris ventured.

'Traps,' frowned Ewart Vaughan, who had been fined a pound in his time for landing a salmon, undersized though it was; 'I expect Jane Morgan was put there as a trap.'

Did he mean a trap to catch poachers or to dazzle a student or licensed angler for mother or daughter's own purpose? They were debating this when, at about nine, T. D. Watkins, owner of the flannel mill and a close friend of Sergeant Pryse, came in and gave the facts.

'No,' he replied to dismayed inquirers on the stools and benches, 'Tudor isn't handcuffed or in a cell. But it's serious. Owing to the college.' It was understood he meant that the incident might put thoughts into the heads of the students.

'Clawdd was here long before the college,' observed Ewart. 'What was Jane doing,' he asked insinuatingly (and was not answered), 'bathing and sleeping like that in the glade? Trees full of leaves don't hide everything—no, not even when they're fig leaves.'

Since Sergeant Pryse didn't come into the inn for his customary refreshment, the affair certainly looked important, and, after ten o'clock closing time, men whose way led past the police station shivered in sympathy for Tudor. Such is the solidarity of old communities. But no one had given credit to the Morgans for their courage in going to the police and thus making public that, private land though she was on, Jane bathed and lay about in that state.

Tudor, who had been hauled out of his mother's cottage three hours earlier, was still inside the police station. He was sipping a cup of tea, an obstinate scowl on his face. Now and again he stroked the back of his head, where a lump had grown to the size of a bantam's egg.

Sergeant Pryse, also with tea, sat irritably making corrections on long sheets of ruled blue paper on his desk. He had wanted to deduct a year from Tudor's exact age. Twenty, and of full stature bodily, nevertheless the face of the accused showed that he had not yet quite emerged from those lunar thickets of youth where incalculable creatures roam bemused, sometimes stamping their hooves in fury.

Pryse suddenly pounced—'Sunday, May 1st, you said it was? Well, May 1st wasn't a Sunday! You're telling me lies.'

'It was a Sunday night,' Tudor maintained. 'I had been looking at her in chapel that evening, and I heard the clock in the college tower strike midnight when I took the ladder out of the Morgans' barn. The moon was full and the blossom was out. It was the first time I had gone there, and I remember thinking. "It's the first day of May".'

'You weren't safe in bed dreaming you did this?' suggested Pryce entincingly.

Tudor shook his head. It was as though, having suffered the pangs of undeclared passion for a long time, he wanted to bellow about them from the housetops. He had told Pryse of behaviour which need not have been applied to that day's offence of loitering on enclosed land and peering from behind a tree while a young lady bathed. In the dead of night, when no other soul was outside the sheets, he had gone many times to the Morgans' house and climbed a ladder to the window of Jane's bedroom. Several reconnoitring visits were made before he discovered which was her room. But all he had done aftewards was sit for a while on the window ledge.

'What did you say your motive was?' the sergeant pressed, returning to this bewildering idiosyncrasy for the third time.

'I just fancied sitting there. The curtains were closed, but I was hoping one night they wouldn't be and Miss Morgan would come to the window and speak to me.'

'To ask if the fine weather was going to change, I expect?' Pryse blew angrily on his tea-damp moustache. 'I wouldn't be surprised,' he said, going beyond his jurisdiction, 'if Mrs. Morgan would say you were after her silver, not her daughter. Do you appreciate you could be had up for trying to break in?'

'They haven't got any money. I'll be the one with money after my mother is gone.'

The long interview had got out of hand once or twice. From its start, Pryse, doubtless with Clawdd's prestige as a theological haunt in view, had done his utmost to coax Tudor into admitting that really it was salmon he was after. Poaching for the expensive fish, though liable to prosecution, was a moot offence in the social and moral spheres; people indigenous to the district felt that local wild fish and fowl, if it was possible to consult them about it, would not be so narrowly selective of their captors as was the law. It was merely bad luck when a poacher was nabbed.

'No,' Tudor, adamant on the point, spurned this reiterated blandishment to the end, 'no, I do not know anything about salmon, and I never want to eat it any time of the year.'

'Anyone would think,' Pryse grumbled (and he couldn't be blamed), 'you'd had your gumption knocked out of your head by bumping it on those cobbles.' He looked over the heavily corrected foolscap, and grieved, 'As far as I can tell now, the charge will be breach of the peace. Your Dad wouldn't have liked this.' And after a final version of his statement was read to the accused he signed it and was freed into the moonlit night. On the telephone, the Rev. A. C. Powys had consented to stand bail for this young member of his flock.

A different ordeal awaited him at home. When he got there, his mother didn't ask him why he had done this extraordinary thing or what was the point of it when he could have approached Jane in a more moral way, especially since the girl attended the same chapel. She laid a poultice on his swelling, then drew a starched cloth off a tray of cold food.

'Now, eat the meat and pickles slowly,' she said, 'or you'll be having

299

nightmares tonight.' She resumed her knitting, sitting in the rocking chair in which her only child used to be sung to sleep.

A small woman with a politely mild face and a voice that rarely darted up into anger, she had never got too big for her boots, though her husband, a builder's repairs man when she married him at eighteen, had later done well for himself in buying up old properties in Marlais, the nearby town. But a policeman—and on such an errand!—had never darkened her threshold before; as she told Mrs. Powys later, she would hear for many years the sound of those feet coming to her cottage door. Her knitting was faster than usual.

'Mam,' Tudor said, the meal rapidly finished, 'I'll have to stand up in court next week.'

'I am surprised you have let yourself be gone on Jane Morgan,' she commented. 'There's half a dozen goodminded girls in Clawdd would be glad to know you've clapped eyes on them.'

He pondered, and said, meekly, 'Well, I thought to myself, Jane's like me, the same age and with only a widowed mother and no brothers and sisters. Except she's got no money. The four of us, I thought, could sit here in Clawdd in comfort, with Jane fetching the rents after you've gone.' Every first of the month his mother went off unobtrusively to Marlais and collected the rents of the eight houses which had been expertly renovated by his father.

Although admiring his sentiment, she objected, 'That dressy mother of hers is a proud one, front and back, and Jane's got the same mighty way of walking, in her fine clothes which they can't afford. If you had been a young man from the college, very likely Jane would have taken you into the house to tea when she found you on their land.'

'Yes,' he sighed, after another gloomy pause, 'I ought to have gone to a college and been made a B.A.'

Still not showing signs of being very cast down, she said, 'While you were in the police station I thought I ought to go and plead with Mrs. Morgan and Jane not to let this business go any further.'

Tudor reared up, like an angry turkey-cock. 'No.'

She nodded approvingly, briskly stuck her needles into the ball of wool, and said, 'Mind you don't do anything foolish after this. Men have drowned themselves over women. But not men with full-weight heads.'

She knew better than to upbraid him in dire terms. He was not a wild one, but had always gone his own way. Stubborn against his father's wish to educate him for work entailing pomp and circumstance, he had dropped school as soon as the law allowed and begun work as a ploughboy on one of the ancestral local farms, where he had quickly progressed. He was able to judge a cow or ewe at market expertly. With help from her, he could buy a farm of his own presently; there was a plan that they would acquire one owned by an ageing relative in North Wales, far over the mountains. And nothing had seemed to rankle in him until lately.

'I won't be going to chapel tomorrow,' he said, as midnight put an end to the disastrous Saturday.

Supporters and inquisitive natives of Clawdd who were able to attend the court in Marlais travelled the seven miles by bus, cars and bikes; dressed in best clothes, the contingent was of sufficient strength for a distinct odour of camphor balls to fill the eighteenth-century court-room. Mrs. Morgan and her daughter were there, although told they would not be called to witness, since the accused was pleading guilty; both of them wore new hats.

Tudor's case was the last of the morning's ration of district ill-doings, which had included theft of a sheep, assault and battery during a Saturday night brawl in Marlais, and a summons concerning the father of a bastard. 'It is unusual for us to find such a charge as this one from Clawdd,' began the chairman ominously, after Tudor was called to the dock. It was a hint that the good status of the scholastically religious village was in jeopardy.

But of the three magistrates on the bench, one was a woman. She was comfortably stout, wore flashing, very observant glasses, and it soon became clear that she was dubious of the case. That Tudor was pleading guilty shortened the proceedings, but nevertheless, after Sergeant Pryse had related the arrest and admissions of the accused, this Mrs. Ellen Jones, J.P., bristled.

'Boiled down,' she said, 'what is this charge but the paltry mis-demeanour of a lovesick farmhand? Why, not a hundred years ago there was a custom in these parts of a suitor being admitted to a young lady's room from a ladder at night, and such courtships were acceptable to families of the best repute. A young man was trusted in those simple days—but God help him if he betrayed that trust! The accused may have heard of this custom of our respected forefathers and—'

'We are not living a hundred years ago,' interrupted the chairman rudely. 'Terrible things were done in those days. A man could be sent to Australia for stealing a sheep.'

301

'It is our bounden duty,' said his elderly male confrère, 'to distinguish in this case between a genuine need to court and something much more vulgar—' Looking annoyed by someone's loud titter, he corrected himself, 'Something that is very vulgar in comparison.'

The chairman took a long, beady look at the accused. Tudor's mother had insisted that he wear a starched white collar and the black suit—now very tight—bought for his father's funeral. But the effect of respectability was spoiled by his fierce scowl—due, perhaps, to Jane being there to view his public humiliation. A tuft of unruly hair shoved down on his forehead somehow added to the surliness. Yet Mrs. Ellen Jones, also giving him a scrutiny, seemed even more impatient that the charge had been brought. She jerked about in her seat. But she had two against her.

'What were your intentions towards Miss Morgan?' the chariman demanded.

'To see her,' Tudor replied, omitting 'sir'.

'We know that,' sniffed the other male beak, cynically. 'Were you aware that she was in the habit of bathing in her private pool?'

'Yes.'

'Ha!' said the two men, almost simultaneously, and the elderly one commented, 'To stare at an unrobed young lady for forty-five minutes from behind a tree in broad daylight shows a very warped mentality to say the least.'

'This sitting on her window ledge late at night,' Mrs. Ellen Jones persisted, encouragingly, '—what were your intentions in that?'

'Only to sit outside her room, Your Worship.'

The chairman barked, '*Not* to go inside, of course, of course! . . . Stand down.'

Mrs. Jones pouted at the short-shrift chairman. But she gave way. No doubt the chairman felt this was a case men could judge best. The three consulted together in lowered voices. Then the chairman announced judgement. A very old law—it was the Peeping Tom Act of 1361—was quoted to the extreme detriment of the accused. But on account of his youth and previously unblemished character, he was to be let off light. 'You are fined fifteen shillings,' the chairman told him, 'and I warn you not to let us see you here again.' The court closed, and the smell of mothballs evaporated.

Opinion in The Hawk Inn that evening was that the charge would have been dismissed if the theological college hadn't been part of Clawdd. Commiseration was expressed by everybody; if Tudor had gone into the inn he would not have been allowed to spend a penny on whatever he fancied. Sergeant Pryse openly remarked, 'I did my best to make him see sense. He could have pleaded to me he had bad eyesight and thought it was a big fish dipping about in that pool.'

The damage was done, however. He had stood in a dock of malefactors; his name had gone down in police records; the case was reported in full in the Marlais weekly newspaper. On the other hand, his behaviour certainly got him Jane's awareness in full measure.

He went about in a watchfully saturnine way, like a man who waits to pick a quarrel with anyone. He bit his nails, shaved less often, didn't take to drinking, and went for morose walks on his own in the evenings, sometimes carrying his licensed gun for rabbiting. Either the gnawing beetle of love hadn't been killed by the magistrates or else he was belatedly feeling the disgrace of the prosecution. He might have been in that state of thwarted passion which men of other days sometimes tried to forget by disappearing into Indian jungles to shoot tigers.

His mother made efforts to repair him; she baked his favourite dishes and, in a roundabout way, drew his attention to several Clawdd girls who were in the pink of condition. He scowled down his strong-rooted nose and had nothing to say. And on the first Sunday after the court apearance he became difficult just as they were about to leave for chapel.

'I'm going to become an atheist,' he announced, resolutely sitting down.

'There's plenty of those in our chapel,' she said, pulling on lace gloves. 'I wouldn't try to coax you if it wasn't that Mrs. Morgan and Jane will sure to be there—and won't they be glad they've driven you from where your dear father was made a deacon the year before he died! Are they to see me sitting alone in our pew like a woman who's lost everybody?'

'I can't help staring at Jane right through the sermon,' he lamented.

'Well, stare at her,' she said firmly, and gave him the hymn book they always shared. 'Though what there's left for you to see I can't think.'

Owing to his humming and hawing they were the last to enter the full chapel. Their seats were a good way down, on a raised side-portion where the pews stood crosswise to the middle ones. The ghost of a commotion stirred in the air; Jane, sitting in a middle pew, was observed to lower her head. As soon as mother and son were seated, the organ, played by Ewart Vaughan, burst into a Handel piece like a fanfare of trumpets, and, until the Rev. A. C. Powys, D.D., opened with his prayer, it was unavoidable that most people couldn't help thinking of Jane lying in a Garden of Eden state beside her pool. It was a brief ordeal endured not only by the characters most concerned.

'Things will be easier for you from now,' his mother comforted him, when they got home. 'Soon everything will be forgotten.'

He pursed his lips. But always afterwards, as on that Sunday, he succeeded in keeping his gaze away from Jane's in the chapel. *Her* seat, though, was so placed that her small, gone-in eyes could rest on her melancholy victim without a turn of her head. And in small country places even the bitterest enemies are likely, sooner or later, to come face to face at a quiet spot. One evening in August, as he neared a humped stone bridge over the river, about a mile from the village, Jane came looming up towards him from the other side. The puce after-tint of sunset had not yet darkened into night, and a sickle moon lay flimsy above the lonely woodlands.

Her spaniel, running ahead, recognized Tudor instantly and offered a saluting leap and lick; he bent to return the greeting with a pat. Jane, in a thin, low-cut dress because of the warmth, halted when she got a step past him on the shady bridge, and turned.

'Tudor Edwards,' she said. ' I forgive you.' She put her head on one side and continued, 'My mother and I ought to have thought twice before going to the police.' He carried his gun, and a limp rabbit was slung over his shoulder; since he said nothing, she asked, chattily, 'Been rabbiting?'

He took the rabbit from his shoulder, looked at it in great surprise, and said, 'Why, it was a salmon just before I came on this bridge!'

Jane fingered a string of coral pieces round her tawny throat and found herself able to smile. 'Oh, well,' she said, 'strange things happen every night and day, don't they?' No apparition, her affluent figure stood clear-cut in the twilight. Her thick-featured face was golden from all the sunshine of that good summer.

He gave her a pondering look, blinked, then slowly turned his head as though what his hardened eyes saw caused him agony which must be conquered at all costs. Yet, stammering over it, he asked, 'Going for . . . for a walk?'

Thereafter, to everybody's surprise, he began to meet Jane frequently for courting walks. And again he seemed a changed man. On the free nights he went up to The Hawk and drank more than he should. Extravagance possessed him. He bought chocoloates and knick-knacks regularly for Jane, and for himself high-priced neckties, glossy shoes, and a fancy waistcoat of canary yellow. It looked as if the demolished pride of a young man was restored. Yet his drinking in The Hawk did not have the ease and calm of one who had climbed into man's estate.

'Courting Jane Morgan now, are you?' remarked Edward Vaughan, who had once taught him the elements of the Gospels in the chapel Sunday-school. 'Well, a lady often likes to scratch a man before she finds out that he's fit for her under the skin.'

Tudor stared into his pewter tankard in a way that might have meant bashfulness or the tight refusal of a man who won't speak. A lot of Clawdd business was done in the Gents Saloon of The Hawk, if only in the way of information and discussion, and Walter Leyshon, a clerk in the Marlais water-rates office, said, 'Well, now, Tudor, you'll have to be the boss and tidy up the Morgans' affairs. Three applications for payment of last quarter's water I've sent to Mrs. Morgan. She'll be cut off one day and have to fetch her water from that pool where Jane splashes about and frightens the trout away.'

'That's enough!' cried Blodwen Lewis, from behind the bar. She always interfered when the men went too far in comment, abuse or revelation. 'I don't blame Mrs. Morgan and Jane for making the best of themselves,' she said. Presumably she meant their habit of dressing in the height of fashion. She served Tudor with another pint of beer— his sixth—in a censorious way, however. 'Taking it while you can?' she asked.

'A gin for you?' he invited, insisting on buying her a drink although she remarked that he'd want a lot of money for his future. And when Police Sergeant Pryse came in Tudor bought him a drink too, before leaving. It was noticed that he always left The Hawk soon after the Sergeant's time of entrance, as if sight of the law's representative gave him a bitter pain he could not forget.

Clawdd, on the whole, was pleased to hear about the courtship. The Morgans, though extravagantly stiffnecked, were as much true local stock as the Edwardses; it wasn't as if strangers had upset the place by calling in the law to Tudor's conduct. It would be a nice development in logic if his doting offence in the glade should be reduced to something seen through the clean circle of a wedding ring.

But it was not to be expected that an affair which had begun to the portentous tramp of a constable's feet would proceed with the delicate smoothness of a minuet. Tudor's mother expressed her forebodings, though she saw that a man in love—especially one who has suffered prosecution for it—must be allowed his excesses, and she had faith in his good sense asserting itself when the humdrum of married life barred these youthful capers. She spoke up in real indignation only after the occasion of Mrs. Morgan's formal visit to the obscure cottage down by Three Saints Well.

The two widows spent half an hour in conclave. Mrs. Morgan had called with the bygone manner of a squire's lady bringing bounty to the hard-pressed, despite the knowledge she had acquired of Mrs. Edwards's circumstances, possession of which she presently disclosed. Living just the same as when she was married, and still baking her own bread in a hearth oven with a Jehovah among wheatsheaves designed on its iron door, Mrs. Edwards had never bought a dress or hat which made other women think.

'I'll be truthful and say he'd not be of my choosing for Jane,' Mrs. Morgan began, a few cool politeness over. 'But times have changed. The bit of trouble can be overlooked. I've made inquiries and I'm told your son is an excellent worker in Treharne's farm—'

'I'll be truthful too,' Tudor's mother put in, 'and say we women can't properly understand what a man sees when he looks at us.'

Mrs. Morgan appeared about to be contentious. But she proceeded, 'Now, what about his means and prospects? A farmhand doesn't earn much. It's not his intention to stay one all his life?'

'Tudor gets full union rate of pay, and he'll get what I've got when I'm gone.'

'You're only about fifty,' Mrs. Morgan quibbled. She paused, then said, 'Mrs. Powys, the minister's wife, has mentioned to me that you own eight houses in Marlais. Is your son to inherit these? If so, surely he should be given some of them on marriage? I intend giving Jane a grazing meadow.'

Not a flicker of surprise or resentment showed in Mrs. Edwards's face. But she asked, 'You didn't know about my houses until after Tudor was fined in the police court?'

'No,' replied Mrs. Morgan, too secure in her social advantage to see a necessity for evasion. 'When Mrs. Powys came to tea after the police proceedings it was natural we should talk about you. Facts must be faced. Jane is accustomed to a good house and table.'

Mrs. Edwards, after a glance at her visitor's clothes, took deep thought, while Mrs. Morgan took admiring stock of the treasure-packed room. There were valuable painted glass plaques and Swansea plates on the walls, the furniture was of old black oak, and there were china effigies, including one of the young Queen Victoria and one of Christmas Evans, the famous divine whose single seeing eye had done the work of forty scarifying orbs. Mrs. Morgan, who knew about the value of such items, had been forced to sell most of her own household rarities

'I've always told Tudor,' his mother said at last, 'that I'll give him the deeds of three houses in Marlais when he gets married. His father wished that. He'll get everything else when I'm gone.'

'Couldn't he be given four houses?' demanded Mrs. Morgan. 'Half the total number would be sensible and just.'

'His father said three. Three it will be.'

The visitor took the hint not to interfere so calculatingly in the love business of the young, rose, praised the Staffordshire effigies, and departed; she looked more or less satisfied. But Mrs. Edwards felt in need of a glass of elderberry wine after the exit; and when Tudor arrived home from work, she fumed, while he sat to a bottle of ginger ale as usual, 'Mrs. Morgan has been here. You're not of her choosing, but she brought a pair of scales with her. In one pan she sat her daughter Jane, and three of my houses in the other. But the scales didn't balance and she asked for another house.'

He remained gazing reflectively down at his farm boots, nodded, then heaved himself up. Dismissing her recital of the interview, he said, 'Now, Mam, leave this to me. I'll manage them. You and I will talk about the houses after I am married.'

She could make nothing of his smile. Had love made a complete dolt of him? Was it possible that he could transform Jane into a pleasingly obedient married woman? She said nothing more, and at eight o'clock, his black hair perfumed with oil, he went out for his courting walk. She watched him disappear up the lane of trees reaching from the cottage. His gait certainly had the strut of a man who knew what he was about.

When he returned from that particular walk he announced with peculiar affableness, 'Well, we settled a lot tonight, Mam.' The hope faded out of her face as he added, 'Jane thinks it ought to be four houses, not three, and I told her I would try my best to make you say yes.'

307

'If the Morgans are not careful,' she said, grim in her disappointment, 'there won't be one house.'

He nodded, sitting down to a piece of her excellent cold veal pie.
Decision seemed to have eased his bones. Smiling at a segment of pie
impaled on his fork, he said, 'We have settled for a wedding on
October 2nd. A Saturday.'

'Tudor,' she allowed herself to shout, 'you've gone off your head.
Those two are a pair of greedy foxes.'

He looked at her, and said, 'A man can teach a lesson to a fox.' And
he went on, 'Jane wants to go to London for the honeymoon.'

She gave up, but protested, 'London!' It might have been Baghdad.
'You ought to go to North Wales and visit my cousin Ellis at his farm.
If he likes the shape of things in this wedding he might let you have
the farm cheap when he's ready to sell.'

'Jane,' he said, a note of teasing in his voice, 'wants to see shops in
London. She doesn't know anything about your cousin Ellis's farm.
Time enough for seeing about that later on . . . She wants a motor
car,' he continued, 'and a refrigerator for when I've bought my own
farm. Her mother's got her mind on old Will Mansell's place.'

'There'll be a big mortgage to raise for Will Mansell's farm,' she
warned.

'Where there's a will there's a way,' he grinned. 'I'll tell Jane you
won't budge from more than three houses.'

She expressed no further important criticism after that night, even
accepting the decision for a wedding as soon as October. From a social
point of view, perhaps it was best for the July disgrace to be wiped out
as soon as possible, and she was comforted by a new realization that he
seemed to have a lot of grown-up fight in him now.

'I'm going to be master,' he assured her. 'The Morgans have trod on
me once.'

In addition to the three houses she had decided to present the couple
with two pairs of linen bedsheets, a tapestry quilt made by eighty-
year-old Jessie James, and, as a reminder of the sterner matters in life,
the china statue of Christmas Evans. These articles she sent up, like the
true Christian she was, to Mrs. Morgan's house on the day before the
wedding. Jane wanted him to live there until the gift of the three
Marlais houses was turned into cash for the purchase of a farm. He
had agreed to this with a jaunty readiness.

It was a fine Saturday for the wedding, the autumn sun clear and warm, and at about one o'clock he said to his mother, 'Some of the men want to give me good wishes in The Hawk. So I'll be off now. See you in the chapel.'

'It's last night the men should have done that,' she expostualted. 'You'll be smelling in the chapel.' She was hurt that he was allowing her to proceed there alone, though the distance was short and no car had been hired.

He promised not to allow the well-wishers to incommode him, praised her silk dress, and went off up the lane of russet trees. Did he need drink and male jests to give him courage after all? But he hadn't been at all jumpy or excited during the morning. At noon, dressed in his expensive new suit, and his fresh-cut hair glistening with oil, he had eaten a substantial meal.

The ceremony had been fixed for two-fifteen on the holiday afternoon, to allow as many people as possible to attend. Just after two, closing time in The Hawk until the evening session, a dozen or so men crossed the road to pay respects by attending. The unusual courtship had brought in other people besides formally invited guests; five theological students were there, too, supposedly to see how wedding ceremonies in Nonconformist chapels were conducted. The groom's mother sat alone in her pew. Jane, with her mother and a male escort from Marlais, waited in the vestry for Tudor's arrival. He should have been standing by the vase of white chrysanthemums under the pulpit, and at two twenty-five the Rev. T. C. Powys came out of the vestry, crossed to Mrs. Edwards, and asked why her son was late.

'He left home at one o'clock to go up to The Hawk,' she mumbled, very flustered.

There was a tightening of silence among the congregation when, a few minutes later, she was called into the vestry. It had been easy to discover that Tudor hadn't visited The Hawk; and his mother, eyes as agog as everybody's, had barely entered the vestry when Blodwen Lewis, the barmaid, hastened in with her gaping nephew, a boy of ten who was still carrying a glass jar with a huge frog in it.

'I saw Tudor Edwards running on the river bank about half an hour ago,' he blurted, encouraged to it by his aunt. 'He had a bag and went climbing up to Howell's Spout.'

Everybody knew that at two-fifteen a bus to Marlais and its railway station passed the Howell's Spout crossroads outside the village.

'His new bag,' declared his mother, at once, 'was in my house when I left. Packed ready for London.'

Cross-examination of the boy revealed that it was the same bag. 'Then he must have gone back to the house to fetch it!' deduced the Reverend cleverly. He was distracted at the prospect of a nasty vendetta developing between two valued families of his flock.

Jane, sitting on a hard chair in a flounced-out dress of pearly grey, did not swoon. But she gazed fixedly into the air, her strong jaw dropped, this contest lost. Mrs. Morgan pranced about on high heels. But, because of the sacred nature of the adjoining edifice, rising tempers had been kept in check. Then the minister returned from announcing to the congregation that the ceremony was postponed.

'Tudor is gone out of his mind and is wandering!' the groom's mother cried, her distress so wholehearted that no one could accuse her of a taunt as she gasped, 'Tell the police!'

'Postponed?' the bride's mother burst out, while the minister poured a glass of water for her silent daughter. 'He'd marry her across my dead body!'

The Reverend quickly took out his watch. 'Baptism of the Leyshon's baby is in fifteen minutes,' he said, more peremptorily than was usual with him. 'So now I must get ready in quiet, please.' Outside the chapel people stood babbling in close groups as if some big event, such as declaration of another war, had happened.

Opinion in The Hawk, early that evening, was cautious. No one denounced Tudor, and neither was he praised. Dirty tricks should not be countenanced, but it was vain to sit in judgement on the eternal slipperiness of love. As well sit on the meaning of the vanishing rainbow or a kingfisher's flight down a stream.

Sergeant Pryse said, 'His mother hasn't reported to me that he's missing, and till she does that I don't know anything.' Always a sign that he was speaking as an ordinary man, he laid his helmet on the bar counter. 'People say a fellow can't help coming back to where he's done a deed, but I dare say we won't be seeing Tudor in these parts again. It's been the old Adam coming out in him today. He grew up on that day in court.'

'Old Adam fiddlesticks!' sniffed the listening barmaid, who didn't care much for Pryse. 'It's hard on his poor mother—*she'll* be there, bearing the brunt. I expect she's collapsing in her cottage, and if I was a policeman, I'd be down there trying to find out what I could.'

The absconder's mother wasn't really collapsing. She had found a token of his regard in an envelope on her dressing table when, still

310

panting a little, she had gone upstairs to change into everyday clothes. He never had been a boy to write letters and, in his outsize scrawl, all he said was,

'Dear Mam, I am catching the three o'clock train in Marlais and I will be looking over Cousin Ellis's farm before dark. You see, Mam, I thought to myself how Jane and her mother liked to show off and have things done for all the people of Clawdd to see, same as before the magistrates in court last July. So they can do the same today. Jane asked me for twenty-five pounds to help to buy her clothes for today, and I gave it. So I haven't robbed her—not of money—and she's got the engagement ring costing thirty pounds. She bought a fine dress. I didn't tell you about this because you had been very upset when they wanted four houses, and I was upset too and I began to make up my mind about today then. Jane pretended.

from Tudor.'

She sat for a while in reverie. He had known she would not have allowed him to do the act of that day! No good woman would have approved it. Yet she couldn't help admiring his angry rigour now. A young man worth his salt mustn't be a worshipping angel all the time. How stupid of Jane to let herself ask for cash before the permission of marriage! And how that day had been a highpriced one for everybody concerned! She stroked the lovely silk of her own dress.

After giving the Morgans decent time to recover, she put on her costly hat bought for the wedding and went up to their house. Opening the porch door, off which the paint was flaking, Mrs. Morgan admitted the silent visitor. 'Where is he?' she demanded, as they went into a room off the gloomy hall. 'I'll track him to the ends of the earth and sue.'

A three-tiered cake, a whole ham, dishes of sandwiches, small pies, and bottles of drink, were spread on a white-clothed table. Tudor's mother looked at these festive things in horror. Why hadn't they been put out of sight?

'The expense I've gone to!' Mrs. Morgan continued her bombast. 'But I'll get every penny back!'

Mrs. Edwards glanced at a board erected on trestles in a corner; on it were displayed the wedding gifts, which included two clocks not yet going, a set of saucepans, an electric iron and a tea-cosy. 'Your daughter?' she asked, looking about her in the fading light.

311

'Jane, come down,' Mrs. Morgan shouted into the hall. 'His mother's here.'

She came in at a run, wearing a crumpled new dressing gown, as if she had been lying on her bed. 'He's come back?' she cried.

Mrs. Edwards shook her head. 'I wouldn't be surprised to hear he's gone to join the Army,' she said.

Jane sank to a chair. 'I'll sue him for breach of promise!'

'Tudor's got no money or property to pay for breach of promise. The business of the three houses was put off till you were settled.' Mrs. Edwards took a long breath, turned her back on Mrs. Morgan, and addressed Jane, 'I have come to say I am sorry . . . But you were hard and foolish in getting the magistrate to fine a man that only wanted to look on what had taken his fancy, strange though that was. Tudor is a boy that gets queer notions. I have noticed that when the moon is rising—'

'The moon has got nothing to do with it,' Mrs. Morgan cut into what seemed the beginning of a long speech of humble defence. 'The plain fact is that he's a born clod and needs a good thrashing.'

'Then what he's done is best for Jane's future,' Mrs. Edwards said, still meek.

Jane's hands seemed to be trying to push an awful outburst back down her shapely bosom. She succeeded, and only exclaimed, 'You've been in league with him, you humbug, and egged him on in what he's done!'

Mrs. Edwards looked at Jane's foreshadowing chin, and at the solid face that should have been eased by true love. She shook her head again, as at some erroneous piece of judgement on nature's part, and asked, 'Would I have paid twelve pounds for this silk dress if I knew what he was going to do? And three pounds for this hat?' She crossed to the display of gifts and picked up Christmas Evans. 'Would I have given you this, and the sheets and quilt?' She held aloft the effigy of the celebrated divine. 'I swear by Christmas Evans that I did not know!'

'Put that ornament back!' commanded Mrs. Morgan, stepping to her.

Mrs. Edwards held the preacher against her chest. 'He was one of my wedding presents,' she said, and suddenly her demeanour became so steely and menacing that Mrs. Morgan, as if fearing Christmas Evans would be smashed on her head, shrank back. 'He will be more at home in my cottage,' she added. 'You can keep the linen bedsheets and the seven-guinea quilt, in memory.' She walked out of the house unmolested.

She did not uproot herself from Clawdd for several months, occupied with the business of selling her cottage. And Jane did not sue for breach of promise. With their ferretings into privacies and idyllic things that often take place—at least, in Clawdd—under trees in lonely woodlands or on a sweet river bank, when only bats or an owl are unbiased witnesses, such lawsuits can be undignified as well as costly to pocket and reputation. But she got her reward for this self-discipline. In due course a youngish schoolmaster in Marlais stood beside her under the pulpit. A sound man, he played cricket and football, and tore about ancient Clawdd on a roaring motor-scooter, Jane proudly erect behind him. He was not the sort to relish a girl who forgot delicacy so far as to rush to a public court over a love affair gone wrong.

BETTY LEYSHON'S MARATHON

Mrs. Betty Leyshon, an old Welsh countrywoman whose left wrist and ankle were secured by separate lengths of cotton tape to the left-side posts of her canopied bed, lay for a while in calculating thought after the front door slammed downstairs.

Only the tenacious hum of a bee pouncing into the window-posts of begonias disturbed the afternoon silence settling on the cottage. No more traffic was likely to come into the lane that day; the postman, the milkman and the oilman called in the morning, and there was seldom a stray walker or car down that aimless track, ending at a thick beechwood. Blessed peace! Chin resting meekly on the folded-back bed covers, Betty allowed time for her noisy daughter to get well away up the lane to the village. She herself had suggested that an arm and leg should be tied to the bedposts, so that Katrin could go on her customary shopping jaunt to the market town. The friend who came regularly from the village to sit in the cottage on Friday afternoons had gone to Swansea for a fortnight, and Katrin always became more cantankerous than usual when something deprived her of her weekly spree. She was catching the half-past one bus at the village, and would be back soon after five.

Watching the clock on a tallboy, Betty calculated, 'I've got nearly four hours to do it. Plenty of time.'

She was waiting for an allotted ten minutes to pass. Her nose twitched in amusement. Katrin, who had never been able to manage the simplest exam in school, had not demurred at the daring suggestion that her mother be tied to the bed and left alone. Afer all, nothing ever had happened to wreck the cottage or put the fear of God into its occupants. Betty had pointed out that the tapes would only be a reminder that she must not think she could take a walk about the house and garden. More important, she often slept in the daytime, and in these restless dozes she had fallen out of bed twice, bruising her rump and—so they *said*—weakening her heart.

Dr. Vaughan, she recalled, had laughed when she told him she thought the shaking-up of those falls had done her good. But wasn't her appetite back? She was eating like a wolf now. Why wouldn't they realize what the restlessness meant? She wanted to be up and about.

314

After her stroke, the long obedience in bed had done wonders. Strength had been returning since the winter had gone. And full use had come back to her right arm. Even Dr. Vaughan wouldn't see that she was more than just 'better'. But he and Katrin were in league. Katrin wanted her kept everlastingly upstairs, out of the way, like a nuisance. Not enougth strength to go downstairs, indeed! She'd show them!

She chuckled, remembering how, with today's project in mind, she had tested her strength in the middle of a night earlier that week. While Katrin snored in the next room, she had got out of bed, crept downstairs in her nightdress, and walked several times up and down the back garden. How the fruit blossom had shone in the bright moonlight! The next day, she asked Katrin what the date was. It was the first of June. So she'd been six whole months in bed! Six months of an angel's patience and a saint's forgiveness! But she *knew* her body's everyday powers were back in full measure now. She'd prove it.

Furtively, as though a supernatural eye watched, her gaze left the clock and roved to the open door. She allowed a couple of extra minutes to pass. Then her free right hand groped under the bolster for a tiny scissors of Victorian silver hidden there. A spare pair, it had been in the work-basket she had asked for the previous day, saying she wanted to try her hand at embroidery again. Stupid Katrin, whose brain was no bigger than a wren's! Stupid, and hard, hard! She had seemed to enjoy tying her mother down securely to the bed, no hesitation at all in those clumsily strong hands.

The knotted tape snipped from her wrist, Betty pushed back the bedcovers and, furtiveness gone, cut the other length from her ankle. She lowered herself carefully out of the bed and sat on its edge until the loud beating of her heart—wasn't it due to excitement?—eased. She listened to the bee's industrious booming among the window flowers. A companionable sound, it seemed to renew her energy. And the day was beautiful—oh, she would be able to do the deed on such a day! She found that her feet took to the floor like a girl's at a dance; hitching up her nightdress, she pattered to the window. The bee, as if scandalized, flew to the ceiling with a rasping buzz. She peered out, and saw that three last camellias remained on the bush close to the corner shade of the front garden lime tree.

Congratulating herself on her unimpaired eyesight, but wasting no more time, she prepared for her marathon. It took nearly an hour, though everything she needed, including shoes in good condition for walking, lay in the wardrobe, the tallboy and a cupboard. Not once was she obliged to sit on a chair, except to draw lisle stockings on the unblemished legs that had never let her down. She decided against a corset, chose her best voile dress, blue as the day's sky, and rummaged among several hats in the cupboard. She pondered over a black toque. Had she bought it for her husband's funeral—was it as old as that? She rejected it—*not* black for that day—and found a lilac straw bonnet that had a bunch of cherries fixed to its poke. Was it tremendously out of date? But, pleased with the gay cherries, she chose it. After all, she reminded herself, arranging the hat on her short crop of silver curls, she was very old.

'I'm eighty-five.' She spoke with a loud vehemence that could not meet with any opposition from her daughter now. 'But it's no good Katrin saying my mind's going the same way as Lady Pencisely, in Rhobell Court—*she's* nearly a hundred, and her head was never sixteen ounces to the pound.'

The completed figure she saw in the wardrobe mirror was not the thin, small-statured woman of reality, but one arrayed for a gala day and therefore filled out to celebrating size. She wore her beads of real amber, a large gold-rimmed cameo brooch, dangling garnet earrings, and a bracelet of gold medallions. Gloves of mauve silk covered the three jewelled rings she had taken from a heart-shaped plush casket, now empty. She noticed the roused blue of her eyes. They shone with eager resolve. Yes, her long obedience in bed had preserved her! Nobody could deny she had been a champion patient . . . at least, she amended this bragging, a champion in the matter of swallowing Dr. Vaughan's medicines and her daughter's meals. She deserved her treat.

Finally, she tied a length of ribbon to a miniature bag of dirty calico and dropped this rather weighty treasure inside her bodice, securing a loop of ribbon to the broochpin. Smiling as she imagined the amazed face that would greet her before the sun reached far down the sky, she crept noiselessly as a marauder down the stairs and, a minute later, after an unnecessarily cautious peep round the front door, stepped into the silent garden. There was not even the sound or flight of a bird there.

She carried a child's three-legged stool, taken from the kitchen, and was able to mount it and tear away the three high stalks of dark shining foliage bearing the last camellias. That she could balance herself on the stool surely was proof that her old steadiness was back? But presently she found herself sitting on the stool. She gazed at the camellias on her lap as if their softly glowing colour hypnotized her. Memory came of the day her firstborn brought the camellia root to her for a birthday present. A dab hand at gardening, Megan had selected this sheltered spot for it, and the bush had flourished and blazed regularly with these crimson splendours. How long ago was the root planted? But she couldn't remember that. She tied the three stems together in a lace-edged handkerchief, got up in a sudden flurry, and made off at once into the lane, the open cottage door and the stool forgotten. Time was passing, and she had far to go.

Oh, the glory of being out! The release brought to her feet, with conniving readiness, a preliminary briskness. Her eye darted; she sniffed hedge and field odours of spacious air. Wasn't it much longer than six months since she had gone beyond the garden gate? She couldn't remember. She smiled a greeting to a crab-apple tree in blossom not far down the lane. The pots of jelly that tree had provided over the years! But she musn't linger in this lane to enjoy the old pleasures. She must be on the watch against being seen hereabouts.

Luckily, it wasn't necessary to go near the village; to reach the road she wanted, there was a winding path up through the nearby beech-wood, then a detour over heathland, with two stiles to negotiate. Memory of these unfrequented tracks came back without lapses. And the Lord was with her; she saw nobody. Within an hour—in other days it would have been half that time—she had got well beyond the village purlieus and its stray, tucked-away cottages and farmsteads. She walked as though propelled by the remains of a tough old energy summoned into important service by the undefeated will; and she was treading native ground. The finery she wore aided her too; the rhythmic swing of her two-inch earrings, that she hadn't worn for many years, especially assured her. The first stile was crossed without fuss. But she kept glancing over her shoulder, and pausing to listen.

She took small notice of a faint pounding in her head; it seemed less a threat of disaster than throbs of guilt because of her trickery with Katrin. Her feet kept compliant, and when she rested at last on the top bar of the second stile, to draw breath, the pounding stopped. She remembered that she used to dawdle on this well-wooded heathland with Bran, her husband, in their courting days. She could see, far away beyond it, ribbed fields, clean-cut segments of last year's hayricks, fat sheep nibbling the unceasing grass, and the steeple of St. Teilo's church, in the yard of which Bran was buried. Nothing was changed. Yet all she saw was different. She seemed to belong to it much less. It looked unsubstantial, like some prospect in a dream. Even when she heard the whirr of a bird's wing close at hand, the sound was strange. But she blessed her hearing, that had never failed.

The warm sunshine shimmered full on her. Vaguely aware of the red camellias on her lap, yet almost forgetting where she was making for, she mused for a while. 'I had a stroke on Christmas Eve,' she told herself, 'and I'm sitting here free as a squirrel. But it's not a miracle—it's just making up your mind to *do* a thing. I'm not one of those grizzling women that take to a bed to be difficult and upset a house.' She corrected this self-praise. 'It was only a bit of a stroke. I kept in bed all that time so that Katrin could feel she was the boss of things, foolish girl. She's got her lesson to learn, like the rest of us. Nobody's boss of anything except themselves.'

Her eyelids shot up. Had she heard a cough? But there was nobody in view. Revived, she guided herself down the two criss-crossed steps, shook out her dress, and felt for the solid little bag inside her bodice. Her trot on the bridle path still did not lag. There was no more climbing now; she was on a flat stretch of glades, and beyond it lay the road to Isaf, her destination. Acclimatization to this outside world came back in greater measure now; she entered a dim alley of hazels, where branches intertwined overhead, and burst into a hymn. 'We plough the fields and scatter the good seed on the land—' she began. Then she remembered she was a fugitive and might be overheard.

Sure enough, as she rounded a turn of the valley she saw a presence blocking the hazy green space ahead. She halted in fear, backed a step, peered again, and saw the apparition more clearly. 'Ah, you duffer,' she scolded herself, her heart less loud as she advanced, 'it's only a horse!' Head dropped, oblivious in half-blind dozing, he was a scraggy old farmhorse that must have wandered from the open patches of the heathland. A glassy eye remained unaware of her when, giving him a greeting, she paused beside the low head. She saw the patient endurance in that diminished eye. Stroking a patch of dry hair on his forehead, she crooned, 'Did you want the shade, then? Were the flies out there aggravating you?' But he did not stir from his deaf musing, and no warmth came from his body as she edged past.

She trod the remaining length of mossy path with a slackened step. Dismay came when she saw, beyond a fence, the endless tarred road stretching down the broad valley. There were no more shortcuts to Isaf. But she would do it! Why should sight of a failing old horse have

318

daunted her? The thing to keep in mind was the tremendous surprise she was going to give Megan. She heard her daughter's shrill cry. In a thrice, the kettle would be filled and the best tea-service brought out. Her son-in-law, Glyn, would come in and shout too at this outrageous antic—'You *walked* here! A miracle!'

Of course, she thought, unlatching a five-barred gate on to the road, there'd be the matter of Katrin's insults to clear up—that nasty scene when Katrin lost all control of herself and accused her sister of conceit, selfishness and neglect of their mother. Megan couldn't really be blamed for not visiting her old home since. But she wrote letters— she never failed in that; and of course she'd be over next Boxing Day, as usual. But December was long months ahead. A peacemaker was trotting out now. This evil warfare between sisters must stop.

A sense of virtuous crusading revived her steps for a while. Sight of a red mail-van hurtling past as she walked the quiet road made her think of the last letter Megan had sent, with a pound note enclosed. Was that neglect? Megan, unlike her sister, never forgot a birthday gift. Oh, yes, Katrin needed to be shown that patience and love paid dividends in the long run! But with this thought came guilty awareness that peacemaking was not the true motive of her flight today, wearing all her jewellery and with the little calico bag inside her dress. Her steps began to slacken again. The faint pounding in her head was coming back.

She saw a flat stone, placed conveniently on the roadside in the shade of a hornbeam tree, and sat on it. Very few vehicles or walkers used this road, she recalled; the way to the market town forked off it not far from the village. She could take another rest, now that the first mile was done. Short spells of them always brought her powers back. She watched a pale butterfly hovering close above her. It seemed to be unsurely considering the cherries on her hat. She held out the back of her silk-gloved hand, wanting to feel the touch of this pretty creature. Its prancings and flutters rallied her. She'd get up in a minute or two, she thought. But her hand fell slowly to her lap, her eyelids drooped, and she was off into the afternoon sleep she hadn't missed for many a long month.

'Do you want a lift somewhere?'

Her eyelids flew up in alarm. She hadn't heard the car's arrival. A young man leaned from its open door a yard away. Faculties not yet assembled, she stared at him in silence. He glanced smilingly from the camellias on her lap to the cherries. 'Having a snooze in the heat?' he called. 'Can I take you anywhere?'

Galvanized, she was on her feet. 'God above!' she babbled, 'I thought you were a policeman!' Without a moment's further delay, she found herself on the soft seat beside him. He asked where she was bound for. 'I'm going to see my married daughter in Isaf,' she replied, jubilance in her fully-wakened voice. She knew at once that this smiling young man would take her all the way.

'Isaf?' He looked at her. 'Were you going to walk there? Over the mountain?' He leaned across her and slammed the door secure.

She had forgotten about the mountain. A long-flanked, craggy mound far down the valley, less a mountain than a sprawling hill, there was an ancient pass over it; a newer and much longer road to Isaf meandered for miles around its base. 'But I haven't visited my daughter since the war started,' she added at random, even with a hint of roguishness. Gloriously fast, they were on their way, and her mind became as headlong as the speed.

'The war has been over a long time.'

'Oh, yes, so it has! I fell asleep just now, you see, and I was dreaming.' Becoming a little less vivacious, she gave him a sidelong peep. He had a clean, gentlemanly face, and well-kept hands to match. He looked a man that would keep his own counsel. Sure that he didn't belong to the valley, she decided he had to do with selling up-to-date farming implements; she had noticed books and a leather portfolio on the back seat when she scrambled in. Why had she thought he belonged to the police?

'It's a rough road over the mountain. But we'll go and see the famous view. I haven't been up there for a long time myself.'

'Until I had my breakdown because of nerves—they said it was a stroke, but it wasn't a proper one—I was always strong as a mule. I'm small and bony and spindly in the limb, and women like me last longest . . . *providing*,' she plunged on, assurance mounting into her manner, 'they don't allow their *minds* to be put to bed, whatever their kith and kin say and do to shut them up out of sight.' Deferential, as if to the superior sex, yet also with the autocratic prodding of the ripely aged challenging the dubious young, she demanded, 'You'd agree, sir?'

'Yes, that's sensible enough.' The driver, an estate agent's partner, spoke in the politic, half-absent way of a man scenting a voluble woman. But he glanced more attentively at this now surprisingly animated passenger. He saw an enthusiastic old village woman whose

finely arched nose had the outgoing eagerness of a hawk's swooping
beak. Despite the animation, though, she had the obdurate and
elusively nefarious calm often possessed by the very old. There was no
moony laxity in her pure blue eyes, that became even more alert as she
quickly turned her head away from him, raising her sheaf of camellias
and burying her nose in it, apparently to smell the flowers.

A car had been coming towards them. When it passed, Betty
lowered the sheaf. 'I've got another daughter, you see,' she resumed,
'and she and Megan in Isaf don't love each other . . . "Katrin the
Puss", Megan calls her,' she confided, maternally deprecating this, 'and
Katrin—she's fifty next birthday, I think, though nobody would
believe it—well, *she* says that Megan was always favoured by me and
had the best of everything because she was firstborn. You've got
opinions on daughters, sir?'

'I'm not married yet. And I never had sisters. All I can think of is
King Lear's bad opinons of daughters.'

'Ah, a king! I expect he owned a lot of jewellery.' Betty tittered,
and, in a burst of still more headlong confidence, said, 'I'm taking my
bits and pieces to Megan in Isaf, while I've still got my wits about me.
It's true that children often cling to silly old grudges all their lives. So
they must expect the punishments children get. Oh, the wickedness of
temper and words!' She shook her head, and the long garnet earrings
swung vigorously. 'Forgiveness comes. But not forgetting.'

'It should,' the young man remarked, sounding forbearing. 'But
we're human beings on the wrong side of Paradise.'

'What's a sovereign worth today?'

'A sovereign? You mean the coin?'

'A gold sovereign. I had an argument at home, with a talking woman
who comes to sit with me sometimes. She's kept forty sovereigns by
her since the days when a pound changed to paper money. I've heard
that a sovereign is worth five pounds today. That comes to two
hundred pounds, so it's a champion profit, isn't it! But she kept saying
a sovereign is only worth three pounds.' In a detachedly forgiving tone,
Betty added, 'Her tongue drives me mad.'

'I've never even seen a sovereign. Any bank will advise her.'

Betty pressed a hand on her chest, to feel if the little bag was safely
there. 'She could buy herself a fur coat.'

'Am I going too fast for you?' The gesture of her hand had been
noticed.

'Oh, no; go faster!' she cried, in relish. Another car approached, and she held the sheaf of camellias before her face until it passed. 'These are the last of many dozens this year. I'm taking them to my daughter.' She chuckled to herself, and lapsed into a reverie for a full minute. Their car ate the miles with a lovely purr. She could feel a warm freshness whipping into her cheeks. Oh, the pleasure of being with a man! Whatever his age. She was sick of women. For reliable confiding in, and for providing true understanding and respect, one man was worth a whole meadowful of women. A man did not ask a lot of foolish questions, a man had knacks of easy but real sympathy denied to inquisitive and distrustful women. A man could put a woman right. She'd always admired the whole lot of them, good and bad.

'Bran,' she said, out of the blue, 'my husband, was with me for nearly sixty years. It wasn't a game of skittles for him all the time, but he didn't go down into St. Teilo's churchyard with his soul in his boots.'

'Any grandchildren?' The question was asked with just the right amount of interest.

'No.' She sighed, briefly. 'Megan talks of adopting a love child from Taliesin Home. There was a hitch. But I'll hear more today.' Her earrings leapt as the car jerked over a swelling on the road. 'Ah, I'm enjoying myself!' she giggled. 'I've never been a woman to make the bed my bible.' She darted another swift look at him. 'Are you thinking I'm a chatterbox?'

'Yes. But I like it, from you.'

'Well, then,' she continued, the prodding back, 'I ask you, what's the worst fault in people?'

'Greed?'

Jealousy! It stays longer in us than greed, and there's never forgiveness in it. It keeps full of revenge. My second daughter, Katrin, *can't* help trying to get revenge because she thinks she *always* stayed second. She *can't* forget she had to wear Megan's cast-off clothes when they were growing up. The wicked words and deeds that come from jealousy! I let her tie me down to my bed after I had my bit of a stroke, that wasn't a stroke, so that I could stay in peace upstairs and let her think she's boss and lady downstairs. But she bangs pots and drops china. Oh, she's a dropper! There's something wrong with people that make bad noises. Then, when I call out for something, she takes half an hour before she decides to thump her feet up the stairs to me. And she hates cooking.'

'You've managed to get away today, haven't you!'

'Katrin *drove* me out.'

She did not develop this misstatement. The car was climbing the mountain now, and, gleeful at the mastery over distance and scene, she peered down excitedly at the sinking valley where she had spent all her life. Ah, she'd been bedded much too long. Take a leap out, and see how one was rewarded with adventure! Here she was, flying up a mountain with a good-looking young man. When they had reached a little way past the crest, and he stopped the car under an overhanging crag of wrinkled stone, she cried, 'There's wonders!'

'Everybody should go up a mountain now and again.' He seemed pleased she had given him a reason to climb there. 'A perfect little kingdom on its own down there.'

An even more secret valley than the one they had left, it was only a five-mile stretch of God's rough handiwork, tempered and matured by man. Along the stretch were three neat grey villages, flower and vegetable gardens, disciplined orchards, scattered white farmhouses, trim walled pastures, cattle in eternal pausing, measured patches of grain-sown fields, precisely arched bridges over a turbulent blue stream, woods giving shade, and gloomy old Isaf Castle standing on an eminence, unoccupied, but its towers and swirl of battlements defying time yet. Farther off, the deceptively mild contours of protective outer mountains could be seen.

'It would be a credit to any land!' Betty exclaimed, with conviction. 'Thank the Lord I've kept my eyesight! I've never needed glasses. I can see two jays flying down there.' She shook her fist, not without approval. 'Thieves! Where there's an orchard coming to fruit there's sure to be a jay. Same as where there's a chicken-run there'll be a fox at night, and where there's a woman there's a—' She checked this flightiness. 'We had a damn fox steal another chicken the other night. Katrin—she's one of my two daughters—wants to buy a gun. Ever since she was jilted she's wanted a gun. She went to see the vicar of St. Teilo's about the fellow. "Katrin," the vicar told her, "a man that jilts a woman has got a reason for it. You're well rid of him. Go down on your bended knees and give thanks you've escaped." . . . Oh, her escape has made her evil-tempered, though!' she ran on, obsessively. 'I often think that a full-length lot of trouble with the fellow might have given size to her mind.'

'Does she vent her temper on you?' He spoke in a far-away tone, as though he had established no real contact with his passenger.

'I'm a nuisance,' Betty admitted. 'Katrin gets a bad time with me.' Acceptance of the eternal cleavage between the irritated young and

323

the tiresome old made her sound punctiliously just. 'She says I'm a liar as well as a chatterbox. But it's only that I get muddled sometimes.' The vivacity was beginning to flag. 'It's Bran, my husband, I remember best after all these years. A good husband can work marvels on us, sir. Children go away, in one way or another, and often we're glad to be rid of them and their everlasting expecting things from us. But a proper husband keeps solid in his mind for ever.' After this testament to conjugal felicity, she said, a little fretfully, 'Well, we've seen the view.'

The young man took the hint and started the car. 'Is your daughter in Isaf expecting you this afternoon?' he asked.

Suspicious of the casual question, she gave him a sharpened look. Had he realized she was on the run? Had she said too much? 'A mother is always expected,' she replied, with a touch of patrician aloofness. 'Isn't the castle over there looking grand and strong? Those Roman conquerors in the history books knew how to build for ever.'

'The Norman invaders built Isaf Castle. But it's all the same today. There's only the English to bother us now. I expect they'd like to drown this valley in another reservoir for their Midlands—it's the right size, with that stream.'

She became silent at last. They were approaching the first village below. She sagged on the comfortable seat, staring out at familiar landmarks in a perplexed way, her brow puckered. The young man asked the whereabouts of her daughter's house. Starting out of her reverie, she murmured, 'The next village. Megan will give you a cup of tea.'

'I won't be able to stop for that. I must get on to the coast.'

She did not insist. But presently, as they speeded into the middle village, all the buoyancy came back. She sat up, gave a glance of astounded recognition at the driver, and paid her tribute to this benefactor. 'Why, you look exactly like a handsome young man we've got in a stained glass window in St. Teilo's! Except there's a halo big as a cartwheel back of his head and flames are reaching up his bare legs. I dreamt of him only the other afternoon—it's all coming back to me now! . . . Down there!' she cried. 'That turning by the whitewashed Baptist chapel.' And while they coursed through a lane of hawthorns, she pointed in triumph to a lazy thread of smoke coming from a chimney visible above the trees. 'Megan's at home! She's lit a fire in her kitchen stove—bakes her own bread twice a week. Here!' The car stopped before a wicker gate under a chestnut tree in flower. 'Brought in a motor car!' she shouted. 'I've cheated.'

'I won't tell anyone,' the driver laughed.

Did he wink at her? Breathless, she leaned to him and hurriedly nipped his cheek; ashamed of her haste to get rid of him now, she drew one of the camellia sprigs from the twist of lacy handkerchief and laid it on his shoulder. 'What's the time, boyo?' she whispered, hoarse with agitation. 'No, not ten past five!' she exclaimed, aghast. She needed no help to get out, stood waving frantically to him as the car began to back up the narrow lane, and forgot him.

All that time to come the few miles to Isaf! In about a quarter of an hour Katrin would be staring at the empty bed and the cut tapes. The chase would begin very soon. But wild horses couldn't drag her back now. Her hand was unlatching the gate. She had a sense that this too had happened in a dream one afternoon not long ago. Surely these chestnut petals covering the ground had been in the dream? She closed the gate stealthily as an intruder, slowly mounted three steps, and half-way up the long, gilly-flower borderd path, halted and swayed. Then the square house became a solid fact again. She saw the familiar brass door-knocker ahead, and resumed walking. Megan always kept that knocker sparkling, she remembered; anyone could tell there was a good housewife within. And all the garden showed her dab hand. There were pheasant-eye narcissi, yellow auriculas, and runs of grape hyacinths. The leafy climber beside the living-room window was much more abundant since her last visit. Never mind that nobody was at that window to see a ghost walking up the garden.

She gave the knocker the unhesitant rap of a visitor with every expectancy of a great welcome. Her sly smile, ready for Megan's startled cry, faded when the door opened. A stout, youngish woman in a bibbed white apron looked at her inquiringly from horn-rimmed glasses. Inside the house, a child bawled something, shouting for shouting's sake, à boy's clamour from sturdy lungs. He began to beat a toy drum. The woman called to him to be quiet.

'Where's Megan?' Without waiting for a reply, she added peremptorily, 'Megan . . . Mrs. Powell.' Transfixed by the sudden thought that this woman in white apron was a nurse, she said, louder, 'Megan's not ill in bed?'

'Megan Powell?' The woman looked surprised, but not especially put out. 'Why, Mrs. Powell died close on six years ago.'

Wariness, deep and guarded, instantly possessed Betty. It gave her faculties the stiffening needed to deal with this crisis. She looked at the woman with the blank stare of a visitor hearing unexpected news. 'Died?' she said. Only a slight panting betrayed tumult; quickly, even with authority, she added, ' I hadn't heard from her for a long time—I am an old friend of hers, you see.' Already there was flight in the shifting of her feet on the doorstep.

Concern came into the woman's face. 'We took this house after Mrs. Powell died. Will you come in? I'm just preparing my husband's tea. He'll be here any minute.'

Betty shook her head, gave a rapid glance over her shoulder, and, still without bewilderment, said, 'Where's Glyn Powell, then?'

'Mr. Powell? He took a job on a farm in Pembrokeshire after his wife died. I heard he married again. Megan Powell caught the Spanish flu a lot of people had that winter, if you remember.' At this, the visitor's eyes blinked, her face wincing; and the woman urged, 'I wish you'd come in for a cup of tea. You must be a stranger here.'

'Dad's coming!' the boy yelled. He beat a smart tattoo on the drum, blessedly short.

'I know the vicar's wife,' Betty lied, on the instant again. 'I'll go and see her.' She turned away. 'Thank you, thank you. I must go on to the vicarage straight away.'

She reached the gate without stumbling, and did not look back, though she knew the woman remained staring at the front door. Slowed down in the lane, she gazed up and down the indistinct hedges Her heart plunged threateningly, and her mind spun in confusion. But a need to hide herself dominated all else. Her sight cleared. She went a few yards up the lane and took the first opening she found in the hedges. A footpath lay there, winding among pink-budded briars. It brought her to sight of a square, ivy-covered church tower. But she avoided entering the straggling village street by this short cut over bushy common land. Another path ran off it, leading, through a gate, to a field of buttercups where a flock of black-faced sheep, quickened nostrils pulsing at her approach, suddenly scampered away. The churchyard wall skirted the field's far end; reaching this, she went along it and found an unlocked side gate, in its low, creeper-hung length.

She had not paused once, though all the time she kept looking back over her shoulder, like a culprit. But nobody had come into view. In the spacious churchyard, she gave no attention to the several new gravestones standing, white and secure, beyond crooked old slabs and lichen-patched stone urns nearer to the cypress-fringed path. When

the worm-eaten door in a side porch of the chuch yielded to her turn
of the rusty latch-ring, she panted in relief. Her gaze darted up and
down the dim interior. There was no feel of a human presence inside.
Odours of lilies, dank stone and dust lay in the silence. She crept up
the nave and went behind an octagonal baptism font placed near the
shadowy main entrance. A dark bench was fixed against the mildewed
wall there, its end stacked with prayer books and hymns. She sank on
it with a long sigh.

She could think about the disgrace now. Humiliation at the total
failure of her afternoon's prank had gone. Something much more
important daunted her. That she had committed the treachery of
forgetting her daughter's death brought a guilt that made her feel as
though a horde of malicious devils was at her heels. A crime against
her firstborn! Oh, what had time done to her? Had she lived too long?
The miserable deceptions time could play! It was only when that
woman said 'Spanish flu' that memory of the death returned in full.
Distinctly now, she recalled Dr. Vaughan telling her of this plague that
mowed thousands down. 'The germ comes from Asia, not Spain,' he
had said, as though that explained the wholesale evil. He was
attending her for shock and nerves. Bran had died only a few months
before. She hadn't been able to go to Megan's funeral. And Katrin—
she realized it now—had never mentioned her sister's name after the
death. Had she been ashamed of those jealous insults when Megan
used to come home?

Katrin? She'd be justified in her hard lecturing after this! Only the
other day, she had said, 'You *can't* go out. It's not your arm and body
now, you silly. It's your mind. You'll soon be fancying Queen Victoria
is still on her throne in black, the same as Lady Pençisely thinks.' What
else had she said? Yes—'You ought to be glad it's only your mind.
Forgetfulness can be a blessing. I often wish I could forget a lot—and
if I can stay Christian long enough, perhaps I will.'

The guilt did not ease. She told herself she must entreat forgiveness
here and now; she must plead that Megan had been truly alive to her
all these years, her love never forgotten. But even as she waited for the
strength to walk openly to the chancel steps, and not stay skulking in a
hidden corner like this, she drifted into oblivion of guilt and prayer, of
pursuit, of fear of discovery. Her eyelids drooped, and the two camellia
sprigs fell from her hand to the floor.

A harsh clanging woke her. Her head jerked up; she was on her feet before the noise finished. But it was only the tower clock striking the hour. Had there been six chimes, or seven? The lozenges of colours in a nearby lancet window looked darker. Surely the church would be locked up at any moment? Or else people would be arriving for choir practice. She'd be caught. There was a police station everywhere in this world, and she hadn't any strength of mind left to tell more lies or to face public exposure. By now, Katrin would have run to Dr. Vaughan's house. Vaughan would phone the police. They'd be scouring everywhere.

She picked up the camellias in their lacy wrap, went to the chancel, and laid them below the communion rail. There was not time to pray. But she went back to retrieve the handkerchief of fine lace, tucked it into her sleeve, and left by the side door at once. Somewhere among the mounds of the yard lay Megan's grave. But it wasn't safe to loiter here either. She made for the gate by which she had entered, and self-preservation gave her feet the alert quickness the chimes had brought to her senses. Voices of children at play on the village green came from beyond the main lych gate facing the tower.

It wasn't bedtime for anyone yet, she thought. The tyranny of bed! She understood the resentment of children snatched from the active day and forced between smothering blankets. She became aware of the huge boredom she had endured, the endless hours of golden daytime in her close little room, while Katrin fumed and fretted downstairs, banging pots and pans, speaking irritably to the milkman, the postman and the oilman. Preoccupied with this, she did not hear immediately a high-pitched voice calling to her; she had gone a pace or two beyond a large, half-toppled memorial stone under a cypress before she heard the repeated question:

'What's the right time?'

She stopped. Wariness came to her aid instantly again. Turning, she saw a lanky girl of ten stepping on to the path from beside the gravestone. The child stood gazing at her measuringly from enormous dark brown eyes. Something less recognizable than calculation seemed to lurk in their gleam. She kept a hand behind her. She looked ready to be aggressive or docile, according to the challenge offered her. Her face and her frock needed a wash, and a ripe stye disfigured an eyelid.

Relief had brought a clear focusing on the small figure. Her heart ceased plunging. 'There's a clock on the tower, my dear,' she pointed out.

'I can't tell the time by the clock. My mother sent me out for
caraway seeds.'

'You won't find caraway seeds here, will you! If your mother's
making a cake, you'd better hurry before the shop closes.'

'She's not making a cake. She chews them as they are. I heard her
tell Mrs. Howells next door she's got a craving for caraway seeds.'
Unstinted approval of this stranger came into the girl's unflickering
eyes. Her hand came from behind her back. 'It's for you,' she said.
'Johnny Parry's got seven of them.' In the open palm lay a white china
rose. 'Johnny Parry is a fool,' she said, dispassionately. 'He lives down
by the river.'

'You shouldn't steal those from the wreaths, my darling!' Betty
scolded. A bygone authoritativeness refreshed her. She wanted to stay
a while with this admiring child. All the censure in the world
suddenly seemed foolish and vain, and she liked the dirtiness and the
stye and the thieving. But she must not stay.

'The glass over the wreath was smashed.' The grubby hand was still
held out invitingly, its sculptured white flower filling the palm. 'What's
the time?'

'Oh, my dear, I don't know at all,' Betty cried in despair, forcing herself
to turn away. 'Put that back, put it back!'

She could feel the child's eyes on her as she went through the side
gate. The lingering regard brought companionship. But all the way
down the buttercup field, where the full-bellied sheep had lain down
in evening meditation, thought of Katrin couldn't be shaken off.
Remorse came. Had it been a cruel trick to suggest that Katrin tie her
to the bed? Everybody would gossip about it now. Katrin would never
forgive her. Taking the sovereigns and jewellery to Megan too! There
would be a long punishment for this. Her step became quicker. A dim
awareness of justice in operation banished the remorse. Let Katrin
learn a lesson, if she could; let her learn it was wise to gamble on
sweet conduct bringing reward. But thought of her wouldn't go.
Remembrance of Megan was already slipping away. Her face wasn't
clear any more. That was what happened to the dead, she brooded,
her eye on a thicket of trees at the bottom of the field. It was the
powerful loving that couldn't be forgotten. Yet even that seemed as of
small account now as the weighty bag of sovereigns inside her dress.

Although her chest began to burn disagreeably, still her feet did not
falter. Guilt no longer undermined her. Instead, upholding her, came

a contempt for the treacheries of body and mind. And she had mastery over her body yet; she could force it on a while longer. But when she reached the thicket of hazels, she found it was not nearly so dense as she had imagined. There were open patches of grass in it. Sight of a crumpled paper bag and cigarette packet among pale-berried clumps of wood-strawberries made her continue through the thicket. It was very silent there. Why couldn't she hear any birds at their evening chirpings? She wandered on, her thoughts as rambling. Pleasures of the day came back. She recalled the mountain ride a kind young man had given her. The day became a victory after all. Kindness of strangers was the only true kindness. Families couldn't help keeping their eyes on property, couldn't help flying at each other's throats over never-forgotten trivialities—it was deep in their nature, she decided, drawing up at a fence of loosely strung wire.

For a time she rested against a post of the fence, peering into the lane lying beyond a ditch of curled young bracken. Then she went effortlessly on her knees, crawled under the bottom strand of wire into the ditch, and remained on her knees among the bracken, gazing assessingly up and down the lane. She got up with much less ease than she had gone down. But she began to walk the lane with undiminished steps, going upwards, towards the last of the three villages, beyond which the mountains closed round. No house in sight. But where there was a lane, rough or not, there would be a passer-by or vehicle sooner or later. Wheel-ruts were visible in the dried mud.

Her eyes searched the bordering hedges of closely-woven briar. The light seemed much darker in this solitude below the golden village where children played. Why couldn't she hear any birds singing? Her hands felt cold in their silk gloves. She forced herself on, and, suddenly, halted. There was something beyond the lane's dim bend ahead. What was it? No sound came. Fear held her heart. But she did not turn to hasten back the way she had come. She went compulsively towards the threat.

A figure came round the bend. Her vision cleared. When she and the man drew abreast, she saw Bran's swarthy face. The very same bold nose, high cheekbones, and dark eyes! 'Nos da,' he said, and passed on with the slow measured tread of a man who has walked that way for a lifetime. She could hear the shuffle of his footsteps now. She chuckled. There were plenty of men in these valleys with that strong-boned dark face. They belonged to an old tribe, and this one had wished her the

330

native good night. He had found nothing extraordinary in a woman walking alone there; he knew she had trod lanes like this thousands of times. She was of his kindred. But somewhere ahead there was a farm. She must avoid it.

Sight of the stranger, who was not a stranger, restored her. She had long passed the bend in the lane before she found what she had been seeking. But she had to peer closely. At one moment the hedge was a cloudy haze; the next, she saw distinctly the small, tightly-folded buds of dog roses that presently would garland this lane. She had enough energy left to crawl into the small bough-strewn gap low in the hedge. A thorn-spiked bough fastened on her hat; another tore her dress, and she thought, 'There goes my Sunday best voile.' But she got safely inside. She remained on her hands and knees until enough strength returned for her to ease herself into a sitting position. It was pleasant in this secret green shelter. Was there honeysuckle somewhere near? Less with her eyes than from memory of delicate wild scents familiar to her from the time she first walked, she apprehended her bed of fresh moss, wood violets and soft primrose leaves. Deep and certain and true, the recognition came that she must yield and rest at last. She was able to lower herself on to her side, and, before she knew it, the gala day faded.

Her hat, with its cherries, dangled above the gap until the farmhand passed that way again, the next morning.

EDITOR'S NOTE

Apart from their regular and widespread appearance in anthologies, the short-stories of Rhys Davies (1901-78) have long been out of print and his books found only in second-hand bookshops. The hundred stories which he published in ten collections and eight private press editions during his lifetime, together with one that appeared posthumously in the magazine *Planet* in 1991, are once again made available in this new comprehensive edition of his *Collected Stories*. They include all the stories he chose for his *Selected Stories* (Maurice Fridberg, 1945), *Collected Stories* (Heinemann, 1955), and *The Best of Rhys Davies* (David and Charles, 1979). Not collected here are a few which appeared in magazines during the author's lifetime but which he chose not to publish in his books, often because they were early versions or reworkings with which he was not satisfied. The purpose in republishing these stories is to demonstrate, for the student and general reader of today, the achievement of Rhys Davies as a writer of short-stories and one of the most distinguished Welsh practitioners in this literary genre.

I am grateful to Dr. Dai Smith, Chairman of the Rhys Davies Trust, of which I am Secretary, for suggesting that I should undertake the task of compiling this edition. The Trust, a charity which I founded in 1990, has as its principal aims the commemoration of Rhys Davies and the fostering of Welsh writing in English. Its patron is Mr. Lewis Davies, the writer's brother, whom I should like to thank for his remarkable generosity, warm friendship and kind co-operation. I should also like to thank members of the Trust for their advice and encouragement.

All enquiries regarding copyright on the work of Rhys Davies, whether short-stories or novels, should be addressed to me in the first instance.

MEIC STEPHENS